HEART OF STONE

ALSO BY JAMES W. ZISKIN

Styx & Stone

No Stone Unturned

Stone Cold Dead

HEART OF STONE

An Ellie Stone Mystery

JAMES W. ZISKIN

SEVENTH STREET BOOKS®

AN IMPRINT OF PROMETHEUS BOOKS

59 JOHN GLENN DRIVE • AMHERST, NY 14228
www.seventhstreetbooks.com

Published 2016 by Seventh Street Books®, an imprint of Prometheus Books

Cover images © iStock.com/YinYang; Kristy Pargeter/Media Bakery (radio)
Cover design by Jacqueline Nasso Cooke

Inquiries should be addressed to
Seventh Street Books
59 John Glenn Drive
Amherst, New York 14228
VOICE: 716–691–0133
FAX: 716–691–0137
WWW.SEVENTHSTREETBOOKS.COM

20 19 18 17 16   5 4 3 2 1

Library of Congress Cataloging-in-Publication Data

Names: Ziskin, James W., 1960- author.
Title: Heart of stone : an Ellie Stone mystery / James W. Ziskin.
Description: Amherst, NY : Seventh Street Books, 2016.
Identifiers: LCCN 2016006974 (print) | LCCN 2016011563 (ebook) |
    ISBN 9781633881839 (softcover) | ISBN 9781633881846 (ebook)
Subjects: LCSH: Women journalists—Fiction. | Murder—Investigation—Fiction.
    | Nineteen sixties—Fiction. | BISAC: FICTION / Mystery & Detective /
    Women Sleuths. | FICTION / Mystery & Detective / Historical. | GSAFD:
    Mystery fiction.
Classification: LCC PS3626.I83 H43 2016 (print) | LCC PS3626.I83 (ebook) |
    DDC 813/.6—dc23
LC record available at http://lccn.loc.gov/2016006974

Printed in the United States of America

To Kunda, for support and encouragement beyond compare.

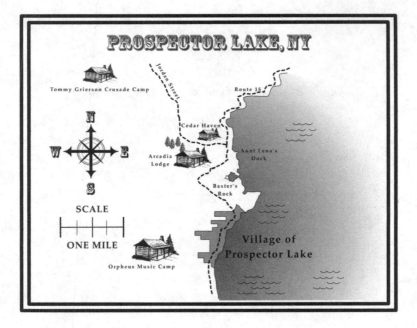

PROSPECTOR LAKE, NY

Tommy Grierson Crusade Camp

Jordan Street

Route 15

Cedar Haven

N
W E
S

Arcadia
Lodge

Aunt Lena's
Dock

Baxter's
Rock

SCALE

ONE MILE

Orpheus Music Camp

Village of
Prospector Lake

I remember the cool breath of the night woods on my neck. I see the glow of moonlight on the highest boughs, filtering down in a pale cast, weak and washed-out, fading into darkness. I smell the moss and the decay of the forest floor, heady, damp, musky. And I can taste the earthy mushrooms and bitter berries on my tongue. But most of all, I hear the pines whisper and sigh, their needles, like millions of tiny blades, carving voices into the breeze.

CHAPTER ONE

FRIDAY, AUGUST 18, 1961

That night I was at the wheel of my car, nosing my way through ever-narrowing Adirondack back roads, in search of a dirt-and-grass lane leading to my aunt Lena's cabin, Cedar Haven. It was past midnight, and the woods were deserted. At least I hoped they were. When I was a girl, the deep north woods had filled me with alternating sensations of awe and fright. Even in daylight, the forest hid mysteries, always just out of sight, but never out of earshot. If ever I was caught out after dark, I would sprint back to our cabin *à toute vapeur*, as my polyglot father was wont to say. Other dads would have simply said "at full speed."

I must have missed a turnoff, perhaps two or three miles back, so I pulled to a stop to consult a map. The night was still and pitch dark, with the moon either below the horizon or obscured by clouds. Silence all around me. I switched on the radio. Nothing but static. I was out of range of the Albany stations, so I fiddled with the knob and found a crackling voice barely audible at 800 on the dial, but the man was speaking French. Montreal. I hunted some more, finally locating a faint bit of music that might have been Del Shannon. Then an announcer broke in and issued a bulletin. I missed the first half, due to the low volume.

"... *escaped this morning from the maximum security Great Meadow Correctional Facility in Comstock. It is not known if Yarrow is armed, but Washington County Sheriff T. T. Buckley advises the public to exercise extreme caution if confronted by the escaped prisoner. Donald Yarrow, a convicted double murderer* ..."

The radio reception faded out, and I didn't wait for it to come back. I floored it, shooting forward into the night—*à toute vapeur*—tires spinning on the gravel shoulder in search of a firm foothold.

SATURDAY, AUGUST 19, 1961

I lay reclined on the wooden slats of the dock that stretched some fifty feet from shore into the lake. The water rolled gently in the breeze, and I closed my eyes, letting the warmth of the afternoon sun spread over my cheeks and my bare limbs. I imagined the world slipping away. Nothing to disturb the calm but the buzz of an outboard motor passing close by as it headed to shore. I ignored it, concentrating instead on the sound of water lapping against the wood. A shadow crossed my face, and I opened my eyes. A bird hovered on the wind above me for a brief moment before alighting on the edge of the dock a few feet from my toes. He folded away his wings. A seagull. Or rather a ring-billed gull, to be precise. My late father's cousin Max, bird-watcher and amateur water-colorist, was a font of knowledge in such matters. I was, in fact, spending a week on the western shore of Prospector Lake in the Adirondacks with him and my aunt Lena, my father's younger sister.

The gray-and-white gull regarded me with one eye, then ducked his head to view me with the other. I drew a lazy breath and made the most momentous decision of the day: ignore the bird and soak in the sun. Time for a nap.

But just then my friend leapt into the air, taking flight, frightened away by a gentle splashing nearby: Aunt Lena. I shielded my brow from the sun with my right hand to see as she reached the ladder and climbed aboard. A low gasp caught in my throat. Of course I had known of her preference to swim au naturel, but the actual witnessing of it gave me a jolt.

"We've discussed this, Ellie," she said in all her naked glory, towering over me, obscuring the sun as she dripped cool lake water on me.

I squinted up at her, my face surely betraying feelings of discomfort and embarrassment. She stood there wearing nothing but a white rubber swimming cap festooned with multicolored flowers atop her silvering head. She was fifty-five, nearly ten years younger than my late father, and well preserved. Which only made the experience even more troubling.

"I've been swimming nude here since I was a young bride," she said.

"It's healthy, and I'm not putting on a suit for you. Since when did you become such a prude?"

For my part, I was tastefully decked out in a navy maillot with white piping. Two years out of date, perhaps, but hardly prudish. It did, however, provide some measure of modesty, which appeared not to concern my aunt. At least not until she noticed the thump of advancing footsteps on the wooden boards beneath us. She turned to see a man approaching from the shore. While perfectly happy to parade about in the altogether in front of her late husband, me, and even her cousin Max, Aunt Lena seemed determined to maintain the veil of mystery between her nudity and the eyes of strangers. She grabbed my beach towel and yanked it out from under me, nearly flipping me over the side of the dock and into the lake.

"Is this pervert one of your friends, Ellie?" she asked, wrapping herself in the towel.

I sat up cross-legged and squinted at our visitor. A large man in dungarees and a sleeveless undershirt was lumbering toward us like a bear emerging from his cave after a long winter. About forty, unshaven, and unwashed, he'd been beached somewhere between portly and flabby on the physical continuum. And he could have used a little sun. His oily, graying hair flapped stiffly in the breeze, like a loose shingle on a roof, while his boots tramped over the planks, trailing wet laces behind him. As he drew nearer, I noticed the stock of a handgun squashed between his considerable belly and the waistband of his trousers, as if it had been trapped and suffocated trying to squeeze its way out.

"You know that nude bathing is prohibited here on Prospector Lake," he said as he came to a stop and stared us down from ten feet away. He spoke with a slow upstate twang. I thought perhaps he'd suffered an aphasia of some kind. Then I realized he'd been drinking.

"And what about voyeurism?" asked Aunt Lena in her unthreatening way. She wielded a stinging wit, but her delivery was so sweet you hardly realized she was cutting you down to size. "I don't believe I've had the pleasure. Who are you?"

The man squinted at her, then glanced down at me, allowing his eyes to linger a second or two over my bust before running down my legs. His lips spread into a contemplative grin, and he blinked slowly before turning his gaze away.

"I'm the chief of police," he said, almost expecting applause. "Not that I have to answer to nudists."

Aunt Lena chuckled. "Oh, I know who you are. Max told me we had a new chief of police on the lake. So you're Tiny Terwilliger."

"Ralph Terwilliger," said the man as if it pleased him to say it. "Tiny is a pet name from my younger days."

"*Homo habilis* with scabby knuckles, according to Max," Aunt Lena said to me, cupping a hand over her mouth.

"What's that?"

"What can we do for you, Mr. Terwilliger?" she asked, ignoring his question.

"For starters," he said, "you can stop swimming nude in the lake. And for seconds, I want to ask you ladies if you seen or heard anything out of the ordinary earlier today."

"I saw a gull," I said. "Just a minute ago."

Terwilliger rolled his eyes and sighed. "Did you happen to see anything over toward Baxter's Rock or the Hebrew kee-boots?"

"*The Hebrew kee-boots?*" asked Aunt Lena. "What kind of thing is that to say?"

"The Arcadia Lodge," he said. "The Jew Communists. You know what I mean."

"Mr. Terwilliger, my niece and I are Jews."

"That's real nice," he said. "Anyways, I didn't come out here to talk religion or politics. I wanted to know if you seen or heard anything unusual in the direction of Baxter's Rock."

"I heard those drag racers again last night," said Aunt Lena. "Why don't you do something about them? They're a menace."

There had been a spate of loud cars speeding through the village and surrounding areas for the past week, she'd told me that morning. It was getting on her nerves.

"We're working on that, don't worry," he said. "I've set up a speed trap about a half mile south of here on Route Fifteen. I was there for three hours this morning watching for them. We'll catch them."

"Please do," she said.

"Now back to my question. Did you see or hear anything over by Baxter's Rock?"

"When?" I asked.

He consulted his wrist and, discovering he wasn't wearing a watch, asked me for the time.

I dug into my canvas bag to retrieve my watch. "Just after two," I said.

He did some calculations in his head, then double-checked on his fingers. "Maybe about an hour and a half ago."

"I swam a bit when I got here," I began. "Then I ate my lunch."

"Did you happen to see or hear anything from that direction?" he repeated, pointing to the southwest.

"I was probably dozing on the dock around half past twelve. I heard some motor boats off in the distance, but I can't say for sure which direction or when."

Terwilliger nodded knowingly. "That makes sense," he said but didn't explain why.

"How else may we help you?" asked Aunt Lena, clutching my towel ever more tightly to her breast.

"I noticed that the young lady had a camera," he said, indicating me with a jab of his left forefinger.

Even from my vantage point ten feet away, I could see that the digit was missing the tip, fingernail, and distal joint, surely lopped off while disemboweling a squirrel for Sunday dinner. Or perhaps he'd lost it in a drunken game of mumblety-peg.

"How do you know I have a camera?" I asked.

He looked me up and down a second time. "I seen you taking pictures with it this morning before you came out here for your sunbathing."

That was a lot of creepiness to process in one go. I certainly hadn't seen him, and I wanted my towel back from Aunt Lena. I had risen early on my first day on the lake to shoot some Kodachrome of the sunrise. Then I'd headed back to Cedar Haven for breakfast. I packed a basket with some lemonade and sandwiches and returned to the lake around eleven for my rendezvous with the gulls and my naked aunt. And now a horrid man named Tiny Terwilliger was polluting the air in the general vicinity. He asked if I still had the camera.

"Yes, in my bag."

"Is photography also prohibited on Prospector Lake?" asked Aunt Lena, still in her saccharine voice.

"No, ma'am," he said. "I don't have a camera, you see. And I don't know how to use one. At least not a fancy one like she's got. So I need the young lady to help me take some pictures over there below Baxter's Rock in the cove."

"Pictures of what?" I asked.

The chief turned back to me. "Two dead bodies."

CHAPTER TWO

Baxter's Rock, a flinty promontory of broken shale and slate, towered some seventy-five feet above a deep pool on the western shore of Prospector Lake. Just a third of a mile from the dock attached to Aunt Lena's property, with Arcadia Lodge, the "Hebrew kee-boots" in between, Baxter's Rock was accessible only on foot through the woods or via a long, narrow road that wound through the hills above the lake.

Arcadia Lodge was a cooperative made up of ten family cabins, grouped around a central gathering facility–cum–dining hall known as the Great Lodge. Once one of the more modest Great Adirondack Camps, the Arcadia had been bought in the early thirties by a group of New York Jewish intellectuals and artists, much to the dismay of the local gentry. The New Yorkers were immigrants from Germany and Eastern Europe, chased out by pogroms, wars, and poverty. They'd brought their music and art with them from the old country, along with their radical politics. I knew all about Arcadia Lodge from the summers our family had spent on the lake with Aunt Lena and her late husband, Uncle Melvin, a thoracic surgeon who'd been on the staff of Mount Sinai Hospital in Manhattan. Over the years, he and my father, too became friendly with the Arcadians, played chess and cards, and engaged in thoughtful political and cultural discussions with them. My brother, Elijah, and I used to play with the children who spent their summers at Arcadia Lodge.

Aunt Lena wished Chief Terwilliger and me luck, claiming that dead bodies were not to her taste. She pushed off to find Cousin Max and fill him in on the news. I stepped into my sandals, grabbed my camera kit from the canvas bag, and followed Terwilliger to the shore, grateful for the breeze that kept me upwind of him. There was nothing to be done, however, about the unrestricted view I had to endure of his rear end. Despite myself, I couldn't help watching it twitch back and forth as he waddled along the planks. He led me to a small launch waiting on the beach, surely the one I'd heard pass earlier as I dozed on the dock.

At his invitation, I climbed into the boat. Then he pushed it into the lake and jumped inside, nearly capsizing us in three feet of water. Once he'd settled into his seat astern, he lowered the outboard into the water and set about trying to start the motor. He yanked the pull cord at least ten times, nearly knocking himself out from the exertion and resulting hyperventilation, before the outboard finally coughed to life. He leaned back, satisfied with himself—red face, perspiration, and all.

Terwilliger steered us around a crag, chugging toward the narrow ingress that opened into the cove below Baxter's Rock. He lined up the bow of the boat between two outcroppings that guarded the entrance, gunned the engine to give us some forward momentum, then cut the power and lifted the outboard from the water. We glided into the cove, skimming over the sharp rocks submerged just below the surface.

"Nice bit of navigation," I said, and he grinned.

"Lots of people break a propeller or get stuck on the rocks trying to come in here," he said. "But I grew up on the lake. I know it pretty good."

The cove stretched perhaps a hundred feet from the stone beach to its narrow exit into the lake. The steep walls of the cliff blocked the afternoon sun's direct rays, giving the pool of captive water a deep-black hue. We approached the beach where I could see two canvas tarpaulins spread out on the ground. I wouldn't have given a second thought to the lumps in the fabric if the chief hadn't already told me the purpose of our visit. I knew that two dead bodies lay beneath the tarps.

Below the cliffs of Baxter's Rock, a ledge of flat shale no more than twelve to fifteen feet wide formed a narrow beach of sorts. It was difficult to reach, accessible only by boat, as we had come, or by climbing over some high, sharp rocks along the shore. And, of course, there was the express route from the top of the cliff. . .

Adventurous divers had long enjoyed testing their nerve and skill by leaping into the pool of water from above. The trick was to clear the shale beach and hit the cove's deep water. In all the years I'd vacationed on Prospector Lake, I never once heard of an actual diving accident at Baxter's Rock. Still, our parents treated us children regularly to horror stories of young fools who'd misjudged the leap and plunged to their doom on the rocks below. Cousin Max, an eloquent man who never used a simple phrase when a convoluted one would do, once warned Elijah and me that two objects cannot occupy a space at the same time. He topped it off with a supplementary caution: "Gravity unleashed is a risky proposition at best."

Working as a reporter for the *New Holland Republic*, I'd seen a few dead bodies in the previous year and a half. Still, I didn't relish the prospect of aiming my camera at a couple of corpses, especially on my summer vacation.

Tiny Terwilliger climbed out of the boat and secured it to a rock with a length of frayed rope. Then he watched closely as I scrambled from my seat onto the shore in nothing but my bathing suit. Pervert.

He told me again that he didn't own a camera, almost as if he was proud of the fact.

"Don't need one." He smiled.

"I believe my presence here right now invalidates your assertion," I said.

He ignored me and lifted the tarp closest to the wall to reveal the first body: a young man in hunter-green gym shorts, a white T-shirt, and a worn pair of low-top Keds, lying facedown on the rocks. His face was turned away from me, and a pool of sticky, nearly dried blood had spread in a two-foot irregular oval around his skull. His right arm was trapped beneath his body, while the left extended at a forty-five-degree angle, the elbow bent another twenty degrees as if waving good-bye. Upon impact, his legs had come to rest crossed at the ankles: an almost peaceful, somnolent pose. Holding my breath and suppressing the urge to vomit and weep, I loaded my camera with Tri-X, wound the film, and snapped several frames of the body from head to toe and back again.

"That T-shirt is from Camp Orpheus," said Terwilliger as if to make conversation. "That's the music camp south of the village."

"I remember their concerts from when I used to come here as a girl," I said, stepping around the boy.

I knelt by his crushed face and gazed at him. He was good-looking, tall and wiry, black-haired, and tanned. He looked to be all of sixteen or seventeen. I bowed my head and touched his left shoulder.

"What the hell are you doing?" asked Terwilliger.

"Just give me a minute," I answered, brushing a stray lock of hair away from the boy's left eye.

Terwilliger snorted. "He'll get a funeral, miss. So for now, just take my pictures, will you?"

I pushed up off the slate, wiped my eyes, and focused my Leica on the young man's face, lifeless and dented, almost caved-in. I squeezed off ten more shots before I turned away to compose myself. After several deep breaths and a splash of cool lake water on my cheeks, I felt ready to face the next body.

The chief pulled the tarp over the boy then peeled back the second one nearer the edge of the water, exposing the other body. The first thing I noticed was that he was wearing nothing but ordinary striped men's boxer shorts. He was handsome, slim, and fair-skinned with a bad sunburn. I figured him to be in his mid-thirties, about five feet nine or ten. A gold watch was strapped to his left wrist. He was lying on his right side, no blood on the rocks, but you couldn't miss the large bluish bruise along his torso against the ground. Another bluish blotch, smaller, was visible on his left rib cage, hip, and thigh. I imagined he'd bounced or rolled after impact on the sharp rocks. His hands were clenched in a death grip, frozen as if in a last, desperate grab at fleeting life. His lips were twisted in an ironic grimace that belied the finality of his demise. Or perhaps affirmed it. What a brutal realization death must be when visited with such abruptness.

I photographed the body from all the requisite angles, shooting two more rolls of Tri-X, before I took a second look at his watch. Why was he wearing a wristwatch? I knew about waterproof timepieces, of course, but I'd never seen one with a leather strap. I knelt down and tried to turn his wrist to see the crystal. The underside of his arm was white.

"Don't go touching the body like that," said Terwilliger. "What do you think you're doing?"

"I want to see if his watch was damaged," I said.

"You like playing detective, do you?" he asked, but I ignored him.

Having read my share of mystery stories as a girl, I knew that the first item to check was the victim's watch. It always seemed to stop at the precise moment of death due to some incidental impact. And though this clichéd artifice often succeeds at the expense of verisimilitude, smashed crystals and frozen watch hands are hot stuff in pulp novels. In this case, however, a broken watch was to be expected, since the dead man's impact with the ground could hardly be categorized as incidental.

But the watch, a LeCoultre Réveil, was ticking away on his wrist as if nothing had happened, its second hand sweeping gracefully around the silver dial. A splendid testimonial for the durability of the product, though probably not one the LeCoultre company would have cared to use in its advertising.

It looked like an expensive model. The casing was a light-yellow gold, and the band, as I'd already noticed, was made of leather or some kind of lizard skin. I stood and reconsidered the dead man. His hair was styled if uncombed, his fingernails manicured, and his physique toned. My interest was piqued. Why no swimming trunks? Why not remove the watch? Who were these two men, and why had they fallen to their deaths together?

"When did you find them?" I asked Terwilliger, rewinding my third roll of film.

"It wasn't me. A vacationer and his son were in a boat, fishing out there," he said, pointing to the water beyond the cove. "They heard a yell and looked over here just in time to see one of them dive off the cliff. That was about two hours ago now."

"Who put the tarps over the bodies?"

"You sure ask a lot of questions," he said. "I did. The guy and his son showed up at the station to report what they saw, and I came out here right away to have a look."

"So they saw him hit the ground?"

Terwilliger shook his head. "The rocks block the view."

"Then how did they know he missed the water?" I asked.

He curled his lip. "No splash. And they heard the splat on the rocks." He paused, seemingly picturing something in his head. "Probably took a second or two for the sound to reach them out on the water."

I felt green.

"Any other questions?" he asked with a smirk.

"As a matter of fact, yes," I said, considering the man in boxer shorts. "Do you suppose he left his clothes at the top of the cliff?"

Terwilliger frowned at me. "What do you want to know that for? This isn't any of your business."

"Things like this interest me. I'm a reporter for a newspaper in New Holland. About an hour and a half south of here."

"You don't say."

His sarcasm stung. I blushed, realizing that I should have expected it. This was, after all, the same enlightened soul who'd referred to a collective of artists and intellectuals as "that Hebrew kee-boots." Still, I was curious about what was at the top of the hill. I waited a couple of beats then asked as nicely as I knew how if I could go along with him for a look at the top of Baxter's Rock.

"I don't need your help. Don't want it either," said the charmer. His tone wasn't exactly rude, but more matter-of-fact, as if he were answering a question about the weather. "I can manage my own investigation. If you're finished, I'll take the film, and you can go."

"Who's going to develop the pictures?" I asked, not quite ready to throw in the towel. "I'll process the film for you, if you like. My cousin has some equipment here that I can use."

"No thanks," he said, holding out his calloused hand with lopped-off finger for the film. "I'll take it to Philby's in Prospector Lake and get the pictures developed myself."

"Have it your way," I said. "If you want it, you've got to buy it. Three rolls of Kodak Tri-X, twenty-four exposures each. That'll be nine dollars and sixty cents. Plus my time. That's another ten dollars. I don't come cheap."

Terwilliger glared at me. I'd just kicked the hornets' nest. He took a step toward me and tried to grab the Leica from my hand. I pulled my precious camera back out of reach, shielding it with my body and a straight-arm. Terwilliger renounced his claim to my property, if temporarily.

"Suit yourself," he said with a sigh. "I'll just arrest you for withholding evidence in a police investigation. We'll see how you like our jail. Let's go." And he started for the boat.

His mulishness was galling me, and I realized I needed to take a different tack or wind up spending a few nights in stir. And he'd still get my film.

"What if we compromise?" I said. "Don't you need photographs from the top of the cliff anyway?"

Terwilliger stopped and turned to squint at me as he chewed on that for a few moments. He shuffled his feet and scratched his cheek. At length he admitted that he did indeed need some photos from the top of the high dive.

"Okay," he mumbled. "But no more compromises. You take the pictures and then scram. I don't want a girl getting in the way."

He watched me climb into the boat, tilting his head to see better as he did; then he pushed off and hopped in.

The blue paint on the beaten-up Ford truck had faded to a grayish patina, bleached by the sun and cracked by the ice and snow of at least twenty years. Dented and scraped, the door panels were a different color altogether. The passenger's side headlamp was smashed and the fender crumpled. But as bad as the truck looked on the outside, the interior presented new horrors. The foul smell inside Ralph "Tiny" Terwilliger's truck was a mélange of sweat and dirt and spilled beer, but I couldn't quite identify the musky odor lingering underneath the general effluvium. If forced to guess, I'd say rotting moose entrails and old socks. I was sure I would never get the odor out of my bathing suit and resigned myself to burning it in the fireplace later that evening.

Terwilliger drove his bucket of bolts up Lake Road for about a quarter mile then turned onto a bumpy asphalt road that petered out some two hundred yards farther along. From there we turned right into a winding dirt-and-grass trail. The truck scraped through the encroaching over-growth on both sides of the road, heaving and bouncing over the dips and ruts until we arrived at a small clearing five minutes later. I slung my camera over my shoulder and climbed down from the cab. Terwilliger was already halfway through the grassy field and nearing the edge of the cliff. I set out after him, but a flash of metal to my right caught my eye. I stopped in my tracks and turned to see. There, partially obscured in the weeds, sat a brown, rusted 1949 Plymouth station wagon. A woody in dismal condi-tion. I knew it was a 1949 model because it belonged to my cousin Max. A quick glance through the open window confirmed my suspicions. The keys dangled from the ignition. Despite repeated admonitions from Lena and me, Max insisted on leaving his keys in the car. An easel, tripod, box of oil paints, and a fishing rod were stashed in the way-back. There were a couple of fresh canvases and some brushes on the backseat. These were the items I'd helped him pack into the car that very morning before I set off for the dock to photograph the sunrise.

Max loved to spend long hours in the woods, painting forest scenes in oil or watercolors, depending on his mood. I noticed now that his water-color kit was missing from the front seat of the car, where I'd placed it that morning, but his lunch basket and thermos of wine were still there. A pair of black trousers was folded neatly on the seat, a leather belt coiled tightly on top, like a snake. Two shoes lay on the floor.

"Are you coming or not?" called Terwilliger from twenty yards away. Then he noticed the car and scurried back to join me.

He rubbed his chin, a little out of breath, as he studied the Plymouth. Then he shook his head and wondered out loud what it was doing there.

"Must belong to one of those two men," he offered.

"Afraid not," I said. "This car belongs to my cousin Max. Those are his paints and brushes inside."

"What's his car doing here?"

"I don't know. But there are some clothes on the front seat, and they're not his."

Terwilliger peered inside and shrugged. "You sure?"

"My cousin is a corpulent man. Heavyset, you might say. Um, fat. And he's sloppy. He wouldn't fold his clothes so neatly."

"Then maybe the clothes belong to one of the dead men," he said. "The older one, I'd say. Those aren't kids' things."

"It would appear so," I said. Perhaps Terwilliger wasn't as dim as he looked. "But what are they doing in Max's car?"

"Maybe he gave them a ride up here. You say he paints? He's probably off in the woods somewhere nearby, painting another useless picture of a bunch of trees."

I thought that was likely, since Max had set out in the morning to do just that.

"Aren't you going to check the trousers?" I asked. "There might be a wallet or some kind of identification inside."

Terwilliger hesitated a moment, probably debating whether it was advisable to listen to a woman, then yanked open the front passenger's door. He bent over and ducked inside, giving me a long, unwanted view of his posterior. When he righted himself again, he was holding the pair of men's trousers, which showed wrinkles and patches of dirt. He dug into the pockets one by one, elbow deep, like a magician reaching into a silk hat. There was no rabbit inside. The trousers were empty.

"Why do you suppose there's no shirt or jacket or wallet among his clothes?" I asked.

He stuck his head back into Max's car and rooted around, rear end in the air again, prompting me to turn away and admire the view of the lake until he'd finished.

"Nothing else in there," he said, scratching his neck. "I wonder what he did with the rest of his clothes."

I said nothing, waiting for a pearl of wisdom from the oracle. At length he shrugged and offered that maybe the older man had taken off his shirt near the cliff, and it had been blown away by the wind. Terwilliger seemed satisfied with this explanation and put it to bed with a bob of his head followed by a deep, protracted dig into his left nostril with his shortened forefinger. He examined the fruits of his mining effort then flicked his find into the gentle breeze.

"I suppose it will show up eventually," I said. "It can't have gone far. Not much wind today."

Terwilliger waved his nose-picking hand at me. "Doesn't really matter anyways. Whether we find his shirt or not, he shouldn't have been diving off cliffs. There are signs posted everywhere. Diving is prohibited here."

"Like nude bathing?" I asked.

"You're funny," he said. "But I don't get what the draw of this place is. The kids just can't help jumping off no matter the danger."

"Of course, only one of the two down there was a kid. I wonder what a grown man was doing diving off a cliff with a local teenage camper."

At this point, Terwilliger had decided to ignore my musings. Surely he wanted a pat conclusion. No niggling questions or missing shirts.

"So where's this cousin of yours staying on the lake?" he asked. "I'm going to want to talk to him about the car."

"With my aunt and me," I said. "At Cedar Haven, just to the north of the dock where you found me."

"Yeah, I know it," he said. He looked around at nothing in particular then asked if Max was married to Aunt Lena.

"No. He's her first cousin."

"I see," he said, nodding. "She's a nice-looking lady."

Oh, God, I thought, wondering just how sharp Terwilliger's eyesight was and how much of Aunt Lena he'd seen.

"But don't forget she's Jewish," I said, hoping to discourage any interest from him.

"Yeah, no danger of that happening," he said. "Now can I expect to find your cousin clothed when I talk to him, or is he a nudist, too?"

"Clothed," I said, expressing a silent thanks in my head.

"All right," said Terwilliger. "Let's go get those pictures of the cliff."

For the moment, I pushed the puzzling presence of Max's Plymouth to one side and trudged through the high grass to the edge of the precipice. But I felt a knot in my stomach that would not unravel until I knew for sure that Max was safe and sound.

I approached the lip of the cliff with care, while Terwilliger stayed a safe distance back. The grass tapered off to dirt near the edge, just where a worn sign warned of danger and promised a fine for illegal diving. I focused my camera on the sign and squeezed off a couple of shots. Force of habit. Establish the scene first. Then the nose-digger inched up behind me and coughed, nearly propelling me over the edge with fright.

"Careful," he said. "I don't want to clean up your mess too."

I drew a deep breath then, standing atop Baxter's Rock, peeked over the edge to see the deep pool of water seventy-five feet below. But I couldn't see the rock beach, at least not without leaning past the tipping point and falling into the void. I don't suffer from acrophobia, but I don't have a head for heights either. All things being equal, I'd rather not dangle off cliffs without a harness and perhaps a parachute. Terwilliger, on the other hand, had retreated again to his safe distance from the edge. He tried to joke about it (deliberate humor was not his long suit) and waved me on to take the necessary photos of the scene without his help.

Using my best guess, I screwed a 90mm lens onto my Leica and estimated a focal length of about seventy feet. Next I identified a well-anchored rock near the lip of the precipice and, holding on for dear life with my left hand, stretched as far forward as I could, the toes of my right foot actually peeking over the edge. I extended my camera beyond the cliff with my right hand and aimed it down at the rock beach. I fired off a shot, pulled back, and wound the film. I repeated the exercise about ten times, hoping at least one frame would capture the bodies below in clear focus. Without looking through the viewfinder, I had no idea if I'd shot the pool of water, the eastern side of the lake, or my painted toenails. But that was enough; I had no intention of risking a fall. Terwilliger would have to wait to see the developed photos to know how I'd done. Of course he hadn't had to wait to watch me performing photographic gymnastics in my bathing suit. As I pulled back from the edge, I found him ogling me, head cocked to the right, with a dumb, open-mouthed stare on his face. I cleared my throat, wanting to spit my disgust at him, and he snapped back to the present.

"Fine job, miss," he said, red-faced with his customary drawl. "That will do for now."

It was nearly five when Terwilliger pulled to a stop on the road next to the dock. I tried to give him the four rolls of film I'd shot, three of the bodies and one from the top of the cliff, but his attention was otherwise occupied. There was a state trooper's cruiser and a hearse waiting for him.

"I've got to get those bodies out of the cove," he said, not even looking at me. "Why don't you develop the pictures like you said? I'll come get them later. Or maybe tomorrow. Those two fellows aren't in any rush."

He pushed open the door and climbed down. I followed suit.

Terwilliger scooted over to the pair of troopers and the hearse driver and began gesturing toward the cove around the bend. The troopers regarded him queerly, their facial expressions betraying some kind of disgust or disdain, as if Tiny Terwilliger smelled (which he did) or they couldn't believe someone had made him chief of police of this, or any other, godforsaken end of the earth. The driver, a short young man in a dark suit, edged away from the lawmen and took up a position against the hearse, throwing occasional appalled glances at the chief.

I made my way to the dock, tucked my camera and lens into my bag, which I placed carefully on the slats. Then I kicked off my sandals and dived head first into the lake. I had to get the funk of his truck off my body and out of my hair.

I paddled around in the water for a few minutes—I'm an excellent swimmer—then climbed out of the lake onto the end of the dock: the place where I'd had the pleasure of making Chief Terwilliger's acquaintance. I spread out to dry in the late-afternoon sun, trying to shake the images of the dead men from my head. After a while, I sat up and considered the majestic view to the east. The Green Mountains dominated the eastern shore of the lake from the Vermont side. Bathed in the magic light of a sinking sun to the west, the peaks rolled gently, one into the next, with more in the distance beyond, fading gradually to blue then gray.

Prospector Lake had been carved out of the earth's crust by the retreating glaciers of the last ice age. Eleven miles long and three miles across at its widest, the crescent-shaped lake hung like a moon north to south between the shoulders of two ranges of mountains. A popular vacation spot in summer and a desolate sliver of ice in winter, Prospector Lake offered pristine water, stony beaches, and stunning sunsets. The village was a quaint, homey place, with souvenir shops, family eateries, boat rentals, and ice cream parlors. The sun stayed up until eight in August, and, as long as you didn't mind the mosquitoes, it was safe and pleasant to stroll through the village, even after dark. An idyllic spot, nestled in the Adirondack Mountains, about forty-five minutes north of Lake George.

For the sportier types, northern pike, rainbow trout, and walleye attracted anglers from far and wide. In the fall, grown men in red-checked jackets tramped through the local woods shooting deer, rabbits, ducks, and sometimes each other. They strapped their prizes onto the fenders of their station wagons and drove back to their homes, startling unsuspecting motorists along the way.

Each summer when I was a girl, my family spent three weeks on the lake with Aunt Lena. My father loved the fresh air and swimming. He also sketched landscapes in pencil and worked on his papers and books. My mother appreciated the calm of the lake and enjoyed preparing communal meals with her sister-in-law, Lena. They all were fond of drink: wine, gin, and whiskey. My brother, Elijah, and I used to look forward to our Prospector Lake holidays all year long. It was a magical place for us. We swam and baked in the sun, suffered the black flies, caught frogs and fish, and, of course, romped with the children from Arcadia Lodge.

My bathing suit was mostly dry. I stood to survey the view one more time, rotating to take in all 360 degrees of the lake's beauty, when I noticed three men watching the police operation unfold at the other end of the dock. I wrung out my long curls—no easy feat—and wrapped a towel around my waist before approaching them. They looked to be about thirty or thirty-five. One of them smiled and waved to me.

"Is that really you?" asked the curly-haired one with sunglasses, the youngest-looking of the three. "You are Ellie, aren't you? Ellie Stone?"

I surely blushed. "Yes, but I. . ."

He smiled a crooked grin and cocked his head to the right. I noticed the brown speck in his green eyes. He touched his right hand to his chest in a self-conscious gesture of identification. "It's Isaac. Isaac Eisenstadt. And you must remember Simon and David," he said, pointing to his companions.

In an instant their faces came back to me, along with a flood of memories. During my family's summer visits to Prospector Lake, we had shared many meals and parties with them. I was the youngest of the children, but the other kids took me in, allowed me to join them in their games of badminton, tetherball, and water tag. The summer before we entered the war, when I was five years old, the older boys and my brother, Elijah, all decided to shave their heads for some obscure end. Wanting to belong, I demanded they shave mine as well, and they quite nearly did. My mother happened upon us just as they were tying the sheet around my neck to begin the shearing. Elijah, four years older than I, got cuffed on the back of his shorn head for his trouble (and his objectionable haircut), and I was dragged off by my arm back to Cedar Haven, my long, curly hair intact.

Now, seeing them again after so long, I broke into laughter and gave each of them a warm hug. They were all slim and tanned, relaxed and happy, from what looked like weeks of summer vacation. Simon had lost most of his hair, some weight, too, and grown a little goatee, reminiscent of Lenin's tapered beard. David's right leg still stood crooked and withered, just as I remembered it. He had borne the handicap from a young age with the insouciance and lack of awareness that only a child could manage. I remembered him running lopsided, a brace on his leg, playing harder than the rest, laughing louder, too. He defied pity.

Isaac was closer to my age than the others were, probably four or five years older than I. His hazel eyes sparkled in a way I didn't remember. He wasn't tall or particularly muscular, nor would you consider him classically handsome. But his smile and wavy hair called to mind Tony Curtis.

We stood on the dock, chatting and laughing for nearly an hour. David Levine was a pediatrician, working as a staff physician at the Harlem Hospital Center. Simon Abramowitz wrote political pieces and art and music critiques for *Commentary*, the *New Republic*, and the *New Yorker*, among others. He always had his nose in a book. And Isaac taught math at Bronx Science and still played the piano and violin in various chamber groups.

"Why don't you join us at Arcadia tonight?" he said. "Miriam and Rachel and Ruth are here, too. We've got a quartet and the correct number of strings." That made me giggle. "We're going to play some music we've been working on. There's always wine and food. It'll be great fun."

"That sounds lovely," I said. "I'd like to come, but I'm here with my aunt Lena and cousin Max."

"The more the merrier," he said. "Bring them along. My father's here. He'd love to have someone closer to his age to talk about the old days."

David Levine snorted a laugh through his nose. "You know Ellie's aunt is Mrs. Suskind, don't you?" he asked Isaac. "The object of your adolescent fantasies." Then he turned to me. "Isaac spent a couple of summers watching your aunt swim nude in the lake."

Isaac shoved him playfully, nearly knocking him into the water. David's stance was tenuous, after all, even when he wasn't on the receiving end of a push.

"Don't listen to him," said Isaac.

"He had a huge crush on your aunt back then," David said. Isaac was blushing crimson.

"Well, she was quite attractive, and I was a teenager," he admitted, flashing his crooked, Tony Curtis smile. "And no one could convince her to wear a bathing suit. My mother tried for years."

Nothing had changed.

"Your mother was against nudity?" I asked. "I seem to remember a lot of naked swimmers back then."

Isaac shook his head. "She had nothing against people swimming nude in theory. Just your aunt. I think she objected to my dad's admiration of her, er, form."

"It sounds as if you were an admirer as well," I said and immediately regretted it. Why was I gossiping about my naked aunt with an attractive man who'd just invited me to dinner?

The moment grew stale, and everyone's smile dimmed as we looked for something to say. Finally Isaac cleared his throat and repeated the dinner invitation.

"Come 'round the Great Lodge at seven thirty. We'll have trout and sweet corn. Lots to drink. And pork chops, of course. We're good Jews, after all."

Simon frowned. "Speak for yourself. I won't be eating pork."

"That's right," chided Isaac. "Simon keeps kosher these days."

They joked back and forth for a bit, with Simon denying he kept kosher and Isaac insisting that he did.

"So you'll come?" asked Isaac once their bickering had run its course.

I felt a bit shy intruding on their celebrations, but I wanted so much to attend. I told him I'd check with Lena and Max. The three of them were cajoling me some more, insisting that I come, when Tiny Terwilliger and the troopers chugged around the bend in two boats, one of which bore two shrouded bodies. My mood soured.

"What happened anyway?" asked Isaac. "We heard someone was killed."

"Two men," I said. "A man and a teenage boy. They were diving from Baxter's Rock and missed the water."

"Both of them?" asked Isaac "Despite all the warnings and what everyone says, no one ever misses the water."

"Do the police know who they are?" asked Simon.

"The boy seems to be a camper from Orpheus. They don't know who the man is yet."

"Wasn't he carrying any identification?"

"Nothing in his trouser pockets."

The driver loaded the bodies into the back of the hearse, while Terwilliger and the two troopers talked things over. The chief was droning on about something or other. The state cops kept nodding slowly, as if he was putting them to sleep. Finally they threw him a salute, in lieu of shaking the hand he'd offered, and climbed into their cruiser. Terwilliger stepped back and waved as they pulled away from the shoulder and followed the hearse north on Lake Road.

Isaac, David, Simon, and I watched in silence. Once the law had decamped, Terwilliger turned his gaze in our direction and waddled over to join us.

"Well, that's over with," he said to me. Then he sized up my cohorts with a glance and a curt bob of the head as a greeting. I didn't think he was quite used to having Hebrews on his lake.

"Anything new on the identity of the man?" I asked. He shook his head. "What about the boy?"

"I'm going over to Camp Orpheus now to make inquiries."

"What a sad story," said Isaac. "Poor kid."

Terwilliger shrugged. "Yeah, too bad," he said, convincing no one. "That's why we don't want people jumping off cliffs."

He turned to me, nodded, and set off for his truck.

CHAPTER THREE

I scolded myself for having lingered so long at the dock, not knowing if Max was safe or not. It was past six when I arrived at my cabin at Cedar Haven. After peeling off my bathing suit, I ducked into the outdoor shower and hosed off the last of the lake and Tiny Terwilliger's truck smell. Feeling human again, I stepped into a yellow-and-white cotton sundress and a pair of flats, then dragged a brush through my unruly hair. Disgraceful, but nothing to be done about it without a hairdryer. I found Aunt Lena in the kitchen in the main cabin, squeezing limes and preparing some canapés for cocktail hour.

"Tell me what happened out there," she said. "Who was it who was killed?"

I explained that one was an unknown man, possibly a stranger to the area, and the other was a teenage boy from Camp Orpheus. Then I asked casually about Max, who was nowhere in sight.

"Not back from his ambulations," she said. "I swear he's crazier every day. Like Jean-Jacques Rousseau."

"Is it usual for him to stay out so long?" I asked.

She shook her head, sliced some pimento loaf, and placed it on a cracker. "He's usually back in time for a nap around three or three thirty. And he likes to go for a swim about five." She reconsidered her words. "Well, he likes to sit in two feet of water around five."

I peered out the window and chewed my lip. "We're invited to Arcadia this evening," I said, scanning the path that led to Jordan Street in front of our camp, looking for signs of dear Max.

"I haven't seen them in a couple of years. Who invited us?"

"Isaac Eisenstadt. He's here with his father and some of the old gang. Simon Abramowitz and David Levine."

"We'll have to see if Max feels up to it after his long day," said Lena, and I decided I had to tell her the whole story.

I explained that I'd found his station wagon in the clearing above Baxter's Rock. A belt and a pair of trousers belonging to one of the dead men were folded on the front seat.

"That's odd," she said, her cheek twitching just a tad. Aunt Lena wasn't a panicker, so this was a dramatic reaction for her.

"I'm taking my car to go find him," I said. "Do you know where he was going to paint this morning?"

Max had been painting for the previous two days in the woods just west of Grover Road. There was a pretty copse of birches he'd found, and he was working on a series of forest-scapes there, about two miles from Cedar Haven. Aunt Lena gave me directions.

"He's been parking his car off the road that leads to Stu Haller's place," she said. "Just a few yards from Lake Road. You can't miss it."

There was no telephone at Cedar Haven, and only a few phone booths in the village, so I wouldn't be able to call Aunt Lena with any news. I promised to hurry back as soon as I'd located Max.

The evening sky was still light, even if the sun had already disappeared behind the mountains to the west. The light was fading fast, though, which wouldn't make my search any easier. It was seven forty-five when I found the spot Aunt Lena had described. I knew Max's car wasn't there, of course; it was still sitting in the grass a mile away atop Baxter's Rock. The dirt lane leading to Stu Haller's place showed recent tire tracks and a flattened area of wildflowers and weeds a few yards off Lake Road. I figured that was where Max had parked his car. But why had he moved it? Or had someone taken advantage of Max's habit of leaving the keys in plain view and stolen the car? Assuming the latter, I couldn't tell which way Max might have gone on foot. After a few moments' search in the falling light, I found what looked like a narrow path through the woods. Along the trail, I came upon two or three spots that might have matched Aunt Lena's description of birches, but there was no trace of Cousin Max.

It was now eight, and the sun had set. The night had gone dark, with roiling thunderheads tumbling across the sky. I felt a chill on my neck. God, I hated the woods at night. And I didn't relish getting soaked in a down-pour, which was threatening to let loose at any moment. The prospect of rain heightened my anxiety for Max's safety. Where had he gotten to?

Picking my way through the trees, I headed back the way I'd come, searching for the clearing where Max had parked his car. A flash in the sky lit up the black clouds overhead, flickering twice. I stepped up my pace, scratching my cheek on a low-hanging bough as I hurried. A few seconds later, the sky boomed as if breaking apart, and I tripped over a root and hit the ground. I scrambled back to my feet and brushed the pine needles from my hands and the front of my dress. Another crack sounded through the woods, but this time no lightning flash had preceded it. I wasn't alone.

"Max?" I called, holding my breath. No answer. I called his name again and waited. But the only response I got was another, softer snap somewhere behind me in the dark trees. I weighed my options. Run or hide? Climb a tree? Not in a lightning storm.

I heard another crackle and took off on a run. Hands out in front of me to protect my eyes, I tore through the branches, stumbled over rocks and tree trunks, and leapt over fallen logs. Gasping for air, I tripped two more times but was back on my feet instantly, almost without missing a stride, sprinting through the pines and expecting a cold hand to corral me at any moment. I wasn't even sure I was following the correct route back to my car, but stopping to find my bearings was not an option. I would run into the lake and swim to the other side, I told myself, if that was what it took to get away from my pursuer. If, in fact, I was being pursued at all. What if it had been just a deer?

After some time, I emerged from the black woods onto a dirt road. I didn't recognize it as the one I'd arrived on, but it had to be. I must have exited the thick trees farther up the road, closer to Stu Haller's place. Lake Road was surely to my left, unless I'd been completely turned around in my panic after one of my falls. Why hadn't I brought bread crumbs? Wheezing and huffing for breath, I felt the first big drop of rain on my head. Then another. And another. Then the skies opened up, and the rain pelted the ground and me, roaring like a waterfall. I set off in the direction I supposed would lead me to Lake Road and my car. The clouds flashed again, and almost immediately, another thunderclap boomed like a cannonade. I ran, and, as the rain beat down upon me, I was well aware that my pursuer might be standing between me and my car somewhere ahead on the very path I was following.

Then, like an oasis shimmering in the distance, a true road—paved and shouldered—appeared before my eyes. I fumbled for my car keys as I covered the last fifty yards at a dead run, determined to jump inside, start the car, and gun the engine before my pursuer could slit my throat.

Dripping wet I climbed into my Dodge Lancer, which, thank God, was still there on the side of Lake Road, and locked the doors. Rain drummed on the roof, and all was darkness around me. Still panting for air, I turned the ignition. The engine roared to life. I patted the dashboard in sincere appreciation—my car had occasional problems answering the call—and switched on the windshield wipers and the headlights, throwing a pale glow over the flooded black tar. The yellow dividing line, seemingly painted down the middle of the lonely road by a drunken driver, weaved its way around a bend some fifty yards ahead. I shifted into drive and pulled away from the shoulder onto the road. Glancing into the rearview mirror, I could see no threats, no one emerging from the woods. I wiped the foggy windshield with my hand and drew an easy breath, the first, it seemed, in hours. I turned my attention back to the road before me and stamped on the brake. The car skidded across the asphalt, skating over the crooked, yellow dividing line, before finally gaining traction and shuddering to a halt in the middle of the opposite lane.

I leaned on the steering wheel, my heart pounding, as the wipers sloshed back and forth over the windshield. I watched as a fat raccoon waddled across my path, unconcerned or unaware of how close he'd come to greasing the undercarriage of my car. My headlights shone on his tawny fur, as the engine ticked and growled, waiting patiently for him to get out of the way. Happy in his coat of soaking-wet fur, he stepped over a long skid mark, most probably left by another surprised motorist who'd narrowly missed him the night before, and completed his crossing in one piece. He disappeared into the darkness of the brush on the other side without ever having looked back at me. I took my foot off the brake and eased back into my lane heading south.

Keeping my eyes peeled for Max, I continued on into the pouring rain. About a mile and a half later, having driven through the village, I slowed to a stop before an outlet on the west side of the road. A cheerful wooden sign in the shape of a lyre proclaimed, "Camp Orpheus: Never Look Back." My curiosity wrestled with my conscience. I wanted to ask about the young camper who'd fallen to his death, but Max's disappearance was more pressing. I decided to inquire if anyone had seen a lost old man. An innocent question or two about the boy wouldn't hurt a soul. That satisfied the guilt. I flicked the turn signal and made a right into the unpaved lane.

*

"It's been a horrible day," said Norris Lester, director of Camp Orpheus, as he rubbed his temples with his forefingers. "I've just returned from the police station where I met with the Kaufmans, Jerry's parents. They drove up from Albany when they heard. They're disconsolate. Just devastated by the news. We all are."

A slight man with thinning brown hair, horn-rimmed glasses, and a prominent nose, Lester was sporting a Camp Orpheus T-shirt similar to the one the dead boy had worn for his final dive. His eyes were red, his face lined and pale.

"Is that his name?" I asked, ever the reporter. "Jerry Kaufman?"

Lester nodded. "Jerrold, yes." Then he wiped his mouth with a handkerchief, nudged his glasses higher on the bridge of his nose, and offered me a lemonade and a towel. I was soaking wet from my run through the woods. I accepted the towel gladly and the lemonade with a tepid smile; I wanted something stronger.

"It's a terrible story," I said. "Tell me about him. What was he like?"

Lester took a sip of his lemonade. "A talented young man. Sixteen years old. Upstanding boy. He played the violin and piano. Loved Mozart and Saint-Saëns in particular, his instructor tells me. And he wanted to learn the zither, of all instruments. Of course we don't have one here, so he had to settle for the autoharp." He paused, seemingly considering the differences between the two instruments. "Not quite the same thing," he concluded wistfully. "And Jerry was an excellent tennis player. One of the top players in camp."

"What do you suppose he was doing diving off Baxter's Rock at half past noon?" I asked.

Lester shook his head. "I've been told that he missed all his activities today, including breakfast. That's at seven thirty. Apparently he snuck out of his cabin before dawn and never returned."

"Would you mind if I spoke to some of his bunkmates?"

Lester regarded me queerly; he'd just realized I was interrogating him.

"Excuse me, miss," he said, vexed but trying to maintain the civility of a host. "What exactly is your business here?"

"I told the boy who met me outside that I'm looking for an elderly relative of mine. He went missing this morning not too far from here."

Lester spluttered something incoherent about an old man in the infirmary before rising and striding over to a door marked "Secretary." He entered without knocking and reemerged a few moments later with a sandy-haired young man on his heels.

"What's the man's name?" asked Lester, looking exercised. I gave him Max's name. "Pete, here, says he's in our infirmary. Stumbled out of the woods about two hours ago, dehydrated and confused."

CHAPTER FOUR

ousin Max was reclining on a cot, looking like a pasha reigning over the camp's infirmary, smiling and sipping what appeared to be a strawberry milkshake through a paper straw. Upon spotting me in the doorway, he waved jovially but refused to cut short the monologue he was delivering to a middle-aged woman in a white nurse's uniform.

"So you see, the human body doesn't bounce," he declared. "At least not with the spring of, say, a properly inflated basketball. And while there are many moments in life when our natural lack of rubberiness proves to be an asset, falling off cliffs is not one of them."

I crossed the room, planted a kiss on his forehead, and whispered in his ear that his comment was in poor taste.

"Perhaps, my dear," he granted. "But as truisms go, it is unassailable. And I doubt anyone could substantiate it better than those two poor souls who fell off the cliff. But, unfortunately, they died proving it."

"That's enough," I scolded. Then I apologized for him to the nurse, citing fatigue, disorientation, and advanced senility. Max objected vigorously to all three characterizations. Truth be told, he was known for his irreverent ramblings, to the alternating delight and horror of his interlocutors. In the case of the camp nurse, he'd achieved full marks for the latter. She suggested that he seemed recovered enough to get the hell out of her infirmary. Norris Lester, Pete the sandy-haired secretary, and the scowling nurse stood in the doorway watching as I packed Max into my car and drove off into the rain.

⤜⤛

It was nearly ten when we reached Cedar Haven. Max was tired, but I prevailed upon him to fill us in on the travails of his day. He said he'd parked his car off Lake Road a little before 7:00 a.m., precisely where I'd looked for him. He then spent a productive morning fashioning the peeling bark of a birch in his painting. He described the umber-and-sienna mixture he'd whipped up as the finest he could remember. I prompted him to concentrate on his story. Finding the thread again, he told us he was famished by the time he'd worked his way up to a particularly difficult branch of the tree, and he set off back to his station wagon in search of the liverwurst sandwich, egg salad, and thermos of Beaujolais Lena had prepared for him that morning. It was a little past eleven, he said, when he arrived in the clearing where he'd left his car, only to find that it was gone. With the benefit of hindsight, he opined that it had been unwise to leave the keys in the ignition. In the moment, however, he wasn't so much worried about the car or his sandwich, brushes, palettes, and paints inside. But the thermos of Beaujolais might just as well have been a jolly jumbuck stolen by a hungry swagman. He wandered through the woods in search of sustenance for some time until he lost his way. Then he lay down and fell asleep. Hours later, as the sun was going down, he stumbled into a clearing where an orchestra of adolescent children was sitting in folding chairs playing what sounded like Holst's "Jupiter." Max swore he had been hallucinating at that point, as such a scene was impossible. For a brief moment, I entertained the idea of explaining that his recollection was most certainly correct, but in the end I thought better of it. Max delighted in our pity until he'd inhaled his second glass of port, at which point he excused himself and went to bed.

"While you were out looking for Max, that Chief Terwilliger stopped in to ask about the photographs you took," said Lena once we were alone. "He stood here in the kitchen staring at me open-mouthed until I offered him a cup of coffee. He told me he'd never really met a Jewess before. I told him that was nice, but he wasn't my first bigot."

"I trust you threw out the cup he used," I said.

"Smashed it into a million pieces. By the way, that Isaac fellow came by about a half hour ago, asking what had happened to you. He looked disappointed."

I checked my watch. Twenty past ten. I wondered if the Arcadians had turned in for the night. They were on vacation, after all. I was still keyed up from the events of the day: two dead bodies, a wayward Cousin Max, and a terrifying close call with God-knows-what in the woods. And I hadn't forgotten the news report about the escapee, Donald Yarrow, either. But the rain had stopped, and, though I dreaded the woods in the dark, I figured I might be up for a quick gallop over to Arcadia Lodge. It was no more than four or five hundred yards, after all.

I yawned and rose to take my leave.

"Good night, Aunt Lena," I said, the hint of a smile curling my lips.

August is hot in the Adirondacks, with temperatures regularly reaching the upper eighties. But the nights can be cool, especially when a thunderstorm has just passed. After a quick change into a fresh dress, I reestablished dominion over my bird's nest of hair with a little water, a brush, and a couple of bobby pins. I dabbed some Touch and Glow onto my cheek to conceal the scratch I'd suffered during my escape earlier that evening. Then I rolled just a hint of pink onto my lips and slipped out the door.

The night was still. No crickets after the rain. At the end of our short lane, I stepped onto Jordan Street and considered my options. I could turn left and follow the street for a quarter mile and circle around on Lake Road to reach Arcadia Lodge. I could avoid the woods completely with that route, but it would take me twenty minutes unless I ran. And that would put my hair back in the seaweed category. I didn't want to take my car in case I got cold feet or the Arcadians had turned in. The headlights would be noticed. And, of course, Aunt Lena would surely hear. Cutting straight through the trees on the opposite side of Jordan Street would get me to Arcadia in four or five minutes on foot. I weighed the pros and cons of each route. Then, shaming myself for my timidity, I marched across the road and ducked into the woods.

A soupy mist rose from the forest floor, testing my resolve from the very outset. The pine needles, sodden and sticky, caked my shoes as I snaked my way through the trees, but at least I heard no snapping twigs and encountered no marauders. My skin tingled nevertheless as I rushed through the last of the trees. Finally, having saved at least fifteen minutes with my shortcut, I emerged onto Lake Road. By all appearances, I was alone. The moon shone above, partially obscured by banks of clouds racing across its face. I smoothed my dress, brushed a rebellious strand of hair out of my eyes, and made my way up the path that led to Arcadia Lodge.

I could hear music coming from the Great Lodge where the Arcadians shared meals and social events. A violin and piano. Bartók. Romanian folk dances, I was sure of it. I have this uncanny and rather useless talent for remembering music. My father used to show me off at dinner parties to his friends. A parlor trick. Bartók wasn't exactly what I would have chosen for a sing-along, but the duo—especially the piano—was acquitting itself remarkably well.

The doors and windows were all thrown open wide, and a warm light spilled out into the night. I paused at the entrance to listen and to watch and wait until they'd reached the end. The hall was a large building with high rafters and a pitched roof at least three stories high. Built completely of pine, it achieved the appropriate rustic look without compromising on fine workmanship and intricate touches. Exquisitely carved flourishes adorned the lintels and stanchions. A mezzanine of sorts, accessible by a wooden stairway and its magnificent balustrade, dominated the room on the north side. At the southern end of the room, an immense stone fireplace rose six feet high. Mounted above the hearth, a proud buck's head, eighteen points, as I later counted, surveyed the room as if it were his realm. Poor thing. Someone had shot, stuffed, and posed him, then hung him on the wall for the pleasure of whosoever enjoyed gazing upon the severed heads of regal beasts. He was indeed a handsome specimen. I only wished I could have caught the fleetingest glimpse of him bounding through the forest—an instant and no more—instead of admiring him forever in his frozen beauty.

Isaac was seated with his back to me, playing the violin. Simon was to his right, a cello resting in its case by his side, as he listened with his eyes closed to the duo. A young, raven-haired woman played the spinet piano a few feet away. She looked familiar. It had to be Miriam, I thought. David was also present, as was Isaac's sister, Rachel, and a few older folks.

A hand touched my shoulder, and I loosed a scream, just about jumping out of my shoes. The music stopped. I reeled around to defend myself against my aggressor and nearly knocked over a small old man wearing a Greek fisherman's cap. The musicians and others rushed to investigate. I apologized repeatedly; the man who'd touched my shoulder was Isaac's sixty-five-year-old father, the painter Jakob Eisenstadt.

Once it had been determined that no one was hurt, I was escorted into the hall, smiles all around, just as if I hadn't almost bashed in the head of the oldest and most famous man in the room. Isaac introduced me to everyone. I knew David and Simon, of course, but I hadn't seen Miriam Abramowitz née Berg (the pianist and Simon's wife) since I was ten years old. That was a year after the war ended, the last time I'd visited Aunt Lena and Uncle Mel on Prospector Lake.

Two or three years older than I, Miriam had never been chummy with me. As a young girl she had been inscrutable, always staring but saying little. She had grown up to be a striking creature in an unusual way. Her mane of jet-black hair and beguiling figure inspired envy in women and lust in men. Her face, however, was closer to plain than beautiful. In no way unattractive, her features struck me as somehow ordinary. My brother, Elijah, once said that it would help if she smiled more often. Or knocked off the creepy stare. But her intellectual and physical intensity attracted people of both sexes and of all ages. She was standing before me now in a faded summer dress that, for all its plainness, couldn't hide her abundant bosom, flat stomach, and curvaceous hips. A head of beautiful hair and a statuesque physique more than compensated for her did-not-place beauty and cheerless personality.

Isaac's sister, Rachel, was about my age, unmarried and unlikely to follow the path of matrimony. She was the dutiful daughter, dedicating her life to taking care of her aged widowed father. Rachel and I had played together as children on the lake. My father was fond of telling the story of how Rachel and I had formed a club with three other girls, Ruth and Sarah Hirsch, and Shelly Leonard. At the first meeting, I convinced the girls to elect me president of the club. That settled, the first order of business, I proclaimed, was that there would be no more elections. The other girls went along without protest. Despite his aversion to fascistic governance, especially given that this had all taken place at the height of the war, my father still chuckled over my moxie.

Once I'd been welcomed by all, some of the older folks retired for the evening. I explained to the remaining Arcadians why I'd nearly KO'd Isaac's father, that I'd been quite frightened earlier in the woods. But by then few were listening. Isaac took my elbow and showed me to an armchair. He pulled up one of the chairs the chamber group had been using and sat down with me.

"Sorry I interrupted the music," I said.

"Don't worry about that. We were almost finished anyway." He paused to reflect. "Not that anyone could tell." I laughed. "I was afraid you wouldn't come," he said and grazed my hand with his so no one else would see.

"I was otherwise detained. My cousin Max went missing this morning, and I only located him this evening."

Isaac showed what looked like true concern. "I remember him from so many evenings here at Arcadia. He used to drink port, I think, and have long discussions with my dad and Herbie Schwartz. Is he all right?"

"Max is fine. Resting comfortably at Cedar Haven. And he still enjoys his port. He was well enough to enjoy a couple of quick glasses when he got home. But I'm so sorry about your father. I'm afraid I gave him a shock just now."

Isaac smiled at me. Such an infectious smile. My eyes surely sparkled, and my skin tingled again, this time without the terror I'd felt in the woods earlier that evening. His gaze held mine for several beats until I blinked and looked away. He asked if I wanted a drink.

The evening's musical program had ended with my awkward arrival, but the assembled seemed happy to continue the revelry. Isaac managed to scare up a glass of whiskey. Not my usual Dewar's, but a reasonable substitute in the circumstances. (I had an unopened bottle in my suitcase back at Cedar Haven.) The others were well into a third bottle of Mateus, and soon Miriam sat down at the piano against the wall and started playing the "Brindisi" from *La Traviata*. The assembled joined in in full voice, clinking glasses and making merry. I was drinking too fast and, since I'd missed dinner, felt a rush to my head and a rumble in my stomach. The singing continued with a stream of popular arias chosen seemingly at random. From Puccini ("Parigi o cara") to Verdi ("La donna è mobile"), ending with Mozart. With no mandolin in the house, Isaac plucked his violin on bended knee as he serenaded me with "Deh vieni alla finestra" from *Don Giovanni*, thrilling and embarrassing me at the same time. He had a lovely voice and did justice to the "Serenade." He segued into "Là ci darem la mano" but butchered it, inadvertently creating an obscene result by changing *le pene* ("pains") to *il pene* ("penis"). I suspected I was the only one who noticed.

"That's enough," said Isaac, coughing and laughing in highest spirits. He packed his violin into its case and suggested the group show some consideration and play something Ellie could enjoy. My heart sank.

"Play 'The Twist' for her," said Simon, giggling like an idiot. "That won't go over her head."

The others laughed as well, and Miriam rose to switch on the radio.

I struggled to maintain a smile for public consumption. How I wanted to fit in with these remarkable people, but they clearly considered me a dilettante. Their laughter stung me hard, humiliated me, and I felt the blood drain from my cheeks. Half of me wanted to slip away and dissolve into the night, run fast and far from the chair where I'd received Isaac's irresistible romantic serenade. I wanted to disappear, especially since I'd demurred like a coward and—like a good girl—said nothing to contradict or correct their impressions. But the other half of me wanted to prove my worth. To be fair, they had no reason to suspect I knew the first thing about modern orchestral music, the operatic canon, or even Italian. But the fact that I could recite chapter and verse on Bartók and correct Isaac's Italian meant nothing as long as I kept my mouth shut.

Isaac flashed his white teeth and sparkling eyes at me. From the radio, Nat King Cole sang "Don't Try," accompanied by what sounded like three squares in checkered jackets. I swallowed my whiskey in one go, trying to pass my frown off as the result of the strong drink.

After the opera singing, everyone collapsed on wicker chairs and lumpy sofas and refilled glasses with various libations. I continued sipping whiskey. I knew if I let myself go, I could drink the men under the table, but that's not a good impression for a girl to make. I wanted to be accepted. I'd missed that feeling of belonging since losing my own family, and I longed to find it again. I craved Isaac's approval most of all.

We discussed everything from the fence the Soviets had thrown up in Berlin that week to Eichmann's trial in Israel to books we'd been reading. Simon had just finished *To Kill a Mockingbird*, which had made quite a splash the previous summer, and he pronounced it "a balm for white guilt." Everyone else said they'd loved it.

We talked of the old days, with the men dominating the conversation. Miriam, Rachel, Ruth, and I nursed our drinks while the boys argued over exactly who had capsized Mr. Wasserman's dinghy on an unauthorized fishing expedition twenty years earlier. The boat sank and was never recovered. David said it had been one of the older boys, but Simon insisted it was young Isaac's rocking that had tipped the boat over.

My family had known the Arcadia bunch well, and I remembered my father having praised Simon's dad, a poet and novelist, for his vociferous support and fundraising for the Republicans in Spain. Isaac's mother had died a few years before, and his father, Jakob—the man who'd startled me at the door—was a painter of note. My mother, an art dealer, had admired his paintings, which were deeply rooted in German Expressionism. Jakob had grown up in Dresden, and, given the paucity of his work, his paintings were highly sought after by some collectors, who paid extraordinary sums to acquire them. Shortly after the Kristallnacht pogrom, during which his family's business was razed to the ground, Jakob was interned for a month at Buchenwald before he and his wife were forced to emigrate. Thanks to a wealthy patron's sponsorship, Jakob Eisenstadt managed to sneak under the quota and secure a visa to the United States. He arrived in New York with his wife, Lisa, their young son, Isaac, and daughter, Rachel, in February 1939.

"Whatever happened to those friends of yours?" I asked the group. "There was one named Andrew something. He was always very funny."

"Andrew Kline," said Isaac. "He served in the navy in the Pacific during the war. I heard he met a girl in the islands and stayed there."

"That's not true," said Simon. "He had psychological troubles after the war and is in a sanitarium somewhere in Oregon."

"His parents passed away," said Rachel, "and nobody knows for certain what happened to him."

"Of course, poor Howie never made it back," said Isaac. "Remember him? Howard Feingold?" I did but only vaguely. "He was the oldest of our generation. Killed in action in North Africa."

The mood grew melancholy, and a long discussion of the scourge of the war ensued. It had touched everyone in the room, everyone across the country.

"What about the one named for Lenin?" I asked, trying to move the subject back to more pleasant memories. "I don't remember his name, but his mother used to call for him at suppertime."

No one volunteered.

"You know, it was something like 'Vladimir Ilyich Ulyanov Lefkowitz, you come in for supper!'"

Isaac's smile dimmed ever so slightly, while Simon cleared his throat and frowned outright. Apparently I'd tripped over some old bones.

"I'm sorry," I said, thinking he must have met some tragic end. "Have I said something wrong?"

Isaac made an effort to relight his smile and brushed off my apology. "Not at all, Ellie," he said. "It's just that Karl—that's Karl Marx Merkleson—moved to California many years ago, and we haven't stayed in touch."

I drew a sigh, relieved it wasn't a more woeful tale. But then Simon stood up and poured himself another drink.

"Karl betrayed his family, friends, and his faith," he announced. "He converted to Christianity, for God's sake. As far as I'm concerned, he's dead. And good riddance."

I stiffened in my seat. The story was a little bit woeful after all.

"Not with the faith again," moaned Isaac. "Simon, we're all atheists here except for you."

"That's right, Isaac. And you're all wrong. What are we doing here if no God exists?"

"Not now, Simon," said Miriam, his weary wife. "No one wants to hear it again."

"Sorry to disappoint you, old friend," said Isaac, staking claim to the last word. "But there is no God."

Then, perhaps realizing that he knew nothing of my beliefs, he turned to me and apologized if he'd offended me.

"It's all right," I said, thinking he should apologize to Simon instead. "My father loved debating God with others. Jews and Christians alike. It didn't matter. He loved the exercise."

"And what about you?"

"My mother used to say that arguing with a passionate believer of any tenet is a losing proposition. You'll never win the argument. But even if you do, you destroy something much more important in your opponent than his case."

"Destroying the argument for atheism won't hurt anyone," said Simon. "Quite the opposite. If I could convince you all to embrace God, you would lose nothing. You would win in the bargain and be enriched."

"Enough," snapped Miriam. "How do you reconcile your God and all his warts with socialism? You're such a hypocrite."

"Socialism and God are not mutually exclusive. We Jews aren't like those crazy evangelicals in the village who preach love in Jesus's name, but in practice act more like bigots and fascists."

The room fell silent after that. It seethed and hissed emotionally, especially between the married couple, but no one spoke for at least a minute. A long minute. I actually heard bullfrogs croaking outside the hall. As the silence wore on, I wondered if I could slip out without being noticed. That was impossible, of course. Adding to my discomfort was the knowledge that my question had provoked the fight in the first place.

I was about to excuse myself when Isaac's father wrestled himself out of his chair and, unhappy with the strife that had ruined the end of a fine evening, announced that he was turning in for the night. He stopped to grasp my hand in his bony, wrinkled grip. His eyes smiled at me, and he wished me good night.

"I hope to see you again tomorrow for supper, despite this ugliness," he said.

Then he shuffled out of the Great Lodge. Rachel excused herself, saying she would see him to his cabin and be right back.

After several more minutes had passed with no conversation, Simon offered me a limp apology for having made such a fuss in front of a guest.

"I'm a passionate person," he said. "I get a little excited sometimes. If I made you feel uncomfortable or unwelcome, I'm sorry."

I thought that as long as he was saying he was sorry, he might as well apologize for the "Twist" crack he'd made earlier, but I let that sleeping dog lie.

The general mood started to improve after that, until David Levine outdid my faux pas by asking me apropos of nothing what Elijah was up to these days. That was a haymaker. Miriam actually gasped. I caught my breath.

"What? What did I say?" he asked.

No one answered him, perhaps in deference to me. Maybe they thought it was my place to respond. I tried to put on a brave smile, but it must have looked as stiff as cement.

"Didn't you know?" I asked, trying to swallow the lump in my throat. "Elijah died four years ago. A motorcycle accident."

David rose from his chair and limped to my side. He took my hand, apologizing for his gaffe and expressing his shock and condolences all in one breath. I told him it was all right, that he couldn't have known. Besides the tightness in my throat, there were tears welling in my eyes, but I willed myself not to weep, convinced that a breakdown at a party was not the way to mourn my brother.

The evening devolved further into Grand Guignol, with my family as the tragic subject. Everyone present seemed to know of my mother's death from cancer four years earlier, and they mumbled their sympathies. The girls reminisced about how sweet and kind she had been to them, how she used to offer them a lemonade on a hot day. Rachel said my mother had accompanied her to the dock one day for a swim when the other adults were too busy to do so.

"She was a wonderful soul," she said.

The boys echoed her thoughts, and I just sat there, not sure what to say in return. Then, just as the awkwardness was abating, Simon decided it was the right moment to express his condolences for my father's death. I should have expected it, of course. It was only natural after the discussions of Elijah and my mother to move on to my father. Yet it took me by surprise. I stifled my emotions, pushed them down, promising myself I would let them out later, when I was alone. I somehow managed to maintain my composure, but I felt my cheeks flush and a vein throb in my forehead. I thanked Simon but gave no details of the attack on my father in his New York apartment or the coma from which he never emerged.

I cleared my throat and waved my hands before me, feigning good humor, as if to clear the sad tidings still hanging in the air. They were all staring at me with eyes full of pity. Thankfully Isaac leaned forward and touched my wrist. He took my hand in his and smiled into my eyes. He whispered to me.

"Do you remember when Elijah slid down that embankment and cut his ass on a rock?"

I blinked at him, startled by the sudden change of tone and the unvarnished vocabulary. Then I found myself smiling back at him.

"He was too embarrassed to tell my mother," I said. "The blood dripped down his leg for hours and soaked the insole of his sneaker."

"And when your father finally took him to Dr. Newcomb for stitches, Elijah insisted on wearing his swim trunks so the nurse wouldn't see his bare rear end."

"I'd forgotten that part," I said. And I laughed.

Isaac gazed into my eyes, still holding my hand, and let loose a good chuckle himself. Then the others joined in, not without a few tears mixed in, but the worst was behind me.

"Your glass is empty," said Isaac, snatching it away and refilling it in a trice. "Now let's sing the 'Brindisi' again."

"That sounds grand," I said, my eyes surely sparkling at him, but not with tears. "*Libiamo nei lieti calici.*"

Isaac did a double take, and his expression betrayed a doubt. Perhaps he'd underestimated me?

"You . . . You know the words? In Italian?"

"Her father was a famous professor of Italian," drawled Miriam, already sitting at the piano, poised to begin.

In that moment, after the story of Elijah's stitches, it was hard to resist the urge to throw my arms around him and kiss him. But I restrained myself. He extended a hand to help me out of my seat. I took it and, holding his gaze with mine, thought, "*Più caldi baci avrà.*"

I earned a small measure of respect and surprise from the gang during the evening's second round of musical numbers. Not only had my upbringing exposed me to a fair amount of Italian, I knew more arias, in both German and Italian, than my linguistic talents might have suggested. My memory for words—even foreign words—qualified as remarkable, and years of listening to grand opera in my father's study had prepared me well for the game. Rachel complimented my Italian after we'd sung "Ritorna vincitor" from *Aida*. My accent was much better in song than in speech; I'm not sure how that was possible, but it was true.

"We'll have to find a more challenging game for tomorrow evening," said Isaac with a wink, and he wrapped a warm arm around my shoulder. It must have looked like an innocent brotherly hug to the others, but I felt the gentle squeeze and received the message loud and clear.

It was after 1:00 a.m. One by one, the assembled faded and began retiring for the night. Simon called to Miriam to follow him to bed, but she shook her head and said she wanted to stay up. He scowled and told her to suit herself and not to wake him when she came in. He trudged back to their cabin alone.

Soon only Isaac, Miriam, and I remained in the Great Lodge.

"You're not tired, Miriam?" asked Isaac a few minutes later.

She ignored his question and stared at the buck's head over the huge fireplace. Isaac nudged me and raised his eyebrows in what looked like a silent invitation to follow him. But I'd surely caused enough gossip for one evening and didn't want to set any records.

"It's late," I said. "I should be going now."

Isaac tried to dissuade me, insisting that the night was young. Miriam just stared at the stag on the wall. I thanked them both and headed for the exit. Isaac followed me, offering to accompany me back to Cedar Haven. Once we were outside the lodge, out of Miriam's line of sight, he grabbed me around the waist and pulled me close, pressing our hips together with great insistence. Then he kissed me, long and hard. A mite too rough, I thought, given our brief acquaintance, but not so hard that I didn't enjoy it. Or reciprocate.

"Come with me to my cabin," he whispered.

"I can't," I said, nearly breathless. "My aunt will worry."

Isaac persisted. "I'll sneak you back before sunrise. You don't want to leave, I know it."

I said nothing, and he kissed me again.

"Isaac?" Damn it. Miriam was standing in the doorway of the lodge watching us. "There you are. I'm going to bed. Good night."

Cursing myself for my forward behavior in front of people I barely knew, I pulled away from Isaac.

"I've got to go now," I said.

"Don't mind her. She's harmless. Come with me to my cabin."

CHAPTER FIVE

SUNDAY, AUGUST 20, 1961

It was still dark outside when I rose and crept across the room. I gathered my dress and underthings from the floor, then grabbed my shoes. I looked back at the bed. Isaac was asleep, facing the other way. I turned the handle on the door—no creaking—and slipped into the next room. There, I dressed and scribbled a brief note that I left on the breakfast table.

Leaving before daybreak to avoid scandal. Ellie

The first blush of dawn broke in the eastern sky as I stepped off the porch of Isaac's cabin. I glanced at my watch—just after six. Scanning the surrounding cabins for early risers, I saw no one. I crossed the compound and disappeared into the woods unnoticed. My worries of being seen escaping Arcadia now behind me, I could concentrate on my fear of crossing the thick woods in near darkness. The trees were, in fact, blocking all but the faintest glow in the sky to the east, so it might just as well have been midnight with a crescent moon. I couldn't see more than a few feet in front of me, so I had to go slowly. Despite the gloom, I could hear the first birds of the day chirping their morning songs. Soon it would become a chorus. But until the sun peeked over the mountains across the lake to the east, I would feel no comfort.

I stepped gingerly over the pine needles, trying to move in silence, but I was no Indian scout. If I could hear my footsteps, so could a marauder or an on-the-lam murderer. My skin felt cold and clammy, and the dew of the forest floor, kicked up by my shoes, soaked my toes and sprinkled my ankles.

I paused and listened. Had I heard something to my left? Squinting through the darkness was useless. I couldn't discern anything but gray and black pine trees. Carefully, I took a first step then another, treading as if fearing to detonate a landmine underfoot, and resumed my long, unnerving journey.

My father came to mind. His life's work was dedicated to the study of Dante, especially *The Divine Comedy*. I remembered a spooky drawing of his of the dark wood of *The Inferno*, thick with gray and black trees, bare but for their sharp, brittle branches, some tapering into winding tendrils or long, bony fingers. That sketch, and many others, gave me nightmares as a girl. Weaving through the trees, I felt now that, like the pilgrim Dante, I was in a dark wood and the right path was lost to me. Perhaps not a spiritual crisis in my case, but I was experiencing serious doubts of whether I was heading in the right direction to exit the woods. Not a good time for me to recollect childhood nightmares. I pushed on toward the light—the east—and, I hoped, Cedar Haven.

It seemed like half a lifetime, though it was only ten minutes according to my watch, when I finally emerged from the trees onto Jordan Street. I found myself about two hundred yards farther east toward Lake Road, but I was relieved to be out of the dark forest. The sky was brightening, and I knew night had passed. Now free of the woods, I chided myself for surrendering to my childhood fears. The trees weren't going to devour me, after all.

I turned to head up the empty street, reflecting on the night I'd spent at Arcadia. I thought of that song by the Shirelles, "Will You Still Love Me Tomorrow?" I wasn't sentimental over my attachments with males of the species, and I didn't usually worry about being loved in the morning. But that night had been different. I didn't care to enumerate in my mind Isaac's qualities, though they were many, as I believed that attraction was not a formula or a recipe one could mix together. Rather it was the sum of the parts, a tenebrous and unfathomable chemistry of warmth, spirit, and desire that can never be known and certainly not explained. I wanted him—that much I knew—and it was all I cared about in that moment.

There was a light in Aunt Lena's bedroom in the main cabin, but the sitting room and kitchen were dark. I felt confident that she hadn't yet embarked on her morning hike to the lake and back, so my late-night tryst was still secret. Aunt Lena wouldn't have judged me, but I preferred to keep my affairs to myself.

There's a time and place to steep oneself in the redolence of intimacy, but daybreak brings other undertakings. With the rising sun, I put all the romance to bed for another day. It would keep until the cover of darkness returned. I stripped out of my clothes and stepped into the cold shower behind my cabin to wash away the indulgences of the night.

I found Max alone in Lena's kitchen, slathering butter on a slice of wheat toast. Given his adventure of the previous day, I was surprised to find him up and about at such an early hour. I told him he should be resting. He dismissed my concerns in typical fashion.

"The earth has rotated on its axis, my dear. The moon and stars have completed their nocturnal peregrinations, and the sun is dispatching its daily duty high in the sky. Why wouldn't I, too, be engaged in fruitful enterprise?"

"Because you got yourself lost last night and nearly died in the woods."

He waved his hand. "A leisurely stroll through a sylvan glade, my dear." And he smiled at me over his eyeglasses.

"Do you still have that Kodak home-developer's kit?" I asked, changing the subject. He nodded. "May I use it? I need to develop a few rolls of film I shot yesterday for the chief of police."

"Help yourself," he said. "Everything is in order. The chemicals are fresh, and there's plenty of Velite paper. But the enlarger is broken."

Max had set up a darkroom inside the small powder room off the kitchen. I took forty-five minutes to run the film through the roll tank, add the developer then the fixer, then rinse off the negatives and hang them to dry.

I returned to the kitchen for some coffee and toast. Max was still at the table, now slicing a banana. Aunt Lena was sitting beside him, nursing a cup of coffee. She gave me a sly look.

Damn it. She knew.

Isaac showed up on foot at half past eleven, just as we'd agreed in the small hours the night before. We'd rehearsed an act, intended to throw Lena off the scent and preserve my good name. Isaac was to arrive at Cedar Haven with the innocent goal of finding out what had prevented me from attending the gathering at Arcadia Lodge. As soon as he began, I signaled to him to cheese it; we would have looked ridiculous.

Aunt Lena prepared a light lunch of vegetables from her garden and some frozen northern pike that Max had caught a week earlier on the lake. She claimed he'd nearly been yanked out of the boat when the fish took the bait and would certainly have ended up as the fish's supper, instead of the other way around, had it not been for the quick thinking and assistance of Bennie Wilson, the young man who graciously took Max fishing from time to time. Max disputed her account of the events with the vigor of a fiery defense attorney, which, of course, he was.

"My dominance over the fishes of river and sea has yet to be challenged by the slippery little bastards," he said in conclusion. Aunt Lena rolled her eyes.

Isaac seemed to enjoy Max's peculiar turns of phrase, idiosyncrasies, and genial oddness, if back-slapping and joking like a couple of old cronies meant what I thought it did. He invited Aunt Lena, Max, and me to Arcadia for dinner and entertainment that evening and wouldn't let go of the bone until they'd agreed. He offered to send a car for them, but I said that wouldn't be necessary.

"I'll drive them," I said.

"A woman driver," Isaac said to Max, nudging his ribs. "Are you sure you want to take the chance?"

Max frowned. "I don't know what you mean, my boy," he said. "In my experience, Ellie is an excellent driver. Fine hand-eye coordination, quick reflexes, and perfect vision. I have no reservations about her abilities behind the wheel."

I said nothing. Isaac's grin wilted, and he mumbled an apology.

"Don't apologize to me, my boy," said Max. "It's Ellie, here, whose driving skills you've impugned."

"He's pulling your leg," said Aunt Lena. "Ignore him."

"What were we talking about?" asked Max, feigning befuddlement, something he liked to do regularly.

"Dinner at Arcadia Lodge," prompted Isaac. "Will you join us?"

"I'd love to," said the old devil. "But how do you propose we get there?"

The sun was burning high in the sky when Isaac and I reached the village. We stopped at the bakery run by Mrs. Ingve Enquist, a transplant from Norway who used butter as if it was melting in the back room. Isaac offered me a couple of almond cookies for dessert after our lunch, and we enjoyed them in two chairs on the front porch facing Lake Road and the water on the other side.

"What are you up to, Ellie?" he asked as I snapped a photo of him with the eastern mountains as a backdrop. "What's your grand plan in life?"

I shrugged and slipped the camera back into its case. "No grand plan. I work as a newspaper reporter. I find it very rewarding. That's enough for now."

He nodded then asked why I wasn't married. "You're twenty-five. Why hasn't anyone snatched you up?"

"I'm quite good at avoiding capture," I answered. "Why aren't you married?"

He smiled and said it was different for a man.

The village of Prospector Lake straddled Lake Road, also known as Route 15, for about a half mile. Small quaint businesses lined the thoroughfare, catering mostly to the summer tourist trade. Ice cream parlors, a couple of taverns, gift shops, and eateries on one side, the post office, library, and sporting goods on the other. At the center of the village was a square that served as the fulcrum of community activity. A green with a large bandstand, a gazebo, spreading chestnut trees, and rows of boxwood hedges, Palmer Square presented a postcard-perfect image of an Adirondack idyll. As Isaac and I strolled across the grass, we passed a pushcart selling popcorn and another with cotton candy. There was a man flying a kite, inviting curious children to take turns holding the string. And there were groups promoting various activities and causes.

"Look over there," said Isaac, pointing to four sorry-looking specimens, flanked by two American flags, manning a small booth piled high with pamphlets. A sign stenciled in black read, "John Birch Society of America."

"I've heard of them," I said. "They're the rabid anti-Communists."

Isaac nodded. "They march around like they're saving the Free World, but Prospector Lake isn't exactly the State Department."

"No card-carrying Communists to root out?" I asked. He smiled and shook his head. "What about the Politburo of Jewish Bolsheviks at Arcadia Lodge?"

"No, we're not Communists," he said with a wave of his hand. "Not all of us, anyway." He paused, watching the John Birchers across the square. Then he added, "Not anymore."

"You should steer clear of those fellows. They look like a rough bunch."

"No, they're all bark and no bite," said Isaac. "Do you see the skinny kid standing in the back?"

I located the object of Isaac's interest: a bleak, gaunt sluggard in a tattered Mickey Mouse Club T-shirt and brown corduroy slacks. (In this heat?) He stood rooted in place, like a timid dog who'd been ordered to sit. His head hung several degrees below the perpendicular as he peered dully from beneath a Neanderthal brow.

"See him?" Isaac asked again.

"The one who looks like a gargoyle fetus? What about him?"

"That's Waldo Coons. He does odd jobs for us at Arcadia."

"Shrinking heads?" I asked.

Isaac chuckled but didn't answer. "Last year, the other lodgers wanted to get rid of him, but my father said he was harmless. As a matter of fact, he'll be helping out at the supper we're hosting tonight. Come on. I'll introduce you."

We approached the John Birch table, causing a minor seism among the pamphleteers. They didn't quite know how to react to interest in their cause. The first man, seated at the table, jumped to his feet and turned to his comrades, who were standing behind him, signaling furiously that they should close ranks with him. I picked up a pamphlet, the *Communist Next Door*, and examined it with feigned interest. Isaac waved to Waldo Coons, who stared blankly at him for several seconds as if he'd been anesthetized by the whack of a shovel to the back of the head. Finally the penny dropped, and he moved his hand in some kind of primate greeting.

"How are you, Waldo?" asked Isaac once we had initiated a palaver behind the pamphlet table.

"Okay," he said.

"This is a friend of mine. Ellie."

I said hello. Waldo didn't speak. He gaped at me and shuffled on the grass, raking his gnawed-off fingernails over his scabby arms.

"Well, just wanted to say hello," said Isaac. "We'll be going now."

"Nice chatting with you," I said, and we moved away.

About twenty yards past the John Birch table, a large group of men, women, and children dressed in their Sunday finest were handing out pamphlets of their own. There were three skirted card tables, manned by unsmiling, middle-aged ladies. Above each table, a different banner announced the good news: "The Tommy Grierson Crusade" with smaller slogans trailing underneath: "Jesus is the Way!" and "Jesus Died for Us. Let Us Live for Him," and "There Are No Reds on the Green of Palmer Square!"

We stopped a short distance away to observe. A tall, thin man of about forty, dressed in a rumpled white suit, shuttled from one end of the three tables to the other, whispering instructions or admonishment—it was hard to tell for sure which—to his charges. He was handsome, with a long, thin face and a mane of prematurely silvering hair. Quite dramatic looking. The ladies nodded at him, all serious, lips pursed, as if poised to defend all Christendom from invading hordes of Red infidels. A little old lady with bluish hair asked one of them for a pamphlet. Then an old man in coveralls approached and read the banner for a long minute without saying a word. He looked more a lonely soul than a lost one. Several children milled about near the tables, some picking their noses, others scratching their rear ends. None was saved that day.

"Look at that girl," I whispered to Isaac. "The one sitting behind the tables near Billy Graham, there," I said referring to the man in white.

"Where?" he asked, scanning the group. Then he spotted her. "She's pretty. And quite bored. Bored to tears, I'd say."

I shook my head. "That's not boredom. She's been crying, poor thing. I wonder what happened."

"I still say she's bored. I'd weep too if I had to sit in the sun all day peddling religious pamphlets to lonesome old farmers."

"I'm going to talk to her," I said and started toward the tables.

Isaac caught my arm and asked if I was really serious. "Let's go down to the dock and have a swim instead."

"This won't take a minute," I said, well aware that it was going to take much longer.

I approached the tables casually and was set upon as if by a swarm of starved mosquitoes, only these blood-suckers attacked with outstretched arms and mimeographed pamphlets. I excused myself, pushed past them all, and arrived face-to-face with a girl of about fifteen or sixteen. She was dressed in a gray skirt and white blouse, buttoned up to her neck. Her light-brown hair was tied back in a low ponytail with a piece of yarn.

"Hi," I said, smiling. She stared off into space. "I'd like some information about Jesus."

She continued to gaze, catatonic, at nothing in particular. I waved my hand before her eyes, and she turned to look at me.

"That's rude," she said.

"Sorry about that," I offered. "I wanted to ask you a question, and you seemed distracted."

"Yes, well, not a good day," she said. "I'd like to be left alone, if you don't mind."

"Of course. I just thought you looked like you wanted to tell someone your troubles. I'll push off and leave you to yourself." I didn't push off.

She looked up at me from her seat, squinting into the bright sunlight of the day. Her hair was sun-bleached, her nose sunburned. And her eyes were red.

"You're not with us. I can tell," she said. "I've never seen you before."

"I saw you and thought you might like a friendly ear."

"Really? You'd actually listen to me?" she asked, her eyes darting from side to side, gauging the scrutiny of her fellow crusaders. I nodded. "I can't talk here," she said. "Will you meet me at the ice cream parlor in twenty minutes?"

⋙

I ditched Isaac, promising to see him later that evening at Arcadia. He didn't understand why I needed to talk to that girl, but, in the end, he shrugged and wished me luck.

The girl was sitting alone at the last table inside Harvey's Double-Dip ice cream parlor, staring miserably at the floor. I slid into the chair opposite her and noticed her left hand, resting languidly on the white-and-gold Textolite tabletop. She was wearing a friendship ring on her ring finger.

"My name's Ellie," I said. "What's yours?"

"Emily," she mumbled. "Emily Grierson from Youngstown, Ohio."

"Any relation to Tommy Grierson?"

"My father," she said, as if a little embarrassed.

A round lady of a certain age, wearing a colorful apron, appeared and asked what we'd have. Emily said nothing for her, and the waitress's face pinched. I ordered a scoop of butter pecan for me and a Coke for Emily.

"Oh, no," she said. "I'm not allowed to drink cola."

She settled on lemonade instead

"I'm not allowed to speak to strangers either," she said. "But I just can't keep this to myself any longer."

She snatched a paper napkin from the tabletop dispenser and wiped her eyes. Then she scanned the room, presumably looking for anyone she might know. I waited. The worst way to get someone to talk is to talk yourself.

"My father won't let me breathe," she whispered across the table. "He won't let me see my friends, boys, nothing."

"That's tough," I said. Not much more I could contribute at that point.

"And now Jerry doesn't want to see me anymore."

I froze. Jerry. It couldn't be.

"I'm sure it's because of my father," she continued. "It's awful. He keeps me on a leash. I have to sneak out to meet Jerry. It's just not fair."

"Jerry doesn't want to see you anymore?" I asked, fearing her answer. "Are you sure?"

She shrugged and looked down. "We always meet just before sunrise. He said it was kind of like Romeo and Juliet, only the opposite. You know."

"You meet. You don't part at dawn."

"Right. So he didn't come today as he promised. I waited and waited, but he never showed up."

"Oh, God," I said. "You're not in trouble, are you?"

"Of course not," she scoffed. "And please don't take the Lord's name in vain. Are you a Christian?"

The waitress reappeared and set down Emily's lemonade and my ice cream. My appetite was gone.

"When did you last see him?" I asked.

"Early yesterday morning. We spent an hour together. There's a place halfway between our camps where we meet. It's in the woods above the lake where no one can see us. Then he had to rush back to camp at seven like always."

"Did he seem upset? Give you any reason to think he wanted to break it off with you?"

"No. We had a nice time. He did say he was scared of my father, but he says that every time we meet there. He doesn't like the sneaking around."

"What does Jerry look like?"

"Handsome, athletic. Nice curly brown hair and sweet eyes."

"Does he play the violin?" I asked, closing my eyes in silent dread.

"Why, yes, he does. How did you know that?"

The round waitress escorted us to the back room where Emily dissolved into a flood of tears. I tried to comfort her, but the only thing I could manage was to hold her tight and let her sob. She wept until she started hiccoughing, gently at first, then violently for several minutes, and I thought she might injure herself. We tried salt and lemon to stop the attack, but nothing worked. I have my own remedy that I'd learned from a bartender, but Harvey's Double-Dip had no aromatic bitters handy.

After about twenty minutes, she'd worn herself out and the hiccoughs slowed and weakened. She blotted her eyes on the sleeve of my dress, mumbling to her lost beloved. I stroked her hair and let her mumble, wondering if I'd done the right thing in telling her. I certainly hadn't wanted to break the terrible news to her, but I couldn't take the coward's way out either. She would have learned of Jerry's death anyway, probably later that same day, as it was sure to be the talk of the village. Still, young minds are fragile, and I hoped I hadn't made the wrong choice.

She wanted to know how it had happened, but I shook my head. "There's no use going over it," I said. "It was an accident. And now you see that he didn't want to leave you. You see that, don't you?"

She nodded, and more tears fell. Then the door burst open, and the tall, thin man in the rumpled white linen suit entered the room.

"Emily!" he barked at her. "What are you doing here? I've been looking all over the village for you." Then, noticing her tear-streaked face and swollen red eyes, he took a step closer. "Who are you?" he asked me. "And what's happened to my daughter?"

I told him my name and urged him to lower his voice. He didn't like my suggestion and demanded to know what was going on.

"Your daughter has had a shock," I said.

"What kind of shock?" he asked.

I let go of Emily and invited her father to join me across the small room for a private talk. There, I explained that a friend of hers had fallen to his death from Baxter's Rock the day before.

"A friend?" he nearly shouted. "I heard that a man and teenage boy died there yesterday. Surely neither of them was a friend of Emily's."

I looked him squarely in the eye, and he softened just a touch. I could see that he wanted to discipline his daughter, tear off his belt perhaps and beat some Jesus into her, but he wasn't so hard a man after all. He glanced over his shoulder at Emily, who was weeping softly on her chair, her arms wrapped tightly around her shoulders as if to console herself.

"Who was this boy?" her father asked me in a low voice.

"A young man named Jerrold Kaufman. He was from the Orpheus music camp."

"Kaufman," he repeated slowly. "A Jewish boy?"

"Does it matter?" I asked.

He shook his head and made his way over to Emily. He reached out a hand and told her to come. She looked up at him, fat tears rolling down her chapped cheeks. And she rose to her feet.

"Forgive me, Father," she sobbed.

He folded her in his arms and patted her back, his face impassive. His gaze bored into me from across the room.

"Come, child," he said. "Let us go back to camp and pray for your friend."

CHAPTER SIX

The Reverend Tommy Grierson whisked his daughter out of Harvey's Double-Dip, clutching her to his side, practically concealing her under the panels of his white linen jacket. I watched them disappear behind a flock of summer vacationers posing for photographs on the sidewalk of Lake Road.

Poor Emily Grierson, I thought. How much and for how long would she pay for her sin? She'd lost Jerry Kaufman, and now she would have to win back her fire-and-brimstone-breathing father's good graces. I sensed she might never succeed. And this episode would draw her deeper under the control of his church, sucking her in like an eddy. I had grown up godless. My parents were confirmed atheists. Culturally Jewish, for sure, but Elijah and I had rarely set foot inside a temple or synagogue. And, as the previous night proved, I still didn't discuss my beliefs with others, even those I agreed with. Faith, or lack thereof, should be personal, not a badge or an advertisement. Or a public crusade lakeside, handsome head of hair or no. I felt a deep sadness for Emily Grierson and hoped her faith, imposed or coming from within, would provide her solace.

I wiped my eyes, turned to head back to Cedar Haven, and bumped smack into Chief Tiny Terwilliger.

"Whoa," he said as I bounced off him like a pinball off a bumper. "Watch where you're going. What's your hurry?"

I apologized, thinking he should do the same for his hand that had taken advantage of our collision to gauge the softness of my right breast.

I readjusted my brassiere. "Excuse me, I'm in a hurry."

"Wait a minute," he said. "I've got to talk to you."

I squinted at him. "About what?"

"The pictures you owe me." He smiled gap-toothed. "And I got your ten dollars, too."

"I believe it was nine sixty plus ten."

"Okay, okay," he said, a smirk on his lips. "I should know better than to talk money with a Jew."

I gaped at him, brows arched, but he didn't notice. I didn't believe he thought he'd said anything wrong. As if he'd said that tall people were closer to the ceiling than short people were.

"You do remember that I'm Jewish," I said finally.

"Of course," he scoffed. "That's why I said it. It's a compliment."

"I guess I'm not used to your brand of charm."

"No need to apologize," he said, waving a hand at me. "I'll get you your money. Now when can I get my pictures?"

"I still have to develop them. And I'll give them to you free of charge since it's been such a pleasure working with you," I said, wanting to wipe the stink of his anti-Semitic stereotypes off me.

"No, no," he insisted. "Business is business, isn't that right? So when can I get them?"

"You seem to be in a hurry."

"I want to show them around town to see if anyone recognizes the man. We still don't know who he is. And the state police want them, too."

That made sense. I told Terwilliger that I'd go back to the cabin to finish developing the film, and he could drop by to retrieve the prints around five.

"Five o'clock? I'm just finishing my supper at that hour. I'll stop by at seven thirty."

"Seven thirty?" I asked. "I'm just finishing my second cocktail at that hour. And I'll be at Arcadia Lodge this evening, so it will have to wait till tomorrow."

He pulled the cap off his head and wiped his face with it. He huffed and frowned then said he'd stop by Arcadia after eight. "And have my pictures ready."

It was just three when I got back to Cedar Haven. My negatives had dried, and I set about making prints for the nose-picker. Max's photo enlarger was buried under some old newspapers in the storage shed, and, as he had told me earlier, it was indeed broken beyond repair. One of the lenses was missing. Simple contact sheets would have to do. I decided not to bother with the roll I'd shot atop the cliff. Those photos, along with the longer shots of the bodies, would surely turn out too small to be of any use to Terwilliger. I would just give him the negatives to do with as he pleased. But I'd taken several tight shots of the unknown man's face that were large enough for anyone who knew him to recognize him.

I made short work of the prints, three sheets for each roll shot on the stony beach, in case I'd botched one or two of them. In twenty minutes flat, I'd mixed the developer solution, printed, fixed, and washed my three sets of prints. I hung them to dry in the pantry and went for a nap. I hadn't slept much the night before, of course, and I wanted to be rested and presentable for that evening's gathering at Arcadia.

Inside my small cabin, I threw open the windows and lay down on my bed. A gentle breeze provided welcome relief from the heat, and soon I was asleep and dreaming of a lake and a cat A red tabby named Rusty. The cat was afraid to swim in the water and paced the edge, searching for a dry spot to cross. He circled around and around, even dipping a tentative paw into the water from time to time. He recoiled and shook it vigorously and backed off. Emily Grierson arrived from behind the cat and walked into the lake as if in a trance. Then the cat turned into me. I jumped into the lake after Emily and disappeared under the waves I didn't come back up for air.

I awoke in a sweat, not so much from the dream as from the heat of the afternoon. Still, the nightmare hadn't needed to dive too deep into my subconscious to latch onto the thing that had upset me so recently. It was just below the surface. I tried to shake Emily from my thoughts, like the cat shaking the water from his paw. She was with her family, after all, and they would see to her well-being. As for poor Jerry Kaufman and the stranger who'd died beside him, there was nothing I or anyone else could do for them.

It was already five. I showered and washed my hair properly in anticipation of the evening ahead. Dressed in a light-blue sundress with a deep square neckline that showed my bust to good advantage, I joined Lena and Max in the big cabin in time for evening cocktails. Max mixed drinks for us all while I collected my dried contact sheets for Chief Terwilliger and slipped them and their negatives into a brown envelope. I hadn't even looked at them and had no intention of doing so now.

I was feeling refreshed from my nap and shower, but something was missing. Max handed me a double White Label on the rocks, and that put things right. I wanted to wash the foul taste of dead divers and grieving girls out of my mouth. Max finished his duties at the bar and joined Aunt Lena and me in the small parlor. They sipped their gin and tonics and munched on crudités and onion dip. I rose to pour myself a second glass of whiskey.

"Dear girl, did you spill your drink?" asked Max.

"Yes, that's it," I said. "There's a large hole in the top of the glass."

"Take it easy, Ellie," said Aunt Lena. "You'll want to have your wits about you later on."

After the emotions of the day, I felt I'd earned the indulgence, but she made a good point. I savored my second drink slowly, lost in thoughts of my own, as the old folks prattled on about other matters.

"Sing, O muse, of the photographs you developed this afternoon," said Max, rousing me from my coma.

"What's that?" I asked.

He took a draw on his drink and regarded me from the sunken depths of his comfortable armchair. He would need help getting out of it later. "What snapshots did you take for the long, knuckle-dragging arm of the law?"

"It's a sad story," I said, lighting a cigarette. "Those two men who died yesterday diving off Baxter's Rock. The ones who didn't *bounce*, as you so delicately put it."

"Poor fellows," he said. "Not a pretty sight, I'd wager."

"Still no idea who the older one was?" asked Lena. I shook my head. "And you say his trousers and shoes were in Max's car, but no shirt or billfold?"

"That's right. He must have removed his shirt near the edge of the cliff. Maybe the wind blew it away."

"That makes sense," she said.

"Do either of you know the drag coefficient of the average wallet?" asked Max. "I believe that a mighty wind would be needed to lift a man's billfold off the ground."

Aunt Lena and I ignored him. Acknowledging him only encouraged more of the same talk. Instead she asked me about the boy.

"His name was Jerrold Kaufman," I said. "Sixteen years old."

Again I thought of Emily Grierson and lost any élan I might have had for the discussion. "It's a sad story," I said, draining my glass. "Let's change the subject, shall we?"

Isaac met us at the mouth of the drive leading to Arcadia Lodge. He directed me to a parking spot that was convenient for the elders in my car, then lent an arm to Aunt Lena and escorted her into the Great Lodge. Adorable little pervert. I wondered what he thought of his boyhood obsession now. I entwined my right arm around Max's left, and we followed. I watched Isaac from a few paces back. He was attentive, sweet, and chatty with Aunt Lena, surely making her feel welcome and special. I heard snatches of their conversation. He was sharing some details about the farmer's stand on Route 15 and the tomatoes and sweet corn he'd bought there that afternoon. Such a fine, well-mannered young man. I entertained some stray unladylike thoughts about his more ungentlemanly behavior, but I chose not to share them with dear Cousin Max.

Jakob Eisenstadt, still wearing the Greek fisherman's cap, greeted me from his seat. "Eleonora, how lovely to see you again."

I cocked my head. "You know my full name?"

"Your father told me once," he said in his sweet German accent. "We used to talk from time to time when you kiddies were playing or mischief-making. I enjoyed our conversations. It was nice to speak the old language. His German was superb."

I nodded and drew a sigh. "Yes, he was quite good at just about everything."

"You enjoy the evening with the young people," he said. "I want to talk with my old friends Max and Lena. Lena, my dear. I haven't seen you in years." His eyes sparkled as he beheld her, and I sensed he had little interest in speaking to Max.

Dispatched by the old man with a smart shove, I scanned the room for Isaac. What I got instead was Miriam. She was standing there with a man and a woman. Outside guests. He was tall and slim, in his mid-forties, chewing on an olive. A little horsey in the face, with teeth like Citation. His companion, however, was a stunner. Dark-skinned and exotic-looking, she was at least fifteen years younger than he. When I looked back at Miriam, she was eyeing me, a glass of sangria in her hand.

"Hello, Ellie," she said in her usual languid tone. "You're back. How nice."

"Yes," I answered, not knowing what else to say.

"I'm Nelson Blanchard," said the man, stretching out a hand. His eyes, peering through black horn-rimmed glasses, twinkled, and his smile hinted at an unabashed eagerness that was off-putting. "And you're Ellie," he informed me, holding my hand tight in his clammy grip.

"Yes, I am," I said, tugging to get my hand back. "Are you a diviner, or did you just hear Miriam say my name?"

His toothy smile cracked, but he managed to prop it up a little longer. "Yes, well, as a matter of fact, I did hear Miriam say it just now. Clever you."

He was still holding fast to my hand, making the situation even more uncomfortable. For me, at least. Finally he released me and introduced his companion.

"This is my wife, Lucia," he said, pronouncing her name the Italian way.

"How do you do?" she asked, offering her dry hand. She was in her late twenties, maybe thirty, and spoke with just a trace of a Spanish accent. Her Ds brushed softly between her tongue and the cusp of her incisors.

"These are my friends, Nelson and Lucia," said Miriam, for all intents and purposes closing the barn door after the horse had run off, if horses were introductions. "Nelson is a gynecologist, though he fancies himself a playwright, and Lucia is an actress and a talented cellist. We play together often."

"Do you play any instruments?" Nelson asked me, his smile blazing once again at full power. I shook my head. "Neither do I," he said. "These days, I don't practice medicine. I'm a *scénariste*. Films, you know."

"Anything longer than one reel?" I asked. He laughed.

"Clever you," he said again. "Perhaps I could find a part for you in one of my movies."

Lucia rolled her eyes. "Ignore him," she said. "He thinks he's funny. But he's harmless. All bark and no bite." She leaned in for dramatic effect. "Trust me."

Lucia took her husband by the elbow and led him away, claiming they had to say hello to Jakob Eisenstadt. Nelson Blanchard turned his head and undressed me with his smiling eyes as Lucia dragged him off.

"What was that?" I asked Miriam.

She shrugged and told me as a matter of fact that the Blanchards were old friends. And wife-swappers.

"They have a very modern outlook on marriage," she said and sipped her sangria.

"How did they end up here on Prospector Lake?"

"Nelson's a summer regular. He's been coming here since the forties."

"So how did an old pervert like him bag a young lovely like her?"

"I think they met in California. About seven or eight years ago. Lucia was trying to make it as an actress. Nelson's stinking rich and has a mansion in the Hollywood Hills."

"She's very pretty. Did she ever get into any movies?"

Miriam shrugged. "Maybe a stag reel or two. Nothing you've seen." I choked.

"She decided Nelson could offer her a better life than the lying casting directors and sleazy producers."

Once I'd regained my composure, I made small talk with Miriam about our lives, but it was awkward. When you spoke to her she would look over your shoulder or off into the distance. And when you were otherwise occupied, you would catch her, chin lowered, peering out from below her heavy eyelids, staring at you as if you were the subject of an experiment.

Miriam and Simon had married five years earlier, I learned. They lived in Brooklyn, and had no children. She volunteered for Hadassah, raising funds for the Ein Kerem Medical Center in Israel. And, of course, she was a brilliant pianist, active in local chamber music groups. But for all of her interests, she walked through life like a mummy, as if tranquillized.

"Where's Simon?" I asked when the conversation ground to a halt.

"I suppose he'll be here shortly," she said, looking away. "He's always here." And she wandered off.

That was enough for me. The two drinks I'd inhaled at Cedar Haven were not going to cut it if I had to make chitchat with the likes of Miriam Abramowitz. I spotted the refreshment table across the room and made a beeline for it. Good thing there were only two children in the room, and they stayed out of my way. Someone—Isaac, I hoped—had procured a fifth of White Label, prompting a not-quite-silent "Thank God" from me.

"What are you praying for?" came a voice behind me. Isaac, finally.

I turned, took a sip of my whiskey—personality in a bottle—and flashed my brightest smile. He leaned in to whisper in my ear.

"Can I convince you to stay again tonight?" he asked, and the skin on my neck tingled.

"Not if you abandon me to Miriam again. You're on the bench at the moment."

"Let's see if I can win first chair by the end of the evening," he said, clearly confounding my sporting metaphor with a musical one. I didn't really care; he was in the driver's seat either way.

We found a quiet corner to talk, but soon Isaac's friends joined us. While we all drank and chatted on one side, a huge dining table set for twenty was being loaded with food on the other. I caught sight of Waldo Coons lugging heavy platters and glasses to the table. He was wearing the same corduroy slacks from that afternoon, but he'd been issued a white waiter's coat two sizes too big. Anything that covered his scabby arms was all right by me. His eyes still betrayed little sign of cognition, but he seemed content enough to dispatch his duties in silence.

At eight thirty, Rachel announced that dinner was ready. The Arcadians numbered fourteen. That evening they'd invited a couple of vacationers from nearby camps, plus Lena, Max, and me. And, of course, the Blanchards. Someone had prepared a giant smorgasbord, with everything from fish to roast chicken to steak. Hors d'oeuvres, breads, and a cheese board. Potatoes, corn, creamed spinach, and even spaghetti and meatballs. And there was plenty to drink. Chianti bottles in straw flasks, Inglenook red and white, and Mogen David for those keeping kosher. Or perhaps that was there just to rib Simon. There was whiskey and vodka and gin, as well as sherry, port, and mixers of all kinds.

"Who organized all this?" I asked Isaac. "There's so much food."

"Rachel is the heart and soul of these Sunday suppers," he said. "But everyone pitches in to help. We all share the costs. It gets paid for out of our dues."

"And you said you're not Communists. You'd need a five-year plan to put this evening together. And you said 'suppers' plural. Do you mean you do this more than once a year?"

He sipped his wine. "Every Sunday during the summer. Whenever we're here."

After dinner, before everyone got too happy on drink, we were invited to adjourn to the area beneath the great stag's head where Waldo Coons had set up chairs and rolled the spinet into place. He stood like a ghoul, half in shadow, off to the side, watching the proceedings. Isaac had his violin. Miriam was at the piano, Simon on cello, and Ruth Hirsch on viola. We had a piano quartet in our immediate future, that much I knew.

The musicians flipped through their sheet music; then Miriam tapped on the A above middle C, and the others tuned their instruments accordingly. Max, who was seated beside me, leaned in and repeated the same joke he dusted off every time he went to a concert: "I've never particularly enjoyed this piece." I rolled my eyes. He also had a favorite companion joke to that one. If we were listening to a modern piece, he never failed to tap me on the shoulder halfway through it to ask when they were going to finish tuning their instruments and get on with it.

Once the audience was seated with drinks in hand, Isaac stood to face us.

"Good evening, everybody," he said, his violin tucked smartly under his left arm. "We're so happy to be among family and friends for another installment of our Sunday Bacchanalia. About ten years ago, a few of us had the idea of organizing these orgies and inviting all our nearest and dearest to share good food, wine, and music with us. Just a bunch of sunburned Jews from New York looking for an excuse to get drunk and play the instruments our parents guilted us into learning." Laughter rippled through the room.

"Tonight we're going to play a piece that we've been wanting to do for years. We haven't had the nerve to perform it in public till now, so please don't be too hard on us; we're just amateur hacks, after all." He retook his seat then turned to the audience again. "I nearly forgot. As always there's a prize for anyone who can name it. The folks staying here at Arcadia Lodge are ineligible, of course, since they've heard us rehearsing it for weeks."

Everyone applauded. Isaac turned to his fellow musicians, made eye contact with them, and on a silent count of three he dipped his head. They launched into the first movement of an energetic piece in a minor key. I knew it instantly. One evening, shortly after VJ Day, I had taken notice of this piece of music as it drifted from my father's study. I had heard Fauré many times before that, of course, as my father particularly enjoyed his chamber works. I could recognize it at the drop of a needle. But that evening in 1945, a couple of months after my ninth birthday, was the moment when listening to music became less of a parlor trick for me and more a true joy. I remember creeping up the corridor where I stationed myself next to the study's open door, invisible to my father inside. The smoke from his evening pipe burned like incense, wafting through the air, out into the hallway, as if on the music. I breathed it in deeply, unconsciously. It wasn't that I loved the smell of pipe smoke; it was just there, part of my world. Daddy's smoke. Cavendish tobacco, sweet-smelling with hints of vanilla and walnut. An intimate, familiar scent that pervaded the rooms I inhabited as I child. And it was usually accompanied by its partner, lingering just underneath: the sharp, but not unpleasant, odor of alcohol. If the sweet pipe smoke represented the mildness in my memories, the whiskey was the spice.

The four movements spread out over about thirty minutes. Miriam's precise, at times powerful, at times gentle, playing stunned me. Not only was she good, she was playing in a room with thin acoustics on a modest old upright that had spent God knows how many humid summers and bone-chilling winters untouched in the Great Lodge. It was clear to me that she was by far the most talented of the amateurs, who were all fine musicians in their own right. I felt a new willingness to accept her oddness as the price to pay for her talents. Who said remarkable people had to be normal? I resolved to try harder to get to know her.

When the fourth movement drew to its spirited end, I realized I'd hardly taken my eyes off Miriam the entire time. The audience rose to its feet and roared with applause. The musicians stood and laughed and took exaggerated bows. All except Miriam, actually, who remained seated on her bench, looking back at the assembled with an expression akin to indifference, but not quite. Perhaps it was vague curiosity. It looked as if she were studying us under glass.

I smiled brightly as I clapped till my hands hurt. Aunt Lena applauded vigorously as well. And Max, still holding onto his long-since-drained glass of port in his right hand, thumped his left against his thigh in appreciation. My eyes darted around the room, taking in the reactions of the crowd. Everyone approved, including Jakob Eisenstadt, who bounced his cane on the wooden floorboards and laughed, his face glowing red. Then my gaze snagged on the shadow against the far wall. Waldo Coons was staring at me, loose-jawed, with hollow eyes, looking like Frankenstein's monster's ugly brother. I shook a shiver off my shoulders and turned to the enjoyment. When I glanced back a moment later, Waldo had evaporated, leaving nothing but a smudge on the wall where he'd rested his greasy head.

"Thank you, everyone," said Isaac. "That wasn't so bad, was it?" A chorus of nos replied. "So who can tell me the piece we just played?"

No one volunteered.

"You must have some idea, Irv," he said, chiding one of the guests. "I thought you liked music. Surely someone has a guess."

"Ellie knows the piece," said Max. There was silence.

Isaac looked surprised. I blushed. "Really?" he asked.

"Of course," said Max. "I know it myself, but I just can't remember the fellow's name or what it's called. But Ellie knows."

The entire audience fixed its eyes on me. Isaac waved his bow like a sword and pointed at me. I still said nothing.

"Max is right," said Aunt Lena. "Don't doubt her. She's uncanny at this thing."

"Ten dollars says she doesn't know," chimed in Simon.

Isaac drew himself up and, acting like a game show host, asked me again. "Ellie Stone, for ten bucks and . . ." he searched his mind for another prize, ". . . and Simon's toothbrush, can you tell us all the piece we just played?"

"It was Gabriel Fauré," I said. "'Piano Quartet Number 1.'"

"That's it!" said Max. "That's what I was going to say, only I couldn't remember it."

Simon's face told the tale, and Isaac jumped for joy. "That's absolutely correct."

The assembled applauded politely at my parlor trick. Even Simon congratulated me, handing a wadded mess of bills to Isaac to award me. The ceremony took place immediately. I accepted the money on behalf of the UJA. I thanked Simon for the cash but told him he could keep his toothbrush.

"You'll need it to wash the taste of crow out of your mouth."

Max looked up from his seat. "Congratulations," he said, holding up his glass. "Oh, look at that. Finished my drink. Be a good girl, Ellie, and fetch me another?"

"I'll help you," said Isaac.

I was so happy that I didn't mind Max's transparent ploy. In fact toasting with an empty glass was one of his signature moves to finagle a refill. Basking in Isaac's adoration, and still tingling from Miriam's exceptional performance, I floated across the room to fill Max's glass with port, not even noticing the giant ground sloth blocking the drinks table until I'd practically run into him. Ralph "Tiny" Terwilliger stood before me, a half-drunk glass of beer in his hand.

"Nice party," he said, then sloshed down the rest of his beer and wiped his lips with the back of his hand. "You look surprised to see me."

"Not surprised," I said. "Startled."

"I told you I was coming here to get my pictures. Do you have them?"

"Give me a minute," I said, leaving Isaac with the chief, and recrossed the room to retrieve the envelope I'd left on my seat.

Max gaped in horror at my empty hands. His lower lip began quivering, and I told him to hold his horses. I'd bring him his port in a moment. I rushed back to the drinks table just in time to hear Terwilliger compliment Isaac on the fine spread they'd put out.

"Glad you're enjoying it," said Isaac.

"I didn't care much for the music, though."

Isaac shrugged. "Sorry about that. The accordion's on the fritz."

"Don't get me wrong," said the charmer. "You all played real good. Just not to my taste."

"Here are your photographs," I said, holding out the envelope. "I didn't have an enlarger, so the pictures are small. You can get some prints made later with the negatives."

"I doubt I'll need to do that," he said, tearing open the envelope and stuffing his bearish hand inside to get at the photos.

"Please, Chief Terwilliger," I said. "Don't pull those out here. They're quite gruesome."

"Are those pictures of the divers?" asked Isaac. "I'd like to see them, if you don't mind."

"I mind," I said. "They're terrible to look at. Why would you want to ruin this perfect evening by looking at two dead bodies?"

Terwilliger looked on expectantly, hand still inside the envelope, waiting for a final verdict of thumbs-up or -down. Isaac apologized, and the chief withdrew his empty hand from the envelope.

"I'll look at them later," he said, clamping the photographs under his right arm. (So much for the envelope ever being used again.) "They're just for the state police, anyway. I'll get you your money tomorrow."

I didn't care either way and, in fact, doubted I'd ever see a penny from him. He turned back to the table and poured himself another glassful of beer.

"Real nice party," he repeated, gazing out across the room.

"You're not on duty, are you?" asked Isaac.

Terwilliger regarded him queerly. "Of course I am," he said and took a gulp of beer. "Why else would I be here?"

Isaac mumbled something about getting back to the others, and we excused ourselves. Terwilliger didn't seem to mind, at least as long as the beer held out. We rejoined Aunt Lena and Cousin Max, who again nearly swooned when he saw no glass of port on my person. I rushed back over to the table to fulfill my promise and his glass. The chief was still there.

"Was that your fellow I was talking with before?" he asked me to make conversation.

I didn't know how to answer that, so I asked him why he wanted to know.

"No reason. Just curious. A pretty girl like you must have lots of suitors."

A little creepy, especially after he'd ogled me the day before in my bathing suit. I poured Max's port and excused myself.

"And I'm curious because he's got a shortwave radio," said Terwilliger.

"Is that prohibited here on Prospector Lake?" I asked. "Along with photography and nude bathing."

He chuckled. "You're a funny one, do you know that?"

"I wasn't joking," I said. "What's wrong with having a shortwave radio?"

"There's nothing necessarily wrong with it. But some people use them to listen for instructions from their handlers."

"I beg your pardon? What handlers?"

"You know, back in the mother country."

I gaped at him.

Terwilliger leaned in and whispered, "KGB."

I put Max's drink down on the table and stepped back to look him up and down. "Now you're the one who's funny," I said. "Do you really think these people are Soviet agents?"

He shrugged and sipped his beer. "Probably not, but . . ."

I excused myself a second time and returned to Isaac, who was entertaining my aunt and cousin. Damn. Max's port. I turned on my heel and made my way back to the drinks table. This time Terwilliger was nowhere in sight. I snatched Max's drink off the table and noticed the brown envelope with the photographs inside. The chief's empty glass of beer sat on top of it, leaving a ring. I didn't want an unsuspecting reveler to discover the horrible photographs by accident, so I picked up the envelope and carried it back to my seat. Max reached out for the glass of port with both hands, trembling with exaggerated avidity. He took a large gulp. Then a smaller one. He expelled a great sigh.

"If ever I fall overboard into the lake, my dear, remind me not to ask you for a life preserver."

"You won't need one," I said. "Not with all that hot air. You'll float."

"Flatterer. Now, if you please," he said, downing the last few drops, "will you go fetch me another?"

The evening had taken an unpleasant turn for me. I hated running into that ogre of a policeman, and Isaac's ghoulish enthusiasm for viewing photos of two poor souls who'd fallen to their deaths soured my mood. It was past ten thirty, and I wanted to go back to Cedar Haven and to bed.

Isaac tapped me on the shoulder and asked what was wrong. I didn't want to spoil the party, so I shrugged and said I was tired. He handed me a Scotch on the rocks.

"Come chat with us," he said.

David, Ruth, Rachel, Miriam, and Simon were seated on a sofa, huddled around a bottle of Chianti, deep in conversation about the fence in Berlin. Isaac and I pulled up a couple of chairs, parked ourselves, and joined in.

"Who cares about Berlin anyway?" asked Simon. "Let the Russians have it. I have no love lost for the Germans."

"Come on, Si," said David. "Don't be so myopic. It pains me to say it, but it's not only about Berlin. I just can't back them anymore. Not after Hungary."

"The Soviets think they can just steamroll Eastern Europe," said Ruth. "They've made a mockery of international socialism, and you know it."

The discussion remained spirited but friendly this night. Simon hadn't drunk as much as he had the night before. Then the topic turned to Donald Yarrow, the escapee from Comstock.

"It's pretty scary," said Rachel. "The latest report I heard was that he'd been spotted near Hague last night. He's heading north, and we're right in his path."

Some were skeptical about the hysterical reports proliferating since the escape. Rachel and Ruth were inclined to believe the news, the men were less sure, and Miriam suggested he was dead.

"If the wolves or mountain lions haven't got him, he's probably starved to death by now. I'll bet he's rotting in a pile of leaves somewhere in the woods."

"What do you think, Ellie?" asked Isaac. "Are you afraid to sleep alone?"

I threw him a reproachful look. "I heard the report Friday night on the radio. I confess that I'm a little scared walking through the woods alone. Especially in the dark."

"Poor Ellie," said Miriam. "Didn't Isaac see you home last night?"

Simon laughed. No one else did. I blushed.

"I can handle myself," I said.

Isaac tried to change the subject by suggesting we pull down the rusty old hunting rifles over the stag's head and oil them up.

"Don't joke," Rachel said. "That guy's a murderer, after all."

Everyone promised Rachel they'd monitor the situation and take action if Yarrow came any closer to Prospector Lake. Then Ruth added that the chief of police might be able to protect them.

"He's useless," said Simon. "Stood there drinking our beer for an hour, uninvited."

"Actually he came to see Ellie," said Isaac. "She took photos for him of the two men who died at Baxter's Rock yesterday."

"How awful," was the first reaction from the group. And the second was, "Can we see the pictures?"

"Don't bother asking her," said Isaac. "She wouldn't even give me a peek. And she doesn't have them anymore."

They expressed disappointment, but I sensed they'd get over it. I was actually sitting on the brown envelope with the photos inside at that very moment. Having nowhere else to stash it, I'd slipped it under my right thigh and could feel it burning through my dress as the silence grew.

"She's got them right there," said Miriam, indicating my legs with a nod. "Why are you hiding the photos, Ellie? We'd like to see them."

Soon Simon and Isaac joined in, and it became a chorus.

"You really don't want to see them," I said. "There's blood and two poor dead bodies. They're terrible images to see. I was nearly sick when I shot them."

Apparently thinking better of it, Rachel grimaced and withdrew her request to see the photos. The others held fast, though, brushing off my warnings and insisting they could take it.

"I've never seen a dead body," said Ruth. "Except my *zeydie*, but he was in a coffin."

"Come on, Ellie," said Isaac, touching my arm. "I promise we'll all be respectful. We're curious."

I shook my head, half in disgust, half in pity. They weren't as tough as they thought, I was sure.

"I tell you what," I said. "I'll show them to one of you. If that person can stomach it, fine, you can all see them."

They agreed, and the nomination process began. Everyone was eager to volunteer, except for Miriam, who just sat there watching. In the end, they settled on Ruth. I questioned the choice, but they insisted. Finally, throwing in the towel, I grabbed Ruth by the arm and led her to a spot against the wall a few feet away.

"Please reconsider, Ruth," I said, but she smiled and insisted she wanted to see.

The group watched from a distance as I reached into the envelope and pulled out the first contact sheet. The one with the tight shots of the two victims. I drew a deep breath and handed it to Ruth. She took it in her hands, still smiling, and her eyes scanned the print. First her smile cracked. Then her cheeks drained of all color. And she choked, a look of horror spreading across her face. Finally she melted and dropped to the floor in a dead faint before I could catch her.

The others ran to her, all diving to the floor to assist her, and I just stood there breathless. I knew the photographs were difficult to look at, but her reaction surpassed even my worst fears. Rachel and Miriam lifted Ruth's head and patted her hand. Simon waved air in her face and offered water. And Isaac grabbed the photograph that had floated to the floor when Ruth fainted. I watched as he looked upon it. His eyes grew as he pushed himself slowly to his feet.

"My God," he said. "It's Karl." Then shouting, he said it again. "It's Karl!"

CHAPTER SEVEN

Karl Marx Merkleson was the unknown man on the rocks. There was no doubt. One after the other, starting with Ruth's faint and Isaac's shout, they all looked at the photos and confirmed the terrible news. Their old friend was the man crumpled and crushed on the shale below Baxter's Rock.

The party broke up quickly. Aunt Lena took my keys and drove Max to Cedar Haven. I stayed behind to help organize everything that needed to be done. For starters I called Chief Terwilliger from the community phone in the Great Lodge and gave him the news: we'd identified the unknown man. He sounded put out. It was after eleven, and he'd probably just bedded down in his pen for the night. He grumbled that he'd come back over right away.

"What the hell kind of name is Karl Marx Merkleson?" he demanded once he'd taken a seat under the stag's head, a fresh beer in one hand, my prints in the other. "Are you people Communists?"

"Of course not," said Isaac, who'd assumed the helm. There hadn't been any vote, but he was the leader. "Karl's parents were of a different generation. You understand, things were different in the twenties."

Terwilliger frowned and took a swig of beer. "So this fellow was a friend of yours?"

"Yes, but we haven't seen him in years," said Isaac. "We had no idea he was here. He didn't contact any of us to let us know."

"He just showed up and decided to take a dive off Baxter's Rock?" asked Terwilliger. No one had an answer for him. "All right, then. If any of you has an address for him, I'll contact his next of kin."

There was a pause. Finally Isaac explained that Karl had changed his name. "It's Charles M. Morton now. He lives in Bel Air, California. I've got the address in my agenda."

Isaac left to retrieve the address from his cabin, and Terwilliger finished his beer and half of another before he returned. The chief seemed satisfied with the resolution. No more loose ends to tie up. He stood to take his leave, advising the rest of us to obey posted signs and not to go diving off cliffs.

"That's it?" asked David, leaning on his crooked leg. "There's nothing else?"

Terwilliger shrugged. "That's it. Now that we've identified both men, that's the end of the story. Unless you think someone pushed them off the cliff."

"Of course not, no. I just expected . . . I guess it's as you say. That's the end of the story."

"Sorry about your friend," said the chief, and he left.

He'd forgotten the photographs again. I grabbed the envelope and ran after him, catching up just as he was climbing into his truck. I handed him the envelope through the window. He took it, tossed it onto the seat, and drove off.

Once the chief had gone, and the older folks had retired, we all sat under the stag's head and reviewed the sad development. Ruth and Rachel wept, as did David. Isaac was white. Simon paced the floor, stroking his beard, looking more angry than anything else. Miriam sat impassive, her face a blank. They expressed their disbelief, their bafflement, and sorrow.

"What was he doing here?" asked Simon, not expecting an answer. "He must have been up to something. Showing up secretly like that."

"Come on, Si," said David. "Leave it alone. Poor Karl is dead. Can't we remember the good times?"

"I can't," said Simon. "And now he comes back here to die, just to open up old wounds and ruin our last . . ."

"That's enough, Si," said Ruth. "He didn't kill himself. It was an accident. Surely he was on his way over here, maybe to try to patch things up."

Simon said nothing. He just seethed.

"What did he do, after all?" asked David. "He moved on to a new life. People change. He fell in love and got married."

"He changed his name to Charles Morton, for God's sake," said Simon. "Married a *shiksa*, threw away his Jewish name, and got baptized."

"He was our friend, Simon," said Isaac softly.

"Turned away from his people. People who have been chased and persecuted for millennia. Isaac, your own family was kicked out of their home, lost their business, lost everything. Your father was thrown into Buchen-wald. How can you forgive Karl?"

"I forgive him because he never hurt my family or my people. Or yours."

Simon stiffened. His mouth twisted into a grimace, and his lips trembled as he spoke. "Karl did indeed hurt my family. For his own selfishness. I'm glad he's dead."

"Si, you can't mean that," pleaded Rachel. "You loved him like a brother."

"I do mean it," he said, turning on his heel to leave. "I'm glad he's dead precisely because once I loved him."

There was silence after Simon had stormed out. Then Miriam rose and said she was going to bed. Isaac reached out and took her hand. He looked into her eyes, and they exchanged a sad nod. The others stayed, sharing thoughts on their old friend. They wept, held each other, and wondered. No one could explain Karl's mysterious reappearance on the lake. At length grief and confusion succumbed to fatigue, and Ruth, Rachel, and David excused themselves, leaving Isaac and me in the cool lodge. I wanted to curl up in my bed and sleep, forget about everything. The beautiful evening that had turned so tragic.

I was about to announce my intentions when I remembered the woods. It was after midnight, and I had no car. The prospect of crossing the dark forest alone, terrifying under normal circumstances, was even more menacing now. I felt like a coward for wanting to stay with Isaac, to comfort him and feel his warm arms around me, because some part of my motivation was selfish. He was staring at the floor, lost in thought, mourning his lost friend. I touched his cold hand, and he sighed. He caressed my cheek, gazing into my eyes.

"Come, Ellie," he said. "Let's get some sleep."

"I should go," I said, hating the taste of the words as they left my mouth. What if he agreed?

His eyes, sparkling with unshed tears, pleaded with me. He said nothing, but I understood, and I had to wrestle my heart into submission before I blurted out a stupid declaration I might regret later. This was too powerful, too quick. I had to tread with care for my own sake. At the same time, I couldn't deny what I felt: danger and exhilaration all at once.

"Come," I said, rising to my feet. "I won't leave you."

CHAPTER EIGHT

We lay awake for hours. Isaac whispered the story of Karl Merkleson to me in the darkened room. His parents, Hiram and Esther Merkleson, immigrants from the Ukraine, had made their way in America writing and producing plays for Yiddish theater on New York's Lower East Side. They acquired a hall on Second Avenue in the early twenties and staged original dramas and musicals. Some of the productions qualified as artistic works with far-reaching influence, while others were lighter fare, roundly criticized as *schund* by aesthetes. But the Merklesons believed the theater needed both tragedy and comedy in order to flourish and have a lasting impact on the community's life. In 1926 the Merklesons co-wrote and staged their most enduring hit: *Chaim Yankel*, a musical comedy about an idiot who manages to succeed despite his feeble-mindedness. The lead character, Chaim, a fool reviled by serious critics, nevertheless delighted thousands of theatergoers for six years and made the Merklesons wealthy. They were never able to reproduce the success of *Chaim Yankel*, and their subsequent serious efforts were never given the credit they deserved, this according to Isaac. I had certainly heard of Hiram and Esther Merkleson, and my father had a framed theater bill of one of their acclaimed dramas, *Di Chasseneh* (*The Wedding*), from 1922, in his study. But I had never seen or read any of their work.

Karl Marx Merkleson was born in 1925, grew up on East Seventh Street, near Tomkins Square Park, in Alphabet City. His little sister, Rosa, was born five years later. I asked Isaac if, by chance, her middle name was Luxemburg, and, smiling, he confirmed that it was. Then his mien darkened again, and he told me Rosa had been born with Canavan disease and died before her third birthday.

The Merklesons and Simon's father met through some political organizations they belonged to and became close friends. When a group of families including Isaac's found the Arcadia Lodge for sale in 1931, they formed a cooperative, complete with a charter emphasizing social and artistic goals, and purchased it. At the time, most Jews preferred the open doors of the Catskill resorts in the Borscht Belt and their proximity to the City. Few Jews vacationed in the Adirondacks, which had remained a white Christian retreat. There were, nevertheless, notable exceptions. The fantastically wealthy banker Otto Kahn and the mining magnate Daniel Guggenheim, not exactly bohemian intellectuals like the Arcadians, had bucked the anti-Semitism of the super rich and built their own magnificent Great Camps, Jewish outposts in the white-bread Adirondacks.

Isaac explained that Arcadia Lodge wouldn't pass muster even as the servants' quarters for the Kahns or Guggenheims, but it was a beautiful property all the same, one worth a fortune in 1960s' dollars. The member families had bought shares when they first acquired the property and had since paid dues for decades. That built up an endowment of sorts that covered maintenance costs and even some of the social activities, including the Bacchanalia Sundays. The original group of owners included seven families: Eisenstadt, Abramowitz, Levine, Berg, Merkleson, Leonard, and Hirsch.

When Karl Merkleson's father passed away in the late forties, his mother decided to move to a smaller place near Hudson in Columbia County, and the cooperative agreed to buy her out. By that time, Karl was in his third year at City College. He shared an apartment on 106th and Amsterdam Avenue with Simon Abramowitz for four years while they were in school.

"It sounds as if they were once very close," I said.

"Like Damon and Pythias."

"What happened between them? It can't have been that Karl changed his name and married a gentile."

Isaac shrugged. "It's sad but true. A beautiful friendship ended."

"When was the last time Karl spent time here at Arcadia?" I asked.

Isaac didn't have to search his memory; he had the date ready. "End of August 1954. He left for California for some business opportunity. He was supposed to return by October. We had a weekend planned to close up the camp for the winter. A big party with most of the families. We do it most years, sometimes in September, but there's always an autumn farewell." Isaac shook his head. "He never came back. And he never said why."

"You mean in all those years, he never contacted any of you? None of you tried to reach him?"

"I tried. Simon did, too. I think we all wrote to the address he'd left us.

But after a month, the letters came back, 'return to sender.' He simply disappeared. Went to ground."

"How did you have his address to give to Terwilliger?"

"About four years ago, Miriam was in Los Angeles for a Hadassah fundraiser. She ran into him in a restaurant."

"That's quite a coincidence," I said.

"He was with a strawberry blonde and an older couple. Karl seemed put out, uncomfortable, embarrassed. Miriam said he did everything he could to avoid introducing her to the people he was with, but finally he had to. It was his wife and in-laws."

"Awkward," I said.

Isaac nodded. "Their name was Pierce. Doesn't get any more *goyishe* than that, does it?"

"So Miriam got his address?" I asked.

"Not exactly. She got his new name. Later she looked up the address."

"That must have come as a shock to her," I said. "Did her face actually move?"

Isaac chuckled. "That's mean, Ellie. I didn't know you had it in you. But don't be so hard on Miriam. She's really quite a remarkable person."

"Sorry," I said. "I didn't mean anything by it. She's quite impressive. She played so beautifully tonight. Why didn't she pursue the piano more seriously?"

Isaac didn't know but thought she wasn't cut out for that kind of life. "She had other interests, I suppose."

"So what happened in Los Angeles?"

"The wife, Gayle—her name was—kept calling Karl 'Charles.' Naturally Miriam was curious about that. Karl told her he'd changed his name to Charles. Said it was for business purposes, but who would believe that? A good Jewish name in Hollywood can take you far. You can imagine how awkward it was when he told her his last name was Morton."

"What exactly did Karl do in Los Angeles?" I asked.

"He started out as a script assistant for one of the studios. He worked on one of those biblical pictures. *The Robe* or something like that. Then he made some connections. He was a good-looking man, which doesn't hurt out there. He met the daughter of a producer, Owen Pierce, and fell for her. The next thing you know, they're engaged."

"And that's when he changed his name?"

Isaac nodded. "A few years later, actually. In fifty-six or fifty-seven. Karl became Charles."

"I'm guessing he dropped the Marx along with the Karl."

"Like a hot latke," said Isaac, chuckling. "My understanding is that he changed his name in order to please his future father-in-law, who asked his daughter if Charles was 'one of those good-looking Jew boys.'"

"And of course he was, or she wouldn't have chosen rye over white."

"Exactly," said Isaac.

"But where did you get all this information?" I asked. "Surely not from Miriam. Karl wouldn't have told her all that."

"You're right," he said. "I managed to get in touch with him a few times about a year later. It was awkward at first, but then he seemed to want to talk to me. We continued communicating every week or so for a while. I tried to reason with him. Bring him back into the fold. We didn't really care that he'd married a *shiksa*. But he was wary."

"Still, he told you all that dirt."

"I sensed he was lonely," said Isaac, staring off into the distance. "He may have been in love or infatuated with Gayle, but he missed his old life too. I could tell."

"How did you leave it with him?" I asked.

Isaac turned his focus to me and said he'd left the door open for reconciliation. "I invited him to join us on the lake the next summer. That was fifty-nine."

"But he gave it a miss?"

Isaac nodded and said nothing.

We lay there in the dark until past two. I wanted another drink, but the bottle was across the compound in the Great Lodge. Why hadn't I brought it with me? I knew I had to steal away again before dawn, but for now, I was happy to be lost in Isaac's arms, even with the awareness that daybreak was approaching. My head resting on his chest, I breathed in his scent. All people have a smell. It's part of what attracts us to and repels us from one another. On the one extreme, there was Isaac. On the other, Terwilliger. What draws two people to each other sexually? A multitude of elements, of course, but it is sensual: beauty in the eye, melody of voice, touch of a finger, taste on the lips, and fragrance of the nape of the neck. The hedonic intoxication of the senses that defies logic and explanation. It's little wonder so many children disappoint their parents with their choice of spouse. They see an irresistible mate, while their parents see a sex maniac. Attraction is visceral. It's an animalistic reaction that has nothing to do with the faculties of the mind. It's in the nose and mouth and skin. It's what drives lovers to madness and extravagance. Makes them lose sight of the practical and opt for the headfirst dive over a cliff.

I knew the feeling well enough from the missteps of my youth. And still my rationality was powerless to dampen or temper my emotions. In Isaac's company, in his arms, I felt rudderless in a wild sea. He could make me do anything he desired, if I didn't ease the ship.

"I can't quite accept the fact that he's gone," said Isaac, stroking my hair.

"I'm very sorry," I offered. "It's hard to lose a loved one. And to find out in such a way . . ."

"He was part of us. Not my best friend by any means, but a friend. An Arcadian. Like a brother."

I looked him in the eyes and, in the low light, saw the sparkle of tears. He smiled and pinched my nose.

"But your evening must have been worse," he said.

"How can you say that?"

"You had to put up with that old satyr, Nelson Blanchard."

I laughed. "Come on. He's not so old."

"A strutting ass," said Isaac. "I told Miriam not to invite him. But she's friendly with his wife, Lucia. She's a nymphomaniac, by the way. The two are perfectly suited for each other. Wife-swappers. You'd better steer clear of him."

"He was pretty creepy," I said. "I'll just stick to you, if you don't mind."

God, what a stupid thing to say. I must have come off sounding desperate. I lay there, wishing silently that I could take it back somehow. I racked my brain for a witty remark to cut the legs out from under the stupid comment. But there was nothing.

"I'm already stuck on you," said Isaac, and I nearly jumped. What a stupid thing for him to say. A wonderfully stupid thing to say.

We lay there contentedly for some time, neither one making any more stupid pronouncements. Then the echo of a thought, having nothing to do with Isaac or me or the stickiness that bound us, crossed my mind. I sat up. He asked me what was wrong.

"It's just that boy who died next to Karl," I said. "How could Karl have known a sixteen-year-old violinist from Albany? A kid who wanted to learn the zither."

Isaac agreed that it was odd.

"And why was Karl diving off cliffs in his underwear? Didn't he own swimming trunks? And he was wearing an expensive watch on his wrist."

Isaac shook his head. He didn't know.

At length we fell silent, and Isaac drifted off to sleep. Then the rain began, first with some booming thunder and lightning. Then, as the front coursed eastward overhead, sheets of rain fell from the sky in great torrents. It wasn't so much a drumming as it was a cascade on the tin roof. I took advantage of the noise and Isaac's deep slumber to rise from his bed and dress. I kissed his lips softly then slipped out the door into the driving rain. I almost looked forward to the protection the dark woods would offer from the downpour. But then, remembering the danger that lurked therein, I shuddered and reconsidered my decision to leave the dry safety of Isaac's cabin.

A bright flash of lightning lit up the sky like a carnival then blinked off, followed instantly by thunder overhead. I entered the woods and slithered through the rain, winding along a path that was becoming all too familiar. I wondered how wise it was to be so near tall trees in an electrical storm.

But I was moving deftly through the forest, much more quickly than on previous crossings. As I pushed deeper into the woods, my nerves loosened. I told myself there was no reason to fear. In all the years I'd visited Prospector Lake, I'd never once been set upon by beast or bogeyman. I smiled.

I stopped beneath a pine to catch my breath and wipe the rain out of my eyes. Then the sky cracked open again, and a bolt of lightning sliced a jagged path through the darkness. A deafening clap of thunder shook the earth. I unleashed a shriek, though not out of fear from the noise. There, not twenty feet in front of me, stood a man. And he was staring directly at me.

CHAPTER NINE

I took off on a run due east, I believe, praying that my eyes had deceived me. It might have been a tree stump or a large rock. But I knew in my thumping heart that it was neither of those things. I'd seen a man, gaunt and pallid, peering out of the rain in my direction. Close enough to catch me if he were a fast runner and inclined to pursue me. It was also possible, of course, that the man was in the woods for reasons other than murdering me; though, in that moment, as I ran, I could think of none. Maybe he was as frightened by our meeting as I. I didn't know, and I had no interest in finding out. I ran.

Why hadn't I turned straight around to head back south toward Arcadia? I knew I was more than halfway home, and, once I'd pointed myself east toward the lake, there was no question of changing course. Running as fast as I dared, given the thickness of the woods, I wanted to look back over my shoulder to see if he was following me. But it was too dark, and I would risk crashing into the trunk of a tree at full tilt. So I tore through the pines, not knowing how close the danger was.

The forest floor was uneven, with roots arching out of the muddy ground, threatening to trip me at every turn. And one did. I sprawled headfirst into the slop, skidding through the wet pine needles and colliding with the base of a tree. My side absorbed the collision, but at least I hadn't broken anything. I pushed myself up slowly, scanning the dense woods behind me, when another flash of lightning blazed across the sky. The thunder exploded, and I saw the man. Following me. Picking his way through the trees, searching for my trail. He seemed to have lost sight of me. I wiped my eyes again, unsure if the water streaking down my face was just rain or a mixture of rain and sweat and tears, brought about by fear. I pushed off north again, confident he hadn't seen me and hoping he would continue east toward the lake's edge.

Assuming that the man was now to my right, on a bearing approximately ninety degrees away from me, I pressed on. The rain muffled any sounds my footfalls might make, but I knew I had to be careful not to trip or crack a fallen branch. The sky lit up again. I crouched down and looked to my right. I thought I saw the figure receding into the distance, but the light had flashed for just a second, and the trees were thick, obscuring my view. Still unsure of my safety, I crept forward. The rain continued to pound the forest and soak me, but perhaps ten minutes later, I reached the edge of the woods. Hiding behind the boughs bordering the road, I peered out onto Jordan Street. I scanned the road through the downpour to my right then left. It seemed I was alone. I drew a deep breath, as if preparing to dive into cold water, then dashed out into the street and ran hard for the lane leading to Cedar Haven. With no trees to block its path, the rain pelted me furiously now. That was the least of my concerns. I was water-logged anyhow, my fingers pruney and shoes soggy. I pulled them off and ran the last hundred yards barefoot, a shoe in each hand, as if carrying two batons toward a finish line.

I reached my cabin, yanked open the door, and darted inside. Dripping large puddles of water on the floor, I bolted the door and leaned against it, huffing for air. I left the lights out. At length I regained my breath and listened for noises outside. There was nothing but the driving rain.

MONDAY, AUGUST 21, 1961

The thunderstorms passed, but the downpour continued off and on all through the morning and afternoon. Barely confident of my safety, I had slept fitfully until eight when I rose and joined Lena and Max in the big cabin. There was a chill in the air, so, at Max's behest, I piled some logs into the fireplace and lit a fire. He sat in the armchair, wrapped in a knitted sweater over an ascot over a scarf and two layers of shirt, topped off by an afghan. Once the fire began to roar, he doffed the afghan then the sweater and finally the top shirt. He refused to remove the ascot, I knew, because he fancied himself quite dapper in it. Then, about a quarter of an hour after I'd lit the fire, Max was so hot that he dispatched me unceremoniously to open all the windows wide.

The three of us enjoyed a lunch of fried fish and boiled potatoes with salad. There was wine as well. We were relaxing in the sitting room, reading as we listened to Mahler's *Titan Symphony* on the record player. The third movement, with its distinctly Jewish themes, made me think of all of us: Aunt Lena, Cousin Max, my parents, Elijah, Isaac, and the Arcadians. All of us Jews. All of us connected. I didn't consider myself a very good Jew, of course. Indeed I was as secular and assimilated as they came. But I recalled my father telling Elijah and me about the Haskalah when we were young. We dismissed his talk as the dry ramblings of someone who'd never read a comic book. But he persisted, explaining how important it was for us to appreciate the contributions of the Jewish Enlightenment of the eighteenth and nineteenth centuries, the importance of the Maskilim, who strove to educate Jews, to convince them that integration into European society and culture was the path to follow. Ours was not a religious family, but we maintained our Jewish identity with careful attention to and respect for tradition and ritual. From the time of my great grandparents, the Stones had integrated into society as well as any Jews. Our family's place, my father said, was at the forefront of society's culture, not just Jewish culture. At the time, Elijah and I merely shrugged, waiting for *Amos 'n' Andy* to come on the radio.

There was a knock at the door. Aunt Lena was in the kitchen, mixing up the beginnings of afternoon tea slash cocktail hour, and Max was too firmly ensconced in his chair to get up to answer, so it fell to me.

"Chief Terwilliger," I said, surprised to see him standing there on the porch. "Please come in."

He shuffled in, looking uncomfortable, but accepted my offer for a cup of tea on that rainy afternoon. Aunt Lena threw me a nasty look when we entered the kitchen, and I shrugged an apology her way. I saw her count the cups and shake her head in woe. Another would need to be sacrificed.

"I've come to tell you some news," he said once we were all seated around the kitchen table with steaming tea before us. "That Merkleson fellow. His wife is here on the lake; she showed up at the station this morning."

"From California?" I asked.

"That's right," he said. "It seems she was staying with him here at the Sans Souci Cabins, not far from here on Route Fifteen. Near the village."

"Yes, we know it," said Aunt Lena.

"She said he disappeared Saturday morning without a word and never came back," continued Terwilliger. "She thought maybe I could help her find him."

"How awkward for you," I said. "What did you tell her?"

Terwilliger sniffed. "I told her I'd look into it."

"You said what?" asked Aunt Lena, who stopped stirring the milk into her tea to express her surprise.

Terwilliger fidgeted in his seat. "Well, I couldn't exactly break the bad news to her all at once like that, could I? I figured I'd let her know slowly, but she ran off before I had the chance."

"That's awful," I said. "The poor woman. She's here, three thousand miles from home, wondering what's happened to her husband, and you just let her go on wondering?"

"Look," he said, folding his hands before him. "I'm not proud of it, but I didn't know what to do. I was kind of hoping you'd help me out on this."

I stared him down. "How, exactly, might I be able to help you?"

He smirked, a little too shamelessly. "I thought you could come along with me over to the Sans Souci and explain to her what happened to her husband."

My jaw nearly fell off its hinges. Terwilliger squirmed as he tried to make the best of the situation.

"We don't get many cases like this up here," he said. "Women are good at this kind of sensitive business. I thought you might not mind helping me out on this one."

I shook the disbelief from my head. It was flattering to have the local chief of police soliciting my help, but I was struggling nevertheless to understand the propriety of my doing his job for him. I couldn't believe he'd actually left her with the impression that her husband was alive, fully two days after he'd missed the pool from the high dive and died in his skivvies on the rocks. But at the same time, I was curious. Perhaps it was the reporter in me, but I wanted to know the details of the sad case. Why was Karl Merkleson—or rather Charles Morton—diving off Baxter's Rock with a sixteen-year-old boy from the local music camp? What had happened to his shirt and his wallet? Had they been scattered to the four winds? And why were his trousers and shoes in my cousin Max's station wagon? I sat there across the table from the nose-picking chief of police, wondering if a short meeting with Karl Merkleson's widow might not be something I'd like to pursue. I knew it would never lead to a story in the

Republic, but the draw was strong nonetheless. I wanted to know her side of the story, including her version of the chance meeting with Miriam in a Los Angeles restaurant four years before. And I wanted to know what she thought of her late husband's decision to change his name and turn his back on his lifelong friends.

"I'm only asking because I'm no good at breaking bad news," said Terwilliger, rousing me from my deliberations. "People around here all say I'm a good-news kind of fellow. I just have one of those happy-go-lucky personalities."

I knew that some people deluded themselves, but this was rich.

"Anyways," he concluded, "I'd really appreciate it if you'd do me this favor."

"Okay," I said. "Give me a few minutes to change."

∞

I stepped off the porch of my cabin and noticed Cousin Max's woody station wagon parked across the compound. I must have missed it when I'd dashed to my room to change. Terwilliger was standing next to the car, scratching his backside.

"You've brought back Max's car," I said. "He'll be so glad."

Terwilliger looked confused. Then he got it. "Oh, actually I'm not quite finished with it yet. I'll need it for a couple of days more."

"What for?"

He cleared his throat and mumbled that his truck was in the shop. "Finally getting it fixed. I hit a deer."

"Poor thing," I said.

He shrugged. "I'm okay."

"What did you do with the carcass?"

Terwilliger looked confused. "What do you mean?"

"How do you dispose of such a large animal that gets killed on the road?"

"I eat it," he said. "Well, not all of it yet, but . . ." He patted his belly. "Anyways, I only need the car for a day or two. I figured the old fellow won't mind too much."

∞

Gayle Morton met us at the door of her one-room cabin in a blue seersucker dress. She looked tired but well turned out, wearing her hair teased up in a bouffant. She was slim and pretty. Terwilliger performed the niceties and introduced us. He said I was a friend of his. Like fun I was. We all sat down on the small porch outside her cabin. The place was too small to accommodate us all inside; though, in honesty, Mrs. Morton and I could have managed by ourselves. But Ralph "Tiny" Terwilliger filled the room like a bad smell. And, in truth, with one.

"I asked Miss Stone to come along because she has something to tell you," said the chief. Rather awkward, but that was my cue.

"Mrs. Morton, I'm afraid there's been an accident involving your husband," I said.

She stiffened, and I gave her the news straight but gently, if that was possible. Her reaction was odd. She stood up and crossed the porch, gazing out at the rain. She didn't weep. She just shook her head slowly.

Terwilliger and I exchanged stumped glances. After about a minute, Mrs. Morton turned and asked if she could see her husband's body. The chief shrugged and said he'd arrange it with the hospital in Elizabethtown, where the body had been taken.

"And then I'll want to take him home to California as soon as possible," she said.

"Sure," said Terwilliger. "Whatever you say. We don't have any use for him anymore." I threw him a disapproving frown. "I mean, there's no official reason to detain the body here."

"I wanted to go to Reno," she said with a sigh. There was no real emotion. Just resignation. "But he had to come to this wretched place. This never would have happened if he'd listened to me."

"Why did he want to come to Prospector Lake?" I asked.

Gayle Morton shrugged. "He said he used to spend summers here. He wanted to see it again."

"When did you get here?"

She stared at me. "Friday afternoon. We flew into Albany and rented a car." She scratched her left forearm, which was pink with mosquito bites.

I'm a curious person, and I like to ask questions. As long as she was amenable, I intended to keep her talking. I asked what time her husband had gone out to swim on Saturday.

"I'm not sure," she said. "I was still sleeping from the time difference. He was gone when I woke up around ten."

"Do you know why he went out to swim without his trunks?"

She shook her head.

"Did he like to swim?"

Now Terwilliger was throwing me reproving looks. I ignored him.

Mrs. Morton said her husband swam whenever there was water handy. But he didn't make a habit of it.

"I apologize," I said. "It's insensitive of me to ask all these questions just now. You must be in shock."

She pursed her lips and drew a deep breath. "It's all right. But I'd like to be alone now, if you don't mind. I have some calls to make. My father. I want to let him know."

Terwilliger and I left her in the cabin. We walked back to Max's car and paused to discuss how the meeting had gone.

"All things considered, she took it pretty well." He smiled.

"Good job," I said, though my sarcasm was lost on him. "Maybe they weren't close. Or maybe that's how she deals with grief in front of strangers."

Terwilliger clicked his tongue and opened the driver's side door. "That's that." Then noticing that I was distracted by a stray thought, he asked what was wrong.

"Nothing," I said. "It's just . . . Did you notice that there was no telephone in her cabin?"

He hadn't. "Maybe she just wanted to be alone. Or maybe she's going to use the phone in the registration office."

"I'm sure that's it," I said, and we climbed into the car.

Isaac was lying in the hammock on Aunt Lena's porch when Terwilliger dropped me off. Max was snoozing in the chair next to him and woke up just as the chief drove away again.

"I had the most puzzling dream," he said. "I dreamt that oaf of a policeman was driving my car. So real."

I patted him on the shoulder. "Just a dream, Max." Then, giving Isaac a playful poke, I said, "Hello, you."

"Hello," he said back. "The rain's stopped. Can I take you for a spin on the lake?"

It was a windy afternoon, overcast but drying out. Isaac took me to a small dock on the far side of Baxter's Rock and its diving pool. He said that it belonged to Arcadia Lodge, thanks to an easement deeded to the property dating back almost eighty years. Two rowboats, a canoe, and one aluminum launch with an ancient Mercury outboard sat listing on the stony beach, as if marooned by a violent storm. Isaac piped me aboard the launch, squeezed the hand-primer a couple of times, and wound the starter rope around the flywheel. It took three healthy pulls, but it finally coughed to life.

"I just love sailors," I said as he took his seat at the tiller.

"The fleet's in town." He smiled.

We motored out to the middle of the lake, where Isaac cut the engine and let us drift. I lay back on some dusty life vests and gazed up at the clouds. Just grayness with blotches of darker gray sliding across the sky. I drew a relaxing sigh and closed my eyes. A pleasant, cool afternoon of dolce far niente.

Before too long, I realized that my afternoon was about to get quite busy. Isaac suggested we take a dip in the lake. I pointed out that we hadn't brought our bathing suits, but he had an answer ready.

"So we'll swim au naturel."

"I'm not stripping down to the altogether to swim in the lake," I said. "Terwilliger has already warned me about that. And besides, what makes you think I'd take off my clothes in front of you?"

He grinned a naughty grin at me, and before I knew what was happening, I had pulled my shirt over my head and peeled off my Capris. Isaac was already naked, standing before me.

"For God's sake," I said, giggling. "Jump in the water before someone sees you."

He did, and I followed a moment later.

I was dozing, curled up against Isaac on top of the life jackets, feeling safe and wicked at the same time. He stroked my hair absently. I wanted to spend the entire day there in the dented old boat. I wanted to spend the entire week there.

A fluttering to my left roused me from my reverie. I opened my eyes to see a ring-billed gull settling on the prow of the boat. He ducked his head to watch us with one eye, and I thought it was surely the same bird I'd met two days before on Aunt Lena's dock.

"He's staring at you," I told Isaac, who lifted his head to see.

"I don't think he likes me," he said. "He looks jealous."

Isaac kicked a leg halfheartedly in the direction of the gull to shoo him away. But the bird stood his ground. He watched us for another minute, perhaps waiting for some food, until Isaac stood up to grab his clothes. The gull sprang into the air and, wings beating, flew off toward the shore.

"Aren't you wondering why I brought you out here?" asked Isaac, pulling his trousers back on.

"I thought it was to ravish me. Mission accomplished."

"Yes, but I wanted to ask you about something." He hesitated, seemingly searching for the right way to put it. "I wanted to ask you about Gayle."

I sat up on the dirty life jackets and covered myself. With the discussion now turned to less intimate topics, I became aware of my nudity and felt suddenly shy. "How do you know about Gayle?" I asked.

"Prospector Lake is a small place," he said. "I went into the village this morning, and Tom Waller told me Karl's wife was staying at his motel."

"Terwilliger roped me into breaking the bad news to her," I explained, pulling my shirt back on. I quickly slipped into my pants. "I told her, and then we left. What did you want to know?"

"Just what she's doing here. I thought maybe she wanted to stir up trouble."

"Why would you think that?"

"Gayle never wanted to come here," he said. "She wasn't interested in Karl's past." He paused. "His Jewish past. At least that's what Karl told me when we spoke a couple of years ago. It was like a confession. He told me how horrible his marriage was. His wife made demands on him that he didn't like."

"Such as?"

"Such as she didn't want his mother to visit them. She felt she was too Jewish. Then the last time we spoke, I told him he should leave her. I said she was making him miserable. But he insisted everything was better, that I didn't know her. He got angry and said it would be better if we just didn't speak again."

"Ouch," I said.

Isaac nodded. "I was heartbroken for him and for me. For all of us here, actually. We missed him very much."

"Even Simon?"

"Well, perhaps not Simon, but that's because they had been like brothers. It was easier for me to talk to Karl, because we were just friends. We weren't so close. Also I have a knack for talking. People open up to me. My father says I should have been a diplomat."

"Or a headshrinker."

He chuckled then turned dark again. "So what about Gayle?" he asked. "What did she want?"

I shrugged. "She didn't seem to want anything except to know where her husband was."

Isaac's eyes betrayed a secret. He was holding something back from me.

"I have a question," I said. "You knew Gayle was in Prospector Lake, but how did you know I'd seen her?"

"Your aunt told me. She gave me a lemonade while I waited for you. Your cousin Max is quite a character, by the way. He had me believing you're some kind of hotshot reporter who solves murders."

That hurt. I'm not boastful by nature, but I'm proud of my accomplishments. And I've worked hard to earn them. Twice as hard as my colleagues, but with half the credit. I wanted to tell him that I was indeed a hotshot reporter who solved murders, at least whenever one presented itself. And I wanted Isaac to know and to admire me for it. God, I wanted him to fall in love with me. Damn it. I wanted him to love me. But I didn't want to admit such a desire to myself. I nearly corrected him. But I kept my mouth shut and wished instead that he'd believed sweet old Max's bragging on me. I resolved to pour Max an extra-large glass of port after dinner that evening.

"What's wrong?" asked Isaac, noticing my agitation.

"I was just wondering why you're so worried about Gayle Morton," I said, putting my bruised ego to one side. "What harm could she possibly do? Does she even know any of you at Arcadia?"

"I don't know," he said. "Perhaps you're right. She doesn't know any of us."

"She met Miriam," I said.

Isaac glanced at me, almost in surprise. "Yes, of course. But that was just that one time in the restaurant in Los Angeles."

"Was it?" I asked.

"Was it what?"

"Just one time?"

Isaac laughed. "Of course. What a thought."

"Anyway," I said, returning to the question of Gayle Morton's presence on Prospector Lake, "I met her in her cabin at the motel and told her the bad news as Terwilliger had asked me to do. She seemed stunned, and that was it."

"Her cabin?" asked Isaac. "Tom's Lakeside Motel doesn't have cabins."

"Tom's Lakeside Motel?" I said, realizing that Gayle Morton had fed me a pack of lies. "She was staying at the Sans Souci Cabins."

CHAPTER TEN

Isaac begged me to join him at Arcadia Lodge later that evening. They were planning another musical soirée, but this time folk songs. Just David on guitar and Simon on bass fiddle. Actually Simon didn't have a bass fiddle, but he figured the cello was close enough to get the job done.

"Eddy Arnold and Tennessee Ernie Ford night?" I asked.

"A little better than that. David's quite good, and we all join in the singing. Mostly protest songs. The usual left-wing folk-song conspiracy stuff, as they used to say."

"I'll tear myself away from Max's stories about my journalistic success and try to make it," I said.

Isaac smiled. Then something seemed to snag in his thoughts. He looked at me, his smile a little on edge. I believed he'd received the message.

I helped Aunt Lena prepare a supper of franks and beans, corn on the cob, and fresh tomato salad. Hardly fine dining but warm and comforting in the chilly evening air.

After supper, as I handed Max his brimming glass of port, I thought back to my conversation with Isaac on the lake. Something was off beam. I couldn't figure why Gayle Morton would cover up the fact that she had rooms at both Tom's and the Sans Souci. I told myself it didn't matter to me what she was up to. Still, it was odd.

I patted Max gently on his forearm as he sank into his chair. He took a sip of his port and thanked me.

"You're a fine girl, Ellie," he said. "Why hasn't some smart young man scooped you up?"

Again the talk of scooping up Ellie. "What's the hurry?" I asked.

"She's young, Max," said Aunt Lena. "Let her be."

"She's twenty-five," he said. "It's time she settled down, don't you think?"

"And when are you going to settle down, Max?" I asked. "You're sixty-eight and have never been married."

"Precisely my point, my dear," he said. "I'm old and must now live with the sting of regret for never having taken a wife. I missed my chance. Or should I say that a generation of girls missed *their* chances?"

"Yes," said Lena, rolling her eyes. "Those poor old ladies are kicking themselves, I'm sure."

"Laugh if you will, my dear. There's more to a man than ephemeral beauty, though that once was mine as well."

I'd seen photographs of Cousin Max as a young man. He had, in fact, once been quite handsome. But age and indulgence had worked their magic on him, and now he was bald of head, round of belly, and slow out of a chair. Though his eyes retained their impish gleam, giving him a roguish charm, no one was lining up for the chance to have and to hold him. I thought of him as one of those aging matinee idols from the silent pictures. Once a dashing sheik, he was now a flabby shadow of his former self, dressed in a paisley ascot, subsisting on heaping portions of caviar and booze.

Cousin Max, the personification of avuncular, sipped his port and smiled off into the distance. He said nothing more about men scooping me up.

Aunt Lena switched on the old Philco radio in the parlor. As it warmed up, she said she wanted to find some soothing music before turning in. She searched up and down the dial, braving the static, buzzing, and whining, until she found a voice.

"... reports that he was spotted in southern Essex County early Monday morning. A three-state manhunt is underway, with Vermont, Connecticut, and New York state police coordinating efforts to capture Yarrow. Residents are advised to lock their doors and report any suspicious activity to local police.

"Once again, repeating our top story, escaped murderer Donald Yarrow continues to elude police dragnets in and around the Adirondack park. In the past twenty-four hours, there have been reported sightings in several locations, including Ticonderoga, Schroon Lake, the Essex ferry, and Hinesburg, Vermont."

With a quick turn of the knob, Aunt Lena located the faint signal of the CBC broadcasting Sibelius from Montreal. *Finlandia*. She settled back into her chair and picked up her book.

"I'm going to turn in," I announced.

After the previous night's thunderstorm and the accompanying terror of being chased through the woods, I was resolved not to make the trek on foot again. Even though I'd had a couple of preprandial drinks, I would take my car and drive over. It was only a quarter mile away after all. I had wanted to tell Terwilliger about my close call in the woods but, in the end, decided I'd rather not besmirch my own reputation. The same concern had stopped me from sharing the story with Lena and Max. But it really had happened. Someone was out there among the trees, possibly Donald Yarrow, waiting for me or some other unsuspecting soul traipsing through the woods at night. I needed to tell the authorities before the spook bagged his first victim.

I arrived at Arcadia a little before nine thirty and parked my car on Lake Road, out of sight. I made sure all four doors were locked then capered up the path to the Great Lodge. All the usual suspects greeted me warmly, and I waved back at them. Still, I worried I was wearing my welcome thin. Then I noticed a new face.

"Ellie, this is my cousin, Audrey Silber," said David.

An auburn-haired beauty in black tights and a form-fitting sweater smiled up at me from her seat next to Isaac. I said hello. She just blinked at me.

Once I'd been handed a drink, I asked Audrey when she'd arrived.

"Just a couple of hours ago," she said. "David met me at the Port Henry train station. I came down from Montreal."

"You're Canadian?" I asked. "Do you speak French?"

"We're Anglos," she said. "But, yes, I do. How about you?"

I admitted that I did not. At least not well. Audrey looked disappointed but not surprised. She turned back to Isaac, flashing a brilliant white smile at him, and ignored me for pretty much the rest of the evening.

I'd finished my first drink and filled up another when David pulled his guitar from its case. He tuned it methodically then proceeded to pick and strum something folksy. He played some songs I'd never heard before. Something called "We Met Today in Freedom's Cause" and "Up from Your Knees, Ye Cringing Serfmen." Simon asked why I wasn't singing along.

"Don't tell me you're with the ruling classes?" he said in jest.

I blushed and glanced at Isaac, who was chatting with Audrey. "It's just that I don't know the words."

Simon jumped to his feet and retrieved a red book from inside David's guitar case. He handed it to me.

"*Industrial Workers of the World Songs: The Little Red Songbook,*" I read.

David launched into "Joe Hill," and Simon accompanied him, plucking away on the cello as if it were a bass. I sang along halfheartedly. Isaac was all in in full voice, while Audrey watched him with the love light in her eyes. Or that was what it looked like to me.

The boys took a break, and Isaac sidled up to me. "You're going to spend the night, aren't you?" he whispered in my ear.

"If nothing better comes along," I said, and he went back to his seat next to Audrey.

Try though I did, I just couldn't enjoy the folk music. Some of it was poetic, and a couple of songs were pretty. But most of it was just "unite," "organize," "wake up," and so on. I much preferred the Fauré evening.

Once the music had ended around eleven, Simon cornered me by the makeshift bar. He glanced behind himself as if checking to see who was listening, then asked me about Karl's wife.

"What was she like?"

"Just a grieving wife," I said. "Maybe not quite as distressed as I might have expected."

"Pretty?"

I hadn't expected that question. I wrinkled my nose and asked why he wanted to know. He changed course and said it didn't matter. He was just curious about the *shiksa* siren who'd lured Karl away from his friends and family.

"You could visit her," I said. "I'm sure she'd appreciate the gesture."

"Not a chance," he said. "I don't want anything to do with her. Or him, for that matter."

He had a funny way of showing his indifference. I was beginning to feel that I didn't much like Simon. At least not always. At times he was friendly and sweet. At others he was surly and boorish. Maybe he didn't hold his drink. But whatever it was, when he was in his unpleasant moods, he made broad assumptions about my philistinism and challenged me about my politics. I had no patience for mean drunks.

Miriam joined us at the bar, and Simon quickly changed the subject to Donald Yarrow. Miriam's contribution to the conversation was to stare unblinkingly at me as Simon gave the latest news he'd heard. Apparently Yarrow had been seen as far away as the Vermont–Maine border and Niagara Falls, all in one day. I poured myself another drink and slipped away.

By midnight the soirée was running out of gas. Gone was the revelry of the previous nights, and the pall blanketing the Great Lodge was Karl Merkleson. Even when people weren't speaking of him, his death was never far from their thoughts. It hovered in the air like a specter, an urge to draw a heavy sigh. Just beyond the conscious but not quite forgotten.

I wanted to sleep, but Isaac wasn't finished holding forth again on the fence in Berlin. The Soviets were testing Kennedy, he said. "They wouldn't have tried this stunt on Eisenhower's watch."

"Are you saying you'd rather have Eisenhower in the White House?" said Simon.

Isaac shook his head. "Of course not. You know me better than that. I'm saying that Khrushchev is manufacturing a crisis to see what the new guy is made of. It's like bull elephants fighting for the right to breed with the females."

Simon laughed. "What are you talking about?"

"The dominant male is the only one with the right to mount the females. From time to time, a younger bull will challenge the alpha. Sometimes the younger one is ready to supplant the elder, but often it's only a testing of the waters. The younger male gains knowledge and experience that he will use later on to defeat the leader."

"So Kennedy is the old elephant?" asked Simon in a mocking tone. "And Khrushchev is the young pretender to the throne?"

"Kennedy isn't the old bull. America is. Mark my words, if Khrushchev gets away with this, he'll be emboldened. He'll make a bigger play before too long."

"Let's talk about something else," said Miriam. "Ellie's bored."

"Yes," I said, having had enough of Miriam's digs and perhaps a little too much to drink. "Why don't we talk about Karl instead?"

The room went quiet, and Miriam left the hall. I immediately regretted having said it. But then Isaac piped up.

"Ellie saw Gayle today." Everyone seemed to know the name without further qualification. "She came to the lake with Karl."

"Don't you mean *Charles*?" asked Simon with a sneer.

Isaac ignored him. "So the first time Gayle condescends to visit Prospector Lake, Karl dies."

"Maybe she pushed him," said Simon, and he laughed.

"That's not funny," said Ruth. "Why can't you keep those ugly thoughts to yourself, Simon?"

Silence again ruled. Then Audrey announced that Karl had once kissed her. The general consensus was horror.

"He kissed me," she repeated. "I was young at the time. Fourteen or fifteen."

David stood up to register his disapproval. "Karl kissed you? He's ten years older than you!"

Was ten years older, I thought.

After much outrage, and Audrey's reveling in the attention, especially from Isaac, who exhibited all the characteristics of being thoroughly scandalized, the group quieted again. Audrey dropped another match into the gasoline.

"He wrote me letters after he'd gone to California," she said, almost giggling.

David fumed. He said that he was responsible for Audrey whenever she visited Prospector Lake, and he didn't appreciate Karl taking advantage of her.

"I'm twenty-one years old," she said in Karl's defense.

"Now," answered David in a strained, high-pitched voice. "You were fourteen at the time. I can't believe Karl would do such a thing. It's . . ." He searched for the right word. "It's criminal."

"You'll get no argument from me," said Simon, acting as if he'd been vindicated by Karl's bad behavior.

Isaac seemed truly troubled by the revelation, but he said nothing. He turned away from Audrey, who, for the first time, realized that perhaps she might have considered keeping her mouth shut.

The party broke up quickly. I felt as though I'd pulled the fire alarm. My suggestion to talk about Karl had sent Miriam running for the hills. I'd succeeded in turning David Levine against his cousin, and nasty Simon emerged as my new ally.

"Good idea to shine the light on that rat," he told me as the others were leaving. "Maybe I underestimated you."

"I'm sure you did," I said. "But can I ask you something?" He nodded. "What happened between you two? Why do you hate him so? And don't tell me that he betrayed his religion."

Simon frowned, our alliance seemingly at an end, and said he didn't need to answer to me.

"You don't know anything about me or Karl, for that matter," he said and walked away.

"What did you say to him?" asked Isaac, who'd materialized behind me. "I'd like to go home now."

Isaac begged me to stay, but I'd had enough of the poisonous air for one night. He seemed genuinely worried that I was upset. Where had that concern been when he was flirting with Audrey earlier in the evening? But I kept my thoughts to myself; I don't like to whine to men about their attentions. If I'm not what they want, I certainly don't want to be there. I assured him that everything was fine between us. I just wanted a night alone in my own bed to clear my head. We made a date for the following evening.

I drove back to Cedar Haven without incident and went to my cabin. For the first time since I'd arrived, I pulled the bottle of White Label from the bag under my bed and set upon it. I had no ice, but there was water. I washed away the foul taste of Simon and Audrey and Karl Merkleson from my mouth.

I lay awake for hours, draining one whiskey after another, asking myself what I was getting into, until the tumbler dropped from my hand to the floor as I nodded off.

TUESDAY, AUGUST 22, 1961

I earmarked Tuesday as a day to spend with Aunt Lena and Max, whom I'd been neglecting for the past few days. After my late night with the bottle, I was a little late to the post, but I managed to emerge by nine thirty. As it was another gray day, the old folks wanted to stay close to home. I took my car into the village to pick up some supplies and was driving back to Cedar Haven when I passed a sign announcing the Sans Souci Cabins a hundred yards ahead. I recalled my conversation with Isaac from the day before. Gayle Morton was staying at the Sans Souci when I met her, but Isaac had insisted she'd been at Tom's Lakeside Motel. I flipped on the indicator and turned into the parking lot.

I had no business at the Sans Souci Cabins, but I couldn't resist. My visit was motivated entirely by curiosity. I wasn't sure if Gayle Morton was still in residence, but I hadn't come to meet her. I wanted to talk to the manager.

The Sans Souci bordered the lake on the western side of Lake Road, just a quarter mile north of the village. The accommodations consisted of ten identical one-room cabins, built of cinder block and painted brown to resemble logs. A wooden sign alongside the road advertised vacancy and beach access. I parked my car in front of the registration office.

Inside at the desk, I found a young man in a white short-sleeved shirt, whose collar was too large for his neck. His clip-on tie was crooked and stained with something shiny. I didn't want to know.

"May I help you, miss?" he asked.

"I'm looking for some information," I said. "It's about Mr. Morton."

"The man who died on the rocks?"

"Yes. Can you tell me when he checked in?"

He grabbed the register and began flipping through the pages. Then he stopped and looked up at me. "Aren't you the lady who was here with the chief of police yesterday?" I nodded. "Who are you, anyway, and why are you asking about Mr. Morton?"

I was prepared for that question. "I work for Stephenson's Insurance in Albany. Mr. Morton had a life insurance policy with us. My boss sent me to gather some information about the accident so that we can clear the payment for his widow."

He nodded, uncertain, but without a good argument to refuse. He turned a few more pages then settled on one. "He checked in Wednesday night. Late."

Wednesday? That meant he'd been on the lake for two full days before he died. Gayle Morton had said they'd arrived Friday.

"Did he have a car?" I asked.

The clerk consulted the register again. "Nope. I don't see any mention of a vehicle here. We always make a note of the cars in the register."

"How would one get here without a car?" I asked. "Is there a bus station?"

"No bus station. But there's taxis in Ticonderoga that might drive up here. It would be a pretty nice fare."

I jotted down a note. Wait, why was I jotting down notes? Those two men had fallen accidentally to their deaths. I was just nosing around because I hated unresolved questions. And the question of which motel Gayle Morton had been staying in the past few days was tickling my brain.

"Do you know a place called Toms Lakeside Motel?" I asked.

"Sure," he said. "It's about a mile south of here. In the village next to Edmond's Market."

"Has Mrs. Morton checked out yet?"

"Last night about six."

"Did she leave in a taxi?" I asked.

The clerk shook his head. "No. She left in a dark sedan. I think it was a Ford."

"I thought you said the Mortons arrived without a car."

"That's right. Mr. Morton arrived Wednesday without a car, but his wife didn't check in until Friday evening." Again he consulted the register. "About five o'clock Friday. And here's the detail of her car. Ford Galaxie Starlight, blue. Plate number ALB-3529."

Curious that the Mortons had arrived separately on Prospector Lake. Not quite odd, but curious just the same. What was even stranger was the fact that Karl had landed up in a taxi or on foot. Perhaps he'd hitchhiked. Still, I wondered why the Mortons had arrived two days apart. Married couples did strange things, I reasoned.

I thanked the young clerk and turned to leave. He called after me and joined me at the screen door of the registration office. He asked if Mrs. Morton stood to collect a big insurance payout.

I flashed him my best born-yesterday smile and said I didn't know. "I'm just Mr. Stephenson's girl Friday."

I reversed out of the Sans Souci parking lot and headed back into the village. A steady rain was falling from a darkening sky, and, as a consequence, Lake Road was deserted. The vacationers were either snug in their cabins, waiting out the rain amid their screaming children, or enjoying a hot lunch at Lenny's Diner in the middle of the village. I drove past Lenny's and through the windows could see a full house chewing on hamburgers and french fries as their kids stuffed their sunburned faces with grilled cheese sandwiches washed down with Squirt.

Tom's Lakeside Motel was a traditional, one-story inn, set back about thirty feet from Lake Road on the west side of the street. There were seventeen units, laid out in a U configuration. Out front, a large wooden sign depicting a beaming angler reeling in an airborne trout invited travelers to stop and sample the local sport fishing. The motel also offered televisions and kitchenettes in every room. My windshield wipers skated back and forth across the glass as I idled in the middle of Lake Road, studying the place. A dark-blue Ford Galaxie sat parked in front of unit six. The license plate read ALB-3529. I flicked on my turn signal and pulled into the parking lot.

⁂

So Gayle Morton was still in Prospector Lake. And she'd changed motels, perhaps for the second time. Maybe the curious double booking was not so mysterious after all. Perhaps she'd found the cabins at the Sans Souci moldy or uncomfortable. Or perhaps Tom's had earned five stars from the *Mobil Travel Guide*. One look inside the registration office debunked that theory. The lobby consisted of a crooked desk, leaning to starboard, and a couple of armchairs whose squashed stuffing and threadbare upholstery looked as though they'd been sat upon for generations by burly men in wet swimming trunks. Smelled that way, too. The walls were pine boards shellacked with a high-gloss shine, making them look like a gymnasium floor stood up on its end. The linoleum tile was covered with an old throw rug.

As the lobby was empty, I rang the bell on the desk. After a few moments, a tanned man in an unbuttoned beach shirt and tight bathing trunks shuffled into the room. He took up a position behind the registration desk.

"I'm afraid we're full up, miss," he said. "But I'm sure I could find some room for a pretty thing like you."

"I'm not looking for a room. I just wanted some information about a guest who's staying here."

He smiled and nodded knowingly. "Did you just come from the Sans Souci?"

When I didn't answer right away, he volunteered that he'd just been speaking on the phone to the desk clerk from the Sans Souci.

"He called to tell me a pretty insurance girl was poking around asking questions."

"Yes, that's me. Are you Tom?"

He nodded. "Tom Waller, proprietor. I own this place."

I wondered why he would admit to such a thing, let alone boast about it. But I kept that thought to myself.

"So, what do you want to know?" he asked.

"Mrs. Morton is staying here. I was wondering when she checked in and how long she's planning on staying."

The man's eyes narrowed in concentration. "Morton? We don't have any guests by that name here."

"Are you sure?" I asked. "Her car is outside. The blue Galaxie in front of number six."

"Number six?" He sounded surprised. "There's no Morton in there. It's a man named Pierce. Owen Pierce. And his daughter is in the next room. Gayle Pierce, I believe her name is."

That must be her father. Isaac had said the family name was Pierce. But why would Gayle Morton register under her maiden name? To ward off curious locals after the tragic accident, perhaps?

"So they checked in yesterday evening?" I asked, trying to put the events in order.

The man stared at me blankly. "No, miss. They checked in last Thursday afternoon."

CHAPTER ELEVEN

"W hat exactly are your doubts, Ellie?" asked Aunt Lena back at Cedar Haven. "It's a little odd, as you say, but there's been no hint of anything untoward."

"You're right," I said. "There are a thousand reasons Gayle Morton and her father might have come here on Thursday. And why she lied to me and the chief of police about it."

We both thought about it for a while. "Maybe this Gayle and her father followed Karl here to catch him at something. Or maybe he left her, and they came to talk him out of it."

I nodded. "That's probably it. But why register under her maiden name? And why stay in a different motel from her husband for twenty-four hours?"

"Maybe they'd had a quarrel then made up Friday afternoon."

I chuckled at myself. Seeing nefarious intent in the innocent actions of a woman and her father. From what I'd heard from Isaac and even Audrey Silber, a roving eye would have been perfectly believable behavior from Karl Merkleson/Charles Morton. Perhaps he was on the run from his wife when he fell to his death. A tragic accident at the moment when he was about to escape a loveless marriage. But if that were true, why had he fled to Prospector Lake? By all accounts, he hadn't contacted any of his old friends at Arcadia Lodge, even though he'd been staying in a cabin a mile away for three days before he made the ill-advised leap off Baxter's Rock with a sixteen-year-old boy from a local music camp. Either something didn't add up or Karl Merkleson's death was the last in a remarkable string of unexplained events.

"You're suspicious of everything," said Aunt Lena. "Ever since what happened to your father."

"And I was right."

"What is it? Did somebody else fall off Baxter's Rock?" Terwilliger asked me.

I was seated across the desk from him in his office on Lake Road. The place was surprisingly tidy and clean. I attributed that to the young officer, Bob Firth, who'd shown me in to see the chief. Firth, a patrolman about twenty-eight years old, was one of the three officers on the Prospector Lake police force. The third, Mark Charlebois, was on vacation in Lake Placid, I was told. Coals to Newcastle. But as clean as the small station was, Ralph Terwilliger hadn't bathed for at least two days. And he reeked of beer again.

"No," I said. "No more divers. I just wanted to report a pack of skinny-dippers up at Dribble's Beach."

"Very funny," he said. "Dribble's Beach isn't my jurisdiction. What is it you want?"

"I was chased through the woods the other night. At first, I didn't want to report it because maybe it was my imagination. But it happened again, and I'm worried."

"You think it's Yarrow, don't you?" asked Terwilliger. "Every crackpot from Hudson to Montreal thinks they've seen him. That guy's long gone. Probably in Mexico or someplace else south of the Mississippi."

Geography.

"Actually I don't think it was Yarrow. But it was definitely a man following me. Twice."

"Was this after one of your sleepovers at Arcadia Lodge?"

I bristled but didn't answer. Instead I told him about Gayle Morton's game of musical motels. Terwilliger shrugged.

"It's a free country. People can stay where they like."

"Have you seen Tom's Lakeside Motel?" I asked to challenge. "Who would want to move from the Sans Souci to that dump?"

The chief just stared at me. Maybe he didn't appreciate a girl speaking to him that way, or maybe Tom Waller was his brother-in-law. Who knew? But he didn't seem happy about what I'd said.

"There's no law against changing hotels," he said.

"Did you know that she arrived with her father on Thursday afternoon? She told us she'd arrived Friday with her husband. Then she checked into the Sans Souci on Friday evening. And Monday, she moved back to Tom's."

"Anything else?" he asked.

"She never even checked out of Tom's when she went to stay with her husband. She kept her room. Doesn't any of that seem strange to you?"

"People do lots of strange things," he said. "Unless you've got something more than a lady who changed her hotel, I'm busy."

"I just find it odd."

"Are you suggesting that something's fishy about those two deaths?" he asked. "Because the only thing I find funny about the whole thing is what those two fellows must have been up to when they died."

"I beg your pardon?"

"I think there was some perverted stuff going on. Two men in their undies, not bathing suits, mind you."

That had crossed my mind, but I thought it was unlikely. Karl Merkleson was married and a ladies' man to boot. And Jerry Kaufman had a girlfriend.

"What's the difference between a bathing suit and underwear?" I asked. "And, by the way, one of them was completely dressed in a T-shirt, shorts, and sneakers."

Terwilliger waved me off. "I think they were committing acts against nature. And they fell off the cliff."

I gaped at him. "Fell off the cliff? As they were . . . doing it? In mid . . ." I searched for the word, ". . . thrust?"

"Sure," he said, unswayed by my incredulity. "People get up to all kinds of perversions."

"Jerrold Kaufman had a girlfriend," I said. "She was with him just hours before he fell to his death. And in the same area. So I doubt that poor boy was performing 'acts against nature' with Charles Morton as they stumbled over the cliff."

Terwilliger leaned forward and rested an elbow onto his desk. "Did his girlfriend say anyone pushed them off Baxter's Rock?"

"Of course not."

"Then tell me what you'd like me to do."

"I'm not sure," I said. "I was just wondering if you thought there was even the slightest reason to suspect something untoward."

He shook his head. "It's the law of gravity, miss. Man falls off cliff and dies. If there was anything suspicious, I'd be on that wife like stink on manure. You can be sure of that. But we've seen this kind of thing before. When people aren't careful, bad things can happen."

The rain continued as I drove back to Cedar Haven. The cocktail hour was already in full swing when I arrived. Martini in hand, Cousin Max was standing over the jar of olives, agonizing over which one to select. Aunt Lena was rocking in her chair in the parlor, sipping her usual summer drink, gin and tonic. I dropped some ice into a glass and poured myself a healthy two fingers of Scotch.

We chatted about my day. I shared the same doubts I'd already discussed with Aunt Lena and Chief Terwilliger. Max enjoyed the exercise, fancying himself cut out for detective work. His bet was on the father-in-law.

"Why on earth would he push an innocent kid over the cliff?" asked Lena.

Max chewed on that one, along with his olive, and finally offered the solution. "Children are annoying creatures, after all. I'd shove one over a cliff myself if I thought I could get away with it."

Before Aunt Lena could answer, a knock came on the porch door. Even with ever-nearing sightings of Donald Yarrow, we remained admirably calm in the face of an unannounced visitor. As things turned out, it was Isaac. He said his hellos, refused an offered drink, and asked to speak to me in private. We stepped outside and talked under the eaves out of the rain.

"Something upset you last night," he said. "I was hoping you'd come to Arcadia tonight, and I could make it right again."

I pursed my lips, thinking of how best to answer. I enjoyed spending time at Arcadia. At least I had enjoyed it until the toxic atmosphere rolled in. I didn't care if I ever saw Simon or Miriam again. A day or two earlier, I had wanted to get to know her better. But that was the last thing I wanted now. She was a miserable, unpleasant soul who ruined my mood every chance she got. Plus I wanted to spend more time with Lena and Max. I was scheduled to leave Sunday morning for New Holland, after all, and I didn't know when I'd have the chance to see them again.

"I'm going to stay in this evening," I said.

"But you'll come over later?" he asked. "And you'll spend the night?"

I shook my head. "No, Isaac. I just want to stay in."

He looked as if I'd driven a stake through his heart.

"Don't you want to see me?" he asked. "Be with me?"

"I do," I said. "It's just . . ."

"Then come."

I drew a sigh and found the backbone I'd been looking for. "Isaac, if you'd like to see me, you'll come back here later. I'm staying in."

After dinner we sat down for port and a smoke in the parlor. Aunt Lena checked the radio for the latest news on the escaped convict. Another sighting, this time in Paradox. Donald Yarrow was either a case of mass hysteria or he was circling around Prospector Lake, closing in like a tightening noose.

"Tonight, I think we'll bolt the doors," whispered Aunt Lena as I poured refills of our drinks at the bar. Max was across the room, ensconced in his chair with a book of Longfellow poems on his lap. "And you, Ellie, no more late-night runs through the woods."

I jerked my head to see her. She looked me in the eye to drive home her point. And I thought I'd been so clever and covered my tracks after the first night. I surely blushed crimson. God, who else was aware of my trysts? Miriam, of course, and the nose-picker Chief Terwilliger. I cringed, certain I was the scandal of Prospector Lake.

We switched from the Yarrow report to the CBC's classical broadcast, catching Ravel's *Piano Concerto in G* from beginning to end. Max sat transfixed, eyes shut, ignoring his Longfellow, as he soaked in the Ravel.

Afterward I asked Max which poem he was reading, and he answered in his brightest baritone, "'This is the forest primeval. The murmuring pines and the hemlocks, bearded with moss . . .'"

"Can't you just once answer a question?" I asked.

"Name it, my dear," he said. "Don't let me down."

"Of course it's *Evangeline*," I said.

"The finest American epic poem ever written," he pronounced.

Max read some passages from the poem, and we reminisced about my father and his favorite Longfellow poems, including "Dante" and "Holidays."

"He made me memorize it," I said. "'These tender memories are a fairy tale of some enchanted land we know not where, but lovely as a landscape in a dream.'"

"But this one was his favorite line," announced Max. "'He hears his daughter's voice, singing in the village choir, and it makes his heart rejoice.'"

My throat tightened, and I couldn't speak. The words stung, though I was too stunned to know exactly why. Were those lines for me? Or just something he liked to repeat? He did things like that. And even though I'd resolved to move on from the long, troubled relationship with my late father, there were these powerful emotional talismans that could conjure painful memories. Yes, I'd made my peace with him, but that didn't mean I had forgotten. One thing I knew for sure: I had never heard my father recite the "Village Blacksmith" even once in my presence. Why would he quote such a random line and make damn sure I was never there to hear it?

"That's right," said Lena. "He used to say it often, even at times when it wasn't apropos."

"True enough," added Max. "But the first time he quoted it was after your school singing recital, Ellie. I think you were seven years old."

I didn't know what to think or how to react. Had he recited the lines as a cherished memory of me? Or was it a bitter reminder of how much he disliked what I had become? I would never know. And I reminded myself that I didn't care. I'd buried that torture along with his ashes, and I wasn't going back.

"What's your favorite port, Max?" I asked, changing the subject and swallowing the last of the memories.

"Any port in a storm, my dear," he said. "Any port at all."

Windy nights had always unnerved me as a girl. They still did as a grown woman. The rush and tumble of air, the whispering and whistling of the wind spooked me. I would listen at the window, nevertheless, and watch the trees thrashing and fluttering, fighting the storm. The spectacle awed and beckoned me at the same time.

That night, alone in my small cabin, the wind blew wet and hard from the west, down the mountainside, over Cedar Haven and across Prospector Lake. Cold rain fell for a few minutes then stopped, only to start again a short time later. Then a great branch broke off one of the cedars in the yard, loosing a loud crack and a thud when it hit the ground. That was spooky enough, but things got even worse when I heard steps climb onto the wooden porch. There came a soft rapping at the door, and I sat bolt upright in bed and reached for the robe I'd cast off before slipping under the covers. The rapping came again. Then the latch moved slowly. Up then down. The door didn't budge; I'd had the good sense to bolt it before retiring for the night. But then it shook, as if someone was trying to push it open with a strong shoulder. I leapt from the bed before I'd even wrapped myself in the robe and, completely naked, scurried across the room to grab the iron poker leaning against the fireplace. I raised it over my head and waited, breathless, thinking I'd never felt such terror in my entire life. And curious enough, I discovered, as I stood there, that fear is multiplied tenfold when you have no clothes on.

"Open up," an eerie voice whispered, and I screamed. Then the voice called out my name. "Ellie, it's me!"

I dropped the poker to the floor and threw open the door. Isaac was standing there, soaking wet from the rain. I grabbed his arm, yanked him inside, and bolted the door again.

"My God, you scared me to death," I said, wrapping my arms around him. He tore off his wet clothes, and we wrapped ourselves in the warmth of the dry bed. The night was not all hell and horrors after that.

CHAPTER TWELVE

Isaac padded across the room in his bare feet to retrieve two glasses next to the pitcher of water. We made short work of what was left of the bottle of whiskey I'd dented the night before. Curled up in the sweaty sheets, we talked for hours.

He told me he'd wanted to come earlier, but there'd been some trouble at Arcadia Lodge. Four John Birchers had shown up looking for Simon. They said he'd tried to throttle Waldo Coons, who had been manning their booth in the village green that afternoon. Simon told him he was fired from Arcadia Lodge, and then, in a rage, he upended their table and tore up their brochures.

"They wanted to drag Simon off to jail," said Isaac. "They even brought Chief Terwilliger with them. My father and I talked them out of pressing charges and promised we'd get Simon to pay for the brochures. And of course we gave Waldo his job back."

"How awful," I said.

"Simon got off lucky," said Isaac. "Although it will pain him to pay to reprint those ridiculous brochures."

"No, I meant how awful that you had to hire back that cave dweller Waldo Coons."

Isaac laughed. "Come on. He's not so bad."

"But how can he work for a bunch of socialist Jews when he belongs to the John Birch Society?"

"He doesn't understand the politics of it," said Isaac. "He's just following along with some of his friends."

"I can't believe that," I said.

"It's true. I think he's retarded somehow. For example, he doesn't react to external stimuli. Once, he spilled a lobster pot filled with boiling water on his leg in the kitchen. He was wearing trousers, but still it should have hurt like all get-out. But he didn't scream. Didn't say anything. He's like that. Slow and dull. If you were to ask him for the time of day or kick him in the shins, he would just stare at you the same from those hollow eyes."

Fascinating though Waldo Coons might have been, I pressed Isaac to change the subject and tell me stories about his own life, his work. He taught calculus to bright young students at Bronx Science High School, he said. When the school moved to its new campus in March of 1959, they faced the considerable challenge of moving all the library books from the old campus to the new.

"Someone came up with the brilliant idea to have the students check out five library books each from the old school on Friday, then return them to the new campus on Monday." He chuckled, sipping some Scotch. "It was genius."

We talked more about his job, and then Isaac asked again about my meeting with Gayle. I had new information for him.

"She's been in Prospector Lake since Thursday," I said. "And Karl arrived the day before that, Wednesday."

"I can't believe he was here for three days without contacting us."

"And at the Sans Souci," I said. "Barely a mile from Arcadia Lodge."

"So what was Gayle doing here?" he asked.

"I can't say. She checked into Tom's Lakeside Motel on Thursday afternoon with her father. They took two rooms; then she switched to the Sans Souci on Friday around five o'clock."

Isaac mulled over the news. I tried to cozy up to him, but his mind was elsewhere.

"Tell me something," I said after a while. "How well do you know Gayle Morton?"

It took the better part of an hour for Isaac to admit that he indeed knew Karl's wife better than he was letting on. I assured him that it meant nothing to me if he'd found her attractive, as long as he wasn't still longing after her. I told him half smiling that he was not my first indiscretion. Finally he hung his head and told me the story.

After Miriam's trip to Los Angeles, Isaac took a train across the country and looked up his old friend. Karl was relaxed with him. They had dinner together then lunch the next day, and Isaac thought he'd made progress toward roping in the prodigal son. To clinch the deal, Isaac thought it would be a good idea to convince Gayle to meet the Arcadians and become one of the old gang.

"Did Karl know about your meeting with his wife?" I asked.

Isaac shook his head. "He never would have agreed."

"Why's that?"

Isaac skirted my question and told me instead that he'd met Gayle Morton at the Beverly Hills Hotel for tea. An hour later they drove to Hollywood and checked into a seedy motel on Sunset Boulevard for a roll in the hay. Gayle knew too many people at the Beverly Hills Hotel and feared discovery. Isaac said he would never forget his shame or the name of the place: the Sunset Motor Inn and Resort. Sounded like a grand place.

"I swear to you, Ellie, she tricked me," he said. "She said she'd seen a gossipy friend in the lobby at the Beverly Hills Hotel and didn't want Karl, Charles, to know she'd been talking to me."

"You don't have to explain to me," I said.

"But I do. She had me follow her until she pulled into the Sunset Motor Inn and Resort. I thought that was strange, but I needed to talk to her. The next thing I knew, we were . . ."

I didn't want to hear another word. I couldn't have cared less that he'd slept with some woman. Any woman. Many women. It didn't matter. What bothered me was that he'd slept with his old friend's wife. I was wrestling with that when he told me that it wasn't as bad as I thought.

"Gayle said she and Karl had an agreement. An arrangement. He went his way, and she went hers. No strings."

I put a finger to his lips, silencing him finally. If the Mortons had an agreement, good for them. I only wished Isaac hadn't become a party to it. And failing that, I wished he would shut up. My finger did the trick. Perhaps he thought I was jealous, and I was happy to let him think that. He could think whatever he liked, as long as he left that story buried in the past.

"What do you think she wanted here?" I asked, bringing him back to the sordid present.

"Karl hit it big about a year and a half ago," said Isaac. "He'd gone out to Los Angeles to get into the movie business. Since his family was so active in the theater, he figured it was the logical next step for him. He thought he could out-write anyone in Hollywood, including Orson Welles and Ring Lardner Jr. He got his start in the film business with Gayle's father, who was a fairly successful producer of Martian movies, but he didn't get anywhere fast. Then Karl and his father-in-law agreed to part company, and Karl scored a huge movie deal. He wrote the script for another one of those biblical pictures. Then he got a producer's credit on a Natalie Wood movie. He was suddenly A-list hot stuff."

"And let me guess. He wanted a divorce?"

"Bingo."

"So was Gayle here to save her marriage or rekindle an old romance with someone else?" I asked.

Isaac waved a hand to indicate impatience. "I was a minor diversion for Gayle," he said. "She was after bigger game. She wanted a rich guy, not an egg-head math teacher from New York."

"So you think she was here to get her man back?" I said. Isaac nodded.

I considered the news. Isaac's version of events didn't rule out any of the odd movements back and forth between two motels. Maybe she had indeed come to the Adirondacks to save her failing marriage. I thought it was a curious choice to bring Daddy along on such a quest, but who knew what kind of relationship they'd had? There was still nothing that pointed to anything but an accidental death, especially given the presence of the young boy on the rocks with Karl. What possible connection could he have had with the Mortons?

Still, I am a curious gal. I craved information about all things. And since we were talking about Karl Merkleson, I had more questions.

"What was it that really came between Karl and Simon?" I asked.

Isaac shrugged and took another slug of whiskey. "They were so close," he said. "At City College, they signed up for all the same classes. Political science and history. They thought about law school for a while. They wanted to change the world, lead the Red revolution in America."

"City College was a hotbed of radicalism, wasn't it?" I asked.

"And Simon and Karl were leading the charge. They used to haunt the cafeteria, making speeches and arguing with everyone. It was a different time. The war had just ended, and both were toeing the party line. They felt that the time was ripe for the expansion of socialism. They cheered Stalin's grab of Eastern Europe at the close of the war."

"So they were best of friends," I said. "Comrades. What drove them apart?"

"People change," he said. "Later, Karl was disillusioned by the Soviet invasion of Hungary. But Simon couldn't bring himself to criticize the USSR for anything. He thought that was a betrayal of socialist ideals."

"But that was after their rift," I said. "Hungary was fifty-six. Karl left in fifty-four."

Isaac was about to answer when a gust of wind rattled the window, and we both started. I saw something duck away behind the glass. I shrieked.

Isaac insisted it was the shadow of a waving branch, but my crawling skin told me otherwise. I was sure I'd seen the shape of a head.

We both rose from the bed. I slipped into a robe, and Isaac pulled his trousers on. A glance through the window revealed nothing, so we ventured out onto the porch, iron poker and flashlight in hand. I scanned the campgrounds and bordering woods with the light for five minutes, as Isaac held tight to the poker. There was no one.

WEDNESDAY, AUGUST 23, 1961

I was awakened at nine by a knocking on my door. Isaac was gone, having left just after dawn. So it came as a surprise to find him standing there again on my wooden porch.

"Get dressed, Ellie," he said. "I need you to come over to Arcadia. Karl's mother is here. She arrived about an hour ago."

"What's that have to do with me?" I asked.

"She's saying crazy things. Insisting that Karl was pushed off the cliff. She says it was Gayle."

"I still don't see what I'm required for."

"She wants to talk to you because you saw the body. You took photographs."

Esther Merkleson was by herself in the Great Lodge, quite composed from what I could tell. No mad look in her eyes, no histrionics, no foaming at the mouth. She sat up straight in one of the armchairs, holding a small pug on her lap. Isaac escorted me in to introduce me to the grieving mother. Once a famous playwright and actress on the Yiddish stage, Esther Merkleson now looked like the perfect *bubbe*. Simple and dignified in a plain black dress, she wore her graying hair in a sensibly short cut. She was in her early sixties. But as modest as her appearance seemed, her eyes told a different story. This was a woman who took no prisoners.

"Mrs. Merkleson, this is Ellie Stone," said Isaac. "She's the girl I was telling you about."

"I remember Eleonora," she said, her Rs rolling in the back of her throat; her vowels were clean and precise. "You were a smart and spirited young girl. And so pretty." She pronounced girl "goil."

"I'm sorry for your loss, Mrs. Merkleson," I said, extending a hand to her. She lifted the dog off her lap and placed him gently on the floor. "You sit quietly, Leon," she said to the pug and took my hand. Her fingers were cold and dry.

"Hello, little Leon," I called to the dog, reaching down to him. He sniffed the tips of my fingers then turned away and ignored me.

"Tell Ellie where Leon's name came from," said Isaac to Mrs. Merkleson.

"I named him after Trotsky," she said, petting the dog on the head. "A little out of date, but I was feeling nostalgia when I got him."

Isaac threw me a naughty smile while she was gazing adoringly at the dog.

"Isaac told me that you saw Karl on the rocks that day," she said, turning her attention back to me. I nodded. "I would like you to tell me everything you saw. What he was wearing, how his body was positioned, how far he was from the water. Everything you can recall."

I stared at her. I didn't know where to start, or if I should even start at all. Was she a masochist? Or simply deluded that she could divine what had happened in the last moments of her son's life from my description of his corpse, as if she were reading tea leaves.

"Isaac said you have photographs," she added. "I want to see those as well."

"The photographs are difficult to look at," I said. "And I'm afraid there's not much to glean from them. They're small and black-and-white."

She stared me down. Her eyes, sharp and demanding, commanded me, as if I were in her thrall. I told her I'd bring her the contact sheets later that afternoon.

Over the next twenty minutes, I gave her the details she'd requested. Her son's body had been found in his underwear, with an expensive watch on his wrist. I said I'd thought it strange that he was wearing a leather wristband for swimming, and she pursed her lips together and harrumphed, as if I'd just proven her suspicions true. I described the bruises on his torso and thigh, and that I'd assumed he'd bounced and rolled after impact. He was about four feet from the edge of the water.

"And he was sunburned," I said. "Quite badly."

"Yes, Karl had very fair skin. He didn't like sunbathing. But what about the boy they found with him?" she asked. "The Kaufman boy. Where was his body in relation to Karl's?"

Our discussion had moved from morbid to ghastly. Yet Esther Merkleson seemed detached, unemotional, clinical in her approach to gathering the details of her son's death. I didn't want to tell her about Jerrold Kaufman's crushed skull, but I did. I told her that I'd nearly vomited over the two bodies.

"Where was the boy?" she repeated. "Closer to the water than Karl?"

Ugh. "He was closer to the wall of the cliff. Maybe ten feet from the water's edge. He was in the shade, behind some rocks."

She thanked me once I'd answered all her questions. I asked her where her suspicions lay. She didn't hesitate. She looked me in the eye and said that Gayle Morton had killed Karl as surely as I was standing there.

"That horrible girl tracked him here, stalked him for two days, and pushed him over that cliff," she said with three bobs of her head to punctuate each step of Gayle's plot.

"How can you be sure of that?" I asked. "The clerk at the motel said that your daughter-in-law checked into Karl's room on Friday afternoon or early evening. That means she was with him, not stalking him."

She shook her head vigorously, gathered little Leon in her arms, and stood in preparation to leave. "I spoke to my son Friday night," she said. "He called me from a pay telephone in the village after midnight. He told me he was leaving that awful girl for good. And he never mentioned that she was here on the lake. In fact, he said he'd left her in Los Angeles on Tuesday. I cried with joy. Then I asked him to give me the number of his hotel so I could reach him. He said not to call him there. He hadn't been there in two days and wasn't planning to return there."

"Why would he avoid his motel?"

"I don't know. He didn't say where he was staying. He said he was out of change, and he hung up."

"Have you told any of this to the chief of police?" I asked.

"I met him this morning," she scoffed. "A *shikker* and a *beheyme*. He was drunk at seven a.m. But he gave me the telephone number of the Kaufmans. I want to meet them later."

"Chief Terwilliger doesn't believe there's anything unusual about

Gayle's comings and goings," I said. "I found out that she checked into one motel with her father on Thursday, then moved to Karl's motel on Friday. And back again to the first motel on Monday."

"You're making inquiries?" she asked. "Why?"

"It started with Karl's clothing. His shirt and possibly a jacket were missing. And his wallet hasn't been found. He had no car, and then I heard his wife had been staying in two different motels. It just seemed odd to me, so I started asking questions."

"So that awful girl's father was here too?"

"They're still here. At least they were yesterday afternoon."

"You're a strange girl, Eleonora," she said, her eyes studying me. "But I'm happy for your help."

I asked her what she planned to do in Prospector Lake. She said the first priority was to claim Karl's body. I told her that Gayle wanted the body as well. Esther Merkleson shook her head determinedly and said that she would fight to her last breath to keep Karl's remains.

"I brought him into the world, and I'll take him out of it, too. I told that drunk Terwilliger this morning that I was taking Karl home. He won't dare stop me."

"Is there anything I can do for you?" I asked.

She took a step closer to me and drew me in with her hypnotic gaze. "You like to ask questions," she said. "What would you ask next?"

I didn't hesitate. I knew exactly where I would start.

"I would like to know what Karl was doing at the top of that cliff with Jerrold Kaufman," I said. "Did they know each other? And why did they die together?"

"Yes," she said and gave a short bob of her head to indicate that the matter was settled. "I'll be meeting his parents this afternoon. Perhaps you can ask some questions and report back to me later." I said that I would. "And you'll bring me those photographs."

"How may I help you today, Miss Stone?" asked Norris Lester.

"I was hoping you'd be able to clear up some questions I have about Jerry Kaufman," I said, sitting in the chair across his desk from him.

He arched his left eyebrow. I knew it was going to be a tough sell. Why should he answer any of my questions, let alone ones about a poor boy who'd died? A boy to whom I had no connection.

"I'm trying to figure out what Charles Morton—he's the other man who died—was doing with Jerry on top of Baxter's Rock," I explained.

"Why?" he asked. "What business is it of yours? You didn't know either of them, did you?"

Good question, I thought. "As a matter of fact, I've known Mr. Morton since I was a child," I said, embellishing. "His mother asked me to help her find out what happened to her son. I thought this would be a good place to start."

"'What happened to her son'?" said Lester in his best mocking voice. "He tried to dive off the cliff and missed the water. What do you think happened?"

I could see that this interview was going to require all my skill. "Let me ask you this," I said. "Did Jerry like diving?"

Lester frowned and declined to answer.

"Won't you bear with me for just a few moments?" I asked. "It certainly won't hurt Jerry to answer a few questions."

"I'm not aware that Jerry was fond of diving," said Lester at length. "He was never interested in swimming beyond the occasional dip on a hot afternoon."

"That's one of the details I'm struggling to reconcile," I said. "I know that Jerry met someone not too far from the cliff early that same morning. You told me yourself he was due back at camp for breakfast at seven thirty. But he fell to his death hours later. What did Jerry do from seven a.m. to noon?"

"You're asking me? I had no idea he was missing until the police came to tell me."

I sat in silent thought for a half minute, trying to imagine what the young man could have done in the five-plus hours between his tryst with Emily Grierson and his ill-fated leap from Baxter's Rock.

"Do you think I might speak to some of Jerry's friends here at the camp?" I asked.

Lester refused, claiming the boys and girls were already upset over their friend's death. He wasn't going to make matters worse by subjecting them to a nosy busybody's prying questions.

"How about a couple of the counselors?" I asked, miffed by his characterization of me as a nosy busybody, even though it was an accurate assessment. I was shown the door for my trouble.

The lunch bell rang. The little prodigies, having blown the last of the spittle out of their trombones and sucked the life from their oboe reeds, had stashed their instruments in their cases and run off to feed their faces. Norris Lester, too, must have been hungry for the franks and beans they were serving in the cafeteria, for he scurried away, surely thinking his secretary, Pete, would escort me off camp property.

I found myself unchaperoned outside Lester's office. Never one to miss an opportunity, I wandered across the main compound, past a totem pole of sorts with mimeographed announcements stapled over the faces of the lower figures. There was a dance scheduled for Friday. The motif was Puccini's *La Fanciulla del West*. I could just picture it: a hundred backward boys too shy to ask a hundred forward girls to dance.

I surveyed the buildings. All pine boards and whitewash with forest green highlights on the door and window frames. The cafeteria, full of campers and counselors, sat on the northwest side of the compound. The library faced it from the opposite end, the southeast. There were rows of dormitories to the west and a great concert hall to the east. Some enterprising camper had managed to climb up twenty feet and remove the "I" from "Recital Hall," leaving "REC TAL HALL" in its place. I got a good chuckle out of that, wondering if Norris Lester had noticed the theft yet.

The dormitories were wide open and unsupervised at lunch. I determined that the boys' cabins were on the left side of the long path, and the girls' were on the right. Furthermore, I figured that the cabins labeled Chipmunk and Squirrel were probably for the younger boys, while the Bear and Eagle lodges were for older boys. I thought Jerry Kaufman was probably a Bear or an Eagle. I slipped inside the Bear Lodge.

A schedule of events was tacked to the wall, listing a variety of activities starting with July 30: move-in day. I heard a cough inside the dormitory and discovered a young man lying in his bunk, hands folded behind his head as he stared into space.

"I'm sorry," I said. "I must be in the wrong place."

"Who are you?" asked the boy, sitting up. He was fourteen or fifteen, skinny, with curly hair and pimples.

"Mr. Lester sent me to check on the . . . um, ceiling fans," I lied.

"Go ahead," he said, lying back on his bed and resuming the communion with his deepest thoughts.

I gazed up at the ceiling. There were no fans.

"Did you know Jerry Kaufman?" I asked as innocently as I knew how. The boy sat up again.

"Not really," he said. "Why do you ask? Is he the guy who stole the ceiling fans?"

"Mr. Lester asked me to find out a little more about him," I said, blushing at my gaffe. This kid was sharp. "He wants to make sure no one else is planning to dive off that cliff."

The boy chuckled and lay back down. "Lester the Jester? What an idiot. No one's going to jump off that cliff. We're musicians here, not daredevils."

"What about Jerry?" I asked.

"Lester didn't send you here, did he?"

I gave his question some quick thought. The kid wouldn't have time to go check with the director, so I could continue with my story. But he clearly didn't like Norris Lester. Neither did I, for that matter.

"You're right," I said, playing my hunch. "He just threw me out of his office for asking questions."

He chuckled. "Yeah, he kicked me out of lunch for a week for having a smart mouth. You're in good company."

"So what about Jerry?" I repeated, now that we were confederates.

"What about him?"

"Was he the type who liked to take chances? Maybe like diving off Baxter's Rock?"

"The word going around is that he might have slipped, but no way was he trying to dive. We heard he was fully dressed. T-shirt, shorts, and sneakers. Who goes for a swim like that?"

"You have a point. What else are people saying?"

The kid shrugged. "Not much. Someone from his bunk said he went out every day at six and came back in time for breakfast at seven thirty."

"So it was strange that the day he died he was out for six hours."

"Maybe not," said the kid. "Maybe he fell off the cliff earlier than that other guy."

That was interesting. I hadn't considered it. Terwilliger had said his witnesses saw one of them jump. Or had he? They'd heard a scream then turned to see one man in midair. I made a mental note to double-check with the chief.

"Has there been any talk that Jerry knew that other man who died?" I asked.

He shook his head. I sensed he had no more information for me.

"My name's Ellie," I said, taking a step closer to his bed. "I'm staying at Cedar Haven, about a mile north of the village on Jordan Street."

He sat up again, a toothy grin smeared over his face. He looked me up and down quite thoroughly. "Is that an invitation?"

I sighed. What was it about adolescent boys and me? Moths to my flame.

"I can see why Mr. Lester kicked you out of the cafeteria. You do have a smart mouth. No, it's not an invitation. I wanted to ask you to do a little digging for me. As a favor."

"What do I get out of it?" he asked.

"I'll give you two dollars if you can scare up some good information about Jerry."

"I'd rather have a quart of beer," he said. "Or a date."

"I'm not buying you beer. Let's start with the two dollars, and we'll see if sparks fly between us later."

He shrugged and said okay. He could use the two bucks to bribe some older kid to buy him beer in the village.

"I'm Herbie," he said as he bestowed me the honor of standing up and shaking my hand. "No last names. I don't want to get involved if you're up to no good."

"Deal," I said, happy not to give him my surname either.

"But I can't just get out of camp whenever I want. You'll have to wait till Saturday night."

"I can't wait that long."

"See, sparks flying already," he said. Little charmer.

"I assume you'll still be cooling your heels here tomorrow at lunch? I'll stop by at twelve thirty and meet you here. Try to get me something by then."

CHAPTER THIRTEEN

The day was bright. The wind and rain of the previous night had passed, and the August sun was back in the saddle. It was only half past noon, but Wednesday promised to be an exhausting day. I was supposed to be on vacation, yet I was chasing a story that was surely just an accident. Yes, there were a few details about the diving deaths that didn't make sense. But what did I think had happened? Had the two men been pushed off the cliff? Was this a case of double suicide? Had they struggled atop Baxter's Rock and caused each other to fall? Had they been engaged in "acts against nature," as Terwilliger maintained, and taken things a step too far? I didn't believe any of those scenarios. So why was I wasting time poking my nose into this tragedy? I thought about those questions as I drove back toward Cedar Haven. I acknowledged my obsessive devotion to clearing up remainders and riddles. It's the same reason I'm unable to leave a crossword puzzle unfinished or a missing sock unfound. I promised myself I would stop as soon as I heard back from my little boyfriend, Herbie. I was finished with this useless digging. Then I passed Aunt Lena's dock and pulled over. I grabbed my camera and climbed out of the car.

After stepping into the old rowboat tied to the dock, taking care not to tip it over, I unknotted the rope and pushed off.

I'm no great sailor, but I can swing a pair of oars. Having rowed around the point, I maneuvered carefully through the mouth of Baxter's Cove where Karl Merkleson and Jerry Kaufman had died. I managed to avoid the rocks and soon reached the narrow shale beach. What was I doing here? I wasn't sure. But I wanted to visit the site again and look around at my leisure.

The first thing I noticed was the white paint on the rocks. The outlines of two bodies. The state police had chosen paint over chalk to preserve the scene, perhaps because of the water that splashed onto the beach. I retrieved my camera from its case and started shooting pictures. I needed to adjust the shutter speed to get usable images of the outlines since the surrounding rocks sheltered much of the beach from direct sunlight. Trying to duplicate the angles and distances I'd shot four days earlier when the bodies had been on gruesome display for me, I also took care to measure the distance between the men. Jerry had landed about two and a half shoe lengths (size six and a half) away from the wall. I wondered if he had scraped against the rocks of the cliffs on his final descent. That was too awful to think about, so I put it out of my mind. Karl had hit the ground approximately seven shoe lengths from the water's edge. Esther Merkleson had put the idea into my head to get an exact positioning, though I couldn't imagine what I would use the measurements for. I asked myself again why I was obsessing over an accident.

I walked the entire length and breadth of the rocky beach, searching for any clue that might have been left behind. I hoped to find Karl's wallet or his shirt, but the place was too small to hide such large objects. There was a rusted beer cap, some twigs, and lots of pine needles. Bird droppings, released from a great height if the explosive patterns on the ground were any indication, dotted the rocks every few feet. Looking to Baxter's Rock above, I could see gulls nesting in the crooks of the wall.

There was nothing to see here. I drew a deep breath of clean Adirondack air and looked to the east, past the cove to the lake. Chief Terwilliger had said that his witnesses didn't see the bodies hit the ground. I could see the surface of the lake, of course, but there were plenty of high rocks guarding the entrance to the cove that would have blocked most views from the other side. It all made sense. I shrugged. So why was I on the beach searching for odds and ends? Just another manifestation of my obsession to finish things off? Most certainly. I should give it up, but I knew I was determined to keep scratching until something bled.

It was nearly two when I drove back to the village and parked my car on the side of Lake Road in front of Palmer Square. The popcorn vendor, stationed nearby, perked up when he saw me climb out of my car. I think he was hoping for his first sale of the day. He deflated when I passed him by, making a beeline for the Tommy Grierson Crusade table across the square.

The pastor was there in his linen suit, which blazed white in the bright sun. As I came closer, I noticed the fraying around the cuffs and lapels, and the elbows were browner than whiter. His hair, however, remained in perfect trim despite its length and thickness.

"Good morning, Miss . . ." he said, inviting me to remind him of my name.

"Stone," I said. "Good morning to you, Reverend Grierson."

He nodded, clearly thrown by my reappearance. I felt sure he wanted never to see me again. He wasn't getting his wish this day.

"I wanted to know how Emily was doing," I said.

"She's fine," said Grierson.

"I don't see her here today. I hope she's coping with the shock."

"The Lord provides comfort in difficult times," he said, barely looking me in the eye. "I shall tell her you inquired after her well-being."

"Actually I need to speak to her. Do you think that would be possible?"

He frowned and ran a hand through his silvery mane. He blustered like a horse before telling me no.

"I wouldn't ask, but Emily may know more about the man who died along with Jerry Kaufman."

"Certainly not," said the preacher. "Emily barely knew the Jewish boy. And she didn't know the other man."

"You can't be sure of that," I said. "I'll only take a minute. Please. The dead man's mother is desperate for information. Won't you help?"

Tommy Grierson shook his head firmly and repeated his no. "I shall pray for that poor woman and for her son." Then he turned away.

$$\infty$$

I'd missed lunch with Lena and Max. When I returned to Cedar Haven, I found poor Max grounded without his car, and I promised he could use mine to go paint in the morning if Terwilliger hadn't returned his by then. I also made a note to demand that the chief release the car immediately. He had no right to commandeer it.

I grabbed one of the two remaining sets of contact sheets I'd printed for Terwilliger, slipping it into an envelope and scribbling Esther Merkleson's name across the front. I drove over to Arcadia to deliver the prints to her as promised, but she was out when I arrived. I ran into Simon, who was nose-deep in a book outside the Great Lodge. *Der demokratische Welt-*

markt by someone named Kohlmey. Light reading for the beach. And in German to boot. Didn't this guy ever take a rest from the revolution?

"I'm looking for Mrs. Merkleson," I said.

"Is that for her?" he asked, indicating the envelope. "I'll make sure she gets it." And he extended a hand to take it. I hesitated, and he took note. "I'll give it to her, you know. I'm not a thief."

"No," I said. "I don't think you're a thief."

We stared at each other for a long moment. "You're becoming quite the regular around here," he said finally.

"I feel so welcome."

Simon laid his book down next to his glass of lemonade on the nearby table. "Look. It's nothing personal, Ellie," he said. "You're a fine girl. And I'm sure Isaac is having a nice summer fling. But Arcadia is a special place. We're a tightly knit group of old friends. You should understand why it's hard for an outsider to belong."

"No one is trying to break up that old gang of yours," I said, turning to leave. But he called after me.

"You see? That's one of the reasons you don't fit in here. We enjoy challenging each other. It's fun. You're just not up to it. The women we accept in our circle have to be remarkable or they're just adornments. Like a nice picture."

"How enlightened. Is that the politburo's official stance?"

Simon shook his head slowly, smirking at me as though I deserved his pity. I wanted to slap him. I wanted to slap him hard enough to knock the smirk and the stringy little goatee beard right off his face.

"As long as Isaac and his father and David Levine welcome me here, you'll have to put up with my presence. You're not bully enough to scare me away, Simon."

"It's okay, Ellie," he said. "Isaac can have his fun with you. The summer's almost over."

How I wanted to defend my honor, but I had to face facts. As much as his words wounded me, I couldn't deny them. I wanted to put him in his place somehow without stooping to name-calling or suggestions of his inability to satisfy his frigid wife. But I was boxed in. He must have noticed the defeat in my eyes, because the boor feigned contrition.

"I'm sorry, Ellie. Do you think I meant country matters?" he asked with a theatrical flair.

My spirits rose like a phoenix. He'd at least served up a fat lob for me to smash back at him without sacrificing my dignity.

"*Hamlet*?" I said. "Have you been waiting since freshman English class to spring that one on some unsuspecting girl?"

I took a moment to enjoy his open-mouthed gape then left him sitting there, hoisted on his own petard.

Back at Cedar Haven, contact sheets still in my custody, I was happy to see Max's Plymouth woody parked on the grass outside the main cabin. I was less than thrilled to find Chief Ralph Terwilliger testing the sturdiness of an old wicker chair in Aunt Lena's parlor. Oh, what did it matter? If the chair didn't collapse under his weight, we would have to toss it onto the fire anyway. He was sipping tea from a paper cup when I entered the room. Aunt Lena threw me a conspiratorial look.

"Just the girl I wanted to see," said Terwilliger through a gray smile. "You're a popular one."

"I beg your pardon?"

"Just that everyone wants to talk to you. First that Merkleson woman. And now even the Kaufmans want to meet you."

"And what do you want?" I asked, and with none of Aunt Lena's charm.

Terwilliger cleared his throat and said that his truck was back from the shop and he was there to return Max's car.

"Did you fill the tank?" I asked.

"I put thirty-five cents' worth of gas into it. That's all I could dig out of the seat cushions. And I appreciate your understanding. The shop didn't have a loaner, and I had police work to do."

"Always happy to help the constabulary," said Max.

"Let's talk," I said to Terwilliger, motioning to him to follow me. Once outside I steered him over to my small cabin and told him about my late-night visitor.

"Look here," I said, pointing to the ground outside the window where I'd seen the face peering in. "Do you see it?"

"Pine needles?" he asked.

"The scuff marks. Someone was standing outside my window last night looking in. I nearly died from fright."

"It just looks like dirt," he said. "Maybe you were imagining things again."

I glared at him. "What do you mean *again*?"

He assumed the look of a trapped animal, held his hands up, and told me to take it easy. "You thought someone was chasing you through the woods the other night, didn't you?"

"Yes," I said. "Surely the same person who was peeping into my window last night. And since you're doing nothing to find him, I'm sure he'll be back again tonight."

Terwilliger looked skeptical. "Can't that boyfriend of yours protect you?"

"Why would he be here?" I asked, again aware of the precarious state of my reputation.

He didn't answer, and I had a fleeting doubt that he might have been the face in the window. That was paranoia. But how else would he have known that Isaac had been there the night before?

"When you get a real glimpse of this mysterious guy, let me know," he said. "But until then, there's not much I can do for you."

I fumed, wishing I could stick a couple of the pine needles into Terwilliger's eyes. And then there was the iron poker I'd grabbed for protection the night before. I had some fresh ideas of where the pointy end might be most effective. One was at the base of Tiny Terwilliger's thick skull. The other was farther south. But I needed the oaf for another few minutes before I could impale him, so I resisted the urge to act.

"I had a thought earlier today," I said through my teeth. "Do you think it's possible that the boy and the man fell off the cliff at different times?"

Terwilliger's face screwed into a mocking grin. "No. What gave you a crazy idea like that?"

"I was trying to figure what Jerry Kaufman could have been doing for the five and a half hours before he died. He met his girlfriend before seven that morning. And he didn't fall off the cliff until half past twelve."

Terwilliger dismissed my concerns. "So he took a nap in the woods. Or went into the village for ice cream. Maybe he went for a swim. Who knows?"

"It's a detail that doesn't make sense. At the least it demands an explanation."

JAMES W. ZISKIN   137

"Look," he said, summoning no small measure of condescension. "Two guys ignored the No Diving sign up on Baxter's Rock and belly flopped onto the rocks. It's simple. Why do you have to make things complicated?"

"I don't buy it," I said. "There's surely a good explanation, but until I find one, it doesn't add up. Help me understand what that kid did to occupy himself for six hours on a Saturday morning, and I'll accept your law-of-gravity theory. Otherwise, I'm starting to think he must have died shortly after seven."

"That's crazy," he said. "Just because he didn't go back to his camp right away?"

"He told his girlfriend he was in a hurry to get back. Why didn't he go? I think it's because he fell off the cliff shortly after he left her."

The chief chuckled. "I happened to be on Route Fifteen that morning, from five to eight, hoping to catch the kids who've been drag racing through the village. And I didn't hear or see anything."

"Where were you?" I asked.

"Just about a quarter mile from that road that turns up to Baxter's Rock. I already told you that last Saturday. We never did catch those kids."

"Still," I said. "You might have been there and still not heard anything."

He laughed. "But they fell off the cliff hours later. I got two witnesses who saw that."

"To be precise," I began, "they only saw one person fall."

Terwilliger dismissed my concerns.

I supposed he was right. What evidence was there that one of the two had fallen earlier? It was just the question of Jerry Kaufman's six hours away from camp.

I asked the nose-picker what he thought had occurred atop Baxter's Rock. He mulled it over for a minute then said he had no idea what young Jerry had been doing with the Jew writer.

"Might you try saying 'Jewish' instead of 'Jew'? It's offensive," I said.

"Very sorry, miss," he said. "I'm still learning the right things to say. I should know better, of course, since Jesus himself was a Jewish. I'm trying not to offend your kind, no matter how hard that is."

Before oozing away and leaving a slimy trail, Chief Terwilliger heaped one more misery upon me. He needed a lift to town to retrieve his pickup truck from the shop that had removed the chunks of venison from his dented front fender.

I agreed, if only to rid myself more quickly of his broad-minded discourse. He stuffed himself into my car, taxing the struts, shock absorbers, and tires all at once. His great behind spread across the bench seat like a pandemic in search of victims.

"Nice car," he said, admiring the dashboard. "Much better than your uncle's."

"Cousin's," I corrected, and we drove in silence to Tucker's Body Shop located on a side street on the far southern end of the village.

As I pulled to a stop to drop him off, he turned and informed me that the Kaufmans were intending to call on me that afternoon.

"You don't mind?" I asked. "No objections to a girl interfering in your investigation?"

"What investigation?" he said and popped open the door.

It was past four when I returned yet again to Cedar Haven, and, having skipped lunch, I was looking forward to a sandwich or some cheese. I noticed an unfamiliar Buick sedan sitting outside Aunt Lena's cabin. A man and a woman were sitting inside with the windows rolled down.

"Excuse me," I said, startling them both. "May I help you?"

The man, who looked to be about forty, climbed out and asked if I was Miss Stone. I nodded. He introduced himself as Harold Kaufman, Jerry's father.

"That's my wife, Rose, in the car," he said. "There was no one at home, so we thought we'd wait for you here."

Aunt Lena and Max must have gone out on a groceries or booze run. I invited the Kaufmans inside and made some tea.

"I'm sorry for your loss," I said once we'd sat down in the parlor.

Mrs. Kaufman started to sob, and her husband consoled her. I bit my lower lip. I had no words to help them. All I could do was give them time. After a few minutes, Mr. Kaufman wiped his eyes and began.

"We're understandably devastated by the loss of our son. You'll have to excuse our emotion."

"Please don't apologize," I said.

"We know that you were present shortly after Jerry died and took the photographs. We don't want to see them, of course. We've seen his body anyway." He paused to mop some new tears from his cheeks.

"If there's any way I can help you and your wife . . ." I said.

"That awful man," he began, "the chief of police said you were moved by Jerry's death. He told us that you said some kind of prayer over him and wept."

"That's not exactly true. I didn't recite any prayers, though I did touch his shoulder in a feeble attempt to comfort him. He was a beautiful boy."

"That's why we've come. To thank you for your care and respect of his body. It was a beautiful thing to do for him."

My throat tightened, a sure indication that I was about to cry. I told the Kaufmans that it was nothing, that I'd felt powerless and useless in the circumstances.

"It may sound strange to you, but we feel you helped him in the moment of his death, or shortly after. And that gives us more peace than you can imagine."

Now I was weeping. I could manage no speech. The Kaufmans approached me and wrapped their arms around me. I couldn't explain why Jerry's death affected me in such a powerful way. Of course a young life snuffed out is tragic and sad, but I hadn't known him. The gratitude offered to me by his parents surely heightened the intensity of my response, but there was a deeper, unknown reason that I could not identify. If the sharing of sorrow provides catharsis, it does so by first tightening the stranglehold of the pain, like a garrote around the neck, before finally breaking its grip and allowing solace to take root. While reporting the story of the disappearance and death of a young girl the previous January, I'd experienced the relief that shared mourning provides. It was a pathway to healing that I'd denied myself in the deaths of my brother and my mother and my father. I'd suffered each of those losses alone, never opening my heart to the grief and comfort of others. Now, in the embrace of the grateful parents of a boy upon whom I'd bestowed a fleeting and futile gesture of compassion, I was moved by the healing power of commiseration.

At length we composed ourselves and managed to share a sad smile. Rose Kaufman asked me if I knew anything about her son, the boy with whom I now shared an eternal bond in her heart.

"I know that he played the violin and piano," I said. "And that he was a fine tennis player."

"That we knew," said Harold Kaufman, patting my hand. "But did you know he was selected among all the students at Orpheus to play the violin in a special concert in the village square with some local musicians? Adults." He said the last word with great pride, as if it connoted quality and gravitas. "They played Mozart and Schubert. That was Sunday the thirteenth. Rose and I came up to watch. Jerry was wonderful."

I tried to appear suitably disappointed at having missed the concert. Harold and Rose fell silent. Their moods darkened again.

"Did you know that he wanted to learn the zither?" I asked.

"The zither?" they said in unison. Harold said no, they'd had no idea. Then they smiled at each other.

"And he had a girl."

CHAPTER FOURTEEN

I ran the film I'd shot in the cove that afternoon through Max's developer and hung the negatives to dry overnight. Then I joined Lena and Max for cocktails.

The evening's radio program included Elgar's *From the South* and Mendelssohn's *Scottish Symphony*, accompanied by two rounds of drinks and canapés. Lena and Max had driven all the way to Fort Ticonderoga to restock the bar. They'd presented me with a fifth of White Label and the admonition that I was due to leave Sunday, and that should hold me until then. I did not share their confidence.

After the CBC, Aunt Lena searched for news of Donald Yarrow. The sightings seemed to indicate that he had grown tired of the Adirondacks' mosquitoes and pushed off to parts unknown. One unsubstantiated report put the escaped murderer in Mexico.

"That's welcome news," said Max.

"How could he have been seen in Paradox yesterday and today he's in Mexico?" I asked.

"Very simple, my dear," said Max, savoring the last drops of his gin and tonic. "The airplane. The latest in high-speed travel."

Aunt Lena laughed and took his empty glass. "So Donald Yarrow waltzed into an airport and bought a ticket to Mexico City?"

"That is the substance of my thesis, yes."

"Where did he get the airfare? And the passport?" she asked, handing him a fresh drink.

"Mere trifles for a seasoned criminal like Donald Yarrow," he said, waving his free hand. "Surely he was working with confederates who provided him with the necessary instruments and papers. I shouldn't be surprised if he hadn't already changed his appearance. Plastic surgery in Tijuana and a suntan in Cozumel."

"Tijuana and Cozumel are on different coasts," I pointed out.

Max took a healthy swig of his G and T and smacked his lips. "Again, my dear, the airplane. Pay attention. A mastermind like

Donald Yarrow would have no problem surmounting such mundane obstacles."

"Mundane obstacles?" I asked. "You mean like time and space?"

After dinner I excused myself and went to my cabin to freshen up. Moments later I was debating whether to take my car to Arcadia Lodge or go on foot. I wanted to see Isaac. And I wanted to look Simon in the eye as I took a seat in the Great Lodge, preferably in the armchair next to Jakob Eisenstadt. Given my recent run-ins with my mysterious harasser, though, I should have taken the safer route in my car. But I had other concerns. Aunt Lena was already onto my assignations, and I didn't much appreciate her knowing what naughtiness I was getting up to. She would certainly hear my Dodge roaring to life if I took the car. So I decided to brave the risk and run through the four hundred yards of woods to reach Isaac.

With an eye to evading my shadow, I took a different path through the woods, leaving Aunt Lena's camp fifty yards farther north and circling around to the southwest. The same old fears pounded in my heart as I dashed through the forest, but this time there was no rain, no lightning or thunder, to magnify my terror. And I carried a flashlight, which gave me a small measure of confidence that I'd lacked on previous nights.

My new route took me on an upward slope across a stream about forty yards behind Arcadia Lodge. I swept the landscape with my flashlight, making sure the path was clear. And that was when I spotted the hut off in the distance, at least a hundred yards farther up the hill. It looked like a hunters' shelter. There were so many in those parts. It wasn't hunting season, of course, so I didn't expect to find anyone inside. In fact I had no intention of looking to see if anyone was inside or even near the shack. I pictured the mysterious man who'd been tracking me enjoying an after-dinner drink inside, his feet propped up on an ottoman as he plotted new ways to corner me alone in the woods.

I arrived at Arcadia without incident. The gang had finished supper and was lounging in the Great Lodge. Simon and David were reading, and Miriam was playing scales with great speed and vigor on the piano. Then, without warning, she launched into a gentle, rolling version of Liszt's "Liebestraum." Ruth and Rachel were nowhere in sight, but Isaac and Audrey were sitting together across the room in a shadowy corner. I nearly turned around and left, but Simon called out to me.

"There you are, Ellie," he said. "Come in and have a drink with us."

What was he up to? The smile he'd directed at me seemed genuine, but I trusted him only as much as I would a smiling crocodile. I did want a drink, though.

I upped the ante in Simon's little game; I breezed over to his chair, bent down, and kissed him on the cheek. He nearly choked, but no one besides me noticed.

"Please, Mimi," he barked at his wife. "Stop that saccharine Liszt and join us for some civilized conversation. Or play some Prokofiev or Stravinsky or Shostakovich. Anything but that Tin Pan Alley schlock."

Liszt was not my favorite composer, but I would hardly categorize his music as Tin Pan Alley.

I waved hello to the crowd and made my way over to the bar. The bottle of White Label hadn't given up the ghost yet, but it had reached the autumn of its years. I threw a glance to my left and noticed a glass of whiskey sitting on the pine end table next to Audrey. I emptied the rest of the bottle into a glass of my own just as Lothario sidled up to me. He wrapped a casual arm around my shoulder and kissed my ear.

"Is that the end of the Dewar's?" he asked. "I didn't realize we were running low."

"It's okay," I said, reaching into my purse and producing the unopened fifth that Aunt Lena and Max had given me that afternoon. I also had Mrs. Merkleson's contact sheets and my flashlight inside. "I've learned to take care of myself."

I plopped the bottle on the table and turned to survey the room. Miriam had stopped playing, but she'd remained on the piano bench, leaning an elbow on the fall board and staring at nothing in particular.

Esther Merkleson entered the Great Lodge with little Leon trotting along a few steps behind her. She made a beeline for me at the bar.

"Ellie, why haven't you brought me the photographs as I asked?" she demanded once we'd repaired to a quiet corner of the lodge.

"I tried to find you this afternoon, but you weren't here," I said.

"Why didn't you leave them?"

"I didn't want anyone to snoop through them," I said as I retrieved the envelope from my purse. "These photographs should be private. I'm sure you'll agree."

She took the envelope and tucked it under her arm. "Yes, of course. Now did you make any progress today? Have you found any connection between Karl and the Kaufman boy?"

"Not yet, but I have a source at the Orpheus camp making inquiries for me. I'm meeting him tomorrow."

"Good," she said with her customary bob of the head. "I'm taking my son's body to Albany tomorrow for an autopsy. I will return Saturday. We will talk then."

"An autopsy?"

"I don't trust these bumpkins up here. And I want to know exactly what happened to Karl."

"You still suspect Gayle and her father had a hand in this?"

"Of course," she said. "Nothing has changed."

Esther Merkleson swept out of the Great Lodge. I watched her go, thinking what a remarkably brave woman she was. A woman of extreme talent and strength, she'd swallowed her share of grief and tragedy over the years without asking for pity. She'd lost a daughter, a husband, and now a son. But she stood tall and firm, facing her tragedies with the dignity of a queen. Hers was a horrible fate: to outlive her entire family. I knew exactly how horrible; I was serving the same sentence.

I migrated back to the drinks table to get that whiskey that I wanted now more than ever. The others all gravitated to the bar. I was popular this night.

"What did she say?" asked Isaac.

"I don't want to talk about it," I said. "Poor woman."

"We loved him, too," said David.

"I know." I took that first stinging sip of whiskey. God, that was good. "But you all have each other. She has no one."

Once I'd fortified my spirits with my first glass of spirits, I managed to put Esther Merkleson out of my mind. Scotch always improves my mood. Personality in a bottle, I'm fond of saying. So when Isaac asked me if I had any news of Gayle, I teased him just a bit.

"Not from me. But how about you? Didn't you stop by her motel to chat about Karl?" I said, a wicked gleam in my eye.

To tell the truth, I couldn't say for sure that there was a wicked gleam in my eye, but that was the effect I'd intended. Isaac blanched a little at the recollection of his confession. I touched his arm and told him I was only kidding. He relaxed and assumed his typical, charming ease. Amazing how he could turn it off and on so effortlessly.

Isaac's father, Jakob, hobbled into the hall a few minutes later. The mood was the best it had been in days, in part due to Simon's sudden cordiality. Between heated debates about music and poets, the Arcadians tackled politics and changing mores, but steered clear of talk of Karl Merkleson. Simon, for one, was vocal about the forward behavior of twenty-one-year-old girls. He maintained that the female of the species was better suited for housework and reproduction, instead of provoking adult males with revealing swimsuits on the beaches and tight dresses on the dance floors of America.

"Personally, I don't know how we girls resist a man in swimming trunks," I said. "It leaves far less to the imagination than a girl's bathing suit."

"Bravo, Ellie," said Isaac. "It's about time a girl admitted we're irresistible."

"What if a girl wants more than housework?" asked Rachel, who'd come in at her father's side.

"Please, Rachel," said Simon with a chuckle. "Not the career talk again. Some women manage to rise to respectable positions in the world. Even build careers. But those are not good odds. Most women are not cut out for work."

"They should just stay twenty-one and beautiful forever?" I asked.

Simon nodded. Neither Isaac nor David could summon the indignation to contradict him. I'd given them their chance; now I was going to bear the standard.

"What do you think, Audrey?" I asked. "Are you happy just to raise a family and cook their suppers?"

"God, no," she said, and I thought I had an ally. But then she clarified. "I want someone to do those things for me. I'm looking for a rich husband." And she smiled a naughty smile.

"You would be a rich man's whore?" demanded Simon.

"Easy," said David. "That's my cousin you're talking to."

"Audrey, the ruling classes and the idle rich are oppressors, don't you see?" said Simon a touch more delicately. "If you don't struggle against them, you might as well join them."

"I voted for Kennedy," she said in her defense, then clarified again. "At least I would have, but I'm Canadian and can't vote here."

"Who did you vote for in the last federal elections in Canada?" asked Simon in challenge.

"I didn't vote," she said, and Simon harrumphed in victory. "I was only seventeen at the time," she added, taking back the high ground.

Simon threw his hands up in surrender.

"Why don't you young people play some music?" suggested Jakob Eisenstadt. "At least you won't argue about that."

"I hate folk music," announced Miriam from the piano. "And Simon can't stand Liszt or anything that's not Russian."

"I positively despise Strauss," offered Isaac.

"Which one?" asked David.

"Do you really need to ask?"

"I enjoy those waltzes," said David, sounding hurt. "Not the pinnacle of musical achievement, but they're sweet."

"Dance music," said Isaac. "Of course I can't quite get over Richard Strauss's chumminess with the Nazis either, but the music is damn compelling. Especially the tone poems."

"I like Paul Anka," said Audrey in a burst of élan. "He's Canadian, you know. Can you guys play any of his songs?"

"His daughter-in-law was Jewish," I said, ignoring Audrey, looping the subject back to Richard Strauss. "He protected her from the Nazis."

"True enough," said Simon. "He moved heaven and earth to help her every time they arrested her. But he didn't do anything for the millions of other Jews."

"I have to agree with you there," said Miriam.

"Besides, as a composer, he was regressive," concluded Simon. "Why not just play Wagner?"

"You all are incorrigible," said Jakob with a chuckle. "Arguing over a beautiful thing like music. All music is beautiful unless it carries a message of hatred."

"*All* music?" asked Isaac. "Even country and western music?"

"Even Paul Anka?" That was me. A little catty, but Audrey had annoyed me.

"All of it," repeated the old man. "Provided it is authentic and true to itself. When I was a young man, I had the pleasure of hearing a concert of Mongolian shepherds plucking some kind of stringed instrument. They call it a horse fiddle. It was glorious."

"You've been harping on that Mongolian concert for decades," said Isaac, chiding his father.

Jakob smiled so broadly that I envied him his simple, genuine joy at the memory.

"The same is true of art," he pronounced. "And you young people shouldn't fight like this."

"But, Papa, we *love* arguing about things," said Isaac. "It's not mean-spirited at all. Isn't that right, Simon?"

"Speak for yourself," he answered, but there was the hint of a grin on his lips.

I cleared my throat and said I knew one thing we could all agree on.

"Excellent, Ellie dear," said Jakob. "What is it?"

"We're all firmly and irrevocably in favor of booze."

"Hear, hear!" cheered the whole group.

"Of course, Simon only drinks kosher wine," I added, trying to fit in with the ribbing. Everyone except Miriam laughed. Even Simon managed a chuckle.

"It's not quite so funny if you have to live with him," she said.

"Did anyone hear the latest report on that escaped murderer?" asked Ruth, changing the subject.

"The radio said he might be in Mexico," said Isaac.

"No," said David. "Mrs. Edmonds at the market in the village said someone in an Airstream trailer saw him at the campground outside of Tennyson this morning."

Ruth gasped. "My God, Tennyson is on the eastern shore of the lake."

"He's nowhere near here," said Simon. "It's just another case of a gullible public falling in step with what the government wants them to think."

"Why would the government want the public to believe there was danger from an escaped convict if there weren't?" asked Ruth.

"As usual you're looking at this too simplistically, Ruth. The government doesn't care about Donald Yarrow particularly. I'm sure they don't want him out there murdering people, but that's not why they sow this fear. It's part of the larger plan to control thought and make people accept the lies they manufacture. It's so obvious."

"Explain it to the rest of us idiots," said Isaac, laughing. "We're not as smart as you."

"If you repeat a lie enough times, people believe it. Or at least lazy, ignorant sheep will believe it. The capitalist system is designed to tell us what we need, when to buy it, and how to be happy about it. Junk that no one wants or needs. And the United States government is one of the most powerful tools in the conspiracy."

Isaac laughed harder. The others frowned their disbelief and annoy-ance. Simon bristled.

"Don't believe me then. Clearly you've been brainwashed by televi-sion and radio and the myth of American democracy." Simon's face was turning red, his voice was rising, and he spat and stuttered as he continued. "You've been convinced that your dreary middle-class lives and the Amer-ican Way are heaven on earth." He was practically yelling now. "You've got a washing machine. Congratulations! Now how about a soulless, cookie-cutter tract home in a white, Christian neighborhood? No Negroes, no Jews, no Spanish. Hell, no Italians, while we're at it! You should all change your names like Karl did. Become white and nondescript. Forsake your forebears and marry a blonde, blue-eyed *shiksa*. You're all just stooges of the capitalist oligarchy, doing the handiwork for your masters!"

He'd finally worked his way up to full-throated shouting by the end of his tirade. His eyes were wild, bulging and filled with blood. He was nearly apoplectic.

"Take it easy, Si," said David. "We're just having some fun."

Isaac took no offense at the insults and, in fact, continued to laugh in Simon's face. I sat on my hands, equally horrified by the vitriol Simon had spewed at his friends and the taunting ridicule dished out by Isaac to throw gasoline on the fire, seemingly for his own amusement. I felt sorry for Simon, who was sitting in his chair, fuming, sweating, and nearly out of breath. And I was disgusted by Isaac's cruel mockery of his old friend. Miriam finally lifted herself off the piano bench and made her way over to her husband. She whispered something in his ear, and he nodded and seemed to calm down in a matter of seconds. Isaac's laughter finally fizzled out. We stood by quietly for a full minute before Simon chuckled and said he had only been kidding.

"Don't you guys know me by now?"

I didn't know him, and I didn't believe him.

"So you don't believe there's systemic brainwashing of Americans?" asked Isaac.

"Let's just forget it, okay?" said Miriam quite forcefully, silencing everyone. Except one.

"Wait," said Audrey. "Paul Anka is a Nazi?"

Contrary to what Simon had told me that afternoon, the Arcadians seemed perfectly happy to have me. I was pouring myself and Isaac a drink when Miriam appeared out of nowhere, like a chimera, frightening the wits out of me.

"Hello," she said.

"Hello," I replied. "Would you like a drink?"

"Nothing for me. I came over to tell you something."

"What's that?"

Miriam looked back over her shoulder. She focused on Isaac, who was chatting again with Audrey.

"They're awfully friendly, don't you think?" she asked.

"I hadn't given it much thought."

Miriam stared hard at them, and I fancied she might burn a hole right through their chests. I waited for her to say something, but she just kept on glaring at them. Not that her expression betrayed any malice. She was wearing her usual anesthetized expression, as if someone had clamped a chloroformed cloth over her mouth.

"I know they've been together," she said finally.

That hurt, but I tried not to let it show. "They're together right now," I said in an attempt at wit. "Occupying those chairs over there."

"Sometimes you're funny, Ellie," she said. "But this time you're burying your head in the sand."

"How so?"

"They spend afternoons together," she whispered.

I bit the inside of my lip. "Why are you telling me this?"

Miriam shrugged. "You should know. Isaac is an immature boy, Ellie. He's very charming and witty, but deep down he's a boy. He craves attention and love."

"You talk as if you know from experience."

Miriam touched my wrist, compelling me to look her in the eye. "I do."

I studied her, trying to gauge her intentions and honesty. And I asked myself why I even cared. Isaac was free to pursue other conquests. We barely knew each other, after all. We had no understanding.

"You slept with him, didn't you?" I asked.

She looked at me as if I'd asked whether the sun had set the day before. "Years ago. But that's unimportant. What you need to worry about is Audrey Silber."

"I beg your pardon?"

"I'm ancient history for Isaac, but that girl is what's on the menu tonight."

"Or tomorrow afternoon," I said. "Look, Miriam, I don't really care what Isaac does in his spare time."

"Even if things are developing quickly between you two?"

"I'm happy with the speed," I said.

"Suit yourself, Ellie. But it's more than just little Audrey. Isaac likes girls, if you hadn't noticed. He collects them."

"And I like boys."

"As I said, Ellie. Suit yourself. I'm not in love with him."

Our conversation was interrupted by a banging at the door. We all turned to see who was calling at almost midnight. Isaac excused himself from Audrey, rose from his seat, and, taking his drink with him, crossed the room.

"Don't answer it," said Simon. "It's probably Donald Yarrow."

"Not funny," said Ruth.

Isaac threw open the door, and Chief Terwilliger stepped inside. Behind him stood three men. I couldn't make out who they were in the dark.

"Come on in, boys," said Isaac, smiling and waving his free hand. "You look like you could all use a drink of something."

Terwilliger stepped aside, and the men entered. Dressed in dungarees, T-shirts, and working boots, the men shuffled in looking shy and uncomfortable. I recognized the first two as the John Birchers from Palmer Square, and the one bringing up the rear was Waldo Coons. He hung back, half-hidden by the two men in front of him, scanning the room with his hollow eyes.

"I'll have a beer," said Terwilliger. "The boys will have the same."

Isaac waltzed them over to the bar and retrieved a quart bottle from the icebox. I had to admire the ease with which he handled people, even as I wondered if I was being handled as well. Ever the genial host, he did his best to make the men feel at home. I knew, of course, that he didn't want anything to do with them; he was defusing a situation.

"Is Schaefer okay?" asked Isaac, pouring. They all nodded. Terwilliger licked his lips. "So, what can we do for you?"

"It's that same business from the village. Mr. Abramowitz hasn't paid these men for the brochures he destroyed. And they say their card table's busted too. They didn't realize it at the time."

"And they'd like Simon to pay for the table as well," said Isaac, handing the new arrivals their beers. Then he pulled out his wallet. "Perfectly understandable. How much was the total again?"

The men exchanged glances but couldn't dislodge the number from their throats.

"They said the total comes to twenty-one fifty," said Terwilliger, swigging from his glass of beer.

"Pretty steep," said Isaac, retrieving several bills from his wallet. He counted them then asked David for a five. Finally armed with enough, Isaac presented the wad of cash to Terwilliger.

"What are you doing?" called Simon from the other side of the room. "Don't pay them. I'd rather go to jail."

"Twenty-two dollars," said Isaac, ignoring Simon. "We appreciate how you've handled this, Chief. We'll make sure he doesn't bother these men again."

Simon jumped out of his chair and tried to rush the men at the bar. David and I managed to head him off halfway across the room, colliding with him in a jumble of limbs and torsos. David's crooked leg never stood a chance of holding Simon back, but with me clamping my arms around his waist, we dragged him to the floor, where we lay sprawled as everyone watched. Simon roared for us to let go of him, but we both held him fast. Miriam swooped in. She pressed her cheek to his, holding his head in her hands, and again began whispering in his ear. This time, she struggled to soothe him. She rubbed his red face and whispered furiously, but he seemed unaware of her presence. Isaac arrived and helped us restrain Simon, who was now in convulsions. His face twisted as he shouted incoherent threats and denials and gibberish. He was rambling, thrashing, wailing like a banshee. Then he started sobbing. A violent, raw sobbing from deep inside, from his diaphragm and through his hoarse throat. Ruth looked on from a few feet away, weeping as the scene dragged on for what seemed an eternity.

Isaac spelled David, who was dispatched to get his medical bag. He returned two minutes later and prepared a hypodermic. While we held Simon still, David tugged his stricken friend's trousers down, dabbed his buttocks with some rubbing alcohol, then jabbed him with the needle.

It took about five minutes for the drug to take effect. Either that or Simon wore himself out. He was still, heaving for breath, eyes shut, lying in a heap on the floor. Soon, though, his expression normalized, and he looked completely lucid if embarrassed.

"What was that you gave him?" I asked David as he repacked his medical bag.

"Something called chlorpromazine," he said. "It's a fairly new anti-psychotic treatment for violent behavior."

"Is Simon psychotic?"

"No, but he occasionally has fits like this."

I was horrified. "How lucky that you had some of that . . . Chloroma . . ."

"Chlorpromazine," he repeated. "Not lucky. Miriam asked me to bring some with me from New York. This is the first time I've had to use it."

The John Birchers had decamped. Only Chief Terwilliger remained, sucking the life out of one glass of beer after another. Miriam lifted Simon and, arm around his waist for support, led him out of the Great Lodge. She returned about a half hour later and said that he was sleeping comfortably.

"What's wrong with that man anyway?" asked Terwilliger. "He's gonna hurt someone someday. He's gonna hurt himself."

"He's got some problems, but he's not dangerous," said Isaac. "We take care of him."

"See that you do," said the chief, taking another gulp of beer.

"What are you still doing here?" I asked him, and just as rudely as it sounds.

He laughed and lit a cigarette but didn't answer. Then he started, as if remembering something important. He excused himself and left the lodge only to return a minute later.

"I almost forgot," he said, placing a large paper bag down on the bar. It was a little moist. He opened it and pulled out a muddy white short-sleeved shirt.

"Is that Karl's?" asked Isaac.

Terwilliger nodded. "We believe the shirt is his." Then he reached back into the bag and produced a waterlogged leather wallet. "This, we're sure, is his," he said, referring to the wallet. "Well, Charles Morton's, to be exact. That's what the driver's license says. A vacationer found these washed up on the shore."

Everyone gathered around the table to examine the effects. Sobered by the evidence of their old friend's death, they stared at his wadded-up shirt. Ruth wiped her eyes and turned away.

Assuming the show was over, Terwilliger dropped the wallet back into the bag and reached for the shirt. But I stopped him.

"May I see that?" I asked.

He hesitated but, after a moment, held it out for me. I spread the shirt out on the table. Still a little wet, it was a size-fifteen neck, wash-and-wear, made of polyester. Sears. It was impossible to tell if it was new or old. I stared at it.

"What's wrong, Ellie?" asked Isaac.

"I'm not sure," I said. "It's just odd."

"How so?"

"This is an inexpensive shirt. He had pricey tastes. This doesn't seem like the kind of thing he would wear."

Isaac shrugged. "It looks like he made this trip at the spur of the moment. Maybe he didn't have time to pack and bought this somewhere around here or in Albany."

"Probably," I said, wondering what clothing Karl might have left behind at the Sans Souci. I made a mental note to ask Gayle Morton.

"If you're done playing detective, I'll take that," said Terwilliger. "It's evidence." He wadded up the shirt and stuffed it back into the paper bag.

"Evidence?" asked David. "I thought this was an accident."

"Maybe," said the chief. "Or maybe not. There are a couple of loose ends I'd like to tie up with the state police."

That was new. Terwilliger had never seemed particularly interested in the unexplained details of the case. He struck me as a lazy investigator, happy to file his final one-paragraph report and sneak off to a bar for breakfast. I kept telling myself that my doubts were simply that: doubts and nothing more. Isaac's reasoning about the shirt made sense. And the motel roulette could be explained away, too, I supposed. I still didn't know where Karl Merkleson had been sleeping or why he'd chosen to stay away from the Sans Souci. Why not just check out? Yes, I had these doubts, but I like clean lines and sharp corners. Tiny Terwilliger didn't share my obsession for order. So what had made him change his mind?

"Anyways, I'll keep you folks informed if anything else turns up," he said, clamping the bag under his arm. He turned to look behind him. "Come on, Waldo. Time to go."

I had assumed that Waldo Coons had crawled away with his pals, but he was still there, sweeping up in a darkened corner of the room. He moved the broom across the floor absently, barely grazing the surface. His haunted eyes, peering out of the penumbra like a ghoul's, were fixed firmly on me.

The party broke up after one. I reflected on the direction the evening had taken. After the arguments that had characterized the early part of the soirée, the general mood rose, mine along with it. But Miriam had taken it upon herself to poison the well by drawing my attention to Isaac and Audrey, who had been chatting nose to nose across the room. I didn't care that Isaac had slept with Miriam. And I didn't care that Isaac might have been sleeping with that vapid little French-speaking Anglo Audrey Silber. The girl who thought Paul Anka belonged in the same conversation as Richard Strauss, the greatest composer of the first half of the twentieth century, according to my father. I didn't care. And yet I did. I cared a lot. Then Simon's breakdown had scared everyone out of their wits.

Now, at half past one, I was too drunk and too tired to make the dash back to Cedar Haven. And there was the rumor that Donald Yarrow had been spotted on the eastern shore of the lake that very morning. I didn't want any part of the woods in the dark. But neither did I want to spend the night in Isaac's bed, so I made a pact with Miriam of all people. I asked if I might sleep on the floor in her cabin. She smiled and said sure. She had a cot I could use if I didn't mind Simon's snoring.

"Is Simon okay?" I asked.

"I gave him some pills," she said. "He'll sleep through the night."

Isaac couldn't understand my refusal to come to his cabin. He asked me what was wrong, and I said I was tired. He still wouldn't accept it. I begged him to leave it, and he asked me if it was my little friend.

"Little friend?" I repeated.

"You know. That time of the month. Why else wouldn't you come?" he asked.

"That's it," I said, searching for the path of least resistance. "My little friend is visiting. Maybe Audrey has no friends. You should find out."

I walked with Miriam to her cabin. There was no snoring when we arrived, but Miriam assured me that the show would not disappoint.

She pulled out a canvas cot and gave me a lumpy pillow and wool blanket.

"Do you want a glass of water, Ellie?" she asked before retiring.

"I'd rather some whiskey."

"You're funny," she said.

No, really. I wanted one last drink before I had to face my self-recrimination. I had doubts and I had fears. What had I done? Why had I rushed headlong into a love affair with a man I barely knew? I wanted that drink all right. But I left it.

Miriam turned to leave. I stopped her.

"Is Simon well?" I asked.

"I told you. He's sleeping."

"I mean is he sick?"

Miriam stood there staring at me. Just stared. Finally she blinked.

"Simon has a brain tumor," she said. "He's dying."

She turned away again and disappeared into the dark.

CHAPTER FIFTEEN

THURSDAY, AUGUST 24, 1961

Islipped out of Miriam and Simon's cabin as the sun came up. I opted for the coward's way back to Cedar Haven, sticking to the roads and circumventing the woods altogether. It took me twenty minutes, but I felt safer. The previous night had exhausted me. Haunted by Miriam's good-night news about Simon's prognosis, I had barely closed an eye, at turns regretting my open hostility toward him, then wondering if Isaac knew that Simon was dying. He couldn't possibly have known, or he wouldn't have baited him so mercilessly. A friend would never do that. But he had told Terwilliger that Simon had problems. And as I walked along Lake Road at 6:30 a.m., I reasoned that a friend would never sleep with a friend's wife. Two friends' wives. Who was this Isaac Eisenstadt, and what the hell was I doing in his bed?

By the time I turned off Jordan Street into Aunt Lena's lane, the eastern sky was awash in a spreading pink corona. Thirty minutes earlier, in the dark, I might have missed the car parked on the grass under the old iron tree. A beaten-up, blue Nash Ambassador. I approached and peeked through the driver's side window. There, sprawled across the front seat, shoes up against the passenger's door, slept my dearest friend in the world, Fadge Fiorello.

I tapped on the window. That did nothing. Fadge slept like a bear. Looked like one, too. And, as a matter of fact, sometimes displayed the personality of a bear emerging from hibernation, sluggish and surly.

I didn't bother trying the door; it had been dented shut for more than a year. So I rapped on the window again. Fadge rolled over but didn't open his eyes. Finally I roused him by kicking the driver's door. A couple of more dings wouldn't matter. Once he'd found his bearings, he crawled out of the car on the passenger's side.

"Good morning, sunshine," I said, giving the huge man a peck on the cheek. He was six feet two inches and tipped the scales at over three hundred pounds. "Now tell me what you're doing here."

"I was in the neighborhood, so I thought I'd drop by," he mumbled.

I laughed. "You're a hundred and ten miles from home. What's going on?"

He confessed that he'd been monitoring the reports of the Donald Yarrow sightings and was worried.

"That guy's getting close. The radio said he was seen in Tennyson yesterday. That's right across the lake from here."

I took him by the arm and led him to my cabin.

"Where are we going?" he asked, rubbing his eyes. "It's not even seven."

"I want to show you something," I said. "But first, you're going to shower and change."

ॐ

Lake Road was deserted at seven thirty on a Thursday morning. I parked on the shoulder a few yards from Aunt Lena's dock.

"I'm not seeing a diner or restaurant," remarked Fadge. "This can't be the right place."

"Come with me," I said, popping open the door and slinging my camera over my shoulder.

A few minutes later, with Fadge loaded into the little boat, we slipped into Baxter's Cove. *Slipped* may be overstating the case, as the bottom of the boat scraped over the submerged rocks of the cove's entrance. I didn't recall touching any rocks when I'd run the same route the day before, so I figured Fadge's weight was the variable in the equation.

The sun was up in the east, and it was burning bright. The forecast called for a hot, sunny August day, and the temperature had already galloped past eighty degrees at 8:00 a.m. We disembarked onto the shale beach, somehow managing to avoid falling into the water.

"So this is what you wanted to show me," he said and whistled through his teeth as he considered the painted outline.

"There's another just behind those rocks." I pointed the way.

The rocks were only three to four feet high, so Fadge was able to see the lines by standing on his toes.

He turned around and got a blast of sun in his eyes for his trouble. His face was effulgent orange. He squinted into the light as he watched me take several photos of the painted outline that belonged to the person who'd once answered to the name Karl Merkleson. Fadge stepped around me and turned his back to the sun's rays.

"Haven't you already taken pictures of this?" he asked.

"You're blocking my light," I said. "Your large shadow is covering my subject. Move it."

He stepped to one side, and the sun again washed over the outline.

"So why do you need more pictures?" he asked.

"I'm shooting Kodachrome," I said. "I wanted some color slides of the scene."

As with the black-and-white Tri-X, I had to slow the shutter speed to capture Jerry Kaufman's outline in the low light that was available behind the rocks. But without a flash, these slides were sure to come out dark and grainy.

"Come on, big boy," I said once I'd covered all the angles and stowed my Leica in its case. "Let's get you some breakfast."

Back at Cedar Haven, Lena asked me whose car had spent the night parked on her zinnias. I introduced Fadge, who apologized for the flowers. Lena asked me how many men I was planning to juggle on my one-week vacation.

"He's a friend," I said. "He owns the ice cream shop across the street from my apartment. Besides does it look like I could juggle him?"

"He does look well-fed," she said.

"Actually I was just going to take him to get something to eat."

Lena nodded then asked Fadge if he'd been hurt in the accident.

"What accident?"

"The wreck. It looks like you totaled the car."

I laughed.

"No," he said. "That's the way it always looks."

Fadge suggested we spend the day on the beach or take a boat and a picnic lunch out onto the lake.

"Not today," I said. "You're going to help me on some errands. I need to speak to a couple of people."

I filled him in on the events of the past several days, the two deaths, Gayle Morton's mysterious comings and goings, and Esther Merkleson's escalating suspicions. I also informed him that the chief of police had changed his opinion and wanted to clear up some lingering questions about the putative accident.

"Sounds fishy," said Fadge. "Did those two guys know each other?"

I shook my head. "Not that anyone knows. But you and I are going to meet a boy at noon who might have some new information on that."

"That leaves us four hours to kill," he said. "Let's go for a swim."

"No. We're going to get some answers out of the dead man's wife and get you some breakfast."

We pulled into Tom's Lakeside Motel a little past nine. The blue Galaxie was still there, but a short, gray-haired man was packing some suitcases into the trunk. He finished and disappeared back inside.

"That must be the father," I said.

"Looks like they're checking out," said Fadge. "We got here just in time."

I parked the car, and we followed the man inside. The lobby was empty, but there was activity through a door off to the right side: the Lakeside Restaurant. A moldering diner whose best days were behind it. Still, Fadge perked up when he smelled bacon. We spotted the gray-haired man inside at a table with a young blonde woman: Gayle Morton. They were both dressed in city clothes, reading breakfast menus.

We sauntered in, pretending to look for a suitable table, and wandered close to our targets. Fadge was a talented improviser and excelled in situations like this one. We also picked up on each other's signals as if we'd been doing this stuff for years. I gave Fadge a nod, and we moved in for the game.

"Hello, Mrs. Morton," I said.

She looked up at me and my large escort. Her nostrils flared ever so slightly.

"Hello," she said. "What can I do for you?"

"I wanted to offer you my condolences again."

"Thank you," she said tentatively.

"Did you manage to reach your father?" I asked.

She blushed. "This is my father here." She indicated the man across the table.

"He sure got here quickly," I said.

"Perhaps I wasn't clear when we spoke Monday. My father was already on the lake. He was staying here at this motel."

I nodded. Before she could send me packing, I explained that I was an old acquaintance of her husband's. The more I repeated it, the less it seemed like a lie.

"You didn't mention that the other day when we met," she said.

"I knew him many years ago when I was a girl here on the lake."

She looked alarmed. "You're not one of those people from Arcadia Lodge, are you?"

"No, I was a neighbor. But we used to socialize."

"Well, thank you for stopping by," she said. "I won't detain you." She cast a glance up at Fadge. "Or your friend."

Now came the hard part. How was I going to get the information I wanted without her taking offense and telling me to mind my own business?

"May we join you?" I asked. "Just for a cup of coffee."

The father answered for her.

"It's a difficult time," he said. "I'm sure you'll understand that we'd prefer to be alone."

Fadge had already taken a seat and grabbed a menu. The gray-haired man, Owen Pierce, looked horrified, but we'd played our opening gambit. I sat down next to Gayle and asked her how she was holding up. She inched her chair away from me and said it was a terrible loss.

"Why do you think Karl wanted to dive off that cliff?" I asked. "Did he enjoy swimming?" A brutal, right-to-the-point question for the widow, but I doubted I had enough time to finesse it. She was likely to grow tired of me and storm off at any moment.

She looked me up and down, almost sneering at my poor manners.

"My husband's name was Charles, not Karl. And, no, I don't know why he wanted to dive off that cliff."

"Did he say anything at all before he left the motel that morning?"

"No," she snapped. "And why are you asking me these questions?"

Her father intervened and said that Fadge and I should leave. No more time for delicacy, such as it was. I decided to take charge with a provocation that might well send them running out the door. My hope was that she would circle the wagons instead and defend herself.

"Karl didn't mention swimming to you that morning because he wasn't at the Sans Souci Cabins, was he?"

The father stood, held a hand out to his daughter, and told her they were leaving. Fadge, in turn, reached up and put a bear claw on Pierce's shoulder, applying a subtle pressure that pulled him back down into his seat.

"Where are you going?" said Fadge. "We're just having a friendly conversation. Let your daughter answer the lady's questions. It'll do her good to talk about it."

Owen Pierce was about five six and of medium build. He gaped open-mouthed at Fadge, who easily outweighed him by double, but made no verbal protest.

"Okay, I didn't see Charles that morning," said Gayle, who, I believed, genuinely feared for her father's safety in that moment. "He didn't spend the night at the cabin. I don't know where he was."

"Did you come to Prospector Lake to stop him from leaving you?" I asked.

"That's none of your business."

"The police chief and Karl's mother both suspect that this was not a simple diving accident," I said. "What do you think?"

"His name was Charles," she said more forcefully this time. "And I think that awful woman is an oppressive, vindictive crone."

"Excuse me. Are you saying someone pushed Charles off that cliff?" asked Owen Pierce.

"I'm not saying that. But I'm wondering if your daughter is willing to help us find out exactly what happened at Baxter's Rock that day."

Gayle Morton was flustered. She started to cry and insisted that she didn't know anything. In fact she hadn't seen her husband at all in Prospector Lake. Her father backed up her version of events.

"You stayed in his cabin, but you never saw him?" I asked.

"That's right," she said, wiping her eyes on a napkin. "I checked into the Sans Souci on Friday once I found out he was staying there."

"How did you track him down?"

"It wasn't difficult. I used the phone directory in my room here. I just called every motel on the lake."

Just then the waitress arrived at our table and asked if we were ready to order. Pierce said his daughter needed a few minutes to decide. The waitress rolled her eyes and left. Fadge called her back, though, and ordered the Adirondack Special: three eggs, a tall stack of pancakes, some bacon, and toast, with home-fried potatoes and coffee. And a side order of cinnamon rolls. The waitress didn't blink. Then she looked at me expectantly.

"Just coffee," I said.

Turning back to Gayle, I told her I had two more questions, and then we would leave her alone.

"So ask me," she said.

"Is there any way your husband could have known that boy who died with him?"

"I can't imagine how," she said. "The police said that kid was from Albany, or somewhere near there. Charles didn't know anyone from Albany. And certainly not some sixteen-year-old boy from a music camp."

"Just one more thing," I said. "Do you have Karl's suitcase? Did he leave it behind at the Sans Souci?"

She said she had it, that her father had just loaded it into the trunk of his car. What did I want with it anyway?

"May I take a quick look inside? I won't take anything, I promise."

Gayle's eyes darted to her father, who threw a glance at Fadge, who glared at him.

Outside in the parking lot, Owen Pierce opened the trunk of his car, moved a suitcase to one side, and pointed to a leather bag.

"That's Charles's valise," he said.

I popped it open and examined the contents as Gayle and her father, wondering what I could be looking for, watched intently. Fadge had remained at the table in the restaurant, making short work of his breakfast. Inside the suitcase, I found four carefully folded shirts, professionally pressed, two clean bathing suits, some socks and underwear, three pairs of trousers, and one pair of city shoes. There was a very expensive-looking Dopp kit. I took

a closer look at the shirts. Fine cotton, well tailored, and each one monogrammed with *CMM*. I locked the case and closed the trunk.

"What is it?" asked Gayle. Her curiosity had overcome any hostility
she'd felt for me at the start. She might have been worried or just intrigued.

"The police found Karl's shirt," I said. "At least they think it's his. It
was in the water along with his wallet."

"And?" asked Pierce.

"It was an off-the-rack wash-and-wear from Sears. Did Karl ever buy
clothes from Sears?"

They exchanged glances and shook their heads.

"Charles was a bit of a dandy," said Pierce. "He only wore nice things."

"He started wearing an ascot," said Gayle. "I told him he looked like a
queer rooster, but he wouldn't listen. So, no, I don't think he would buy a
Sears wash-and-wear."

Still, I thought. He might have had to purchase it for some unknown
reason. But why? He had a suitcase filled with clean, well-tailored clothing
in his room.

"Are you finished with us now, young lady?" asked the father.

"Sorry," I said. "Just one more question."

"What's that?" asked Gayle.

"Have you seen Isaac Eisenstadt in the past few days?"

"Who?"

"Isaac Eisenstadt," I repeated. "I believe you met him in Los Angeles
a few years ago when he was trying to reconcile Karl with his old friends."

She shook her head. "Charles might have mentioned him once, but
I'm not sure. At any rate, I never met him."

"I'm sorry," I said, staring into her eyes. "I must have been mistaken."

"Mistaken about what?" came a voice behind me.

I reeled around and came face-to-face with Chief Terwilliger. He was
unshaven, and his breath smelled of stale beer.

"Mrs. Morton and her father were just checking out," I said, dodging
his question if not odor.

"No, they're not," he said.

"I beg your pardon?" asked Pierce.

"I'm going to have to ask you nicely to stay on until I finish my investigation. I can't force you, of course. But how would it look if you disappointed me?"

"But why?"

"There are just a few loose ends I need to tie up before I put this case to bed. It's just a couple of days."

Something about Chief Terwilliger's request to stay put changed Gayle Morton's attitude toward me. Her father, too, suddenly embraced our short acquaintance and treated me as a friend and confidante. Since I was "friendly" with the police chief, they seemed to think that I could help them out of their jam or at least provide answers to their questions. I convinced them to rejoin Fadge and me for breakfast.

By the time we returned to the restaurant, Fadge was studying the menu again, smacking his lips, his face betraying a lingering hunger that the Adirondack Special had not appeased. Once we'd all sat down and ordered (English muffin for Owen Pierce, half a grapefruit for Gayle, and cornflakes for me), Fadge asked the waitress if the steak and eggs were any good.

"What can that revolting man possibly want?" asked Gayle once the waitress had pushed off. Fadge looked up, ears pricked and eyes bulging.

I motioned for him to take it easy and mouthed the name Terwilliger. His alarm subsided.

"I never even saw Charles here in Prospector Lake, I swear," she continued, unaware that she'd nearly offended Fadge.

"I'm sure he doesn't suspect you," I said, confident that my questions had sparked the doubt in Terwilliger's mind. "He said it was just for another day or two. Until he can discuss the details and review the photographs with the state police."

"I wish you'd never met Charles," said Pierce to his daughter. "A leopard can't change his spots."

"If I may ask again, was Charles leaving you?" I asked, opting for his *Christian* name. I was trying to win her over.

Her father didn't like the question, but Gayle answered straightaway. "That's not true," she said. "Charles and I had our troubles like any other marriage. But he wasn't leaving me."

"What kind of troubles?" asked Fadge, surprising us all.

Gayle looked at him in horror. She must have been wondering who this giant man was and why he was asking her personal questions.

"Charles was . . . in demand," she said. "For the past year, people have been seeking him out, hoping he could do something for them."

"Because of the Bible picture?" Fadge had joined the hunt. "Or was it the Natalie Wood movie?"

"Both," she said, appearing bemused. "People sent him scripts to read, begged for meetings, made offers for new projects."

"And there must have been women," added Fadge. "Starlets, ingénues, stage mothers?"

"Yes," she answered wearily. "All of the above. If it wasn't a crackpot or a schemer, it was a nineteen-year-old girl from Iowa or a Spanish whore from the islands trying to ride my husband to a studio contract."

"Gayle," spouted her father. "Some decorum, please."

"Must have been hard," said Fadge.

"Like I said. We had our troubles."

The two of them sounded like an episode of *Dragnet*.

"So what was he doing here?" asked Fadge, continuing his direct examination. "No Hollywood deals going on here, were there?"

"No. I doubt it."

"The two of you arrived on different days, and you weren't staying in the same motel."

Owen Pierce huffed his disapproval.

"Cool your heels," said Fadge. "I'll get to you next."

"We had a quarrel," explained Gayle. "Charles wanted to get away. He had fond memories of this place and his old friends. So he decided to visit them. I came to tell him I was sorry."

"Bunch of Communists," said Pierce. "A damn yeshiva full of Communists."

"I don't understand why you flew across the country to follow him if it was just a quarrel," said Fadge, probing deeper. "It couldn't wait till he got back?"

Gayle mulled it over for a long moment before finally saying that she wanted to turn over a new leaf in their marriage. She wanted to embrace his past and his friends.

"Then why do you still call him Charles?" asked Fadge.

She didn't answer. Her father piped up to tell Fadge to leave her alone.

"Why don't you pick on someone your own size?" he said.

"All right," said Fadge. "I'll ask *you* a question." (I didn't think Owen Pierce qualified as Fadge's size, but I kept quiet.) "If it was a simple quarrel, why did *you* fly across the country with your daughter? Frankly, the whole thing seems like a bigger deal to me."

Good question, I thought. But it was time to let silence go to work. I like to use silence as a carrot when I'm interviewing a subject. Or perhaps it's more of a stick. Nervous people hate gaps in the conversation. They would use a shovel to fill them if shovels shoveled words.

I gave Fadge the subtlest of blinks, and he acknowledged me. We waited. Gayle started to fidget. Her father toyed with his spoon. We watched them.

"I thought he was coming here to meet his old flame," Gayle blurted out finally. "We'd had a fight, and he said he didn't love me anymore. He packed a bag and stormed out of the house that night. When he didn't come back the next morning, I was worried. I phoned our travel agent and found out Charles had booked a flight to Albany. I knew what that meant."

"An old flame," I said. "Who was that?"

Gayle looked me in the eye. "It was someone named Miriam. One of his old friends from that Arcadia place."

CHAPTER SIXTEEN

Philby's Bait and Tackle and Photo Supplies opened at 5:00 a.m. I figured they sold more worms than film at that hour, but I wasn't going fishing. And I didn't land up there until after eleven anyway. I took all my film— the black-and-white rolls I'd shot of Baxter's Cove the day before and the color slides from that morning—and for a five-dollar bill, the lady at the counter agreed to rush everything. She said they'd be ready by three.

Leaving the shop, I bumped into a tall man who was just on his way in. The collision nearly knocked me to the ground, but he caught me in his arms. I apologized, as did he. And that was when I noticed his face; it was familiar, but I couldn't place it straightaway.

"Why, hello, Ellie," he said, grinning at me from behind his horn-rimmed glasses. "Don't you remember me?"

Oh, God. It was the wife-swapper, Nelson Blanchard. I wondered if our collision was accidental after all.

"Mr. Blanchard," I said, smoothing my skirt. "How could I forget?"

"Nelson, please." He bared all his teeth at me. "And it's Dr. Blanchard, actually."

Right. I'd forgotten. This was the pervert whose job it was to examine women's private parts. Talk about the fox guarding the henhouse. He must have taken an aptitude test in high school and scored "degenerate."

"Terrible news about Karl," he said, and I stopped.

"You knew him?"

"Of course. Karl and I go way back. Before he was Charles Morton."

"How well did you know him?"

"Very well from the old days here on the lake," he said. "I've had a cottage here since forty-seven. And I saw him from time to time in Los Angeles. I have a home in the Hollywood Hills. He was in Bel Air. The movie biz, you understand."

"Yes, I do."

"Perhaps you'd like to visit me sometime in California. If you're more the traditional type, you might prefer a time when Lucia is away . . ."

Or when pigs flew.

"Had you seen Karl recently?" I asked. "Since you go way back, I thought perhaps he'd contacted you."

Blanchard shook his head. "Strange, isn't it? But, no, he didn't contact me. And we'd been corresponding about my pet project. Karl was very interested in coproducing *The Scarlett Lady*." He paused. "That's my film." He blushed. "*The Scarlett Lady*. Brigitte Bardot wants in. But it's Lucia's role, of course."

"Bardot? Really?"

He nodded. "Not right for the part."

"Maybe if there's a role for a schoolmarm," I said.

"Going fishing?" he asked, ignoring my contribution.

"Something like that."

"Lucia and I would like to invite you to dinner one night before you leave," he said.

I assumed my best expression of disappointment. "I'm leaving Sunday, you know. I don't think I'll have a free night before then."

He looked crushed but took it like a man. He managed a weak smile. "Oh, well. Perhaps next summer."

"Who was that guy you were talking to?" asked Fadge when I climbed into the car.

"An oddball I met at a party here. He and his wife want to have me for dinner."

"What's wrong with that?"

"No, I mean they want to *have* me for dinner. They're wife-swappers."

Fadge shook his head. "What's wrong with people?"

I started the car and pulled away from the curb.

"What's the wife look like?" he asked.

"Put it this way," I said. "Her husband wants to cast her over Brigitte Bardot in his sexy movie."

"You know, Ellie, we don't have any plans for dinner."

I slugged him on the arm and drove on.

❧

From Philby's, Fadge and I headed south on Lake Road out of the village. A half mile later, I pulled over to the side of Route 15 and parked twenty yards shy of the Camp Orpheus entrance. Fadge asked why we couldn't drive in.

"I'm not welcome here," I said, switching off the ignition. "We'll have to wait for lunch to be served before we can go in. The camp director will throw me out if he sees me."

Fadge sighed. He didn't like walking farther than from the sofa to the refrigerator. "This is the worst vacation ever."

"What vacation?" I asked. "You're supposed to be working. Who's minding the store anyway?"

Fadge shrugged sheepishly. "Nobody. I put a sign on the door that I went fishing."

I shook my head. No wonder he couldn't make ends meet. He was a financial disaster. Who else would close an ice cream parlor in August?

As the day before, campers and counselors and directors all convened inside the cafeteria at noon and tied on their feedbags. Fadge and I climbed out of the car, made our way onto the campgrounds, and crossed the compound to the Bear Lodge. Herbie was lying on his bunk in the same position I'd left him the day before.

"Who's he?" asked the boy, indicating Fadge with a bob of his head.

"A friend," I said. "Do you have anything for me?"

"Do you have my payment?" he asked.

I walked over to his bunk and fished my billfold out of my purse. "Two dollars, wasn't it?"

"We said beer and a date."

"You said beer and a date. I said two dollars, and you agreed."

"Fine," he huffed, sitting up and holding out his hand. "But you're getting the better end of the deal."

Herbie told me that he'd asked around and found some interesting dirt on Jerry Kaufman. But first he told me there was no talk of Jerry knowing Karl Merkleson.

"Okay," I said. "Then what's the interesting dirt?"

"Jerry had a little girlfriend in the village," he announced as if dropping a bomb. "One of those annoying Christians trying to convert the world. They have that big camp not too far from here."

"I already knew that," I said. "The minister's daughter. I even know her name."

Herbie smiled smugly.

"So I gave you two dollars to tell me what I already knew?"

"Hold on," he said. "Did you know he had a crush on an older woman before he met the girl?"

"No," I said, still unimpressed. "Did she push him off the cliff by any chance?"

"I don't know. But word is that he was always falling for some new girl. He was a romantic."

"So what does this crush have to do with any of this?"

"Jerry was quite the ladies' man," said Herbie. "Like I said, she's an older woman."

"Seventeen? Eighteen? How old was she?" I asked.

"Try thirty," said Herbie. "And I heard he met her at Tom's Lakeside Motel."

⊘

Herbie didn't know the woman's name, but he assured me that his information was accurate and that Jerry had been obsessed with her until quite recently. Until he met Emily Grierson, in fact. Fadge thought it was normal for a boy to have a crush on an older woman. I knew that more than one teenage boy had entertained impure thoughts about me, including Herbie with the smart mouth. And I remembered Simon teasing Isaac about his infatuation with my aunt Lena when he was about Jerry's age.

I intended to follow up on the lead, even if I had little expectation of success. I doubted Tom Waller of the Lakeside Motel would remember a young boy meeting an older woman. If the two had trysted there, they certainly would have done it on the QT. But Tom might well remember an earlier visit by Gayle Morton—a visit before the previous Thursday—and I was going to ask him.

"You don't think it might have been Gayle Morton, do you?" I asked Fadge as we drove toward the village. "She's staying at the Lakeside Motel after all."

"Maybe," he said. "Pretty big coincidence, though."

I drove on in silence for a stretch then pulled over to the side of the road.

"What is it?" asked Fadge.

"We've been wondering why Karl Merkleson came to Prospector Lake. It's strange that he didn't even contact his own friends. Then he left his motel once his wife arrived to win him back."

"Yeah, so?"

"So what if things happened the other way around?"

"How do you mean?"

"What if Gayle Morton flew here to meet someone, and Karl followed *her*?"

"But how would Gayle Morton have known that kid? When would she have met him?"

I pondered it as my Dodge's engine growled quietly. Then I released the brake and slipped away from the shoulder.

"So what's your next step?" he asked.

"I'm going to find out if Gayle Morton had ever been to Prospector Lake before last Thursday. I need to see her plane ticket."

"How are you going to manage that?"

I glanced at him as we headed up Route 15. "First stop, the Lakeside Motel."

"And then?"

"Let's see if Chief Terwilliger can't get that plane ticket from Gayle Morton."

※

"You again? Are you trying to sell me insurance?" asked Tom Waller with a wink.

"No, nothing like that," I said, flashing my brightest smile at him. Shameless. But who could blame me? I could hardly resist his sunburned belly, which was two sizes too large for his mustard-stained T-shirt.

I had asked Fadge to wait in the car in case his presence intimidated Tom and discouraged him from talking. I suspected the innkeeper might be susceptible to charm, and I intended to sprinkle some sugar liberally, if necessary, to get what I wanted.

"My boss is angry with me," I said. "He made me drive all the way back up here because I forgot to verify something."

"He did? That doesn't seem right. A pretty little thing like you? I would never get angry with you. Why don't you come work for me?"

"Really, Mr. Waller. How you go on."

"So how can I help you today, miss?"

"My boss wants me to verify Miss Pierce's previous visit to your motel," I said. "Would that be possible?"

"I'd be happy to check for you, hon. But I don't remember her ever staying here before. Do you have an idea of when that might have been?"

If she'd come to the lake and met Jerry Kaufman, it couldn't have been earlier than July 30. I remembered that as move-in day from the schedule of activities posted in the Bear Lodge at Camp Orpheus. And, realistically, she would have had to return to Los Angeles before the previous Tuesday if she'd hopped back on a plane Wednesday or Thursday to fly to Albany.

"It would be from late July to August twelfth or thirteenth," I said.

He opened the register and flipped back some pages. Then he licked his thumb and turned a few more. Squinting to see better, he twisted his head to the right in an effort to force his aging lenses to focus. Yes, I thought, I'll surely find you devastatingly handsome, provided you don't wear eyeglasses. He ran a finger over the names, licked his thumb anew, then looked up at me.

"I'm afraid I can't find her name here," he said.

"What about Morton?" I asked. "Anyone by that name?"

He hunted some more, his eyes scanning the page, even pausing as he dug deep to extract a bit of underwear pinched between the folds of his posterior.

"Nope," he said. "But I can check with her. She's still here. Chief Terwilliger asked her and her father to stay a few days more."

"That won't be necessary," I said. "I'll just tell my boss she hasn't been here before."

"Any luck?" asked Fadge.

"No, not for me. But Tom Waller stuck in his thumb and pulled out a plum."

"What?"

"Never mind," I said, thinking that a far too revolting a joke for me to attempt, even if Fadge would have appreciated it. "Let's go see Terwilliger."

"So you think this Gayle Morton was here earlier this summer?" the chief asked me. He was leaning back in his chair, picking the last of his lunch out of his teeth with a paperclip he'd untwisted expressly for the task.

"Might have been," I said. "It occurred to me that perhaps we were looking at the Morton marriage backward. What if the shoe had been on the other foot?"

"How do you mean?"

"What if *Gayle* was the one contemplating divorce, and Karl came to Prospector Lake to win *her* back?"

"And this boy, Jerrold Kaufman, knew her?" he asked.

"I can't say that. I just think it bears looking into."

"And you and your friend here," he began, indicating Fadge with a nod, "believe she might have been corrupting a minor at Tom's Lakeside Motel?"

"That's a possibility we'd like to confirm or eliminate from consideration, yes."

He thought it over, a process aided by folding his grubby hands, minus half a forefinger, over his belly and staring at the ceiling. Fadge threw me a look that communicated a mix of derision and disbelief. Eventually Terwilliger reached his decision.

"I'll ask to see her plane ticket," he said. "I think it's unlikely, but she has been a little squirrelly about this whole thing. It wouldn't surprise me if she gave her husband a little shove of encouragement for his jump off the high dive."

"And the kid?"

He nodded. "Sure. Why not? Find a teenage boy who's feeling his oats. It wouldn't be hard to seduce him as part of her plan. Then push him off the cliff, too."

"Maybe," I said. "But how would Jerry fit into the plan? Why not just lure the husband to the cliff and do the needful? Why complicate things with the teenager?"

"Simple," said Fadge, speaking for the first time. "In order to get the husband to follow her across the country to the lake, she needed to create a threat to their marriage. Enter the patsy: that poor kid."

"Your friend may be onto something," said Terwilliger. "Makes sense to me."

"Maybe," I said, unconvinced. "But we would need to understand why she came here of all places. If she'd been thinking murder, she could have done the same somewhere in California. Maybe a mountain resort. She's an attractive woman, certainly up to the task of seducing red-blooded men. Why come to his childhood vacation spot?"

Neither Fadge nor Terwilliger had an answer for that. At length the chief said the first order of business was to get a hold of Gayle Morton's ticket and see if it matched up with her arrival story.

"Will you get a warrant?" I asked.

Terwilliger pshawed. "Things don't work that way up here. She'll show it to me. Don't worry about that."

My film was ready. Fadge and I stopped to pick it up at Philby's and, happily, ran into no Blanchards this time. I climbed into my car and handed the envelope to Fadge.

"Let's have a look," he said, going straight for the color slides. "Do you have one of those magnifiers?"

"It's called a loupe," I said, fishing the one I always carried out of my camera kit.

Fadge ignored the vocabulary lesson and examined the slides one by one, grunting and clearing his throat from time to time.

"What do you see?" I asked.

He took the slide away from his eye and looked at me. "What do you mean? You know what's in these pictures."

"Yes, but I'm always hoping there's something more. Tell me what *you* see."

"A nice, sunny morning," he said, squinting into the loupe again. "Some rocks and the outlines of two bodies. Oh, and my shadow's in this one. Man, I need to go on a diet."

"You're most unhelpful," I said, taking the loupe and the slide from him.

I held the slide up to the late-afternoon light shining through the windshield. I stared at the picture long and hard. The colors were beautiful, and I congratulated myself on a fine job framing and focusing the shot. This was a photo of Karl Merkleson's outline. The sun flooded over the rocks. Fadge was right; it was a nice, sunny morning. Too nice a day to die.

"Your friend is a remarkable fellow," said Max, taking the first sip of his first cocktail of the evening. "Excellent idea of his to whip up this Tom Collins. Tall and refreshing."

Fadge was sitting on the chair opposite Max, poring over the *Racing Form*, unaware he was being praised. He was planning to call his bookie with his picks for the next day's races. Or maybe he was considering an early-morning dash to Saratoga in his dented car. It was only about an hour's drive. The horses were Fadge's day job, after all. The ice cream store was a sideline that provided seed money for his terrible gambling habit.

"What's in the news today, Ronald?" asked Max.

"Sorry?" said Fadge, interrupted from his study.

"I asked what was making headlines today? What news from Berlin? How many home runs for Roger Maris? Tell me what's in the funny pages."

Fadge looked at me, perplexed. I shook my head, a signal for him to ignore Max.

"Tomorrow's the Sanford Handicap at Saratoga," he said. "I'm leaning toward Brunette Downs. She's only carrying a hundred and ten pounds."

"Seems like a load to me," said Max. "I slow down when saddled with anything heavier than my lunch."

Fadge looked to me again, silently begging for assistance, but all I could manage was an I-told-you-so roll of the eyes.

"Shall we listen to the Yarrow report?" asked Lena, rising to switch on the radio. Fadge seemed relieved, until the announcer said that the escapee had been spotted three times in or around Prospector Lake in the past twenty-four hours. A report was to follow at seven. Fadge was white.

"Perhaps it's time for some music," I said.

CBC was broadcasting Berlioz, for whom I'd never really cared. I invited Fadge to join me on the porch for a drink instead. I wasn't sure if he was afraid of Donald Yarrow showing up uninvited in our compound or if he knew there was a squadron of mosquitoes lying in wait to siphon his sweet blood out by the gallon, but Fadge didn't want to chance it. He suggested we stay inside with Lena and Max. Then there was a knock on the cabin door. I answered to find Isaac standing before me.

"Ellie," he said. "I really wish you had a telephone here. Every time I need to speak to you, I have to hightail it over here in person."

I offered a vague smile. "And I wouldn't know what that feels like."

"You're right," he said. "Sorry. I know you've braved the elements and all manner of danger on foot through the woods to visit Arcadia."

Just when I'd decided to write him off, when I found him to be insufferable, Isaac always managed to redeem himself in my eyes, at least to a degree. He seemed to care for me, lacked the flaws that one usually encountered in bachelors. He didn't smell, didn't embarrass, didn't snore. He was fit, smart, talented, and cultured. And he had a smile to beat the band. But questions about his character caused me fits. He'd betrayed two of his best friends by sleeping with their girls. Paint me old-fashioned, but that was something I believed friends didn't do to each other. I remembered my own experience in this arena. I'd had a dangerous fling with Stitch Ferguson, who'd been on the rebound from my friend Jackie Rennart. I was sure they'd broken up when I embarked on my ill-timed and ill-advised affair. Stitch promised me they had parted ways. But in the end, I discovered that Stitch had lied. He broke my heart and forever ruined my friendship with Jackie. And he'd taught me to doubt the integrity of the men I frequented.

Why was I tarring Isaac with Stitch's brush? It wasn't the same. Isaac hadn't led me on, had his way with me, only to break it off with the announcement that he'd been carrying on with his old flame all along and was going to marry her, would I like to attend the wedding, by the way? What a fool I'd been. Was I punishing Isaac for another's duplicity? No, it wasn't the same. And yet my antennae were up. The warning signs were there. Did Isaac want anything from me besides a summer fling? I didn't care in principle. But in practice I did. I wanted him. But I wasn't sure if he deserved my desire. I wasn't sure I could trust him. And that was what vexed me.

"Come in," I said. "I want to introduce you to my friend."

Isaac entered and surveyed the room. He said hello to Lena and Max, of course. Then he turned to the big side of beef that answered to the name Fadge Fiorello.

"Isaac, this is my friend Fadge," I said.

"How do you do?" asked Isaac.

"I do fine," said Fadge. They didn't like each other; I could tell right off the bat. But why should they? At the risk of overstating the case, I feared they saw each other as rivals for my affections.

Isaac whispered that he wanted to have a word with me in private. I felt Fadge's eyes on me. Our relationship was friendly, not romantic. Still, I knew he was carrying a torch for me, and I hated to flaunt my boyfriends in front of him.

"I'll just be a minute," I said, excusing myself. Then, trying to prove that my word was good, I asked Fadge to be a darling and pour me another drink.

"You really need to ask your aunt to get a telephone up here," said Isaac once we were outside.

"Okay," I said, a little out of sorts with him. "Anything else?"

"Come on, Ellie. What's happened? What have I done to upset you?"

I thought about it. There were many things. Little things. And some not-so-little things. Besides the virtual parade of women through his bedroom, there was the mean-spirited taunting of his old friend Simon. Sure he'd said they all enjoyed the teasing, that it was part of their usual games, but I found that it grew sour after a while, especially given what I knew about Simon's health. I wondered again if Isaac knew about his friend's disease, and I almost asked him then and there. But I held back. I wasn't risking a major emotional discussion on the cabin porch while my dearest friend, Fadge, sat stewing inside. And what else had Isaac done to estrange himself from my good graces? He'd flirted shamelessly with Audrey Silber, and perhaps done worse. That stung my pride as well as my affections. I did care for this man, after all. I was perhaps throwing up shields to protect myself, magnifying small doubts and suspicions to hold him at bay. Or was I truly over the brief infatuation?

"There's one thing," I said, determined not to show my hand.

"Tell me, and I'll fix it. I swear," he said, almost pleading. I liked that.

"Why did you assume that I knew nothing about the music you all were playing?" Isaac's face fell. "And why did you find it so hard to believe that I'd investigated a couple of murders in my work as a reporter?"

"Well," he began but quickly stalled. He tried again. "It's unusual these days that young people know about music," he said, dipping his spade into the ground and removing the first shovelful of dirt. "I just thought you'd probably be like most girls and like rock and roll. You know, like Audrey." The spade pushed deeper into the dirt. "And how many girls investigate murders? Or have jobs on newspapers? Not many, I'd guess." The hole was growing, and I decided to stop the carnage.

"Perhaps you've said enough. Let's leave it."

"Will you come tonight?"

"I have a guest. I can't abandon him."

"Your aunt and Max are here," he said. "He'll be fine."

I sighed. "Let me rephrase that. I don't *want* to abandon him."

Isaac gave it some thought then apologized. "Where are my manners? Please let me invite your friend as well. We'd love to have him with us. All four of you should join us for dinner."

I laughed. "Isaac, it's almost seven. You can't invite people to dinner like that. Don't you think we've already started preparing our supper here?"

He shook his head, looked away, and apologized again. "I'm being selfish. But it's because I want you to come, Ellie. Please reconsider. Maybe you and your friend could come over after your supper. It'll be fun. He'll have a great time."

"I've got to go," I said. "I'll check with Fadge. If he's game, I'll see you later."

Isaac drew a sigh of relief. I smiled despite myself. Damn it, he still had something of a hold on me. I just wasn't sure if it was slipping or about to get stronger.

I let myself back inside the cabin and saw Lena, Max, and Fadge sitting forward in their seats, hanging on every word coming from the radio. Well, Max had sunk too far into the cushions of his armchair to make any real effort to lean forward, but his attention was fixed on the Philco.

"*The young couple stated that they saw their car being stolen as they emerged from the lake after a swim. Though the car was a distance away, they described the thief as a slight man in his forties, dressed in baggy clothing. Prospector Lake chief of police, Ralph Terwilliger, told reporters that there is no credible evidence to indicate that the car thief was, in fact, Donald Yarrow, who escaped one week ago from Comstock prison in Washington County. Chief Terwilliger urged residents and visitors to remain vigilant in case Yarrow was in the area, but cautioned against overreaction."*

"Did you hear that, Ellie?" asked Aunt Lena, nearly breathless. "Yarrow stole a car from Frenchman's Creek Beach. Just at the southern end of the village."

"He's been spotted everywhere from here to Canada to Mexico," I said. "Max had him in Cozumel just yesterday."

Max frowned and sipped his Tom Collins pensively. "Airplanes, my dear," he mumbled half to himself.

CHAPTER SEVENTEEN

Fadge and I drove over to Arcadia Lodge at nine thirty. I'd convinced him to come along, if only to protect me from marauding escaped murderers. And I told him there would be booze aplenty and a couple of pretty girls.

The Arcadians had just finished their dinner and were relaxing with drinks in the Great Lodge. To my dismay, I spotted that contagion, Nelson Blanchard, drooling over Audrey Silber on one of the sofas. She didn't seem to mind his attentions, but, in her defense, perhaps she didn't fully grasp the depravity of his intentions. Miriam and Rachel were sitting together in silence, Miriam staring at the floor, Rachel watching her father, who was crossing the room, unsteady on his cane. Once he'd found a seat, she relaxed and turned back to Miriam. She still didn't say anything, and Miriam continued her contemplation of the floorboards.

I dragged Fadge over to Jakob Eisenstadt to introduce him. I wanted to visit the bar, of course, but propriety dictated that ceremony be respected. Once we'd exchanged pleasantries with the senior host, we made our way to the drinks table. I was pouring myself a whiskey as Fadge surveyed the room.

"Who's that talking to your friend over there?" he asked, indicating Isaac across the room.

I followed his gaze and saw Lucia Blanchard, leaning over Isaac from behind as he sat in an armchair, talking to David and Ruth. She was drunk, it seemed, close to falling out of her silk blouse. In Isaac's defense, he was ignoring her even as she endeavored to park her derrière on his shoulder like some kind of bosomy epaulette.

"That's the wife-swapping wife," I said, and Fadge's face lit up.

He watched her intently, never taking his eyes off her as he spoke. "Do you know you're selfish sometimes, El?" he said. "Did you ever stop to consider that I might like to meet interesting new people and have dinner on my vacation?"

"Pervert," I said. "Come on. I'll introduce you."

Nelson Blanchard had a better nose than a bloodhound. He appeared behind me just as I said hello to the group surrounding Isaac.

"I hoped I'd run into you here this evening," he said. "Lucia and I were just saying how sorry we were not to see you again this summer."

"Very sorry," slurred Lucia.

"How lucky that we met here," I said through my teeth.

"And who's your big, handsome friend?" asked Lucia, slipping off Isaac's shoulder and cozying up to Fadge, who looked terrified.

"Everybody, this is Ron," I announced. "Fadge."

The gang welcomed him. Lucia took his hand and asked him where he'd been all night. Poor thing. Despite his big talk, he was overwhelmed by the attention. Then Isaac took me by the arm and steered me away from the group.

"I'm so glad you came," he said. "I've been thinking about what you said. You were so right. I've been a fool."

"What's this about?" I asked.

He kissed me, right there in front of anyone who might have been watching. A long, passionate kiss. I kissed him back.

"I'm crazy about you," he said.

"You're mad all right," I said, giggling. "Control yourself. People will talk."

"How can I make it up to you? How can I make it all up to you?"

I thought a moment. "You can start by apologizing for the Blanchards being here."

"Sorry. This time it's my fault, not Miriam's," said Isaac. "Nelson called me this afternoon and invited himself and his nymphomaniac wife to supper. Wouldn't take no for an answer."

I wondered if his telephone call didn't have something to do with his meeting me at Philby's that morning. I wasn't flattering myself; I knew when a man was interested. And I knew even better when a man was rutting like a horny goat.

"So you'll stay with me tonight?" asked Isaac.

I shook my head. "I have my big friend."

Isaac threw a glance back at the group we'd just left. "I'd say your big friend's doing just fine on his own."

Lucia Blanchard was hanging on Fadge's every word, as well as on his sweater. Nelson Blanchard, too, seemed amenable to the match, if grinning ear to ear and licking one's lips meant what it used to.

"Poor Fadge," I said. "I've got to rescue him. He looks miserable."

"Let's slip away," said Isaac, and damn me, I slipped.

We stepped outside the Great Lodge. Isaac led me through the trees to a secluded spot within earshot of the party going on inside. And there he took me on the ground, under the stars, atop the sticky pine needles. It was fast. Too quick for me even to get into the spirit of the proceedings. And then it was over. Isaac leaned against me, heaving for breath in the night air, holding my body tight. He was gentle and loving. Or was it gratitude? I stroked his temples, felt his heart beating against my side, and thought that this was surely the last time.

We brushed the pine needles off my backside and my skirt, out of my hair, and straightened our rumpled clothing. It's one of the inherent disadvantages of being female. We suffer the indignities of occupying the subjacent position in lovemaking. That means supporting the weight of the bucking male of the species as he satisfies his urges, suffering the scrapes and abrasions, the lumps and pinches, on the various surfaces we find ourselves up against. Something surely had bitten me, and I felt a bruise growing on the base of my back.

Before sneaking inside, we agreed that Isaac would go first, and I would follow a minute or two later. Isaac made his entrance with the practiced ease of one who'd done this before. As I waited outside, counting to two hundred in my head before risking it, I became aware of a malaise brewing inside me. I'd never felt that way before, but I was embarrassed. Actually embarrassed. I'd had unsatisfying encounters with men before, but this one bothered me, and I didn't quite know why. With difficulty I pushed the thought to one side. Then I realized I'd lost track of my count and had to start over.

When it was time, I took on the task of reentering the hall, striding straight for the door as if I'd been outside for nothing naughtier than a smoke. All was going according to plan until I crossed the threshold and ran headlong into Waldo Coons, who was wrestling a bin through the door on his way out to the garbage cans. We stood there face-to-face for several beats as I searched for something to say. He gulped, staring at me.

"Sorry," I said, pushing past him.

"I saw you," he said, and I froze in my tracks. I turned back to look at him. He shied away like a beaten dog.

"What did you say?" I asked.

"I saw you the other night," he said in a strangled voice.

"What? Where?"

"It was raining," he whispered. "You were running. In the woods."

"That was you? You nearly scared me to death. Why were you following me?"

Waldo looked down at his muddy sneakers. He swallowed a couple of
times, as if priming the pump in preparation to speak. But he couldn't get
anything out of his throat.

"You've been following me all week, haven't you?" I said to accuse.
"And that was you on the porch outside my cabin Tuesday night."

Waldo sprang to life. "No, I never went to your cabin. Never."

I wanted to ask for a more precise reckoning of his nocturnal activity,
but did I really need to know how many insects he'd de-winged?

"Did you hear or see anyone wandering around in the woods that
night?"

He shook his head and coughed over the trash cans. "Not then.
Before. Last week there was a guy in the woods."

"Who was it? Where?"

"He was in the shed," he said. "The hunters' shed in the woods."

"Will you show me where?" I asked.

I followed Waldo into the deep woods behind Arcadia Lodge, wondering
if I would ever come back out alive. Was I mad? This was a man, after
all, who I suspected bit off the heads of live chickens. And not at some
sideshow, but for dinner. Yet I sensed he was harmless, just as Isaac and his
father had said. And at 10:35 p.m. on a dark August night, we were going
to explore an empty hunters' shed in the woods.

Waldo led the way in silence. He moved quickly and efficiently
through the branches, and I labored to keep up. We reached the lean-to in
less than five minutes. It was the same one I'd spotted off in the distance
the previous night.

"He was staying in there," whispered Waldo. "I seen him come and go."

"What did he look like?" I asked.

Waldo shrugged. "Just a guy."

Our hushed conversation only made the woods seem more menacing in the dark. I wanted to knock on the shelter's door and interview whoever might be inside, but my nerve didn't go that far. I asked Waldo to do the honors.

"There's no one in there," he said. "Not anymore."

I wondered how could he be so sure, but he didn't hesitate even for a moment. He stepped up to the door and yanked the latch. The door stuck, so he pulled harder, and it opened. No bogeyman leapt out. No one screamed. The night remained as silent as it had been before Waldo rattled the latch. I could hear faint voices from down the hill. It was the party at Arcadia, going strong in my absence. I took a cautious step closer to the open doorway. It was dark inside, but it appeared to be empty of marauders at the moment. A bolt of light fired across my nose into the doorway. I jumped.

"Flashlight," said Waldo, holding it out for me.

I came down to earth and took it from him. Why the hell hadn't he used it on our climb up the hill? Drawing a calming breath, I put my fright to one side and entered the small shack.

Inside, a narrow wooden bed of sorts filled half the room. It was just a bench, really, about five and a half feet long. A dark wool blanket was folded neatly at one end. There were shelves on the wall at the other end of the bed with a box of matches, three cans of Sterno, a couple of half-burned honeycomb candles, and some empty quart bottles. A cast-iron skillet hung from the wall next to an antique double burner. Beside the door was a small mirror and lopsided stool with an old, chipped, enamel bedpan on top. And hanging from a nail on the back of the door was a leather Dopp kit.

"The man stayed here three nights," said Waldo as I opened the kit. "Then he didn't come back."

"How did you discover him here?" I asked. "Did he make noise? Start a fire?"

"No. But I notice things."

I rooted through the Dopp kit, retrieving a comb, a safety razor, shaving soap, a styptic pencil, and aftershave. A toothbrush and toothpaste. I placed them on the wooden bed. There was also shampoo, a nail file, clippers, and two handkerchiefs. A pair of scissors and some hair tonic. With the bag now empty, I opened it wide and examined the inside. Nothing but the tag. Swank. Fine leather. On the outside was a monogram. *KMM*.

⁂

"Where the hell have you been?" asked Fadge when I walked into the Great Lodge at eleven fifteen.

"I thought I'd left you in good company. Didn't you want to meet new people?"

He threw a look over his shoulder then turned back to me. "That Lucia is sick. She told me her husband likes 'big fellows' like me."

"Then we must make time for a dinner with them before we leave."

"Not funny, El," he said.

Fadge was the only person who called me that. The only person since my brother, Elijah. I was finally getting used to it. It no longer caused me pangs of sorrow.

"There you are," said Isaac, interrupting our tête-à-tête. "What happened to you?"

Fadge regarded us queerly, and Isaac volunteered that we'd gone outside for a smoke and I hadn't returned. I'm sure I blushed.

"Relax," I told both of them. "I'm fine. Waldo and I made a discovery. Let me tell you about it. I found this." I held up the Dopp kit.

"Whose is that?" asked Isaac.

"I can't say for sure. But it's monogrammed. KMM."

⁂

Chief Terwilliger showed up at Arcadia Lodge yet again, smelling strongly of beer, as usual. I had called him to let him know about the Dopp kit. There was little doubt in my mind whose toiletries were inside, but procedures demanded the police.

"Can anyone actually confirm that this stuff belonged to Charles Morton?" Terwilliger asked the assembled in the Great Lodge.

No one could say with certainty since they hadn't seen Karl in years. Still, the initials were compelling, said Isaac. Everyone agreed.

"Okay," said Terwilliger, stuffing the kit into a paper bag and downing the rest of his beer. "I'll add this to the evidence. Maybe we'll get a fingerprint expert from the state police to have a look at it. But don't hold your breath."

"Just a moment, Chief," I said. "I believe everyone is overlooking one important detail pertaining to the kit."

"What's that?" he asked.

"It looks brand-new, wouldn't you say?"

"Looks new to me," he agreed. "So maybe he bought it recently. It looks like he had money for this kind of thing."

"Of course," I said. "But if he bought it recently, why are the initials wrong?"

Terwilliger pulled the kit back out of the bag, surely slathering his own fingerprints all over it. He turned it over until he had the monogram under his nose.

"It looks right to me. KMM."

"But his initials are CMM," I said, and the Arcadians murmured agreement.

"That's right," said Isaac. "Why would Karl use his old initials on a new kit?"

"And there's one more thing," I said. "Charles Morton had a very expensive leather toiletry bag in his valise at the Sans Souci Cabins."

"So?" asked Terwilliger.

"So why did he have this second, brand-new Dopp kit?"

"What do you make of the two bathroom kits?" Fadge asked me after we'd returned to Cedar Haven around one. We were having a nightcap in my cabin.

"First," I said, "let's remember that Karl Merkleson was traveling with just one suitcase." Fadge nodded agreement. "So I ask myself why he had two Dopp kits but only one valise."

"And what's your explanation?"

I took a sip of my drink. "I think he arrived here with only one Dopp kit. The one I found tonight was new. You could smell it, see it."

"So why did he buy a second one when he got here?"

"He didn't," I said, and Fadge scowled at me. "Someone gave it to him."

"How do you figure?"

"I don't believe you can get your hands on leather goods like that around here," I said. "And even if he had managed to find one nearby, he wouldn't have had the time to have the kit monogrammed. And finally he knew his own name. Whoever bought the kit and had it inscribed was sending a tender nostalgic message to him, hence his original initials."

"So obviously it had to be one of the gang at Arcadia Lodge."

"It would seem so."

Fadge mulled it over. "Isaac? Or that other guy, Simon? You said they were once great friends. Maybe this was his way to needle him."

"I don't think so," I said. "Simon wouldn't give him anything. And Isaac and he weren't that close."

"Then who do you think?"

"Miriam. Simon's wife. She and Karl had a torrid affair many years ago, I'm almost certain. Isaac was very cagey about why Karl and Simon had their falling out. It just never clicked for me. The intensity of the hatred didn't add up. I think it was Miriam who came between them."

"Not sure I'm convinced," he said.

"There's more. Isaac told me that Miriam had run into Karl accidentally in Los Angeles about four years ago. It's a pretty big town."

"But still possible," said Fadge.

"And then Gayle Morton told me she was worried enough about her husband meeting up with an old flame here on Prospector Lake that she jumped on a plane and flew across the country to stop it."

"Could have been any number of women here."

"I suppose you're right," I said. "Any number of women named Miriam."

CHAPTER EIGHTEEN

FRIDAY, AUGUST 25, 1961

The close of summer is a melancholy time. The weather, the best of the season, with magical sunrises and sunsets, makes the farewell all the more bitter. The Adirondacks are particularly difficult to leave; I'd forgotten just how much.

The evenings hinted at the impending fall, which would bring crisp air and exploding colors. It would all end in a few weeks in a blizzard of falling leaves. I had just one night left with Aunt Lena and Cousin Max. They were packing their things for a Saturday noon departure. I had agreed to stay on one more day and close up Cedar Haven.

Friday morning Isaac arrived bright and early and sat down to coffee in the kitchen. He invited all four of us, including Fadge, for a party that evening at Arcadia Lodge to celebrate and watch the lunar eclipse.

"It's our last night together," I said, motioning to the old folks. "We were planning to watch the moon here."

Isaac deflated.

"There's an eclipse tonight?" asked Fadge, who, I realized, lived under a rock.

"Absolutely," said Isaac, pushing the sale hard.

"Only a ninety-nine percent eclipse," I said.

"Read it in the paper this morning. Ninety-eight point six, to be exact," added Max. "I, for one, feel a little cheated."

"I wouldn't mind a night off from cooking," said Lena. "And the view of the moon isn't going to be good from here."

"Will there be music, young man?" asked Max. Isaac shrugged and said there was always music at Arcadia. "Good," he continued. "I'm itching to guess the musical selections. I nearly did last time, but Ellie beat me to it."

"You didn't have the faintest idea," said Lena.

"Jealousy doesn't become you, my dear. It's petty. You should correct that immediately."

"Then it's settled?" asked Isaac, practically chirping. "You'll come?"

"It's supposed to rain tonight," I said. "Hard. There may be nothing to see."

"Scattered thunderstorms, my dear," said Max, the font of all information.

"We're hoping the storms will pass in time for us to have a nice show," said Isaac. "What do you say?"

I glanced at Fadge, who was probably dreading a reprise of the previous night's matchmaking. I wasn't sure if he would push away from a helping of Lucia Blanchard, but as long as her husband was on the menu, he was on a diet.

"Come on, Fadge," said Isaac, slapping the big guy on the back. "I promise to run interference with Nelson Blanchard. Besides, he's got a thing for Ellie and Audrey Silber. You'll be safe. And we're on higher ground so we'll have a better view of the eclipse."

I doubted Fadge wanted to go, but he had an excuse all ready anyway. He said he was leaving for New Holland after breakfast. That was news to me.

"I hate to leave you up here with that murderer on the loose," he said. "But I have to get back to the store."

"Don't worry about me. But I wish you'd stay one more night."

"Then that settles it," said Isaac, beaming. "You're all coming."

I was outnumbered. Max and Lena wanted to attend the last great Bacchanalia of summer, and Fadge was leaving. And if I was honest with myself, I, too, wanted to be there.

Isaac wondered why I wasn't happy. I said nothing, but the truth was that I didn't appreciate his going around the end to box me into a corner. What if I hadn't wanted to go? What if I hadn't been in his thrall? What if I actually could have said no to his crooked little smile and green eyes with brown specks? He annoyed me, and I knew I couldn't trust him. But I also wanted him, the sexy math teacher. And I didn't want to want him, which was a different argument altogether, and not one I had any hope of winning.

"Next time, ask *me*," I said, giving him a playful shove. "A girl likes to feel special after all."

Isaac promised he would. Then, claiming he had preparations to attend to for that evening, he excused himself. The rest of us lingered over our coffee, chatting about the eclipse and the coming storm. I asked Fadge if he really needed to leave, but he was focused on something outside.

"You've got visitors," he said.

We all directed our attention to the kitchen window and the big Cadillac chugging thick, gray exhaust into the fresh morning air. Without consulting the owner's manual, I could only guess at the model year, but it looked like a 1950 or '51 white Fleetwood four-door. It had certainly seen many, many better days. The driver switched off the ignition, but the motor sputtered and coughed for at least ten seconds before finally giving up the ghost and falling still.

I stepped through the kitchen door and crossed the compound to investigate. The Cadillac's hood ornament was a cross. That was the first clue. The second was the blue paint on the doors reading, "Tommy Grierson Crusade: Bear Me Swift Away."

The driver's side door opened with a rusty groan, and the tall man unfolded himself from his seat and rose before me. He yanked straight the lapels of his white coat then smoothed his shock of silvery hair with two careful hands.

"Reverend Grierson," I said. "Good morning."

"Good morning, Miss Stone," he said, taking a few steps toward me. "May the Lord bless you and keep you."

I didn't know what the proper response was to that greeting, so I said, "Likewise, I'm sure." Stupid.

"I've come to make amends with you," he said. "For my unchristian behavior."

"I beg your pardon?"

"After much prayer and meditation, and having received counsel from God, I have realized my error."

"I don't understand."

"Emily is in the car," he said. "You said you wanted to speak to her."

I knew a little beach nearby that I had used to explore with Elijah when we were children. The water was clear, the bottom smooth and squishy between our toes, and no one in the world knew where we were. Sometimes I visited the beach by myself, especially when I was feeling blue or when I wanted to be alone.

Now, I thought the isolation might help Emily open up to me, so I left Reverend Grierson in the company of two Jewish atheists and a lapsed Catholic.

Emily and I walked in silence for a short while then pushed through the last of the trees. Prospector Lake appeared before us. The water was a dark blue that stretched out like a carpet before the Green Mountains on the eastern side. I drew a deep breath and closed my eyes, taking a moment for some reflection of my own. I could see Elijah splashing into the lake, his baggy swim trunks wrinkled from the previous day's swim, his tanned shoulders flexing and rotating, his wiry arms and kicking feet powering him through the water. He was a natural swimmer. At the end of a long day in the lake, my mother would examine his feet looking for webbed toes.

"Pruney, but not a frogman yet," she would say.

She always performed the check with mock seriousness, usually fooling Elijah for several beats before he realized it was the same old joke again.

I was lost in the memory. In moments like that, I felt fluid in time. As if I could travel back and relive the past, just as it had happened then. It was as if Elijah were actually there before me and I were a child again. Such beautiful instants rarely occurred, but when they did, I almost believed his sudden death was the daydream, not my recollections of him. Of course he was still alive. What a terrible nightmare.

"Miss? Hello?" a voice summoned me back to the present.

Emily. I opened my eyes and beheld the lake and the shore where I'd frolicked with my brother so many years earlier. It was an idyll. I marveled at the physical beauty and the emotional hold the lake had on me. And, yes, I realized that the daydream was not reality. Elijah was indeed dead and gone.

"I wanted to talk to you," I said, quietly closing the lid on my memories. "To see how you're doing."

She gave a halfhearted shrug and said she was okay.

"I also wanted to ask you about Jerry," I continued. "I wondered if you could tell me about him and that other man who died."

"I don't know anything about him," she said.

"You knew Jerry. What can possibly explain why he was atop the cliff that day? And why he was with that man?"

Emily shook her head in bewilderment. "I don't know. We left each other a couple of minutes after seven."

"And did he tell you where he was going when you two parted?"

"He said he was heading back to Orpheus like always. He had a lesson after breakfast and didn't want to miss it. He was preparing for his final summer concert at camp and wanted to be ready."

I took a few steps down the beach and picked up a flat pebble. I crouched down and threw it sidearm into the lake. It skipped twice. I'd never had a strong throwing arm. Elijah could skip rocks seven or eight jumps.

"Why are you asking me questions?" said Emily. "It was just an accident, wasn't it?"

"Of course it was," I said, wishing I could accept that. Every time I began to think that my doubts were explainable or unfounded, a new tentacle sprouted from the mystery in the form of another loose end. I wanted to cut off every last one of those tentacles and forget the whole story. But here was a new question.

"If Jerry was eager to run back to camp right away," I began, "then why didn't he?"

"He didn't?" she asked.

"No. By all accounts, he was missing from Orpheus from six in the morning onward. He never returned."

Emily could find no explanation. She maintained that Jerry had set off in a rush to return to camp at 7:00 a.m.

"Did you see or hear anything the morning you met him?" I asked. "Was there anyone else in the woods at that time?"

She shook her head again. "We didn't see anybody. We never did. The forest is deserted at that hour."

Then she caught herself. A vague expression crossed her face. It was one of those looks of recollection mixed with doubt.

"What is it, Emily?" I asked. "What did you see that morning?"

"No, I didn't see anything," she said. "But I heard something. It was maybe a minute or two after Jerry left. I was heading back to my camp, and I heard something."

"Heard what?"

"It was a car," she said. "On the road not too far off. It was skidding tires, you know."

"Did you hear anything else?"

"No. Just the tires screeching on the road. Then everything went back to silence."

Probably the drag racers or a driver avoiding the same fat raccoon I'd nearly run over in the rain earlier in the week.

"Tell me the truth, Miss Stone. What do you think really happened to Jerry and that man on the cliff?"

"I just can't figure anything but an accident," I said. "There are one or two anomalies, of course, that I would love to have explained."

"Like what?"

"Like what did Jerry do from seven a.m. until half past twelve when the witnesses said they saw him dive off the cliff?"

"There were witnesses?" she asked.

"A man and his son were fishing on the lake and heard a shout. They turned and saw one of the two dive or fall off Baxter's Rock. They reported it to the police."

Emily began to cry. I put my arm around her, and she bucked up in short order. She said it was hard to lose Jerry, but Jesus was helping her cope.

"Why do you think Jerry knew that man?" she asked after a few moments had passed.

"I believe there was some kind of connection between the two of them," I said. "Why else would they be there together?" I paused. "Unless they weren't."

Emily frowned and asked what I meant.

"What if Jerry fell hours before the other man? What if he fell minutes after leaving you in the woods? Baxter's Rock was not far off his path back to the camp. Maybe he decided to try to make the dive."

"He wouldn't have done that. He was in a hurry to get back. And I know him. He wasn't interested in that kind of thing."

I looked her up and down, wondering how well she had really known young Jerry. She was full of confidence and certainty about what he would or wouldn't have done, but she had no explanation for why he was diving off cliffs with a man more than twice his age. I decided to test her.

"Emily, when did you and Jerry start seeing each other?" I asked.

She cast her eyes downward. "About three weeks ago," she said, almost in a whisper.

"That's not very long."

"It's long enough," she said. "We told each other everything. I knew everything about him. His dog's name, his address and telephone number, his parents' names."

I told her as gently as I knew how that those were fairly superficial details that didn't rise to the level of deep familiarity between two kindred souls. That seemed to aggravate her. Of course, I should have known it would. I tried to apologize, but she challenged me back.

"You don't know anything about us," she said, weeping. "We shared everything. He even told me about an older woman he was in love with. That's how close we were."

Emily's high-pitched avowal echoed then faded into the north woods. I stepped forward and held her gaze with mine.

"Tell me about her."

◈

I had all but dismissed the story of Jerry Kaufman's older girlfriend. Probably just an adolescent crush like so many others. Like the one Isaac had had for my skinny-dipping aunt. But these crushes never go any further, I reasoned. What kind of woman seduces sixteen-year-old boys? And yet, according to Emily Grierson, Jerry had indeed gone beyond the usual longing and lusting after the beguiling older woman. She told me that his behavior had been sinful, but she'd forgiven him because he repented. He acknowledged his wrong and vowed never to do it again.

"Wait a minute," I said. "Are you telling me that Jerry . . . converted to Christianity?"

"Of course he did," she said. "I baptized him myself. In the lake. It was our secret." She paused a moment. "Of course Jesus knew."

God, that was a secret that I wasn't about to share with Jerry's parents. The poor things had suffered enough. I didn't know how they might react to such news. And the coincidence of Karl Merkleson's conversion didn't escape my notice. Perhaps there was a connection between the two dead men after all. I just couldn't see it.

"What exactly was Jerry's sin with this woman?" I asked.

"I don't like to think about it."

"You have to," I said. "It could be important."

"Who are you, anyway?" she asked. "I know you're not a cop. You're a girl, and there are no girl cops."

"Actually there are female police officers," I said, though I certainly had never met one.

"Then are you one?"

"No, I'm a reporter. And I'm investigating this diving accident for my paper." Okay that was a lie, but I wasn't a Christian, and I had no qualms about lying. Or committing other deadly sins, for that matter.

"He said he'd lain with her," said Emily, covering her face as she said it.

"He'd *lain* with her?" I asked. "You mean in the biblical sense? Or they took a nap?"

"This isn't funny, Miss Stone," she said through anger and tears.

I apologized. We stood there on my beloved secret beach, each one waiting for the other to say something. Finally, once she'd calmed down, I asked how the love affair had ended. Emily sniffled, wiped her eyes, and hiccoughed. Just once, thank God. There was no repeat of the violent attack she'd suffered when I informed her of Jerry's fate.

"It all happened suddenly. In the first days after he arrived at camp. The woman used him for her evil urges. When she'd had enough, she threw him over. Jerry thought he was in love with her. But that's just how Satan uses lust to steal men's souls. He convinces them that it's love, not sin." She stopped, gathered her breath, and recited from memory, "'Let the marriage bed be undefiled.' Hebrews, 13:4."

"For the record, Emily, I'm not a Christian, and I have different ideas on sex."

"Please don't use such foul language," she said. "I'd like to go now."

"Okay," I said. "But just one more question. Did Jerry tell you the woman's name?"

"Yes," she sighed. "He said her name was Mimi."

CHAPTER NINETEEN

Tommy Grierson was sitting with Cousin Max on the porch of the main cabin, sipping lemonade as they engaged in what appeared to be a lively argument. Max had probably goaded the reverend into a debate over what size sandals Jesus wore. Why did people insist on arguing about religion? I made straight for the porch, intending to break up the melee before someone got hurt.

"No," said Max. "I will not accept him. He's a fraud."

"Reconsider, my friend," pleaded Tommy Grierson. "This is a new day. It is inevitable and shall be so. Accept him."

I sped up my pace, just yards away now.

"Never!" shouted Max, trying to wriggle out of his chair. He was unsuccessful. "Roger Maris will never beat Babe Ruth's record. Never!"

I stopped my advance. Typical of Max, I thought. I should have guessed it was something like that.

"Brother, it's only a matter of time. He has thirty-four games to hit eleven homers. Maris will prevail."

"Can you turn a blind eye to the extra games? Maris will have had a hundred and sixty-two games. Ruth only a hundred and fifty-four."

Reverend Tommy reasoned that questioning Maris's achievement, if in fact he reached sixty-one home runs was wrongheaded. All records—pitching, batting, and fielding—even championships, would need to be reevaluated.

"Yes, that's right," said Max. "Just as you did with your New Testament."

❧

"I'll be fine," I said to Fadge, who was sitting at the wheel of his Nash, about to leave. The car had needed a jump to start. "I'm sure Donald Yarrow is nowhere near here. People are highly suggestible. And I'm the one who should be worried about you making it home safely in this bomb."

"Don't be fooled by outward appearances," he said. "This car looks like it was vandalized, but underneath the dents and scratches, she purrs like a kitten."

Just then the kitten backfired.

"Be sure to give those photos to Fred Peruso," I said, referring to the Montgomery County coroner. He was one of my guys back in New Holland, and I knew he would tell me if anything fishy could be seen in the pictures.

"How's he going to get in touch with you?" asked Fadge. "You don't have a phone, and I'm not driving back up here."

"He can send me a telegram if there's anything to report," I said. "Now don't worry about me. I'll be back in New Holland Sunday evening." Fadge looked up at me. "Unless something goes wrong."

"I thought I made it clear that I didn't want you nosing around here," said my old pal Norris Lester.

"I'm sorry to bother you again, but I have new information on Jerry that might be important."

"He died diving off a cliff, Miss Stone," he said. "What new information could you possibly have that would change that outcome?"

"He was seeing an older woman here on the lake. It was a romantic relationship."

Lester the Jester wanted to close the door on our conversation, but his interest was piqued. He asked me how much older she was.

"Thirty," I said. "Or thereabouts."

"And you say they had a romantic relationship?" he asked. I nodded. "But that's inappropriate, isn't it?"

"Possibly illegal," I said.

"But I still fail to see what this has to do with his death."

"The woman in question was also having an affair with the man who died with Jerry on the cliff."

Okay, that was a guess on my part. I had no hard evidence that Karl Merkleson and Miriam Abramowitz were breaking their marital vows, but I was convinced of it. Gayle Morton had pointed a finger at Miriam, suspecting that Karl might have come to Prospector Lake to meet his

JAMES W. ZISKIN   201

old lover, whom she identified as Miriam. And Isaac's account of Miriam's "accidental" encounter with Karl in Los Angeles strained credulity. It sounded more like an ambush to me. Add to that Karl Merkleson's baffling movements in Prospector Lake and his presence in the hunters' shelter, not two hundred yards from Miriam's bedroom window, and the circumstantial evidence was compelling. Even the Dopp kit pointed to Miriam. It had to have been a gift from one of the old gang. A gift that facilitated an adulterous affair.

"What do you want from me?" asked Lester.

"I'd like to speak to the other boys in his bunk," I said. "He must have told them something. Boys can't keep their mouths shut when it comes to sex. Especially sixteen-year-old boys."

"But you already know about this woman," he said. "Why do you need to bother our boys?"

"I'm a reporter," I said. "I'm always looking for corroboration."

Lester seemed to struggle with the idea. I was sure he wanted the whole mess to go away. Be forgotten. He probably wondered what benefit he could derive from granting my request. An expanded investigation into Jerry's love life would only draw attention to the camp. No matter the outcome of my questioning a dormitory full of adolescent boys, things could only get worse for Norris Lester and Camp Orpheus. If it became known that Jerry had bragged to his bunkmates about his conquest, questions might arise about how he had managed to slip his bonds so easily to meet his older lover. Where was the oversight? And who was running the asylum anyway? Norris Lester, Lester the Jester, that's who. I also wondered what benefit Lester could hope to gain by helping me. And yet he did.

"I know that Kenny Partridge was Jerry's closest friend here," he said. "I'll allow you to speak to him and only him."

Lester showed me to "REC TAL HALL," which was empty at ten in the morning. I wondered when it had last been evacuated. He left me in the first row of benches and told me to wait there. He went to fetch Kenny Partridge. The amphitheater seated five hundred, according to the placard in the entrance. For all intents and purposes, it was a large barn. I sat on my bench and looked around the hall. The stadium seating was built on an incline, assuring a good view for the entire audience. The stage was large enough to accommodate a symphony orchestra. I noticed some graffiti carved into the bench in a small hand. I squinted to read it.

Question: What's the difference between a conductor and a sack of s**t?
Answer: The sack.

Oh, my. Sounded like something my little friend Herbie might say.

"Miss Stone," came Lester's voice from behind me. "This is Kenny. Jerry Kaufman's friend."

I looked up at a kid who appeared to be three years younger than Jerry. He was cute, like a little brown-haired cherub.

"May I speak to Kenny alone?" I asked.

Lester pursed his lips. I was sure he was torn between two opposite and conflicting desires: one, to hear all the dirty little secrets, and two, to avoid any knowledge of the dirty little secrets. In the end, he opted for the latter.

Once we were alone, Kenny stared at me.

"Are you the lady Jerry was balling?" he asked.

I choked. "No. I never met him," I said, recalling Fadge's admonition about outward appearances. This kid was no angel.

"Sorry. When Lester the Jester came to get me, I just thought you must be the one. You don't look thirty, though."

"Thanks for the compliment," I said. "Still, you should learn some manners."

"You can't blame me. A pretty chick shows up asking about Jerry. I just assumed it was Mimi."

"I'm not Mimi. But since you brought up her name, what can you tell me about her?"

Kenny looked me up and down, the little pervert. He smiled, and I thought I would never trust first impressions again.

He squinted at me. "Who are you again? Why should I answer your questions?"

"You should answer my questions because I'm pretty, and boys will do anything for a pretty girl. That's a rule." I was a little impatient.

Kenny gulped, and his attitude changed. He scratched his pubescent cheek, which was flush and smooth. Not even the hint of a beard. Like a baby's bottom.

"Jerry was a nice guy," he said finally. "And he was good-looking, you know. Girls liked him. But he wasn't just after a good time. He was different. More interested in love. At least he thought he was."

"How do you mean?"

"Well, it was a little hard to take him seriously, what with him falling in love with a different girl every couple of days. Every time, he swore it was true love."

"Kind of sweet," I said. "Boys your age are usually after just one thing."

"He was a romantic. I'm not sure exactly what that means, outside of music. But Jerry thought he was looking for love, not sex."

"Did he ever talk to you about Mimi?" I asked.

Kenny nodded slowly. "Yeah, he used to tell me about the stuff they did. That was almost a month ago. Right after camp opened."

"How did he meet her?"

"Jerry was picked to play in a concert in the village. He met Mimi while they were rehearsing for the concert. She was one of the musicians."

"How did Jerry feel about her?"

Kenny gave a halfhearted chuckle. "He was madly in love with her. He said they did it in her car after the first rehearsal, but they almost got caught."

"Did they find a safer place to do it after that?" I asked. My God, I was discussing sex with a teenage boy.

"Yeah. A motel in the village. But that was risky, Jerry said. The third time they found an abandoned shack somewhere in the woods."

"Did he tell you anything else?"

Kenny couldn't quite suppress a smile. "You mean the details? Sure."

"No, not the details," I said. "Anything about Mimi?"

Kenny shook his head. "The time in the shelter was the last time. The whole thing lasted less than a week."

"What happened? Why did they stop?"

"Mimi just dumped him," said Kenny with a shrug. "Jerry was broken up about it. But then he met some girl named Emily. He seemed to get over Mimi pretty quick."

"Did he tell you what you wanted to know?" asked Lester.

"He confirmed what I believed," I said.

"Excellent. That means you won't need to come back here again."

I thanked him for his hospitality and set off across the compound toward my car. There were a few campers milling about. Others were rushing to lessons or rehearsals, instrument cases in tow. I stopped in front of the totem pole and looked over my shoulder to see if Norris Lester was watching me. I couldn't see him anywhere.

I turned back around and stared at the totem pole. Flyers of all colors, mimeographed and handwritten, were stapled and tacked onto the face of the thing. I glanced at a couple of them. A lime-green paper caught my attention. "Summer Fête Concert August 13, 1961." I pulled it down from the pole and examined it more closely.

Piano Quartet No.1, W. A. Mozart
Adagio and Rondo Concertante, F. Schubert
Prospector Lake Chamber Players
Miriam Abramowitz, piano
Lucia Blanchard, cello
Lionel Somers, viola
Jerrold Kaufman, violin

I drew an uneasy breath, reflecting on the sum and substance of what Kenny Partridge had told me. And the program spelled it out in black and lime-green as well. I'd heard Simon call Miriam Mimi myself. I had all the proof I needed. The thought of Miriam sleeping with a sixteen-year-old boy in cars, motels, and shacks turned my stomach.

I'd found a close connection between Jerry Kaufman and Karl Merkleson. They had both been having an affair with Miriam Abramowitz, one after the other, it seemed. I wasn't sure how their last dive had played out the previous Saturday morning, but a jealous altercation atop the cliff looked like a good bet. Or were their deaths more nefarious than that? Perhaps Simon had caught wind of the affairs and shoved the two off the cliff. Or Gayle Morton. Or even her father, Owen Pierce.

I folded the concert program into my purse and headed to my car. Norris Lester was probably right, I thought. I didn't have any reason to return to Camp Orpheus, and I wouldn't look back again.

Before presenting the information to Tiny Terwilliger, I wanted to know which motel Miriam had used to debauch Jerry. Tom's Lakeside Motel was the closest inn to Camp Orpheus, and it was on the way to the police station. I pulled into the lot as I drove north on Route 15.

No one was manning the registration desk when I entered the office. I rang the bell to no effect, so I lit a cigarette and waited. Then I noticed the register sitting unattended on the desk, not three feet away from me.

I tapped the bell again. Still no one. I inched closer to the register, at first throwing a casual look at the names. Then, as the office was still empty, I flipped through a few pages. Before I knew what was happening, I had rotated the register 180 degrees and was poring over it. With the prospect of discovery hanging over me, I decided to concentrate on the first week of August, which I figured held the most promise. For one thing, I wanted to see if any names jumped out that might suggest Mimi or Miriam or Abramowitz. Her maiden name was Berg, so I was on the lookout for that. But I was also looking for a name that might be Gayle Morton. Even if Tom Waller had searched the register in good faith the last time I'd visited, how could I be sure he'd done a thorough job? I wanted to check for myself.

The minutes stretched on, and still no one entered the office. I ran a finger down one page then another. I wasn't finding any Mimis or Gayles, but on Sunday, August 6, Lucia Blanchard checked in at 4:03 p.m. That was interesting, but Lucia, oversexed wife-swapper, was not Mimi. My finger resumed its course down the page. It didn't get far. My cigarette dropped to the floor. I strained to read the cursive writing before me. A little past 6:00 p.m., August 6, Isaac Eisenstadt checked into unit sixteen.

I didn't have time to exhale, to grasp the significance of this information, or even to crush out my wayward cigarette with my shoe. I heard a toilet flush in the back room behind the desk. I spun the register back around and feigned interest in the local leisure activities brochures near the door. My cigarette butt hissed from the floor several feet away. A door opened, and Tom Waller entered the registration office. I reeled around, trying to appear casual but probably looking terrified instead. His skin was even browner than the last time I'd seen him. He flashed me another of his lascivious grins, turning on the charm in his open shirt and tight bathing suit.

"Just can't stay away?" he asked.

"I try, believe me," I said, my voice aquiver.

He chuckled, my sarcasm flying high over his head. I had to say something, but I couldn't find any breath. The appearance of Isaac's name in the register had kicked me in the stomach.

"Can I help you with something?" he asked.

I tried to smile but still could find no voice.

"I think you dropped your cigarette," he said, making his way around the desk to retrieve it. "We like to use ashtrays around here. 'Smokey says care will prevent nine out of ten forest fires.'"

I forced a stiff laugh, and Tom stubbed out the butt in a tin ashtray on the desk.

"I wanted to ask you if any of the Arcadia Lodge folks ever took a room here," I said a mite too hoarsely. I cleared my throat. "Say, three or four weeks ago."

"You seem to have the notion that everyone stays here," he said. "I'm not real comfortable giving out information about my guests."

"I wouldn't ask if it weren't important," I said.

"What do the people from Arcadia Lodge have to do with Mrs. Morton's insurance?"

He had me there, so I lied.

"That's what I asked my boss, Mr. Stephenson. But he said it wasn't my job to question him. He just told me to come back up here and find out if any of them had stayed here this summer."

Tom Waller thought it over, smacking his lips as he did.

"I know it's asking a lot," I said. "Especially since you're friendly with some of them."

He stopped the smacking. "Friendly with who?"

"Isaac Eisenstadt, for one. He told me he spoke to you Monday. He stopped by, and you told him Gayle Morton was staying here."

Waller frowned and scowled at me. I thought I'd gone too far too fast. He was suspicious. I was wrong.

"Look, I know Eisenstadt, but we're not friends," he began. "Nice-enough fellow, but I only know him because he spent a couple of nights here earlier in the month."

"I'm confused," I said, playing dumb. "Mr. Eisenstadt took a room here this month?" He nodded. "But he has a cabin of his own at Arcadia. Why would he need a room here?"

Tom Waller just stared at me. He wasn't going to answer that.

"But did you speak to him last Monday about Gayle Morton?"

He squeezed his lips into a sort of pout and shook his head. "Nope. Last time I saw him was about two weeks ago when he stayed here."

My heart was pounding. "Has anyone else from Arcadia stayed here this summer?"

"Like who?"

"A young woman with black hair." I said, choking up. "Someone named Mimi."

"Nope. But I still don't get why you're asking questions about those people. What do they have to do with insurance?"

"I don't know," I said, wiping a tear before it could fall. He noticed anyway. "I don't know," I repeated. "Mr. Stephenson is a horrible boss." And I ran out of the office.

I was reeling. I ran to my car and jumped in, starting the engine and switching on the radio as if by rote. The station was playing Chubby Checker. "The Twist." Damn Simon. I punched another button and got "Puppy Love." Paul Anka, for God's sake! I switched it off. My temples throbbed even as I regained control of my emotions. Isaac had lied to me, that much was sure. And it looked unlikely that Miriam had taken a room at the Lakeside Motel. It was possible, of course, that she'd taken Jerry Kaufman to a different motel, but I was too rattled in that moment to think or care where.

My face was burning, and my mouth had gone dry. Why would Isaac lie to me? What was he hiding? The answer occurred to me without much coaxing: he had met someone there. A lover. I was sure. But this had happened before my arrival on Prospector Lake. Had he lied to me because he thought I'd be jealous of his conquests? I didn't care what he'd done before he'd done it with me. I'd had flings of my own, after all. Plenty of flings. That wasn't what bothered me. It was the lie.

Sitting at the wheel of my car, I dived deeper into dark thoughts. Who was it he'd met at the motel? Three names came to mind immediately. And they made me feel sick to my stomach. Gayle Morton, Miriam Abramowitz, and Lucia Blanchard. I knew for certain that he'd already slept with two of them. He'd told me about his indiscretion with Gayle, and Miriam herself had confirmed her trespasses with Isaac. And now I had proof that he'd checked into the Lakeside Motel within two hours of the man-eater, Lucia Blanchard.

CHAPTER TWENTY

I followed Route 15 north through the village, past the police station, and didn't stop. The lake stretched out to my right, sparkling this late August day, beckoning me to jump in for a swim. I was in a skirt and blouse, my bathing suit back at the cabin. I drove a few miles north of the village, to the top of the lake, and the road began to turn east. Then south. By the time I'd reached Tennyson on the eastern shore of the lake, I was hungry and exhausted. It had been an eventful morning, and I'd missed my lunch again.

I pulled over to the shoulder and switched off the ignition. Prospector Lake was about three miles wide. Staring west into the afternoon sun, I thought I could see Aunt Lena's dock. And Baxter's Rock must have been the high ground a little to the south of it. I couldn't be sure without a map or binoculars. Funny. Even after so many vacations on the lake, I just wasn't sure where anything stood.

That was true of my investigation, as well. The two deaths no longer appeared to be unrelated, but that didn't mean there was any foul play. Karl and Jerry might still have fallen accidentally. Or had they struggled at the top of the cliff? I revisited that question again as I sat in my car, watching the lake. I wondered. What evidence might point to a struggle? Or, on the other hand, was there any evidence that indicated no struggle had taken place?

For starters, I reasoned, who strips down to his underwear to wrestle atop a cliff? It was absurd. It made no sense. How had these two men died side by side? The more I considered the unexplainable, the more I leaned toward a different time of death for each.

I climbed out of my car and strolled down to the shore. It was a quiet spot, sheltered by overgrowth. There was no beach, just some rocks. I unbuttoned my blouse and stripped it off. Then I shimmied out of my skirt. No sense putting dry clothes on over wet underthings, I thought, and removed those as well. I dived into the lake from a smooth rock and swam for at least a half hour. The cool water felt grand, and I wanted to swim forever.

A motorboat sped by about two hundred yards out into the lake. A water-skier trailed behind, bouncing over the waves. They surely couldn't see me; I was invisible at that distance. But I could see them. And, being downwind, I could hear the buzzing of the outboard and even the shouts of the skier. I watched as he let go of the towline and sank gradually into the lake. The pilot cut the engine, and the water served as a natural brake, slowing the boat as if it were on a long leash. Just a fraction of a second later, the motor's buzzing dropped in pitch to a low growl. It couldn't have been more than a half second's delay, but just enough to be later than what I'd seen. Science, I thought. How interesting.

But then I remembered something Terwilliger had told me about the eyewitnesses' account of the diver they'd seen at Baxter's Rock. If I recalled correctly, they'd said the sound of the impact on the rocks took a second or two to reach them out on the water. That didn't seem right. I remembered my seventh-grade science class and the speed of sound. Eleven hundred twenty-six feet per second. If the sound had taken even just a second to reach the witnesses, they would have had to be nearly four hundred yards away. What could they possibly see from that distance?

It was probably just Terwilliger exaggerating for effect. He seemed to enjoy making me green with his description of the splat. Nevertheless, I decided I had to ask him about what exactly the witnesses had seen and heard. I wondered if I should locate them and speak to them myself. But then I dipped my head back under the water and willed the whole mess away. I didn't care as much about the loose ends and the unexplained details now that I knew Isaac had broken my trust.

I swam to shore and lay on the flat rock to dry myself in the sun, still thinking of Isaac. I realized just how much I loved being with him, just how difficult it would be to say good-bye, how much I would miss his touch. But I knew the end was upon us. A short, torrid affair gone the way of all my other affairs.

I heard a cough. And given my recent musings on the speed of sound, I was sure its owner was not hundreds of yards away. I grabbed my blouse and tried to cover up, twisting around to see who was there. It was that slob, Tiny Terwilliger, standing on top of the embankment, not forty feet away.

"I've told you about nude bathing on the lake," he said. He had to shout since he was downwind of me.

I, on the other hand, didn't need to shout to be heard, but I did. I called him the foulest names I could conjure, demanded that he back off and turn away so I could dress. He laughed as I yelled, but eventually he complied. I scrambled into my clothes, practically in tears. I would have strangled him if I'd thought my hands would fit around his sweaty neck. Now I would never look at my naked body the same way again. It was as if he'd ruined me for myself.

Once I'd dressed and climbed up to the road, Terwilliger lectured me again about swimming nude in the lake. I reminded him that we were not in his jurisdiction, and he could jolly well go to hell.

"Take it easy," he said, grinning from ear to ear. "I'm just having some fun."

"What do you want?" I demanded.

"Nothing. I just seen your car parked on the side of the road and got worried. Imagine my surprise to find you . . ." He coughed, his feeble attempt to appear circumspect. "Well, never mind."

I pushed past him to get to my car, but he called after me. He apologized and said his vision wasn't good anyway. He hadn't seen anything but a shape on the rock.

"I need to speak to you later about some new information I got this morning," I said, wiping my eyes. "But right now, I can't. I just want to be alone."

☙

Aunt Lena told me she'd been worried when I didn't turn up for lunch. Max had no such concerns.

"She's a big girl," he said, turning the page of his newspaper. "She's twenty-five, after all. Not married, but these are modern times we live in."

"Stop with the married talk," said Aunt Lena.

"Perhaps she'll marry that Isaac fellow. I believe he would make a fine husband. Don't you agree, Ellie?"

"I've decided never to marry," I said. "Like you, Max. I want to feel the sting of regret, as you say. It will remind me I'm alive."

"Don't talk that way, Ellie," said Aunt Lena.

"Oh, look," said Max, referring to his paper. "Joe Palooka suspects Peligro has slipped some frog venom to Felipe. This doesn't look good."

"And your weather forecast was off, too," I said. "Look out the window. It's started to rain. It's pouring buckets. Good luck seeing the eclipse."

Max shrugged. "No great loss, my dear. It's only a ninety-eight point six."

⚮

Bags packed and readied for the next day's departure, Lena and Max finished off the last lime for their evening cocktails. We were dressed and ready to go to Arcadia, though I was hardly in the mood for it. My aunt suspected it was something Max had said about my getting married, but she was far off the mark. For his part, Max sensed I was not to be crossed, and he was quite solicitous, offering to pour my drink and passing me the tray of the scraps of cheese and crumbled crackers, which, like the lime, were among the last of the cupboard's stores.

"We haven't checked the Yarrow report, have we?" asked Max. "Would you like your aunt to switch on the radio, Ellie?"

I rolled my eyes. "Sure," I said. "I was wondering what was missing from this wet evening. Escaped murderers."

After the news of the impending eclipse and the Berlin crisis, the biggest story of the day was the frantic search for a missing woman from the campgrounds in Tennyson. She'd disappeared in the afternoon from her trailer. That must have been around the time I was swimming. Her husband reported her disappearance to the local sheriff, who contacted the state police.

The story unsettled me, especially given how vulnerable I had been; I'd left my car unlocked on the shoulder of the road and then jumped into the lake without a bathing suit. The news about Isaac's stay at the Lakeside Motel didn't help my mood either.

"What's the matter, Ellie?" asked Aunt Lena. "You look terrible."

I gulped down my drink and rose from my seat. The whiskey burned my nose and the back of my throat, and I savored it. The rush hit me, and I smiled at my aged relatives.

"Time to go," I said.

CHAPTER
TWENTY-ONE

Isaac realized something was wrong as soon as I arrived. And it wasn't only the fact I'd been drenched walking from the car to the Great Lodge. I'd ceded the umbrella to Lena and Max, who made their entrance dry and comfortable. There was a large group of residents and guests already present, all with a drink and appetizer in hand. Cigarette smoke wafted up to the pitched ceiling, and the chatter of a cocktail party filled the room. Isaac took me to one side to ask what was bothering me. I was through being quiet, holding my tongue, and sitting on my hands. I told him there were two things bothering me, but I had no intention of causing a scene.

"Maybe we should go to my cabin," he said.

We slipped out the side door and raced across the compound, trying to beat the rain. He held the door for me, and I went inside. He switched on the light and offered me a seat on one of the armchairs. I waited.

"So tell me, Ellie. What is it?" he asked once he'd sat down opposite me.

I debated which way I should parry first: Isaac's motel stay or Miriam's seduction of a minor. I chose the latter.

"I discovered something quite disturbing this morning," I said. "I spoke to Jerry Kaufman's little girlfriend."

"Who's Jerry Kaufman?" he asked.

"The young man who died next to Karl."

Isaac slapped his forehead and swore. "Sorry. I forgot his name."

"I had a long chat with Emily," I continued. "She said that Jerry had been involved with an older woman."

"Wow. This sounds juicy. Tell me more."

"It's not a funny story," I said, and his smile disappeared. "She told me the woman was thirty years old. And she said it was Miriam."

Isaac choked then laughed. He said it was impossible, he couldn't believe it. How would she even have known the kid? I opened my purse and retrieved the concert flyer I'd taken from the totem pole at Camp Orpheus that morning. Isaac unfolded it and scanned the details. He jumped a bit when he saw the names.

"I just can't believe it," he repeated. "This doesn't prove anything. Miriam is one of the founding members of the Prospector Lake Chamber Players. She does this every year."

"Seduces young boys?" I asked, and just as sassy as it sounds.

"Why should we believe the hearsay of some girl? I've known Miriam my whole life, and she would never do such a thing. Do you have any corroborating evidence?"

I nodded. "Jerry's best friend at camp gave me her name as well. He said that Jerry had fallen in love with her, that they'd had sex in her car, at a motel, and in the woods."

"He knew her name, or did you prompt him?"

"I find that question insulting," I said. "I did not give him the name. As a matter of fact, he thought I might be Mimi when he first saw me."

Isaac shot out of his seat. "Mimi?" he asked. "I thought you said those kids had identified her as Miriam."

"They did," I said then clarified. "That is, they said her name was Mimi."

Isaac drew a deep sigh of relief. "But Miriam is not Mimi, Ellie," he said softly. "You've mistaken her for someone else."

"I've heard Simon call her Mimi with my own ears," I said. "And Jerry's friend said that Mimi was in the Prospector Lake Chamber Players. Miriam is Mimi, all right."

Isaac paced back and forth, twisting the flyer in his hands as he thought. He frowned and said again that it didn't make sense. "Simon is the only person who ever called her Mimi," he said finally. "I've never called her that. No one here does. It's Simon's pet name for her. He uses it when he's a little annoyed."

I shrugged. "If you have another explanation, I'd love to hear it," I said.

Isaac had nothing to add. He retook his seat, and I thought of how to open with the information about the Lakeside Motel. Isaac looked ill, in terrible pain as he considered the significance of my evidence. I hated to kick him while he was down, but I reminded myself that I was the injured party. So I teed up my second ball and gave it a whack.

"The other thing that's bothering me is more personal," I began. Isaac

JAMES W. ZISKIN   215

looked at me, his eyes sparkling brown with the green flecks. "This is hard to ask," I said. "Why did you lie to me about the Lakeside Motel?"

He cocked his head like a confused dog and asked what I was talking about. I studied his face. His brow was knitted just so to communicate confusion, not anger, his mouth drawn just tight enough to show concern, but not guilt. Then he blinked, and his eyes turned perhaps five degrees to the right for a split second.

"I visited the motel this morning," I continued. "I wanted to know if Miriam had taken a room there with Jerry Kaufman." I paused.

"Well, did she?" he asked in a small voice from the back of his throat. I shook my head. "No, she didn't."

We stared long and deep into each other's eyes. His were soft. They nearly trembled under my scrutiny. Mine were strong, until they started to cloud. His face blurred, but it wasn't until I blinked that I realized it was my tears that were to blame. I looked away and wiped my cheeks. Damn. I'd promised no scenes.

Then Isaac was at my side, on his knees, holding me in his arms. I told myself to stop. This was foolish. Weeping over a man I barely knew. But it was more than the loss of a lover. It was the loss of a trust that I'd granted to him. This hadn't been a mere roll in the hay for me. I was realizing that too late. It had only been a week since we'd first seen each other on the dock, but time was not a factor in my desire for him. Empathy, attraction, pheromones, and intellectual compatibility. I'd liked his face. I'd loved it. I'd loved staring into his eyes, no matter what we were doing or saying. Even if we were doing nothing at all. And my skin jumped at his touch. It was a thrilling sensation, completely unexpected and involuntary, and unlike anything I'd ever experienced before. I was deluding myself if I thought this summer fling was nothing more than a brief indulgence. Simon had seen through me and hit me hard with that label. He knew it would sting more than anything he might say. And I had denied my feelings, even as I felt them growing. Even as I feared them.

"Ellie, I lied to you," he said. I couldn't look at him. Not in the state I was in. "I lied because I didn't want you to get the wrong idea."

I couldn't speak. At length he continued, gazing at me with all the contrition one face could muster. Then he took my hands in his.

"I didn't go to Tom's on Monday as I told you. That was a lie. I knew Gayle was staying on the lake because she came to see me."

When I didn't answer him, he continued. "She arrived Thursday and showed up here that evening. I was shocked, of course. I certainly wasn't expecting her. We hadn't stayed in touch after that time in Hollywood." He wiped a tear from my cheek. "Ellie, don't cry. I swear nothing happened with her."

I pulled away and wiped my own tears. "You're still lying," I said.

"No, it's the truth. Gayle came to me to ask if I'd seen Karl. I said no, of course. No one here had any idea he was in Prospector Lake."

I shook my head. "Miriam knew," I said. "Who do you think gave him that monogrammed Dopp kit? They were meeting in a hunters' shelter behind camp. Not two hundred yards away."

"What? Ellie, what do you have against Miriam? You've accused her of everything under the sun. First the boy and now Karl."

"She's the connection, Isaac."

"What?"

"Miriam is the link between Karl and Jerry Kaufman. Nothing else connects them to each other. Just Miriam. Mimi. She was carrying on with both of them."

Isaac eased himself back into a chair and glared at me. For a long moment, as if trying to see through a fog. He frowned and ran a hand through his hair. I thought he hated me.

"You're saying Miriam, a woman I grew up with, murdered a boy of sixteen and one of her oldest friends?"

"No," I said. He waited. "I'm saying she is the link between the two of them."

"How is that different?"

"They either died accidentally or in a struggle. I don't know why they might have struggled, unless it was over her."

Isaac drew a deep breath. "So where does that leave us? You accuse Miriam of terrible, unspeakable things, but you haven't convinced me. Everything can be explained."

"Karl's presence on the lake? His Dopp kit in the shack two hundred yards away? The boy meeting Mimi in motels and cars? And, yes, in a hunters' shelter?"

Isaac struggled to find an explanation to cast doubt on my conclusions. He said that Karl might have seen her, but that was not proof of an affair. And the boy? "What about Lucia Blanchard?" he asked. "Maybe she was the one who seduced him."

"Mimi is Miriam," I said. "Not Lucia."

Isaac stood and crossed the room. He didn't have an answer for that. But he did have something to say.

"Maybe you should go, Ellie. I'm not feeling very festive after this talk."

That only angered me. After his lies, he was blaming me, the messenger. I stood and smoothed my skirt. I strode across the room to make him look me in the eye.

"I'll leave," I said. "But first you're going to tell me why you lied to me."

"I don't know what you're talking about."

"It was a lie of omission," I said. "But a lie nonetheless. While I was at the Lakeside Motel today, I saw the register. I know you spent a couple of nights there. And you never mentioned it to me."

He tried to laugh it off. "I have to tell you what I did weeks before I met you? I took a room there to free up this cabin for an old friend of my father's. Does that satisfy you?"

He may have been telling the truth, but I still had one more salvo for him. "It'll satisfy me when you admit that you took a room at the Lakeside Motel to meet Lucia Blanchard. She checked in two hours before you did."

He looked surprised.

"Good night," I said. "And good-bye."

∂⊃

Surrounded by three suitors, Aunt Lena was holding court on a sofa in the Great Lodge. She sparkled, a drink in one hand while the men ate out of the other. At the same time, Max looked to be making some important and long-winded point to Ruth Hirsch. I knew he hadn't paused for breath since his glass was full. No one seemed concerned that the sky was completely clouded over and that there would be no view of the eclipse this night.

I didn't have the heart to tear Max and Lena away just because I had to leave. It was their last night on Prospector Lake, after all, and they were having so much fun. I waited for an opportunity to whisper in Lena's ear and told her I had to speak with Chief Terwilliger about something important. I gave her my car keys and said I'd make my own way back to Cedar Haven. She frowned and asked if I really had to go. I hadn't even eaten yet.

"I'm fine," I said, patting her hand. "You and Max enjoy yourselves. I'll catch up with you back at camp."

I started to make my way toward the door, chatting casually with whoever showed up in my path. I came face-to-face with Simon, who was alone near the drinks table. His cheeks were peaked, eyes puffy. He smiled at me.

"Can I get you a drink?" he asked. "Isaac went out and bought a couple of bottles of your Dewar's today."

"Thanks, no," I said. "I'm afraid I have to meet that awful Chief Terwilliger just now. I have to go."

"You're leaving Sunday for home?" he asked. I nodded. "Listen, Ellie," he began carefully. "I wanted to apologize for my behavior toward you this past week. I have no excuse for it. You're a swell girl, and I acted like an ass."

A sad smile crossed my lips. I reached out and touched his hand gently. "Don't give it a second thought. I think you're a swell man, too."

I kissed him on the cheek, and he gave me a little hug. The tension between us was forgotten; I was sure it was the tumor that gave him the violent, antisocial fits. Poor thing. He had such a big heart. Loved big and hated bigger. We said good night, and I headed for the door. I paused at the threshold to look back and throw him a small wave. He had turned to face the party. He was alone, a little stooped in his posture. I sensed I would never see him again. Then I caught sight of Waldo Coons, half-hidden in the shadows. He was still staring at me.

⁂

There exists a reckless urge in humans to suffer harm when they feel they've been wronged. The injury serves as punishment for the person who has aggrieved us. We comfort ourselves with fantasies of how wretched that person will feel when injury befalls us. But it's like an insurance policy: you have to lose to win. That was the state of my mind as I left Arcadia Lodge that night. My death or mutilation or drowning by rain would be fitting reparation for Isaac's having asked me to leave. I imagined myself set upon by Donald Yarrow as I crossed the woods alone under a dark, violent thunderstorm, and the responsibility would be all Isaac's. Of course I didn't actually want to be attacked, struck by lightning, murdered, or drowned, but anger coupled with pain is a powerful concoction. It can make us take chances.

And so I did.

The woods opened before me like a great muddy maw. I dared fate to put an escaped murderer in my wet path. I wanted the headlines to read that I had been sent away from the party by the host despite strong winds and pelting rains. But nothing happened. I was terrified all right, and soaked to the skin. I thought I heard twigs cracking and a man breathing, but that wasn't possible, given the roar of the storm. I made it back to Cedar Haven, pruney, but without incident. After changing into some dry clothes, I locked myself inside the main cabin and poured a stiff drink. I waited for Lena and Max to return.

I wanted to listen to the radio to change my state of mind, but the weather was wreaking havoc with the reception. Switching the dial back and forth between the Montreal classical music program, which blasted static with each thunderbolt, and a station in Burlington, Vermont, broadcasting the latest news on Donald Yarrow, I managed to make an hour pass. Another drink greased the skids. Then, the glare of headlights lit the room through the window. Aunt Lena and Max. Finally. It was a quarter past eleven.

I rose to meet them at the door and frowned at my bad luck. It wasn't my Dodge at all parked on the grass outside, but Tiny Terwilliger's rumbling shipwreck of a truck instead.

"I was looking for you over at Arcadia," he said, standing drenched in the doorway.

"What for?" I asked.

Terwilliger gaped at me. "You said you wanted to tell me something. Some new information you had."

I apologized that I had no beer to offer him, but he waved me off and produced a quart bottle from behind his back. He removed his wet coat and hung it on the rack by the door.

"Snagged this from the good folks over at Arcadia Lodge." He smiled, holding up the bottle of beer. "So what's the big news?"

I poured myself another drink and lit a cigarette. If I had to spend time in his company, I at least wanted an anesthetic. We sat opposite each other before the fireplace, which I'd lit to fight the chill of the rain.

"I spoke to Jerry Kaufman's little girlfriend today," I began. "And she put me onto something."

"What's that?" he asked, swigging directly from the bottle.

"Would you like a glass?"

"No thanks. I'll manage just fine. What did she tell you?"

"That Jerry had an older girlfriend before she met him. A couple of weeks ago. Someone named Mimi."

"And?"

"And she was thirty years old."

Terwilliger whistled and cocked his head to one side in what looked like admiration. He smiled, sucked some more beer out of the bottle, then let loose a window-rattling belch.

"Sorry about that," he said, remembering his good manners. "Better out than in."

"I also spoke to Jerry's best friend at Camp Orpheus," I said, suppressing a shudder. "He confirmed that the woman's name was Mimi. He said Jerry used to meet her in a motel here on the lake. I don't know which one, but it wasn't Tom's. I checked. And they met in a hunters' shelter, too."

"There's a hunters' shack behind Arcadia," he said. "Isn't that where you found that leather kit?"

"Exactly. I think it's possible they met there, but there are lots of those sheds in the woods."

"So what else did the girl say?"

"She said Mimi was a musician. A member of the Prospector Lake Chamber Players. Jerry performed with them in a concert two weeks ago in the square in the village."

"I remember that," said Terwilliger. "I was there to keep the peace."

"A rowdy crowd, was it?" I asked with a smirk.

He shook his head. "Bunch of eggheads and old ladies. Dullest concert I ever heard. Except maybe for the one the other night at Arcadia Lodge. Just a lot of tinkling piano and sawing on violins. They had three of those. A small one, a medium, and a large."

"Yes, I've seen those big ones," I said. "Hard to hold under your chin."

Terwilliger frowned at me, perhaps catching a whiff of my sarcasm. But maybe not. "So this kid was getting his jollies with an older gal," he said. "What's that got to do with him falling off the cliff?"

"Do you remember who played the piano that day in the square?" I asked.

"No."

"It was one of the women from Arcadia. Simon Abramowitz's wife."

"Is he the one who gave the John Birch boys such a hard time?"

"That's right. His wife is Miriam. She's the one with the long, black hair."

"Yeah, I know who you mean. The one with all those curves."

"The very one," I said, thinking what a revolting man he was.

"I thought you said the older girlfriend was named Mimi."

"That's right. Mimi is a common pet name for Miriam."

"Are you saying her husband got wind of it and pushed the kid off the cliff?" he asked, squinting at me in the low light.

"No, I don't think so."

"Why not?" he asked. The idea seemed to appeal to him.

"For one thing, it doesn't explain how Karl Merkleson happened to die at the same time in the same place."

Terwilliger knitted his brow and sipped his beer. "Maybe this Simon fellow pushed the kid over the edge, and Merkleson saw it. So he had to take care of him, too."

"Did he ask him to strip down to his skivvies first?" I asked. "No, it doesn't add up."

"Then what's she got to do with all this? I don't get it."

I stubbed out my cigarette in the ashtray on the end table. "Miriam was also Karl Merkleson's former lover. I believe he came to Prospector Lake to see her."

"So both of them?" He laughed. "Wow. She gets around."

I tried to ignore his mirth at the demise of the two men. "But my point isn't so much that Miriam gets around, but that she finally provides a connection between the two victims."

The chief interrupted his belly laugh long enough to give my words some thought. Then he threw his head back and glugged down the last of his beer. I couldn't believe my eyes, but he'd choked the life out of the bottle in a matter of minutes.

"So maybe *she* pushed them off the cliff," he said, wiping his lips with the back of his hand. He placed the empty quart on the table.

"No, I don't see any reason for her to have done that. But I do believe that her relationship with those two men had something to do with their deaths. Maybe they were fighting over her. But that seems unlikely as well."

"Why's that?" he asked. "It seems as good an explanation as any."

"Because Karl Merkleson stripped down to his underwear. Why would he do that unless he wanted to dive off the cliff and didn't have a bathing suit with him?"

"I don't see it as a problem. People do all sorts of strange things. It doesn't bother me at all that he was in his underwear. What else doesn't make sense to you?"

"His shirt."

"What's that?"

"His shirt. The one that was found in the lake. It's not the kind of shirt a dandy like Karl Merkleson would have worn."

"Some vacationers found it near his wallet. His driver's license was inside."

"I just don't believe he would buy shirts at Sears," I said.

Terwilliger chewed on that for a while. "Did the kid's little girlfriend tell you anything else?" he asked finally.

"Nothing very helpful. But she did say she heard a car screeching on the road just after she left Jerry that morning. Do you think it might be important?"

"Probably not," he said.

"Maybe the driver saw something."

Terwilliger shrugged but had no answer. He also had no beer. Eyeing my drink, he licked his lips.

"You may have a drink if you like," I said. "But you're not drinking from the bottle. There are glasses on the bar."

"I don't mind if I do," he said. "Just to wet my whistle." And he got up to pour himself a tall whiskey.

Poor Aunt Lena. At this rate, she would run out of teacups, chairs, and tumblers by night's end. I had no intention of washing the glass he was slobbering over.

"A love triangle," said Terwilliger, sitting down again with his drink. "And I thought they were just a couple of queers, committing acts against nature."

The radio continued to buzz softly from across the room, rain drummed on the roof, and thunder boomed above from time to time. We sat quietly for a while. Then I asked him if he had any insider information on Donald Yarrow that the public didn't know about. He emptied his glass, grimaced, and coughed, eyes watering.

"Strong stuff you drink," he said. "You're a different kind of gal, aren't you?" I shrugged. "You know, I've grown to kind of like you," he continued. I was mortified. "You've got spunk. And you're easy on the eyes."

I groaned. He was pretty drunk.

"About Donald Yarrow?" I prompted.

"The state police have been consulting me on that," he said, serious all of a sudden. "We know he's here on the lake. Kidnapped a lady from the campgrounds near Tennyson. We're closing in. We'll get him soon." And he winked at me.

"I had another question for you," I said at length. "Your witnesses, the man and his son who saw one of the two men fall. You said they heard the impact of one of the bodies on the rocks?"

"That's what they said."

"How far away were they when they heard it?"

"I don't know," he said. "Maybe seventy-five yards. A hundred. Why?"

"Because you said the sound took a second or two to reach them. That struck me as strange."

He leaned forward in his seat to scrutinize me. "What are you getting at?"

I explained the speed of sound to him, outlined some rough calculations, and said I didn't think their story made sense. "If the sound took that long to reach them, they would have been too far from shore to hear anything quieter than a cannon."

Terwilliger dismissed my concerns. "They never actually said that. I just told you that to get a rise out of you."

I bristled, which only seemed to amuse him.

"I was annoyed with all your questions," he said. "You got to admit, it kind of turned your stomach, didn't it?" And he laughed.

He was the worst cop I'd ever met. Lazy and ineffective, disorganized and slow. And smelly to boot. I wanted to throw him out, but I wasn't quite finished.

"I'd like to speak to those witnesses," I said. "Could you give me their names?"

"Sure," he said, his laughter dying down. "But they're not here. They left last Sunday and went home. Somewhere in New Jersey or Delaware. I don't remember offhand. But I can get the address if you want."

"What were their names?"

"John something. I don't think I ever got the son's name."

"Do you know where they were staying on the lake?"

Terwilliger frowned at me. "Who's running this investigation anyways? Look, I've been patient with you trying to play detective, but it's starting to get on my nerves."

"You're not exactly winning me over either," I said, feeling a tirade coming on. It came, like a hurricane, and, after a week of his foul company, I was powerless to still my sharp tongue. "You intrude, overstay your welcome, drink everyone's liquor. You're always drunk, even in the morning. You take private citizens' automobiles for your own use. You belch, you smell, and you ogle women in bathing suits, spy on them when they're sunbathing and minding their own business."

I paused for breath. Terwilliger just stared at me, eyes wide. Then he smiled. Then he chuckled. Finally he laughed and rose to pour himself another long drink from my bottle of Dewar's.

"I may not be fancy like you," he said, settling into his seat once more. "I'm just a hick. But I'll let you have your fun at my expense."

I drew several deep breaths, trying to compose myself. I wasn't there yet. "And one more thing."

"Go ahead."

"Your trousers are either too loose or too small to contain your gigantic ass. I wish you would correct that immediately."

He nodded slowly, took a thoughtful sip of his whiskey, and pursed his lips. "Thank you," he said finally. "I will take your advice under consideration."

"And maybe you could shave once in a while?" I asked a touch more gently.

"Anything else?"

"Yes, but this has nothing to do with your appearance. Can you tell me where John the witness and his son were staying here on the lake?"

Surely he didn't think I'd forgotten my question.

He chuckled again. "You're all right, Ellie. May I call you Ellie?"

"If I can call you Ralph," I said.

"My friends call me Tiny."

Great, I thought. How was I going to manage that without laughing?

"Deal," I said.

"Well, Ellie, John Gorman—I think that was his name—was camping with his boy somewhere in the woods south of the village. I can show you, but there's nothing there to see."

"Okay," I said. "But you'll get me his address? Just in case I want to contact him later on. And I think the state police should interview them."

"Will do," he said with a gray smile.

"And you'll check on Gayle Morton's airplane ticket as you promised?"

"I've been meaning to do that. Just keep forgetting. Tell me again why you're interested in her ticket?"

It was a loose end I'd wanted to sew up. But I'd be lying if I didn't admit that I still harbored suspicions about Isaac and Gayle Morton.

"Just to erase any doubt that she came to Prospector Lake earlier than she's been claiming," I said. "Maybe she came here to meet someone. If she had, and her husband followed her here instead of the other way around, that might point to a murkier picture of what happened at Baxter's Rock."

Terwilliger nodded. "Right. Makes sense to find out. And if she didn't come here earlier in the month to meet someone, that means she came here to save her marriage, not push her husband off a cliff."

"Maybe," I said. "There's such a thing as a crime of passion. But I'm not convinced there was any foul play. This still looks more like an accident than anything else."

Tiny Terwilliger rose one last time from his seat and thanked me for my hospitality and whiskey. At the door he said he was going over to Arcadia to have a chat with Miriam. He asked if I wanted to go along.

"I know you like police work."

I begged off, thinking of my worn-out welcome. It was late, it was still raining, and I'd drunk my fill for one day. I intended to go to bed. And, truth be told, even with my newfound *entente cordiale* with the chief, I didn't exactly relish the prospect of breathing the polluted air inside his truck.

"One thing I'd like from you, Ellie," he said. "Can you give me the name of that little girlfriend of Jerry's? I might need to talk to her."

CHAPTER
TWENTY-TWO

Feeling munificent toward my new friend, I actually scrubbed his glass clean with soap and hot water from the teakettle. I dried it and nearly replaced it in the cupboard with the others. But in the end, I decided to stash it under the sink with some chipped bowls earmarked for Aunt Lena's gardening projects next summer.

Aunt Lena drove up about ten minutes after my guest had left. I greeted my favorite relatives at the door. Max was pleasantly soused, but not so much that he refused an offer of the last port of the season. We had arrived at the end of the summer. Almost.

"You missed a lovely evening," said Aunt Lena. "Even if the moon let us down. The younger people played standards, and we all sang our hearts out. The food was delicious, and Max flirted with a lovely young lady. Someone named Lucia. But your friend Isaac looked miserable. Sad boy. He sat off to one side by himself, drinking whiskey and sulking. Did something happen between you two?"

I thought I'd been smarter than that. But Aunt Lena was a clever old bird. She didn't let on, but she was always watching. I remembered how she'd used to know when Elijah and I were lying. Usually about nothing of consequence, but she knew.

"Don't you think stealing is wrong?" she'd asked us one summer when I was nine.

Elijah and I exchanged glances.

"I'll buy you cigarettes if you must have them," she continued. "But poor Mrs. Edmonds is struggling to make a living. The war hasn't been kind to her business."

"We didn't steal anything," said Elijah.

"Didn't you, Elijah?" asked Aunt Lena, smiling at him. "I thought you might have palmed a package of Kools when Mrs. Edmonds wasn't looking."

Elijah fidgeted. He glanced at me. I was no snitch. I just stared at him. At length he bowed his head and nodded.

"Doesn't it feel better to tell the truth?" she asked. Elijah nodded again. "By the way, Kools are revolting cigarettes. If you must smoke, I'll buy you some Chesterfields. That's what Joan Bennett smokes, you know."

She marched us into the village to Mrs. Edmonds's market and watched as we made a full confession. Then she paid for the cigarettes we'd stolen. On our way back to Cedar Haven, Aunt Lena shared with us a Chesterfield that she'd bought. She never betrayed us to our parents. And we never stole again.

"Nothing happened," I said coldly in answer to her question. "I had to meet Chief Terwilliger."

"Don't tell me he used another teacup."

I hesitated. "No, he didn't use a teacup," I said finally.

Aunt Lena pursed her lips. "What, did he use a glass instead?" She still knew when I was lying to her.

"So what did that golem want?" she asked as she poured herself and Max one last port.

"I asked him to stop by. I had to fill him in on what I found this morning."

"What was that?" she asked.

I didn't like the idea of gossip, but she and Max were family, and I trusted them. So I told them the entire story of Mimi, Miriam, Karl, and Jerry. They had known Mimi since she was a girl, of course, but not well.

"With a young boy?" she asked. "Are you sure?"

"I can't find another explanation," I said. "The young man's girlfriend and his best friend at the camp both identified the older woman as Mimi."

"*Mi chiamano Mimi*," sang Max from his armchair, but that was all he could manage. "I confess that I only know the first line." He sipped his port. "Ellie, my dear, surely you know the whole thing. What comes next?"

"I'm tired, Max," I said. "I don't feel like singing Puccini right now."

"Fair enough," he said. "One must be in the mood for opera, after all. As a matter of fact, I can't stomach it in the main. The music is all right, but all that caterwauling gets under my skin. Disliked it since I was a boy. Since the first time I heard that soprano sing. What was her name? La Raimondo. That was it. Screeched like a barn owl and put me off opera forever."

"I adore Puccini," said Aunt Lena. "And La Raimondo was one of the great sopranos."

I'd had my fill for one day. Perhaps for one vacation. I wished them good night and retired to my cabin, where I lit a mosquito coil. Lena always insisted that mosquitoes had never bitten her, but I was different, having donated many pints of blood to the little suckers over the years. I switched off the lamp and curled up under the covers as the rain cascaded on the roof and the wind howled outside.

I slept fitfully. I dreamt of Isaac. Not logical dreams. But not nightmares either. He had invaded my subconscious and was gamboling through my slumber like a puckish satyr. I wanted to call to him. I wanted him beside me in my bed. All the anger and disappointment had evaporated. But then my attitude changed, and I was shooing him away as if he were a gnat. I awoke, stared at the ceiling, tried to sleep, tried to edit the dream into a version of my liking. But that was doomed to fail. I was simply conflicted and confused, angry and sad at the same time.

The rain had stopped. I lay there in the dark, immobile. Just staring and blinking and breathing. I lit a cigarette and glanced at my watch on the bedside table. It glowed three thirty. The cigarette was a foul idea, but I saw it through to the end. Then I switched on the lamp, rose from the bed, and crossed the room to stub out the cigarette in the ashtray on the table. Just inches from my hand, the bottle stood tall and defiant. There was still another drink or two at the bottom. I snatched it by the neck and made my way back over to the bed.

Sitting naked on the mattress, propped up by pillows and the head-board, I drained what liquid was left in my nighttime water glass and refilled it with whiskey. I knew where I was headed, and despite my best efforts to manage it, I could not. I conjured Isaac, and he appeared in my mind's eye. His crooked smile and flecked irises. His soft voice and gentle touch. His scent. My eyes welled with tears, and I punched the pillow in frustration. Then a tear fell, then another and another, rolling down my cheeks, heavy and warm, collecting under my chin. I let them run, refusing to dry them in a ridiculous attempt at self-flagellation through the most minor discomfort I could imagine: damp cheeks. I supposed it was the whiskey and cigarettes on an empty stomach that had contributed to my collapse. My breath caught in my throat, and I sobbed pathetic little gasps.

I could hear the Fauré that Isaac and company had played. It spun 'round and 'round in my head like the theme to a bad melodrama. The power of the piece swelled with the association with my late father. The memory of him smoking in his study blurred with the image of Isaac bowing his violin as his gaze ranged over the sheet music.

Now I had the conflation of Isaac with my father to look forward to every time that music went through my head. Damn it. This man had stolen something precious to me and somehow enriched it at the same time. Turned it into a haunting rondo that would always remind me of how I had fallen for him, and how the affair had ended unhappily ever after.

And I found more creative ways to punish and torture myself. A memory long forgotten: Elijah and Isaac as children, blowing bubbles off their tongues, one after the other. Tiny little bubbles of saliva, one at a time, that, using their tongues, they lifted gently off the floor of their mouths, just behind the incisors. Then with just the softest puff, a bare whisper, the bubble took flight and floated on air, drifting slowly to its rendezvous with the ground and its tiny explosive splat. Each burst provoked a new staccato of giggles. I never managed to do it, though Elijah tried to teach me for years. I would just stand there, eyes crossed to focus on my tongue, surely looking as if I'd suffered some kind of stroke. But I never achieved bubbles. Only drool.

Isaac and Elijah had been chums for a couple of weeks for a few childhood summers. There was something about this man who'd known my dear brother as a child—known me as well. We'd played together. He'd spat bubbles off his dexterous tongue with Elijah. There was indeed something powerfully complex and emotional about my meeting Isaac again after so long. The confluence of history, distance, passion, and now rupture, opened the wound that I'd sealed the day after my brother died four years earlier. The same disbelief that I'd felt when I'd first heard the news of his death crushed the air out of my lungs again. I sat there on my bed, weeping, drink in hand, cheeks still streaked with tears.

And there was a thump.

CHAPTER
TWENTY-THREE

I jumped, spilling what was left of my drink in the bed, and in a single motion, I threw away the pillow I'd been punching and flew to the fireplace. I grabbed the iron poker and screamed, "Who's there?" Silence. Weapon raised and at the ready, I crept naked to the window near the door where the bang had sounded. (I was going to have to start wearing pajamas of some kind if these late-night intrusions continued.) I drew back the curtain slowly, trying to see into the black night. But the only light outside was coming from the dim lamp inside my cabin shining through the window. I couldn't be sure if someone or something had tripped and fallen into the door or if a branch had broken and landed on the wooden porch. Maybe it was a bear. Or that fat raccoon I'd nearly run over. Or was it a man? A murderer? Waldo Coons? Or Isaac again? God, how I wanted it to be Isaac. I dropped the curtain and hissed his name through the door. No one answered. I tested the bolt and congratulated myself for having had the good sense to lock it before turning in hours earlier. Then there was a shuffling on the porch, and heavy footsteps. Then they stopped.

"Who's there?" I repeated. "I have a gun, and I know how to use it."

Still no answer. The night had become a blanket, trapping me, smothering me and all my fears and sorrows beneath its heavy fabric. I thought the prowler may have run off, but I couldn't be sure. I didn't dare open the door to investigate, and the views from the windows showed nothing. All was silent now. Even the wind held its breath waiting for the other shoe to drop. I prayed it wouldn't drop on my porch.

SATURDAY, AUGUST 26, 1961

I waited until six thirty, until the sun had peeked over the mountains to the east, before finally finding the courage to unbolt my door and venture outside. The ground was sodden from the storms that had raged the night before, ruining everyone's view of the lunar spectacle. Fallen branches and pine needles lay strewn across the compound, the detritus of the high winds that had blown through the area along with the rain. If someone had been prowling about in the night, I couldn't tell from the ground. The rain had smeared everything. I saw marks that might have been human tracks. Or a moose. It was anyone's guess.

Standing on the edge of my porch, I peered out on the compound, scanning right and left to see if the coast was clear. Everything seemed normal. Then I looked down at the wooden planks. Mud tracked around the window and in front of the door. They were footprints all right. But it looked as if someone had tried to scratch them out by shuffling and dragging his feet.

I searched the compound again for signs of an intruder. All was still. I was ready to make a run for it. But I wasn't taking any chances. Armed with the fire poker, I scurried across the mud to Aunt Lena's cabin. I rapped on the door and, still on the lookout for marauders, waited for her to open up.

"Ellie, what's the matter?" she asked. "Why are you banging on doors at this ungodly hour?"

"Someone tried to break into my cabin last night," I said, pushing past her inside. I slammed the door behind me and bolted it shut.

"Did you see anything? Are you sure it wasn't the wind?"

"I'm sure. There was a man outside my cabin. He banged on the wall and shuffled around on the porch. It was nearly four a.m."

Aunt Lena brewed a pot of tea and opened a box of digestive biscuits. "I'm afraid this is about all we have left to eat," she said. "I'm saving the last of the bread for Max's toast."

I wasn't hungry. Too rattled to eat. "Nothing for me."

"But you didn't have any dinner last night either. I know because there's nothing left here in the cupboard. I worry about you, Ellie. You eat less than a bird."

"It's a myth that birds don't eat a lot," I said, gazing out the kitchen window for signs of movement.

"Yes, dear. I'm aware of that. But you hardly eat a handful of seeds a day. Why don't we go to the village and have a proper breakfast today? A farewell meal before we leave. And I've had Max on a healthy diet since we arrived. He'll be glad to gorge himself on bacon and pancakes."

I felt little enthusiasm for Aunt Lena's plan, but I figured I'd be safer in the village than in our isolated camp.

Lenny's Diner was hopping at seven thirty on a Saturday morning, but we managed to slip into one of the last free booths along the window looking out onto Lake Road. I stared out at the gray sky. Vacationers were going to miss out on their last day of summer fun.

I tried to buck myself up. My summer fling with Isaac Eisenstadt was nothing to lose sleep over. It had only been a week, after all. And I was being surly to my beloved aunt and cousin on their last day. Enough, I told myself. Put on an ersatz smile and make them happy before they leave.

But just as I was about to do that, I overheard the two men in the booth behind us talking about Donald Yarrow. I turned to see them. Just a couple of locals back from an early-morning fishing expedition on the lake.

"Excuse me," I said, interrupting them. "Did I hear you say something about the escaped murderer?"

They nodded. "They got him last night," said the one on the far bench. "This morning, really. About five a.m."

"Oh, my," I said, my heart jumping. Perhaps they'd caught him just after he'd left my cabin. Might it really have been him lurking about?

"Where did they arrest him? Was it Chief Terwilliger or the state police?"

"Terwilliger?" said the other man, chuckling. "Hardly. He couldn't catch a cold. But Yarrow was captured in Maryland. He was never anywhere near Prospector Lake."

"That's remarkable," I said. "What about the woman who disappeared yesterday from Tennyson?"

The two fishermen exchanged amused looks. "She turned up at Tom's Lakeside Motel," said the first man. "With her brother-in-law. Not sure how happy her husband is now that she wasn't murdered by Donald Yarrow."

I thanked them and turned back around. "What do you make of that?" I asked. "He was never even near here."

"People are funny," said Lena. "They imagine bogeymen everywhere. Mass hysteria, I guess."

"The airplane," said Max, sipping his coffee as he studied the menu. "Prospector Lake, both coasts of Mexico, and now Maryland. What did I tell you?"

"I think we can all sleep more easily now," said Aunt Lena, ignoring Max's contribution.

"Sure," I said. "If you don't worry about who tried to get into my cabin last night. Frankly, I wish Yarrow had been captured here. I'd feel a lot safer."

Max continued to pore over the menu, humming as he did.

"Still with the Puccini?" I asked.

"Can't get the blasted tune out of my head," he said.

⁂

After our farewell breakfast, I drove the old folks back to Cedar Haven, where they set about readying their departure. It wasn't yet nine, and I was feeling curious. When the two fishermen had mentioned Tom's Lakeside Motel, I got to thinking. The previous day's missing woman had turned out to be another in a string of adulterous patrons of the moldering inn. If Gayle Morton was still in town, I wanted to chat with her one more time.

Her father's blue Galaxie was there, parked in its usual spot, and I found Gayle in her room. She had just finished her breakfast and seemed to be preparing to go out.

"Leaving today?" I asked once she'd invited me inside.

"Tomorrow," she said. "That buffoon of a police chief finally gave us the okay this morning."

That was news. "You've already seen Chief Terwilliger today?" I asked. "So early. Probably smelling of beer."

"You would think. But actually he was quite presentable today. Bathed and shaven. Wearing clean clothes, too. An actual police uniform, if you can believe it."

Well, I thought. Maybe my little discussion with him the night before had sunk in. I was happy to hear it.

"I gather you showed him your plane ticket and he was satisfied," I said.

"What are you talking about? I didn't show him any plane ticket."

"He didn't ask?"

Gayle shook her head. "What's this about?"

"Sorry," I said, trying to explain. "He told me he was going to check on your travel dates. He said he'd send you on your merry way as long as you hadn't been in Prospector Lake earlier this month."

"Why would that make a difference?"

"He wanted to be sure you weren't lying," I said, omitting the part about it having been my idea. "Or that maybe your husband followed you here and not the other way around."

Gayle turned white. "Why would I come to this place if not to follow my husband?" she asked in a trembling voice.

I gave a short shrug. "Maybe you came here to meet someone else."

"Is that what he thinks?"

Again I shrugged, never taking my eyes off her. Despite my closest scrutiny, I couldn't read her. There was so much more I wanted to know about her. Had she loved her husband? Had she followed him to the Adirondacks? Or had she come to meet another man she loved? And was that man Isaac?

I was acutely aware of how shameful my obsession had become. But at the end of this affair, I wanted to know just how big a chump I'd been. I hoped that I was wrong. No one likes to be played for a fool, and I was no exception.

"When did you arrive here exactly?" I asked her finally.

"Now I have to answer to you?"

"I can help you," I said. "The chief listens to me."

"But he's already told me I can leave whenever I want. I don't have to answer to anyone."

She was right. I needed to find a new tack, or she'd never tell me anything.

"You're right, of course," I said. "It's just that these backwoods lawmen can be tricky. He tells you one thing then does another. He may pull you over on your way out of town and arrest you on a trumped-up charge. It wouldn't hurt to show me your ticket."

She loosed a nervous laugh. "I'm not showing you or anyone else my ticket."

"I know you and Isaac Eisenstadt had a fling in Los Angeles. You lied to me about that. Why?"

"I did no such thing," she said, but this time I could read her. Maybe because I knew for a fact that she'd seduced a willing Isaac in the Sunset Motor Inn and Resort.

"He told me about the motel in Hollywood," I said.

She cursed under her breath. The jig was up, and she knew it. She sat on the edge of her bed, twisting her wedding ring, staring at the worn carpet pile on the floor.

"It's okay," I said to encourage. "He told me you and your husband had an arrangement. And I'm not one to judge. I'm a liberal thinker when it comes to sex."

"I don't know what to say," she said at length.

"Just say if you followed Karl here, or if he followed you. You don't need to say anything else."

"His name was Charles," she said, a mite peeved.

"Why won't you call him Karl?" I asked. "Are you so ashamed of his Jewish birth?"

She scoffed and looked away. There were tears in her eyes. I gave her a moment to collect herself. She dabbed her nose with a tissue.

"I'm not an anti-Semite, Ellie," she said softly. "I asked Karl to change his name for his own good. Where was he ever going to go with a name like Karl Marx Merkleson? It was for his future."

"Then why not a more palatable Jewish name?" I asked. "We're talking about Hollywood, here. It was founded by Jews. Built by Jews. Jews who were shunned elsewhere, so they made their own industry. It's not as if there were 'Hebrews need not apply' ads out there. Why were you so ashamed of him in a place like that?"

"Stop saying that!" she shouted, surprising me. "I'm not a Jew-hater, for God's sake. I *am* a Jew."

That came as a jolt I'd never expected. Gayle aimed her fiercest glare at me, challenging me to contradict her. I stammered an inadequate defense. How could I have known? What did she mean?

"I am Jewish, Ellie," she repeated, a little more gently. "My real name is Naomi Berkowitz. I changed it."

"But your father . . ." I said. "Owen Pierce?"

"Hiram Berkowitz," she said.

"Why would you hide such a thing?" I asked.

"I don't expect you to understand. You live in your Jewish cocoon. But my father grew up in the Midwest. He faced bigotry every day of his life. He tried to make it with his Jewish name, but some people wouldn't even meet with him, wouldn't shake his hand when they heard his name. No club would have him. He was asked to leave restaurants. He made a choice to assimilate."

I drew a deep breath, urging myself to remain calm and to try to understand. But at the same time, I certainly didn't live in a Jewish cocoon. Not in New Holland, New York. But I held my tongue.

"Did you love Karl?" I asked, trying to force his Jewish name down her throat.

"Of course I did. And so did my father. Even after Charles broke his heart and said he wanted to go out on his own. Yes, we had our problems, like I told you before. We didn't look on sexual fidelity as the be all and end all in a marriage. As long as we came home to each other, there was no harm."

"Save the last dance for me?" I asked.

"Yes, I loved him, Ellie," she said, ignoring my remark. "But he was hard to love. Moody, mercurial, selfish. I have desires, too, you know. I'm not sure it would have lasted much longer. But I wanted to give it one more try to save our marriage."

"You had an agreement with him," I said. "Did that include a love affair with his old friend, Isaac?"

She started to sob, and I felt sorry for pushing her so. But she was close to breaking; I could sense it. I couldn't stop now. I wanted to know the whole truth. I wanted to know exactly who Isaac was before I left him behind for good. It was selfish. I knew that. But my heart was broken.

"Were you going to go home to him?" I asked. "To Karl? After meeting Isaac here?"

"I don't know," she whispered.

"You were here August sixth, weren't you? You stayed at the Lakeside Motel. Isn't that right?"

Gayle's head fell into her hands. I waited. It took another minute. Another minute of her weeping and wondering what she should say. But in the end, she lifted her eyes and looked me straight in the face.

"I loved Charles," she began. "Yes, he was hard to love, as I said. And you were right. He followed me here."

☙

Gayle Morton unburdened her soul. She had arrived in Prospector Lake on August 6, met Isaac at the Lakeside Motel where he had taken a room, and spent two days with him. It was a purely physical thing.

As she spoke, she never noticed my pallor, my dry mouth, my wet eyes. "I could never have left Charles for him. It was just a fling. He's a school teacher, after all. But I just couldn't stay away. I wanted him. I started obsessing over him. Despite everything. Our differences, my marriage, his job. And then, too late, I realized what a fool I was. Hanging around, hoping against hope that things might somehow be different in the darkness of a motel room. But Isaac didn't love me. I didn't love him either, I know now. But ..."

"Did you go back to Los Angeles?" I asked, my voice hoarse. "After your tryst with Isaac?"

She shook her head. "I stayed in a motel on the other side of the lake for a week when Isaac went back to his camp. I couldn't go there, of course. I couldn't show my face there."

"And Karl came to find you?"

She wiped her eyes and nose. "I don't know," she said. "Maybe he came for me. Maybe he came for Miriam."

CHAPTER
TWENTY-FOUR

I reached Cedar Haven at ten thirty. Max's car was all packed except for the two passengers and a small bag each. Their plan was to take Route 9 south, stop at an inn near Hudson for the night, then continue on to Aunt Lena's house in New Rochelle the following morning. Max would set off for Washington the day after that.

As for me, I intended to touch all the bases one more time, then leave the sad story of two diving victims behind. Aunt Lena had already washed the bedclothes and towels, so all that was left for me to do on Sunday was to bring in the washing from the line, switch off the lights, and shutter the place for the winter. I had no intention of visiting Arcadia.

We chatted for a few minutes on the porch, made promises to see each other more often, and exchanged admonitions on health and advice on happiness. The sun was finally coming out again, drying the ground that was moist from the storms. Finally, at a quarter to twelve, the old folks decided it was time to go. I walked them to Max's wagon, kissed them good-bye, and watched them drive off.

I started back to the main cabin to fold some washing when I heard a car approach. I turned to see an old black Rambler wagon pulling into the compound. A little man with white hair and a bald pate climbed out of the car, pulled a worn Western Union cap onto his head, and hobbled over to me.

"I'm looking for . . ." he consulted the envelope in his hand, ". . . Miss Eleonora Stone, care of Lena Suskind, Route Fifteen, Prospector Lake, New York."

"That's me," I said, holding out my hand for the wire.

"You got any identification?" he asked.

I ran inside to fetch my purse then produced my driver's license and signed for the telegram. The little old man drove off, and I opened the envelope. It was from Fred Peruso, the county coroner back in New Holland. Fadge had carried out his orders.

I'd forgotten about the photographs of the bodies that I'd sent to him. I opened the telegram and read.

REVIEWED PHOTOS. NO OPINION ON BOY DUE TO LOW LIGHT AND CLOTHING COVER. RIGOR MORTIS APPEARS PRESENT IN OLDER VICTIM'S FACE AND HANDS. IF RM IS PRESENT, IT SUGGESTS DEATH OCCURRED AT LEAST TWO HOURS EARLIER. PROBABLY EVEN EARLIER. APPARENT LIVIDITY ON OLDER MAN'S RIGHT SIDE NEAR GROUND. NOT CERTAIN GIVEN BLACK-AND-WHITE PHOTO. IF BLOTCHES WERE BLUE, THIS IS LIVIDITY. ALSO EVIDENCE OF BRUISE ON LEFT TORSO AND THIGH. MAY INDICATE LIVIDITY, BUT IMPOSSIBLE TO SAY FROM PHOTOGRAPHS. CONCLUSION: THIS BODY MAY HAVE BEEN MOVED AT LEAST TWO HOURS AFTER DEATH.

FEDERICO PERUSO, MD,
CORONER MONTGOMERY CO

I considered the telegram. Peruso believed that Karl Merkleson had been dead for at least two hours before I snapped my photographs. I did some math in my head. Did his opinion match the timeline of the deaths and discovery of the two men? The two witnesses put the time of death at twelve thirty. I reached the scene around 2:30 p.m. I frowned. Just barely, I thought.

What about Fred's observation of rigor mortis? He didn't seem sure of it but thought Karl's face and hands indicated visible stiffness. Fred only had small, black-and-white photographs to go by. I had seen Karl up close. And I had touched the boy. Touched his shoulder. I tried to remember if Jerry had been stiff. I couldn't say.

But what about Karl? I redoubled my concentration. His face and hands had been as stiff as a two-by-four, that much was sure. I recalled from an anatomy class I'd taken at Barnard that the smaller muscles of the body stiffened first post-mortem, beginning as early as twenty minutes after death. That made sense and did nothing to contradict what I already knew. But what troubled me more was Fred's comments on lividity. He couldn't be sure there were signs of lividity since my photographs were in black and white. But I had noticed the marks on Karl's body. The blotches had indeed been blue. A purple-blue on the right side and a smaller, redder blue on the left. I had assumed his body had bounced on impact. But Fred thought that the body might have been moved after death. I wondered just how long after death. How long would a body need to lie dead for lividity to become evident? Fred hadn't elaborated, and I wanted clarification.

I wondered if any of Uncle Mel's medical books were still around. Once as children, Elijah and I had snuck peeks into an old red copy of *The American Illustrated Medical Dictionary* that Uncle Mel kept at Cedar Haven. Elijah showed me the drawings of male and female parts. That cured me from ever wanting to look again. I knew that Aunt Lena had donated many of the books after Mel died in 1951, but I hoped some remained in her library. I searched the likely locations, but the closest thing I could find to a medical book was a copy of *Doctor Zhivago*. With nowhere else to turn, I knew what I had to do. I had to make one more trip to Arcadia Lodge.

David Levine was the only doctor I knew in the area, if you didn't count Nelson Blanchard. And I didn't. I liked David and thought I could trust him. The hitch was how to see him and avoid Isaac at the same time. In the end, I decided to brazen it out. I drove over to Arcadia a few minutes after noon and located David's cabin without too much trouble. After all, I knew which one was Isaac's, and I'd spent the night in Miriam and Simon's cabin. There were little signposts for others, wooden arrow indicators planted in the ground, so I deduced David's was one of two in the southwest corner of the large compound. As things turned out, I ran into Audrey Silber, who pointed the way.

"Ellie," said David, standing in the doorway. "Hi. Please, come in."

I saw suitcases opened and half filled on the bed. David was packing to leave.

"It's been a bad week," I said.

"Why do you say that?" he asked. "It's been nice seeing you again."

"That's sweet. You always were the one with the best outlook on things. But we both know the week started well and went south after that. Karl, Simon, and, well . . . Never mind."

David's gaze clouded. "You're right, I suppose," he said. Then he summoned a brave smile. "What do you mean about Simon?"

I wondered if he knew. Of course he knew. He'd told me that Miriam had asked him to bring chlorpromazine for Simon. Surely he would have asked why. It wasn't as if she'd asked for aspirin.

"I think Simon is quite ill," I said.

David looked away. He knew.

"Did you come here to talk about Simon?" he asked.

"No," I said, resigning myself to put that sad conversation to one side. There was nothing I could do to help Simon just then. But there might be something I could do for Karl and Jerry. Perhaps clear up some of the ambiguity that would trouble their loved ones. Or maybe not. Did it matter? Did any of my snooping make the slightest difference at all to the lives, to the deaths? I didn't know, but the alternative—forgetting them— was surely the easy way out. And that would never help anyone.

"I came here to ask you about lividity."

"Lividity?" he asked. "Why would you ask such a thing?"

"I saw Karl's body," I said. "You saw the photos of him, didn't you?"

David's face fell. He rubbed his brow and looked to be in true distress. "I saw the photos that night you showed them to Ruth," he said. "When she fainted. But they were so small. And I couldn't bring myself to look for more than a second or two. It was just too difficult. He was my friend."

"I understand," I said. "But I showed the photos to a friend of mine. A coroner. And he thought there were two areas that might indicate lividity."

"How do you mean?"

"There were two areas on his body where the blood had darkened his skin: the entire right side of his body and a smaller area opposite that on his left."

David frowned. "How was his body positioned on the ground when you saw him?"

"Lying on his right side, arm beneath the body."

He seemed confused. He asked if he could see the photographs.

"I'm afraid I sent my last set of prints to the coroner," I said. "And the police have the negatives."

David asked me to show him where the lividity was evident. I lay on the floor, assuming the approximate position in which Karl had been found, and indicated the locations of the bruises. Once I'd stood and brushed myself off, David limped over to a chair and sat down.

"What's your conclusion?" I asked. "Is there anything that can explain the two areas of lividity?"

"Yes," he said. "Just one that I can think of." He stared up at me with sober eyes. "Somebody moved his body after death."

"That's what the coroner thinks. Is there any way to know how long after death he was moved?"

David shook his head. "Not with any precision. And certainly not without the body or the photographs. It's too bad there was no autopsy. That might have given us more information."

"But there was an autopsy," I said, brightening. "Karl's mother took the body to Albany Wednesday. She's due back here today with the results."

"I'd love to see the report."

"David," I said after a brief pause. "If, in fact, Karl's body was moved after he died, why do you think someone would do that?"

He pursed his lips and rubbed the bridge of his nose while he gave my question some thought. "I can't believe I'm saying this, Ellie," he began. "But the only reason I can imagine would be to make his death look like an accident."

"His death?" I asked, inviting him to use a different word.

He sighed. "His murder."

CHAPTER
TWENTY-FIVE

I thought I'd made a clean escape from Arcadia Lodge, but as I looked back over my shoulder and reversed down the dirt-and-grass drive, there was a rapping on my hood. I stopped and turned to see Isaac practically climbing up onto my fender.

"Ellie, wait," he said. "I have to talk to you."

I kept my foot on the brake but didn't shift into park. "Maybe it's better if we just leave it," I said.

"Please. I have to apologize to you. I was wrong last night."

"No, you weren't. I accused your old friend of things I can't prove. And you and I have come to a point . . ." I was trying to be oblique. Why? "I think we both know we've come to the end," I said, correcting myself.

"Ellie, please turn off the car and come talk to me. Don't drive off like this."

I gazed up at his flecked eyes and nearly complied. But I didn't want to go over the same torture of the night before. I'd made up my mind, and it had been hard to do. I wasn't prepared to change it now, only to have to convince myself again later.

"Please, Ellie," he said, reaching an upturned palm through the window.

"I've got to go," I said and took my foot off the brake.

The car slid backward, and Isaac had to pull back his hand or lose it. He chased after me, imploring me to stop. I reached the pavement of Route 15 and wheeled the car around. Isaac reached me just as I shifted into drive. I stepped on the accelerator, and the car lurched forward.

"Simon's been arrested!" he called after me

I quite nearly didn't hear him. In fact it took me a couple of beats to arrange his words in my head and realize what he'd said. I cursed him and myself. Then I stamped on the brake and pulled over to the side of the road. Isaac arrived at a trot from behind. I glared at him and told him to climb in.

"What happened?" I asked, once I'd driven off again toward the village.

"Terwilliger came back to the camp last night after midnight," he said. "He dragged Miriam out of bed to question her. He knew about the Mimi thing."

"Yes, I told him. I had to tell him. It's important."

"I know. I get that."

"So what did she say?"

"She laughed. Told him he was crazy. She'd only met the kid a few times for rehearsals and the concert. And she'd certainly never seduced him."

"Did Terwilliger believe her?" I asked.

"Didn't seem to. But you know how cops are. They shine a hot lamp on you and blow smoke in your face until you confess."

"So how did it end? He couldn't have had any evidence to arrest her."

"No, he didn't. He just said he'd come back again today after discussing the case with the district attorney."

We were coming up on Palmer Square. I had no appointments or any idea of where to go, so I pulled into a parking spot across the road from the park. I yanked the handbrake and opened my door.

"Let's talk over there," I said, indicating the gazebo in the square.

The day was turning into a gem, at least weather-wise. After the rain and wind of the previous night, Prospector Lake was once again a perfect summer idyll. As long as you didn't count the dead bodies and seduced young boys.

"Why did Terwilliger arrest Simon? Did he blow his stack again?"

"Nothing like that," said Isaac, squinting out over the lake toward the eastern shore. A light breeze ruffled his hair, and I felt I was losing my resolve. "Terwilliger came back this morning. Just about an hour and a half ago. He wanted to speak to Miriam again, but she was taking a walk down by the lake. Simon and I met him in my cabin so as not to upset the others."

"And?"

"That idiot cop said he'd spoken to the district attorney, and the two of them had agreed that there was enough evidence to take Miriam in for questioning. Trumped-up evidence, I'm sure. Terwilliger said he was going to arrest her as soon as she came back to camp."

"So why didn't he?"

Isaac gazed into my eyes, and a frisson ran up my spine and over my shoulders. I wondered if he'd noticed. I blinked and looked away. "So why didn't he arrest her?" I repeated.

"Because Simon confessed to killing Karl."

∂◯

Isaac told me the entire story. When faced with Miriam's arrest, Simon had come clean. He told Terwilliger that he'd long hated Karl for his betrayals. First his friends, then his family, and finally his faith. He spoke calmly for once. No paroxysms, no fits or shouting. He simply said he'd seen Karl in the woods near Arcadia that morning, not far from the hunters' shelter above the camp. He engaged him, and the two walked to the beach. Simon asked him what he was doing on the lake, why he hadn't contacted any of them. Karl told him he had come because he hated his wife and wanted to win back the love of his life, Miriam.

"Don't you mean Mimi?" asked Terwilliger.

And Simon bristled. No one called her Mimi but him. That was his name for her. Karl called her Miriam, and he didn't deserve her. And she didn't love him, besides. He had come to Prospector Lake for nothing.

"Then there was nothing going on between them?" asked Terwilliger.

"Nothing," insisted Simon. Sure, she may have helped him. Given him a flea-bitten blanket to sleep under in the shelter, but that was it. Nothing else.

"I understood she gave him a monogrammed Dopp kit?" asked the chief.

Simon laughed. "That was nine years ago," he said. "And it was a gift from all of us. For his trip to California."

"But it's brand-new."

"Not brand-new," said Simon. "Never been used. Karl left it behind in 1954. I took it back to New York with me to give it to him the next time I saw him."

"Why did you all deny any knowledge of the Dopp kit that night? You lied to me."

Simon chuckled. "We're all loyal to each other, not to fascist cops."

"You seem to have an answer for everything."

"No answers," Simon said. "Just facts."

"So what happened next?" asked Terwilliger. "How did you get from the shore to the top of Baxter's Rock?"

Simon shrugged and explained. "I told him I would step aside and let him have Miriam if he could prove his love for her."

"Huh?"

"When we were kids, we used to talk about diving off Baxter's Rock. We always chickened out. I told him if he would risk his life for her, I would let her go."

I had to interrupt Isaac at this point. "What the hell?" I asked. "Are you telling me Terwilliger bought that?"

"Of course not," said Isaac. "He's not as dim as he looks. But it's true that we used to talk about diving off the cliff. But none of us ever had the guts to do it."

Simon insisted he convinced Karl to climb up to the top of the cliff with him. And once there, the two men argued over Miriam. Then their differences devolved into blows, and in self-defense, Simon pushed Karl over the edge by accident. That was it.

"And Terwilliger actually arrested him?" I asked.

Isaac hesitated, casting his gaze upward as if to recall. Then he frowned and said that the police chief had seemed annoyed. "I believe he thought Simon was lying to cover for Miriam. But what could he do? Simon swore he'd killed Karl, even if he said it was an accident."

"What did he say about Jerry Kaufman?" I asked. "Did Terwilliger even ask?"

Isaac shook his head. "Simon said the kid must have shown up later and fallen on his own. He insisted they died at different times, since he, Simon, was a witness to Karl's death."

"And what about you? Did you say anything at all?"

"I kept saying that it was absurd. Believe me, Ellie. It made no sense, and I don't think Terwilliger bought it either. He just shrugged and took him in."

We sat for a minute, digesting the information on the green of Palmer Square, Isaac just inches from me on the bench inside the gazebo. I wanted to run to the police station to appeal to my new friend, Tiny Terwilliger, to see reason and release Simon. But I also wanted to fall into Isaac's arms, breathe him in, abandon everything, including myself, to him. Forget this whole summer and all its heartbreaks. I just wanted to embrace the good, throw away the bad, the doubts, and the pain. I wanted Isaac and nothing else. No one else. None of the lies, none of the betrayals or suspicions. I wanted to be folded in his arms and lose myself forever there.

And I was sure he wanted that too. Even if I held none of the cards, I still knew. And Isaac's desire was unequivocal. I could dictate terms, ask for the moon, and he would capitulate. It would have been so easy to fall back into our love affair. But you can't un-ring a bell. You can't un-feel a burn. It was perhaps possible to heal. But healing took time. I inched away from him on the bench.

"Where's Miriam now?" I asked. "I need to speak to her."

The last thing Miriam wanted was to see me. She'd heard of my accusation, according to Isaac, and couldn't understand my betrayal.

Officer Bob Firth was manning the desk at the police station when Isaac and I entered. Miriam was in an interrogation room, he informed us, refusing to leave without her husband.

"Where's the chief?" I asked.

"On his way over to Elizabethtown to see the DA," he said. "He left about fifteen minutes ago."

"Has Simon Abramowitz secured a lawyer?"

Bob shook his head. "Said he didn't want one. Didn't need one. He's going to sign a confession as soon as the DA gets here this afternoon."

"He's not signing anything," I said. "That man is not going to die in prison."

Isaac's head nearly spun off its axis snapping to the side to look at me. His eyes burned wild, afraid, as if perhaps I knew something I shouldn't. He didn't ask, and I didn't volunteer. Let him wonder, I thought.

"Ellie, I know a local lawyer, Bill Hoch." Isaac pronounced it "hoke."

"Is he good?" I asked. "Or just some backwoods raconteur who likes to sue doctors?"

"Former vice president, fourth judicial district of the New York State Bar Association. He's a quiet, thoughtful man, by the way. So you can drop your stereotypes of small-town lawyers. Of course, his brother, Jim, is another story."

"So what are you waiting for?" I said. "Go get Bill Hoch. Simon's not signing any confessions this afternoon."

Isaac nodded and ran for the door. Hoch and Hoch's law office was across the street.

"Real nice to see you again, Miss Stone," said Bob Firth, smiling.

Miriam glowered when she saw me enter the interrogation room. Her usual impenetrable expression was gone, replaced by an all-too-obvious evil eye. And it was directed at me.

"Put your indignation to one side for now," I said. "We've got to get Simon out of here."

"What do you care?" she sneered. "You came here, wormed your way into our hearts, then showed your thanks by betraying us. Simon is in that jail cell now because you started that lie about me and Jerrold What's-His-Name."

"You listen to me, Miriam," I said, brooking none of her argument. "You have spent your adult life hopping in and out of the love lives of your oldest and dearest friends. I'm no prude. You can love whom you will. But friendships suffer for it. And you, not I, destroyed Simon's love for Karl."

"What?"

"They didn't split over Stalin or Khrushchev or Hungary. They split over you. You loved Karl, he loved another, and Simon loved you. Still does, obviously, since he's willing to confess to a crime he didn't commit. All to save you."

"Don't point the finger at me, Ellie," she said, her hackles up as high as I'd ever seen them. "I love Simon dearly and would never hurt him."

"But you tracked Karl down in Los Angeles just to say hello? I don't believe it, Miriam. I think Karl came here to meet you. To win you back again after all those years."

"That's not true," she said. "I wasn't sleeping with Karl."

"Don't tell me you didn't know he was here on the lake, because we don't have time for games. Not if we want to get Simon out of here before he does something foolish like sign a confession of murder or manslaughter."

"Yes, I knew he was here," she hissed. "He wrote to me to tell me. He told me he loved me. He told me he hated his wife. And I told him it was too little too late. I did not sleep with him. I set him up in that shelter near Arcadia because I hoped he'd come to his senses and rejoin his friends."

"Why should I believe you?" I asked. "You were in love with Karl. He broke your heart and left you waiting. For years."

"I did love him," she said. "Once. And I did hunt him down in Los Angeles. It was stupid of me, I know now. I was obsessed with him. It nearly broke up my marriage to Simon. But that's buried in the past. I told you that I love Simon dearly. He's dying, and I would not betray him now when he needs me most."

She turned to face the opposite wall. I could see her shoulders rise and fall with her heated respiration. But at length, she calmed.

"I know people think I'm cold," she said. "And odd. I can't help that. But I do not fornicate with teenaged boys."

I circled around to see her face. It was flat, expressionless, unless you considered paralysis an expression. I tried to engage her, attract her attention to me. Finally I crouched before her and caught her eye.

"What are you doing?" she asked.

"Trying to see if you're telling the truth. Liars often look away as they proclaim their innocence."

"I don't sleep with teenaged boys," she repeated. "And I didn't sleep with Jerrold What's-His-Name."

"Kaufman," I said.

"I beg your pardon?"

"That poor boy had a name," I said, staring deep into her brown eyes.

"I swear I never spent a moment alone with him," she said, returning my gaze. "And I never spoke to him except to say hello, good-bye, and you're flat."

I must have looked confused, because she explained.

"A violin doesn't have frets. He played well, but he was prone to be flat. Sorry; I have perfect pitch."

"I believe you," I said, standing up.

"Thanks, but I can prove my perfect pitch if you're being sarcastic."

"No. I meant I believe that you didn't seduce Jerry Kaufman."

She cocked her head as a dog might do when confused. "You believe me now? After blackening my name? Why?"

"Because you didn't know Jerry's family name. Only a monster could make love to a boy and not remember his name. And I don't think you're a monster."

"Just a whore," she said. "Thanks."

I ignored her and began to pace the room. She asked what I was doing.

"If you're not Mimi," I began, "then who is?"

"I have no idea. I barely knew the kid."

Mimi, I thought.

We fell silent for a moment, and I heard Cousin Max singing slightly off-key, "*Mi chiamano Mimi.*"

And all at once, the fog cleared. The answer had been there all along, but I had missed the clue. I felt that revelatory crawl of my skin. Over my shoulders and up my neck.

"I know who Mimi is," I whispered.

The answer had been so maddeningly close. Max had, in fact, prompted me for it the night before, but I'd been too tired and full of self-pity to indulge him.

"I confess that I only know the first line," he had said, referring to the Puccini aria. "Ellie, my dear, surely you know the whole thing. What comes next?"

I indeed knew the whole thing. One of the most famous and best-known arias in the Romantic operatic canon: "*Mi chiamano Mimi*" ("They call me Mimi"). What came next, to answer dear, befuddled Max's question, was, *Ma il mio nome è Lucia* ("But my name is Lucia").

Lucia Blanchard, cellist and wife-swapper par excellence, was Jerry Kaufman's Mimi. She'd surely come up with the clever pet name to protect the secrecy of her immoral liaison with a sixteen-year-old boy. I imagined her giggling with young Jerry, instructing him to call her Mimi instead of her true name just before she debauched him in her car. I understood some of her motivation, of course. Just not the part about a sixteen-year-old boy. Secrets add delicious spice to an affair, heightening the naughtiness and cementing the complicity between two lovers.

The unmasking of Mimi cleared up other mysteries for me as well. For one it meant that Jerry had indeed met his older lover at Tom's Lakeside Motel after all. Only it wasn't Miriam, but Lucia, who had checked in August 6, just two hours before Isaac met Gayle Morton there.

Now the question was what to do with this information. I had to find my friend, Tiny Terwilliger, and let him know. Miriam Abramowitz was not the link between Karl Merkleson and Jerrold Kaufman. Whether Lucia Blanchard had slept with Karl, I couldn't say. But I remembered something Gayle Morton had told me about women throwing themselves at Karl. One of those she'd mentioned was a Spanish whore from the islands trying to ride her husband to a movie contract.

CHAPTER TWENTY-SIX

Isaac, Miriam, and I spent an hour and a half consulting with Bill Hoch on Simon's case. Terwilliger hadn't yet returned from the county seat, Elizabethtown. Hoch had managed to get in to see Simon, despite Bob Firth's attempts to stall him until the chief returned.

"Well, I suppose we could wait," Hoch had said in a slow, measured tone. He pursed his lips and gazed up at the ceiling as if putting his facts in order. "Let's see." He rubbed his chin. "Violation of due process, access to counsel . . ." He counted on his fingers, mumbling to himself but loud enough for poor Bob Firth to hear. "It will certainly invalidate any confession he might make." He thought some more, never looking at anything but the floor and ceiling and his ten fingers. "Well, young man," he said at length. "If that's your decision, I think we can live with that. I suppose your chief and the district attorney will understand that you meant well. When the case is dismissed, I mean."

"I'm sure the chief would want me to let you visit your client," said Bob Firth, who'd turned positively green.

Hoch nodded. "I thought he might."

I left Isaac and Miriam to their own devices. They had some business to attend to for Simon's defense. I asked Bob Firth to make sure Chief Terwilliger found me as soon as he returned; then I exited the police station and folded myself into the phone booth on the corner. I flipped through the thin directory, finding what I was looking for in short order.

BLANCHARD, Nelson, MD: Pine Grove Lane, ESsex3-8745.

The house was of recent construction: a ranch-style summer home, set back from the narrow little road beneath some tall pines. A secluded love nest for the wife-swappers and their conquests. I wondered why Lucia had felt it necessary to carry on with young Jerry in motels, cars, and hunters' shelters. But then I figured maybe she didn't want to share him with Dr. Nelson. Or, more likely, Jerry Kaufman wanted nothing to do with him.

The good doctor was pruning some rose bushes in front of the house when I walked up the path. I cleared my throat to signal my presence, and he turned to look up from his kneeling position. His eyes lit up like an H-bomb. He jumped to his feet like a circus tumbler completing a somersault, doffed his gardening gloves, and fired his most lecherous smile my way.

"Ellie," he said. "How lovely to find you in my little garden. Don't worry, I'm not a serpent." And he leered at me.

Oh, God. Yuck.

"I'm looking for your wife," I said. "Is she in?"

"As a matter of fact, yes. She's out back. The neighbors insisted she do her sunbathing out of sight. Something about corrupting the minds of little children. As if the human body were something to be ashamed of." He grinned his toothy smile at me again.

"May I interrupt her?" I asked.

"Only if you're not offended by the nude form. She finds swimwear . . . er, confining."

Oh, God.

"I'll look the other way."

Blanchard escorted me around the house to a clearing among the trees in the back. There, on a chaise longue, flat on her stomach, her hair wrapped in a turban, lay a very bronzed and naked Lucia Blanchard.

"We have a visitor, *querida*," said Nelson, rolling the R like a Tijuana whore.

Lucia lifted her head slowly—perhaps she'd been dozing—and turned to see who had intruded on her leisure. Her tanned buttocks flexed as she twisted. I confess that I stared for a moment because—well—she *was* stunning and quite shameless. But then I averted my gaze and admired the nearby woods instead. Lucia flipped over to side B, and I glanced back despite myself as she provided me with an unsolicited view of her . . . pulchritude. She said hello. Making no effort to cover herself, she wasn't going to make this easy.

"Ellie," she said with her sexy little accent.

"Hello, Lucia," I answered, willing myself to focus on her sunglasses. "I'd like to ask you a few questions about a delicate matter."

"I have nothing to hide," she said, punctuating her words with an open-armed gesture. My best intentions notwithstanding, I found myself staring at her tanned breasts.

"You know Simon Abramowitz," I said. She nodded. "He's under arrest."

Lucia shifted in her seat. Nelson gasped and grabbed me by the shoulders and asked if I was serious.

"He confessed to killing Karl Merkleson. That is, Charles Morton."

"I can't believe it," said Nelson. "Simon and Karl were old friends. They used to be inseparable. Why would he do it?"

"He claimed something had come between them. You told me you'd known him for a long time. Any idea what that something might have been?"

Nelson stuck out his chin, mugging ignorance.

"How about you, Lucia?" I asked. "Did you ever meet Karl Merkleson?"

She was inscrutable behind her sunglasses as she answered no.

"You did meet him once, *querida*," said her husband. "It was your first visit here after our marriage. It must have been in fifty-four."

"Was it? I don't remember him," she said.

"Never saw him in Los Angeles?" I asked.

"I don't believe so," she said. "But so many men try to talk to me. I can't keep track."

"She was a blushing young bride," Nelson said to me. "Just twenty-two years old. I had to beat off all the men who couldn't keep their eyes off her. Karl was one of them. And, yes, *querida*, you met him in Los Angeles. He was the film producer."

"So many producers, *mi amor*. You shop me around like you want to sell me."

She removed her glasses, placing them on the table beside her, and batted her eyes hard enough to create a breeze. Maybe she didn't remember Karl Merkleson, or maybe she'd known him better than her own husband knew. The Blanchards had an open marriage, enjoyed naughty games with new partners, but who knew what really went on? Nelson Blanchard was a horny old goat and maybe an unaware cuckold as well.

Or maybe she was smart enough to deny that she'd known the dead man at all.

"Then you don't remember meeting Karl Merkleson seven years ago either?" I asked her.

"No. Why do you ask?"

"I'm trying to establish some kind of connection between Karl Merkleson and Jerry Kaufman."

"That's the boy who fell off the cliffs with Karl," said Nelson.

"You knew Jerry?" I asked.

"No," he said. "Never met him. But I read about the whole thing in the weekly *Pennysaver*. And the entire village is talking about it. Heard it on the radio, too."

"And you, Lucia?"

She pushed out her full lips in a pout. "No, I didn't know him," she said.

"Didn't you?" I asked as naively as I could manage. "I thought you and he performed together in the Prospector Lake Chamber Players concert a couple of weeks ago. I saw the flyers."

Lucia Blanchard knitted her brow, as if trying to remember where she'd left something long ago. Her virginity, perhaps. Then she grabbed the beach towel from the chair next to her. She draped it over her nudity. At least the burlesque show was over. She smiled up at me.

"Yes, of course I'd met him," she said, chuckling as if to brush aside a misunderstanding. "I saw him a few times for rehearsals. But we weren't exactly chums. He was just a boy, after all."

"Do you like opera, Lucia?" I asked, throwing her for a loop.

"What?"

"You're a classically trained musician," I explained. "You must know a good deal about opera."

"Of course she does," said Nelson.

I sensed he was trying to make nice but only just beginning to understand that my intentions might not be as friendly as he'd thought.

"What are you driving at, Ellie?" she asked, still making attempts to smile, though obviously ill at ease with my questions.

"Don't you just love Puccini?" No answer. "My favorite Puccini opera is *La Bohème*. What about yours?"

"What's this all about?" asked Nelson.

I ignored him and took a step closer to Lucia. "I know that Jerry Kaufman had a girlfriend earlier this month. An older girlfriend named Mimi."

Lucia began wrapping herself in the towel. She knotted it above her left breast and stood. "I don't know anything about that," she said.

"This older woman seduced him. Took him to motels."

"You're not suggesting that I was that woman, are you?" she asked. "That's absurd. And my name is not Mimi."

Nelson Blanchard grabbed me by the elbow, and I wrenched myself free.

"But you are Mimi," I said. "And I'm going to inform the chief of police as soon as he gets back from Elizabethtown."

"I didn't seduce that boy," she said, her eyes laughing at me. "Go ahead and tell the police whatever you want."

"I have proof that you took a room at the Lakeside Motel on August sixth. And you took Jerry Kaufman there. I know it."

"How can you accuse her of that?" demanded Nelson. "You said the woman's name was Mimi. How can Lucia be Mimi?"

I looked to his wife. "You know so much about opera," I said. "Do you want to tell him, or shall I?"

Lucia looked down. I'd made the first dent in her veneer. I had her, I thought. Now impatient and annoyed with the discussion, she explained it to her husband as would a child forced to make a confession.

"She's referring to that famous aria in *La Bohème*. The character Mimi explains that her true name is . . ." She paused to glare at me. Her eyes weren't laughing now. "Her true name is Lucia."

Nelson looked puzzled. "You met this boy for sex?" he asked, betrayed, humiliated, and angry all at once. Or so it seemed. "Without me?"

They both laughed. They made a good team.

"I wanted to invite you, *mi amor*," she said to her husband. "But you know how selfish I am about my teenaged boys."

They laughed some more, but I sensed it was an act they'd rehearsed and planned for years. How better to deflect suspicion than with a good-natured belly laugh? No one would believe she'd cuckolded him with a young man if he dismissed it as a joke.

At length the Blanchards' mirth dwindled to intermittent sniggering and eye wiping.

"Where were you last Saturday at noon?" I asked.

"Last Saturday? I don't know where we were," said Lucia.

"*Querida*, we were right here in the backyard," said Nelson. "Don't you remember? You held a luncheon meeting of the Prospector Lake Chamber Players."

"Of course. Now I remember. We had egg-salad sandwiches and ginger ale."

"Lionel Somers and his wife were here and can corroborate that," added Nelson. "And Beatrice Eberle, the Chamber Players chairwoman, too."

"In fact, even Miriam Abramowitz was here," said Lucia. "But she was a little late."

We stood there in their backyard at an impasse. While I searched for a way to break their story, they locked eyes. Like longtime bridge partners, they enjoyed a silent communication, a channel of understanding open only to them. And they were expert cheaters with secret signals to reveal what cards they were holding. I watched for clues in their eyes, their mouths, their noses. But their faces were blank. They were communicating to each other, I was sure. But I didn't speak their language.

Finally they exchanged a subtle nod and turned to me. Composed and united, their laughing routine over, they assumed serious expressions.

"My husband and I are modern thinkers," said Lucia. "For us, jealousy has no place in love. We understand and support each other perfectly. But I did not seduce that boy."

I had one last ace in my hand, and now was the time to play it. "Then tell me and your husband exactly who you were seducing at the Lakeside Motel on August sixth."

But Lucia Blanchard was a better bridge player than I. She retrieved her sunglasses from the table and slipped them on, obscuring her eyes once again. Then she produced a trump.

"My husband knows all about it," she said, her voice oozing wicked delight. "I was with Isaac Eisenstadt."

CHAPTER
TWENTY-SEVEN

I drove back to Cedar Haven, my head in a fog. In the space of a week, I had fallen hard for a man, allowed myself to dream of a love affair greater than any I'd ever experienced, then discovered he had bedded half the women on the Eastern Seaboard. I was no prude, but this man was testing my patience and my better instincts. Isaac had slept with, in order, Miriam Abramowitz, wife of one of his oldest and dearest friends; Gayle Morton, also wife of one of his oldest and dearest friends; and Audrey Silber, cousin of one of his oldest and dearest friends. Then, if the wife-swappers were to be believed, he'd helped himself to Lucia Blanchard's charms two weeks before he'd had his way with me. It seemed no woman in Prospector Lake was immune to his magnetism. I wondered if he'd also bedded Ingve Enquist, the baker, and Mrs. Edmunds from the market. And I knew he'd lusted after my aunt Lena.

The thought made me laugh despite myself and brought me back to sanity. I had a doubt. If Lucia Blanchard was Mimi, she had seduced young Jerry Kaufman at the Lakeside Motel. Would she also have had the energy and inclination to give Isaac a roll as well? Perhaps. She was some kind of nympho-maniac, after all. But there were holes in her story, I thought as I pulled into Cedar Haven. And I believed she'd made it all up to get under my skin.

What did it matter anyway? I hadn't even met Isaac at that time. But the idea, the accumulation of undesirable partners, gave me pause. It made me feel like the lobster thermidor that's just discovered that the diner who's about to consume me ate a hot dog for an appetizer.

$\partial\!\!\!)$

By the time I'd dragged my sorry carcass into my little cabin, it was four. I threw myself on the bed and set my mind to the task at hand. I had to crack the Blanchards' united front and force her to admit to her illicit affair with Jerry Kaufman. I was fairly certain she also had a notch on her bedpost for Karl Merkleson, but I knew of no witnesses who'd seen her with either of the victims. She'd been careful, covering her tracks and fooling even her husband. I racked my brain, visualizing the village from end to end, looking for a hook that might have snagged her. My thoughts circled 'round and 'round, always coming home to roost at Tom's Lakeside Motel. Had Tom Waller perhaps noticed a teenaged boy in the company of the village's most notorious siren on or around August 6? Wouldn't he have told someone? I intended to ask him.

And once I'd obtained an admission from Lucia Blanchard, I wondered how I would figure out what roles she and her randy husband had played in the deaths of two of her sexual conquests.

The rumble of distant thunder caught my ear. The beautiful August day was going to end with lightning storms, it seemed.

I pushed the weather to one side and thought about the Blanchards. As I did, my eyes grew heavy, and I soon drifted off into a deep slumber. I didn't wake until nearly seven. Feeling hot and wooly-headed, I slipped into the shower behind my cabin. The cold water did me good, bracing my skin and chasing away the last traces of my drowsiness. As I buttoned my sundress, I wondered if Tiny Terwilliger had returned to town and sprung Simon. That was perhaps too much to hope, but I was confident my new information and Bill Hoch's skill would convince the chief that Simon's confession was bogus. I brushed my wet hair into submission and tied it back with an elastic and a hairband. Now it was time to find my pal, Tiny.

Before setting out, I stopped by the main cabin to see if Aunt Lena and Max had, by any chance, left me a cracker or two. The sky was dark with thunderheads, but still no rain. I unlocked the door and pushed it open, discovering an envelope on the floor. Someone had dropped it through the mail slot. I sat at the kitchen table, stuffed a couple of green olives into my mouth, and tore open the envelope. It was from Esther Merkleson. The autopsy report.

Dear Eleonora,
    Please read this report and contact me tomorrow. I am staying at the Sans Souci Cabins.
    Yours truly,
    Esther Merkleson

The pages consisted of a case report, a diagram of the body with injuries noted, and a narrative of the observations and conclusions of the examiner.

The case report gave the details of the deceased: height, weight, and cause of death, which was listed as internal injuries. In the space reserved for time of death, the pathologist had written "Saturday, August 19. Time unknown."

The diagram of the body showed a generic line drawing of the front and back views of a male figure. The examiner had shaded the right side of the torso with dark pencil and labeled it "livor mortis visible." The pathologist had also scribbled abrasions on the right side of the face and arm. He had noted fractures of the frontal, zygomatic, sphenoid, and mandible, all on the right side.

On the left side of the body, the doctor had circled the lateral rib cage and written "blunt force injuries, broken ribs, internal bleeding, ruptured spleen." Also noted were the broken ilium and hip, and at the very end "evidence of livor mortis."

The typewritten narrative provided the most interesting reading.

OBSERVATIONS:

The deceased is a white male in his mid-thirties. Health and condition appear to be excellent. Death was caused by internal bleeding and lacerations, resulting from massive blunt-force trauma to the left side of the torso. Observed intra-abdominal hemorrhage, hemothorax, and rupture of the spleen of sufficient severity to cause death. Other injuries contributing to death include fractures of the left anterior lateral ribs four through nine, the left ilium, and left greater trochanter. Presence of subcutaneous glass fragments discovered on left side.

Additional injuries observed: multiple contusions and abrasions on right side of face, arm, and torso, externally and internally, consistent with a fall from a great height. Fractured greater tubercle, clavicle, and two ribs. No internal bleeding observed on right side, indicating that these fractures occurred post-mortem.

Examination revealed the presence of lividity on the right side of the body, from the upper thorax to the thighs and, to a lesser degree, on the left side.

TIME OF DEATH:

Witnesses reported seeing the victim fall from a height of approximately seventy-five feet at 12:30 p.m. on Saturday, August 19, 1961. No evidence found to contradict the time of the fall.

CONCLUSIONS:

Death was caused by a blunt-force injury to the left side of the body. Postmortem injuries and presence of lividity on the right and left sides indicate conclusively that the body was moved after death. While I am unable to determine if death was accidental or inflicted by another party, it is evident that death occurred elsewhere other than the site where the body was found, unless the body fell twice from the top of the cliff, hours apart.

Submitted this 25th day of August 1961, by Peter Stueben, MD

I stared at the page. The injury to the left side, the smaller bruised area I'd observed on Karl Merkleson's body, was the blow that killed him. The broken bones on his right side had occurred after death. I had assumed the body had simply bounced or rolled when it hit the rocks, thus accounting for the injury to his left side. This new information changed all my preconceptions about the two deaths at Baxter's Rock.

But the biggest surprise in the autopsy report was the presence of glass in the wound on Karl's left side. I didn't remember having seen any broken glass on the rocks where he fell. But then I reminded myself that the report made it clear that death had occurred somewhere else, unless the body had been thrown off the cliff twice, which seemed unlikely. Where, then, had Karl Merkleson died, and how? And what about Jerry Kaufman? Had he died where his body was found? Had he died at the same time as Karl Merkleson? I would probably never know, since there had been no autopsy performed on the boy, and I figured he'd already been buried. I made up my mind, though, to contact the Kaufmans to encourage them to order an autopsy on their son.

I put down the report and crossed the compound to my cabin. There, I retrieved an envelope from the dresser drawer. Inside were the color slides

I'd shot with Fadge on Thursday morning. In light of the autopsy report, I wanted to have a second look at them. I doubted I'd be able to discern any broken glass in the transparencies, at least not without a good projector to enlarge them. And I knew now that Karl Merkleson had died elsewhere, that his left side had most certainly collected the glass fragments in that unknown place. Still, I had to cover all the bases to be sure.

"Any sparkles?" I asked the slides as I peered into them with a loupe. "Come on. Show me some glass."

My examination of the slides was interrupted by a car arriving outside. I looked out the window and saw Terwilliger's pickup truck.

CHAPTER
TWENTY-EIGHT

Tiny Terwilliger showed up at Cedar Haven a little after eight. Dressed in his finest police uniform, he actually looked like a cop. He'd shaved that morning, and his hair was clean. The fabric of his trousers was still engaged in a pitched battle against the broadness of his backside and the volume of his protuberant belly, but one couldn't expect miracles in just one day. I let him inside and told him I didn't have anything to offer him except the last of the gin and Scotch. He'd finished his supper, he said, so he wasn't wanting for food. He did, however, accept my offer of booze. I poured myself a short one as well.

"What's the latest on Simon Abramowitz?" I asked as he eased himself into Max's armchair.

"He's still in the jail," said Tiny, swallowing some gin with a grimace. "Fine stuff."

"He didn't sign any confession, did he?"

"Nope. Changed his mind about that, which was too bad. I was hoping to be finished with this case by now."

"You know he confessed only to protect his wife," I said.

"Yeah, that's what I figure. Still, a fellow can hope for an easy solution, can't he?"

"Then why is he still in jail?"

"He made a false statement to the police. That's a crime. I have to make an example out of him. Besides, it might get his wife to own up to defiling that boy."

"But she didn't do it," I said.

Tiny looked surprised. "But you told me she did. You said her name was Mimi."

"I was wrong. It turns out only her husband calls her Mimi, and she didn't have a relationship with Jerry Kaufman."

He drained his glass and stood to refill it.

265

"We only have time for one more," I said. "I have new information, and I think you're going to want to talk to Nelson and Lucia Blanchard."

"What for?" he asked, draining the last of the gin into his glass. "Does this mix with whiskey?"

I shook my head. "I know now that Lucia Blanchard is Mimi."

"Are the Blanchards those perverts who have a place on Pine Grove Lane?" he asked, and I nodded. "So how do you know that she's Mimi?"

I explained the Puccini reference to him, but he didn't exactly swallow it whole on the first cast. He drank his gin and frowned, telling me that it all seemed like a lot of hooey to him. He asked if I'd spoken to the Blanchards about it, and I told him I had.

"I suppose they denied everything," he said.

"Of course. They even have an airtight alibi for twelve thirty last Saturday."

"Then that shifts the suspicion back to your friends. Especially Miriam Abramowitz."

"Afraid not," I said. "Miriam was with the Blanchards at the time. Unless they're lying for each other, they couldn't possibly have been near Baxter's Rock at half past noon last Saturday."

"Then we're still stuck," he said. "I've got two witnesses who saw them fall to their deaths at twelve thirty."

"But they only saw one man fall," I corrected. "Jerry Kaufman."

"What are you saying?"

"Just that they couldn't possibly have seen Karl Merkleson fall to his death."

"And why not?" he asked.

"Because he was already dead well before twelve thirty," I said with a flourish. "I've seen the autopsy report."

"Autopsy? What autopsy?"

"Esther Merkleson asked for one. Don't you remember releasing the body to her?"

"Sure," he said, taking a gulp of his gin. "But I thought she just wanted it for burial. Did she say why she wanted an autopsy?"

"She suspected her daughter-in-law, Gayle Morton, was guilty of some kind of foul play," I said.

Tiny stared deep into his drink and frowned. "Are you sure about this time of death thing?" he asked. I nodded. He downed the rest of his drink, the last gin of the summer. Then he stood up. "All right, then. Let's go talk to the perverts."

On my way out the door, I stuffed the envelope with the transparencies into my purse along with my camera. The slides were an integral part of my plan to extract a confession from the Blanchards.

Tiny's truck was no less smelly that night, but I figured it would be the last time I'd have to suffer it. On the ride, I explained the Puccini reference again, and Tiny seemed to buy into my reasoning better the second time around. Then I gave him my theory on the perverts' dealings with Karl Merkleson. Nelson Blanchard liked to brag about his Hollywood projects. He'd told me that he'd been working on a movie project with Karl, *The Scarlett Lady*. I had doubted him, of course, sure no one would be interested in making any of his debauched masterpieces into pictures, but he talked a big game. Nelson's dirty movie provided the link I'd been searching for. Surely Lucia had been lying to me about knowing Karl.

Lucia was the bridge between Karl Merkleson and Jerry Kaufman. I still didn't know exactly how the two men had come to die, but it was clear that Karl's death was no simple diving accident. The autopsy had eliminated that possibility.

We were rattling along Lake Road, heading south on Route 15 toward the village, just as the skies finally opened up, and the rain began to fall in earnest. Then Tiny plowed into a pothole, sending a bang and a shudder through the truck. Seconds later we heard the folding rubber and felt the shaking of a deflated driver's side front tire. Tiny swore then apologized to me for his language. He pulled over and climbed out of the cab.

"I'll just be ten minutes to change the tire," he said, throwing a coat over his head to protect against the downpour.

He opened the tailgate and heaved himself up into the flatbed, and the truck lurched under his weight. I could hear the clanging of metal.

It was bad enough being cooped up in the smelly truck when it was moving, but parked at the shoulder with the windows closed was more than I'd bargained for. I wanted to stick my head out the window, but the rain ruined that idea. I needed a distraction from the odor. Then I remembered my slides. I flicked on the dome light and retrieved the envelope and loupe from my purse.

Having located the tools he needed to change the flat, Tiny dis-

mounted from the flatbed, and I'm pretty sure he stumbled and fell on his
face in the wet gravel. I heard a thud, a splash, and more swearing.

"Sorry about that!" he called from behind the truck.

Then he passed the driver's side window and ducked down to deal
with the tire. In no time, he was cranking the jack and lifting the truck off
the ground.

"The rim's ruined," he yelled, convinced that I somehow cared either
way about the wheels of his truck. "I hit that hole pretty hard."

I turned my attention to the transparencies. There was plenty of sunlight in the photographs but nothing looking like broken glass on the
black rocks. Staring at one after the other, squinting through the loupe for
any sign, I shut out the clanking and huffing coming from underneath the
driver's side fender and focused on the images.

The painted lines provided a strong contrast to the black rocks, and
the bright sun gave everything a warm color temperature. What was I
looking for? I scanned the ground for anything resembling glass, even
though I knew that the glass must have come from somewhere else. The
shale was flat, flaked, and gave up no secrets. The sky was clear, already blue
at a few minutes past eight. Nothing helpful there. I zeroed in on a large
shadow being thrown by Fadge, even if he was not otherwise visible in the
photograph, and I lost track of the outside world. I fell into a near trance,
a meditative state of complete immersion, as I gazed at the shadow. And
that was when I saw it. I saw what had been there in plain sight all along.

I slid across the seat to the driver's side, intending to share the news
with Tiny, who was still grunting away as he performed his task. But
something poking out from under the seat caught my eye. It was a brown
envelope. It looked familiar, right down to the ring left by a beer glass at
Arcadia. It was the envelope I'd given to Tiny. The one with the prints and
negatives of the two dead bodies inside. The idiot was supposed to turn
them over to the state police. I couldn't say if it was laziness, incompetence,
or indifference, but he was the worst lawman I'd ever met.

I'd only looked at the photographs once, but now I was curious. Forgetting about my plan to tell Tiny about my discovery, I yanked the black-
and-white prints out of the envelope and pored over them. The images
were sharp and showed some details not immediately evident to me at the
scene. Merkleson was lying on his right side with his head pointing more
or less east. The sunburn covering his back looked even fiercer in the grainy

black-and-white photos. What struck me as odd, though, was how the burn ended at mid-calf, below which his skin had retained its very white complexion. Thanks to the high walls of the cove, the sun's rays would be blocked as it rose high in the sky on its westward journey. And that was the confirmation of my discovery of a few minutes before.

I picked up the slides again and peered through the loupe. Yes, the sun was what I'd missed. So obvious and so bright. I'd shot those color slides a few minutes after eight in the morning on Thursday, and the sun was burning brightly onto the painted outlines left by the state police. I verified one last time. It was a coincidence, to be sure. But like a sundial, Karl Merkleson's painted outline showed me the exact time his body had landed on the shale beneath Baxter's Rock. In several of my slides, the sun was illuminating the outlined figure on the rocks from the top of the head to mid-calf. Someone had dumped Karl Merkleson's dead body off the cliff a few minutes after 8:00 a.m., I was certain.

The driver's door opened, and Tiny climbed back in. I had to slide over to the passenger's side to make room. Drenched in rain, with black hands, he turned the key and looked over at me. Still he managed a smile.

"All fixed," he said, reaching for the gear shift. "Now let's go see those perverts."

"I think I've broken their alibi," I said, quite proud of myself.

"How'd you manage that?" he asked, taking his hands off the gears and leaning onto the steering wheel.

"While you were wrestling with the tire, I was looking at the photographs I took Thursday morning."

He stared at me. "Thursday? You took more pictures?"

"I wanted better photos. I shot some color slides."

He nodded. "Anything interesting?"

"As a matter of fact, yes. I know now exactly when Karl Merkleson went over the cliff."

"From the pictures you took? How could you tell that?"

"From the position of the sun on the painted outline of the body and the actual sunburn on Karl's skin. They match exactly. So you see, he must have been thrown over the cliff earlier than twelve thirty. At a couple of minutes after eight. That's what time it was when I took those pictures on Thursday."

"But I've got two witnesses who say he went over the cliff at twelve thirty."

"Right," I said. "The state police are going to have to speak to those witnesses. There's something fishy about their story. You have their address and telephone number, I assume."

"Sure," he said, the truck still idling in park on the side of the road. "But how do you know Merkleson's sunburn matches the outline on the rocks? Is your memory that good?"

I held up the envelope I'd found on the floor of his truck. "Right here. Tiny, you were supposed to give these to the state police." He assumed a suitably sheepish expression, and I smiled. "Good thing you didn't, though."

"I guess I forgot," he said.

"Just like you forgot to check on Gayle Morton's airline ticket."

That last rebuke appeared to sting him, and I thought I may have taken my ribbing too far.

"At any rate," I continued, "we'll have to get those witnesses back up here to talk with the state police. Their story threw us off the trail for a week."

"Let me see those photographs of yours," he said.

I handed him the black-and-white prints of the bodies, along with the loupe; the contact sheet images were small. He studied them carefully, then asked for the slides and began scanning the images one by one.

"Sorry, which pictures show the sun on the outlines?" he asked, offering the sleeve back to me.

I took it and the loupe and held them up to my eye to find the relevant slides.

"If only there had been a witness at eight a.m.," I mused. "Someone on land, not water like that father and son, who mucked up everything. Jerry Kaufman's girlfriend heard a car on the road, remember. Squealing tires."

"Must have been those drag racers I've been looking for," said Tiny.

"Probably. I wonder if that car did hit something," I said, still looking at the slides, searching for the best one to illustrate my point about the sun. "Karl Merkleson, perhaps. That would explain the glass fragments the coroner found in his skin." I sighed. "But there were no reported accidents, you said. Nothing all week. No one hit anyth—"

I stopped mid-word. My skin went cold. I tried to act as if nothing had happened. I pretended to examine the slides while my mind searched frantically for an out. I knew in that moment that I was sitting next to a murderer.

CHAPTER
TWENTY-NINE

As I stared at the photographs through the loupe, I felt something hard against my arm, followed by a smart, metallic click. I dropped the slides and turned to see the hard steel, quality carbon steel, on my wrist. Terwilliger had just handcuffed me.

Before I could react, the beast snapped the other cuff onto his right hand then threw the truck into gear.

"What are you doing?" I gasped as the speed of our acceleration pushed me back in the seat.

He shook his head slowly with what looked like genuine regret on his face. "You just wouldn't let it go," he said softly. "A simple accident turned into a double murder."

"That's not my fault," I stammered. "It wasn't an accident."

"Yeah, but it was an accident until you stuck your nose into it. I was just hoping you'd go home, forget all about Baxter's Rock, and all this would've been over. Why did you have to meddle, Ellie?"

I had no answer. I just ordered him to unlock the cuffs and let me out. He didn't say anything but made a sharp turn instead. I looked through the windshield, into the pouring rain, and saw that we were on a narrow lane, heading up a slow incline. He was driving fast, bouncing and careening from side to side over the rough, wet road. Then we made another turn, onto an unpaved path that grew steeper and muddier as we went.

"You didn't hit a deer," I said. "You ran over Karl Merkleson on Route Fifteen, didn't you? It was automobile glass in his skin. From your broken headlamp."

"It was an accident," he said, wiping the fogged-up windshield with his right hand, dragging my cuffed left along for the ride. "He was walking along the road just south of Grover Road at about seven in the morning. Just about a quarter mile from here. God knows why. Probably heading back to the Sans Souci after a night in that hunters' shelter with Miriam or Mimi or whatever her name is. But I didn't know that then. I seen a car parked near Grover Road when I passed it, and I figured that was his."

"My cousin Max's station wagon," I prompted.

"That's what I found out later. But at that time, I thought it was his. The guy I ran over."

"So you put him in the car and drove to a spot you knew to dispose of him. Baxter's Rock."

He didn't answer. Just steered, looking straight into the thrashing rain.

"You were drunk," I said to accuse. "You smelled of beer that day, I remember. You always smell of beer. You're even drunk now. You ran straight through that pothole and blew a tire because you'd had two gins and who knows how many beers before that for supper."

"I drive just fine when I've had a few. It's only beer."

"You ran him over," I said again in disbelief.

"Yeah, he was dead on the spot. Or maybe just a few minutes later. I felt real bad about it."

I put the events together in my mind. Jerry Kaufman and Emily Grierson had just parted company at seven. She heard the squealing tires on the road as a drunken Terwilliger tried, too late, to brake and avoid Karl. He hit him hard. Hard enough to cause the fatal internal injuries reported in the autopsy. Terwilliger remembered having passed Max's car just a few dozen yards before he'd crushed Karl Merkleson to death with his smelly truck. Thinking Max's car belonged to the dead man, he put the body into the way-back and drove him to the top of Baxter's Rock, intending to make his death look like an accident. Karl must have lain in the car for some time; that would account for the lividity on his left side. I still didn't know how Jerry Kaufman fit into the picture.

The wipers slapped back and forth, sloshing the water off the glass in sheets, as the truck barreled up the hill.

"The screeching tires Emily Grierson heard were yours," I said.

"Yeah, I'm gonna have to do something about that little girl," said Terwilliger.

My chest tightened. He couldn't be serious. "Are you mad?" I said. "She didn't see anything. She didn't even think there'd been an accident."

"Can't take that chance." He shrugged.

Oh, God. Why had I told him her name? Time was short. I had to slip the cuffs and get away, not only to save my own skin but Emily Grierson's as well.

"What are you planning to do with me?" I asked just as Terwilliger steered into a large branch that whacked the windshield directly in front of me. I ducked, but the glass held. When I lifted my head again, a crack, looking like a bolt of lightning, had spread across the windshield, reaching nearly halfway across the driver's side.

"I've really grown to like you, Ellie," he said, struggling to control the mushy steering in the mud.

Maybe he'll crash into a tree and knock himself cold, I thought. He was a lousy driver, after all. Especially when drunk, as he was now. Not a speech-slurring intoxication, but he was impaired.

"You've got a funny way of showing your affection," I said. "Please let me go and stop this madness."

He said nothing. Just stepped a little harder on the gas.

My best hope was for him to drive off the road, even if it killed us both. At least Emily would be safe. I wondered if I had the courage to grab the wheel and steer us into a tree. Or perhaps I could wrestle his gun away from him. But I'd need to displace his belly first then manage to extract the gun from the waistband of his trousers. I had a better chance of pulling Excalibur from the stone.

"If Karl's death was an accident, why did you kill poor Jerry Kaufman?" I asked, trying to distract him.

"I didn't want to do it," he said. "But the kid showed up in the wrong place at the wrong time. He came out of the woods just as I was rolling the guy over the edge."

"And you chased him down?"

Terwilliger shook his head. "No. I just called out to him, told him I was the chief of police, and he came over. He sure was a well-behaved young man. Respected the law."

"How could you just push him over the edge?" I asked. "At least Karl was already dead, but that poor kid. How could you do it?"

"I didn't enjoy it," he said as a matter of fact. "But I had to. He saw what I did."

I shook in horror at the thought of Jerry Kaufman dutifully obeying his heartless killer when he should have run for his life.

"Why did you dispose of Karl's shirt?" I asked with a bitter taste on my tongue. I had to keep him talking. "Was there blood?"

He nodded. "Yeah. Blood. And the shirt was all ripped and torn from the accident. I had to get rid of it. I couldn't fold it up nicely on the seat of your cousin's car like I did with the rest of his clothes. That wouldn't have looked right."

"When did you throw that wash-and-wear shirt in the water?"

"I had no intention of doing that until you started asking where his shirt was. So I went to the Sears in Elizabethtown and bought a shirt. I thought that might put the question to rest."

A flash of lightning lit the sky, and a great bang of thunder sounded directly overhead. Terwilliger flinched and nearly lost control of the truck. But he steered through the mud, his tires soon found the ruts again, and we were back on course.

"And there never were any witnesses," I said. "No one found the shirt in the lake. You did. And there was no father and son in a boat either."

"Nope. That's why I'm doing this, Ellie. You're insisting on telling the state police about the witnesses. It would've come out that I was lying. I sure wish you hadn't done that."

Me too, I thought. Or, at the very least, I wished I'd kept it to myself.

In all the time since he'd handcuffed me and turned off the main road, I hadn't given any thought to where he was taking me. I was concentrating on distracting him with questions while I tried to figure out a way to get him to run off the road. But suddenly as we spun up the slippery hill, I realized he was heading for Baxter's Rock. One-trick pony. Oh, God. My insides tightened, and I steadied myself by clutching the door handle as if it were trying to run. I knew what was coming next. He was going to throw me off the cliff.

And just as I came to that terrifying realization, with no more time to wrench the steering wheel from his hands or make a grab for his gun, we reached the crest of the hill. Even in the dark, I recognized the clearing where we'd discovered Max's car one week before. Terwilliger skidded to a slippery stop in the wet grass on his bald tires.

"We'll wait a bit till the rain eases up," he said, and I struggled to catch my breath. "I'm real sorry, Ellie. Real sorry. That's why I kept you so close this past week. Once you started asking about loose ends, I had to know what you were onto. And then I grew to like you."

"You don't have to do this," I said. "And Emily Grierson poses no threat to you. She didn't see anything. You're safe."

He switched off the engine.

We waited. It felt like an eternity. My guts churning, my mind ablaze, thoughts and schemes ricocheting off the walls of my skull, I rooted desperately for an idea, an out. I was finding no traction at all, though, as my captor just sat there, waiting for the rain to stop so he wouldn't get his hair wet. Then I caught myself, grappling to gain control of my careering emotions. Panic wasn't working. I had no chance if I didn't concentrate. Calm. I needed to think rationally. God knows Terwilliger was calm, and he seemed to know exactly what he was going to do to accomplish his goals. I had to do the same.

I drew a breath and held it, as if trying to suffocate an insistent case of the hiccoughs. Then I exhaled and drew another breath. I considered the situation. I was handcuffed to the man who was planning to throw me over the cliff. That meant he had to release me, unlock the handcuffs, before sending me to my doom. That was the moment I had to make my move. I had to win one battle in that last fleeting moment of freedom. My options were few, I thought, as Terwilliger watched the rain sullenly. I could try to overpower him, but that was unlikely. He outweighed me by at least a hundred and fifty pounds. He was a strong man, if not fit. And I was as physically unimposing a specimen as you could hope to find. But I was fairly fleet of foot, and it was dark. I was sure I could outrun the ape in the open field.

I weighed my other advantages. He was drunk. I wasn't sure exactly how much of an edge that might prove to be, since he was also cagey and I was chained to him. And he had a gun, the half-strangled pistol he'd ruined for resale by stuffing down his pants. I put that thought to one side and continued my inventory of options.

He clearly liked me, even if he was determined to shove me off a cliff. That was a plus in my column. Could I use my charms to distract or delay him? I didn't see how, short of stripping out of my clothes. And I had no intention of doing that. If I had to die, I was going to die with my dignity intact. What did I have in my purse? Anything that might incapacitate a killer? No guns, knives, or weapons of any kind. I struggled to remember if there was a small vial of perfume. If so, I might, if my aim was true, squirt a healthy dose into his eyes and make good my escape. I knew for sure that my Leica was inside my purse. Maybe I could bash him on the head with it. But how would I accomplish that? Ask him to pose for one last photograph?

None of these ideas was viable, I realized. My only hope was to run when he unlocked the handcuffs.

"I think the rain's letting up," he said, bringing me back to the present. "That's the way it is with these storms. They come in quick, dump a lot of rain, and move on soon enough."

"How right you are. Thanks for giving me something so banal to ponder in the last moments of my life."

"Don't be like that," he whined. "Do you think I want to do this?"

"Listen to yourself," I yelled. "You're about to kill me, and you're asking for my understanding."

He went quiet, perhaps thinking about my words. For a brief moment, I thought I'd reached him. Then he nodded. "You're right. That was wrong of me. You see, you really have taught me a lot of things."

I looked into his lazy eyes, hoping for a change of heart. I was disappointed.

"Okay," he said. "The rain's stopped. Let's go before it starts again."

CHAPTER THIRTY

Ever the gentleman, Terwilliger invited me to leave the cab on my side, and he followed, extending his meaty right hand to provide me with some slack. He nearly slipped in the wet grass. Had my hand been free of the handcuffs, that would have been the moment to run. But tethered to Baby Huey, I had no hope of escape. I had to wait for my chance.

The storm had paused only long enough to get us out of the truck. Not ten paces into the grass, the heavens opened again and favored us with a downpour to impress Noah.

"Too late to stay dry now," said Terwilliger. "Come on."

He led the way through the high, wet grass, pulling me along by the wrist.

The thunderheads raced across the sky, dumping buckets of rain over the land and occasionally exposing the moon. The refracted light made the night brighter than normal, even if the clouds were black and roiling above. Still I could barely make out the edge of the cliff before us. He reached into his pocket and produced a steel key. My last chance was upon me.

"Give me your hand," he said.

I braced myself for what was to come next. I intended to slap him or push him. Poke him in the eyes or stick two fingers up his nostrils and roll him over the cliff like a bowling ball. Maybe I'd kick him in the shins, then run. Which was I going to do? I was panicking again. Drawing one deep, wet breath, I made my decision.

We were about twenty feet from the edge of the cliff. Driven by strong, whipping winds, the rain strengthened as if bent on making my last moments on earth wetter and even more uncomfortable. He squared up to me, pulling me in close, his belly pressing against mine. Holding my arm tight with his right hand, he squeezed the steel key in his left.

"Just hold still now," he said, fiddling with the lock. He couldn't see in the dark, and it took him several tries before he found the hole.

The lock sprang.

I jerked my knee into his groin and pushed away in one motion, taking off on a sprint. He tried to snatch my arm, scratching me in the process, but my wet skin foiled his grip. He shouted for me to stop. The last thing I saw was the approaching void.

In that instant before he'd unlocked the handcuffs, I'd realized in a moment of perfect clarity that my only chance of survival was to dive off the cliff and reach the water below. My only chance. Emily Grierson's only chance. But a successful leap off Baxter's Rock involved not only gaining enough speed to clear the beach below, but also jumping in the right direction. A takeoff too far to the right would send me onto the high rocks that separated the cove from the lake to the south. The same result to the north if I pitched myself over the edge too far to the left. But it was too late for any such doubts. I didn't have the luxury to pause to consider angles and hazards below the lip of the cliff. I ducked my head, closed my eyes, and barreled toward the edge, even as Terwilliger shouted behind me, and the thunder boomed over my head.

One, two, three, four, five strides and I pushed off like a bird taking flight. Reaching out as if trying to grab the moon, I soared skyward before gravity drew me back to earth. I stretched into an arrow-straight dive, aiming my fingertips toward whatever fate awaited me below. Everything went silent. Everything stopped for an instant as I fell. My soul was at peace with my decision to fly, and I was ready to die. Die in a spectacular, adrenaline-fueled leap into the night. My end would be swift. No suffering, no awareness of the impact on the sharp rocks. Just a broken neck and a crumpled—

A boom interrupted any thoughts of consequences. Then a tumbling and bubbles and water up my nose. It was cold and wet. I had hit the cove in a magnificent dive, and I was still alive.

I kicked my way to the surface and gasped for air, eyes still clenched shut. My relief was short-lived, however, as even amid the thunder and the sloshing water and my own desperate respiration, I heard the gunshots. I drew two quick breaths and ducked under the water again.

There were rocks, I knew, at the entrance to the cove. I could find shelter there. Kicking and stroking under the surface, I swam furiously toward the open lake. Swimming in a dress isn't as easy as one might think. The fabric becomes heavy when laden with water. It drags, makes you work twice as hard to move half as far and half as fast. And the dress I was wearing was bright yellow, surely making me an easy target in the water. I had to dive deeper. But first I needed air. I came up for a breath but didn't wait for any bullets to find me. I gasped twice and dived back under.

Twenty seconds later, I surfaced again like a whale breaching. I wheezed, tried to suck in as much air as I could, then plunged into the dark water, kicking deeper, seeking the protection of the depth. But the lake floor had risen, and I found myself in barely four feet of water. I was a sitting duck.

I heard no shots. My feet found the muddy bottom, and I ran for my life. Rather I tried to run, but the water and my dress slowed me as if I were dragging a wet parachute. Finally I reached the rocks that guarded the entrance to the cove, the same entrance that Terwilliger had navigated one week before when I first saw the two dead bodies. Now those rocks provided me with cover. I scrambled behind the largest one protruding from the water and cowered behind it, heaving for breath.

I listened, but all I could hear was rain and thunder off in the distance. I waited more than a minute before chancing a glance over the top of the rock. I could make out the crest of Baxter's Rock against the gray-black sky, but just barely. If Terwilliger was still there, searching for me, I couldn't see him. Then a bolt of lightning streaked across the sky, and he came into view, standing atop the hill, arms akimbo, peering into the night. The light vanished after three quick flashes, and all was dark again. I waited thirty seconds more until the wind, coursing west to east above, cleared a swath of sky and revealed the moon. The clouds lit up, and I could see again. There atop Baxter's Rock, large and menacing, scanning the cove below for signs of movement, paced Ralph "Tiny" Terwilliger.

I heard shouting. My name. He was calling out to me. Other than my name, I couldn't make out his words. I shrank behind the rock, my eyes just high enough to hold him in my sight. He was terrifying, standing there, yelling my name, knowing I was below listening. Then he turned. He wasn't alone. And I saw him stumble. I watched him teeter at the edge of the precipice. And I watched in horror as he plunged palsied into the void. Unlike his imaginary father and son witnesses, I was close enough to hear his scream and the impact on the rocks below. Tiny Terwilliger did not clear the stony beach. He did not reach the water.

CHAPTER THIRTY-ONE

I phoned the state police from Lenny's Diner on Lake Road. It was past eleven by then, and I was soaking wet in my torn yellow dress, no shoes on my feet, with my hair looking like Medusa's after a couple of turns on the Coney Island Cyclone. The place was empty, except for Lenny and the dishwasher. Lenny just stared at me, mouth agape, a wad of chewing gum forgotten somewhere between his tongue and cheek. My conversation with the troopers surely shocked him. Chief Terwilliger dead on the shore below Baxter's Rock, in the same spot Karl Merkleson and Jerry Kaufman had been found.

"Yes, he tried to kill me," I insisted into the receiver. "He handcuffed me and drove me up to the cliff. I have marks on my wrist. He was going to push me off."

At length the doubting policeman on the other end of the line agreed to send a couple of cruisers over from Schroon Lake to investigate.

"Would you like some coffee, miss?" asked Lenny once I'd hung up the phone. "It's a couple of hours old, I'm afraid."

"Thank you," I said, sniffling, trying to keep warm by hugging my wet self.

"That'll be ten cents," he said, placing the cup down before me. "And a dollar should cover the long-distance call."

Forty minutes later, the state troopers still hadn't arrived. I was shivering in a booth near the back, cursing Lenny the cheapskate, who would have to wait for his dollar and ten cents. My purse was somewhere on top of Baxter's Rock. I was also feeling a bit overwhelmed by the drama of the past seven days. Karl Merkleson and Jerry Kaufman, Isaac, Simon, the rest of the Arcadians, and, of course, Tiny Terwilliger. A tightness in my chest, combined with the dunking I'd taken, made me feel lonely and forsaken. I thought of Isaac.

The dishwasher appeared above me. He was a short, square man of about fifty. He had nervous eyes, the kind that dart around in search of a place to rest. His hands were rough and red.

"You look cold," he said, holding out a neatly folded tablecloth. "This is the closest thing we got to a blanket. It's clean."

I wrapped the cloth around my shoulders and thanked him.

"What happened out there anyway?" he asked.

"I'm not sure I should say."

"Did Tiny Terwilliger really fall off Baxter's Rock?"

"He must have slipped," I said, just as four state troopers entered the diner.

The state police radioed for five more cruisers, a lieutenant, four troopers, a hearse, and a photographer. I showed them the scene from the top of the cliff and from the rocks below, explained what had happened, and answered the same questions three different times from three different officers.

"We've recovered his gun," said Lieutenant Miller Sutter as we sat in the backseat of a state police cruiser. Sutter was tall and slim, about thirty-five, with broad shoulders and a deep voice. Gosh, cops are sexy. "Looks like he fired four times."

"I heard a couple of shots once I was in the water."

"And you weren't lying about the cuffs. They were still on his wrist."

Realizing just how close I'd come to dying, I started to cry and wiped my eyes on the handkerchief he'd offered me.

Sutter waited until I'd composed myself. "You took quite a chance, miss, diving off that cliff. And in the dark. That was very brave of you."

I shrugged. "When the alternative is getting shoved over the edge, you kind of lose your reluctance to dive. At least I had a chance with a running start."

"Is there anything else you can tell us about what happened up there?" he asked.

I recalled the figure I'd seen atop the cliff struggling with Terwilliger. He might have been a figment of my imagination, but, no, I knew what I'd seen. A gaunt silhouette, illuminated by a flash of lightning, grappling with the large man who'd tried to kill me. I'd watched as the larger shape stumbled, lurched to one side, and, whirling his arms in a desperate attempt to regain his balance, teetered. His weight had shifted too far into the void, and slowly, like a duckpin kissed by a passing bowling ball and doomed to fall, he toppled over the edge of the precipice.

"No," I said. "Nothing at all."

Lieutenant Sutter accompanied me back to Cedar Haven sometime after two in the morning. My dress had dried stiff and muddy, and it crackled whenever I moved. My hair was a right mess, and, as I later discovered looking in the mirror, I had a dark smudge of something on my forehead and on the side of my neck. I must have looked a fright. Nevertheless Lieutenant Miller Sutter doffed his hat at my door as he prepared to leave, giving me a hungry look I knew all too well. He asked if I wanted him to check on me in the morning. I said that wouldn't be necessary. Then he extended a hand to wish me good night. I took it and held it fast. He gazed into my eyes for a long moment, flexing a muscle in his jaw just so as he did. I scolded myself. I told myself no. And then I released his hand and took a step inside. He tried to follow, and I almost let him. But, instead, I said it had been a trying day. He nodded, replaced his hat on his head, and strode off toward his car. Gosh, cops are sexy.

EPILOGUE

TUESDAY, AUGUST 29, 1961

From behind the mountains to the east, the sun broke pink against high clouds, heralding the dawn of one last glorious day of summer. I'd had to stay on two days longer than planned to tie up loose ends with the state police. For most vacationers, though, the annual exodus had taken place Sunday. Dads had packed their families into station wagons, herding their stray children into the way-back, before setting off for home and their workaday lives. The kids would be behind their school desks within a week. Notebooks, composition pads, pencils, compasses, and rulers. Brown paper-bag book covers, fashioned by Mom with sharply creased corners and tight folds. New shoes and slacks and skirts. For the boys, a fresh haircut and some Vitalis to tame the cowlick. A hairband and ribbons for the girls. Patent-leather Mary Janes. Maybe a new lunchbox. The moms were returning to keeping house, den-mothering their Cub Scouts and Brownies And there would be bake sales, the PTA, and ladies' clubs. But Dad had been due back in the office bright and early Monday morning. I was two days late.

I tossed my suitcase into the trunk of my Dodge, slammed it shut, and surveyed Cedar Haven one last time, ensuring I hadn't forgotten anything. Both cabins were locked and shuttered, linens washed, folded, and mothballed for safekeeping for another year. I drew a lungful of air, willing myself to preserve its pine scent in my mind until the next time.

"Ellie." It was Isaac. I hadn't seen or heard from him since Saturday. "I'm so glad I caught you before you left."

"I'm glad too," I said.

"I wanted to come earlier to check on you after I heard what happened at Baxter's Rock. But I thought you'd left on Sunday. Then I heard from Mrs. Edmonds that you were still here."

"The police needed a few details," I said. "They asked me to stay a couple of days longer."

"I'm here to apologize to you. I really mucked up everything."

I smiled at him. "Don't think that. It was lovely. Truly lovely. Not every love story ends like a fairy tale."

"But why does it have to end at all?" he asked, aiming his crooked smile at me. It was a little less confident now. Tinged with melancholy. He reached out and took my hand. I wanted to resist but didn't have the heart. "We can see each other," he said. "It's not that far."

My silence communicated what I thought of that idea. He released my hand and changed his tack.

"Listen, Ellie. Don't say no yet. We can try."

I brushed his cheek gently with my hand.

"I love you," he said, the speckles in his eyes catching the morning sun. "Please come back with me."

"What?" I said, choking back the urge to laugh.

"Come back to New York with me. Leave those upstate hicks behind and come with me. What do you have there anyway?"

I shook my head and smiled as tenderly as I knew how. Then there was nothing more to say.

∂⟶

It had been a momentous week and a half on Prospector Lake. The first visit in many years for me. I felt saddened by the way some things had turned out but regretted nothing. I wondered for a brief moment if I was destined never to find my mate. Then I clicked my tongue and thought what a fine adventure it would be to find out the answer. My intense affair with Isaac had been at turns delicious and bitter. In the light of the summer's last day, I resolved to remember all of it with good cheer and nostalgia. Despite the short time we'd had together, Isaac had left a mark. Not a scar but an indelible mark I would always carry inside. I was grateful for the passion, the music, the laughter, and even the pain we'd shared. Those things were ours. Might we have been able to work things out and make a go of it? Perhaps. But standing there in Aunt Lena's compound, surveying the grounds one last time, I knew that I wanted better for myself.

And more than that, I knew that I would accept nothing short of better. Maybe those were the same things.

After Isaac left, I strolled down to Aunt Lena's dock with my camera for one last look at the lake. I snapped some photos, wondering if I'd ever come back. Surely, yes. But one never knew. Endings always made me reflect on the permanence of good-byes. I thought of Simon. I'd said my farewell to him. An adieu, not an au revoir. I wondered if he'd realized it. I received word from Miriam three months later that Simon had died. I wept at the news. The world was short one angry, argumentative, uncompromising fighter. And it was poorer for it.

But that final day on Prospector Lake, I stood on the dock, squinting into the morning sun. I turned to look back at Baxter's Rock, clearly visible a few hundred yards to the southwest, and the image of Tiny Terwilliger falling to his death came rushing back to me. And there was the ghostly figure I'd seen struggling with him atop the cliff. As far as I was concerned, that sleeping dog, fleas and all, could lie there forever.

I shook the thought from my mind. It was barely eight, the lake was deserted, and I was seized with the urge to take one last dip. My things were all packed away in the car, and I thought of Aunt Lena. With a naughty giggle, I pulled my dress over my head, stripped out of my underthings, and dived in. The water felt fine cool, restorative. I paddled around for a few minutes, wishing I hadn't soaked my hair. Perhaps next time, I would get myself a bathing cap like Lena's, replete with colorful, rubber flowers. I climbed back onto the dock. With no towel to dry myself off, I lay down on the warm wooden slats and let the sun do the job. I nearly dozed off, but a feathery flutter of wings called me back. I raised my head to see my old friend, the ring-billed gull, staring at me from one eye. The little pervert. Then I became aware of advancing footsteps on the dock beneath me and looked to see a man approaching from the shore. I covered up with my dress in time to deprive him of a proper nudie show. It was Officer Bob Firth.

Blushing crimson, he wished me good morning. I returned the greeting, clutching my sundress to my breast.

He diverted his eyes and cleared his throat. "You know that nude bathing is prohibited here on Prospector Lake."

ACKNOWLEDGMENTS

For their expertise and advice, I am forever grateful to Nancy Deneen, Dr. Hilbert, Lynne Raimondo, William Reiss, and Mary Beth Ziskin. A special thanks to my editor, Jeffrey Curry.

ABOUT THE AUTHOR

James Ziskin is the Anthony and Lefty Award–nominated author of the Ellie Stone mysteries. He lives in the Hollywood Hills with his wife, Lakshmi, and two cats, Bobbie and Tinker.